translation MATTHEW J

lettering and retouch ST

publisher MIKE RICHAF

editor TIM ERVIN

book design STEPHEN REICHERT

Published by Dark Horse Comics, Inc., in association with Shueisha, Inc.

Dark Horse Manga
A division of Dark Horse Comics, Inc.
10956 SE Main Street
Milwaukie, OR 97222

darkhorse.com
First edition: January 2011
ISBN 978-1-59582-662-6

1 3 5 7 9 10 8 6 4 2

Printed at Transcontinental Gagné, Louiseville, QC, Canada

GANTZ
[ガンツ]

Original cover design: Yoshiyuki Seki for VOLARE, Inc.

To find a comics shop in your area, call the Comic Shop Locator Service toll-free at 1-888-266-4226.

低俗霊
デイドリーム

GHOST TALKER'S DAYDREAM

Written by
Sankichi Meguro

Art by
Saki Okuse

Ghost Talker's Daydream tells the dark, sensual story of Misaki Saiki, a young woman with a troubled past, who is a professional dominatrix in one of Tokyo's most exclusive S&M clubs. However, her real money comes from something she likes even less than being a dominatrix. Ever since childhood, Misaki has had the ability to see and communicate with ghosts, and that talent is put to use by the Livelihood Protection Agency, which pairs Misaki with Souichiro Kadotake, a martial artist who happens to be deathly afraid of ghosts. Using her gifts, Misaki is able to help troubled departed spirits resolve what is troubling them and allow them to move on to the afterlife.

Volume One
ISBN 978-1-59307-950-5
Volume Two
ISBN 978-1-59582-186-7
Volume Three
ISBN 978-1-59582-234-5
Volume Four
ISBN 978-1-59582-260-4
Volume Five
ISBN 978-1-59582-666-4

$10.99 each

AVAILABLE AT YOUR LOCAL COMICS SHOP OR BOOKSTORE! TO FIND A COMICS SHOP IN YOUR AREA, CALL 1-888-266-4226.

For more information or to order direct: • On the web: darkhorse.com • E-mail: mailorder@darkhorse.com • Phone: 1-800-862-0052 Mon.-Fri. 9 AM to 5 PM Pacific Time.
*Prices and availability subject to change without notice.

DARK HORSE MANGA

XS

HYBRID

SONG JI-HYUNG 송지형

In a strange future where gifted, "hybrid" humans police the planet, Mina is a likeable tomboy with growing psychic powers. When a young boy falls into a coma after gazing into her eyes, it's clear that there's more to Mina than her pretty looks. This young boy, Inchang, grows up to be quite a daredevil, and his awkward, secret love for Mina fuels his protective fire when mysterious men arrive, bringing the violence of the "hybrid" world with them!

Volume 1 ISBN: 978-1-59307-628-3

Volume 2 ISBN: 978-1-59307-757-0

Volume 3 ISBN: 978-1-59307-758-7

$10.95 each!

AVAILABLE AT YOUR LOCAL COMICS SHOP OR BOOKSTORE! To find a comics shop in your area, call 1-888-266-4226.

For more information or to order direct visit darkhorse.com or call 1-800-862-0052, Mon.–Fri. 9 A.M. to 5 P.M. Pacific Time. *Prices and availability subject to change without notice.

DARK HORSE MANHWA

NEON GENESIS EVANGELION

Dark Horse Manga is proud to present two new original series based on the wildly popular *Neo~
Genesis Evangelion* manga and anime! Continuing the rich story lines and complex character~
these new visions of *Neon Genesis Evangelion* provide extra dimensions for understanding or
of the greatest series ever made!

NEON GENESIS
EVANGELION
THE SHINJI IKARI RAISING PROJECT

STORY AND ART
BY OSAMU TAKAHASHI

VOLUME 1
ISBN 978-1-59582-321-2 | $9.99

VOLUME 2
ISBN 978-1-59582-377-9 | $9.99

VOLUME 3
ISBN 978-1-59582-447-9 | $9.99

VOLUME 4
ISBN 978-1-59582-454-7 | $9.99

VOLUME 5
ISBN 978-1-59582-520-9 | $9.99

VOLUME 6
ISBN 978-1-59582-580-3 | $9.99

VOLUME 7
ISBN 978-1-59582-595-7 | $9.99

NEON GENESIS EVANGELION
Campus Apocalypse

STORY AND ART
BY MINGMING

VOLUME 1
ISBN 978-1-59582-530-8 | $10.99

VOLUME 2
ISBN 978-1-59582-661-9 | $10.99

Each volume of *Neon Genesis Evangelion* features bonus color pages,
your *Evangelion* fan art and letters, and special reader giveaways!

DARK
HORSE
MANGA
darkhorse.com

AVAILABLE AT YOUR LOCAL COMICS SHOP OR BOOKSTORE
To find a comics shop in your area, call 1-888-266-4226 • For more information or to order direct: • On the web: darkhorse.com
E-mail: mailorder@darkhorse.com • Phone: 1-800-862-0052 Mon.–Fri. 9 AM to 5 PM Pacific Time.

NEON GENESIS EVANGELION IKARI-SHINJI IKUSEI KEIKAKU © OSAMU TAKAHASHI 2010. © GAINAX • khara. First published in Japan in 2006 by KADOKAW~
SHOTEN Publishing Co., Ltd., Tokyo. NEON GENESIS EVANGELION GAKUEN DATENROKU © MINMIN 2010 © GAINAX • khara. First published in Japan in 20~
by KADOKAWA SHOTEN Publishing Co., Ltd., Tokyo. English translation rights arranged with KADOKAWA SHOTEN Publishing Co., Ltd., Tokyo, through TOHA~
CORPORATION, Tokyo. Dark Horse Manga™ is a trademark of Dark Horse Comics, Inc. All rights reserved. (BL 7077)

the KUROSAGI corpse delivery service

黒鷺死体宅配便

If you enjoyed this book, be sure to check out *The Kurosagi Corpse Delivery Service*, a new mature-readers manga series from the creator of *Mail*!

Five young students at a Buddhist university find there's little call for their job skills in today's Tokyo . . . among the *living*, that is! But their studies give them a direct line to the dead—the dead who are still trapped in their corpses, and can't move on to the next reincarnation! Whether you died from suicide, murder, sickness, or madness, they'll carry your body anywhere it needs to go to free your soul! Written by Eiji Otsuka of the notorious *MPD-Psycho*!

Volume 1:
ISBN 978-1-59307-555-2 $10.99

Volume 2:
ISBN 978-1-59307-593-4 $10.99

Volume 3:
ISBN 978-1-59307-594-1 $10.99

Volume 4:
ISBN 978-1-59307-595-8 $10.99

Volume 5:
ISBN 978-1-59307-596-5 $10.99

Volume 6:
ISBN 978-1-59307-892-8 $10.99

Volume 7:
ISBN 978-1-59307-982-6 $10.99

Volume 8:
ISBN 978-1-59582-235-2 $10.99

Volume 9:
ISBN 978-1-59582-306-9 $10.99

Volume 10:
ISBN 978-1-59582-446-2 $10.99

Volume 11:
ISBN 978-1-59582-528-5 $11.99

Volume 12:
ISBN 978-1-59582-686-2 $11.99

AVAILABLE AT YOUR LOCAL COMICS SHOP OR BOOKSTORE!
To find a comics shop in your area, call 1.888.266.4226. For more information or to order direct:
•On the web: darkhorse.com •E-mail: mailorder@darkhorse.com •Phone: 1.800.862.0052 Mon.-Fri. 9 A.M. to 5 P.M. Pacific Time. *Prices and availability subject to change without notice.

DARK
HORSE
MANGA

darkhorse.com

Kurosagi Corpse Delivery Service © EIJI OTSUKA OFFICE 2002-2011 © HOUSUI YAMAZAKI 2002-2011. First published in Japan in 2002-2010 by KADOKAWA SHOTEN Publishing Co., Ltd., Tokyo. English translation rights arranged with KADOKAWA SHOTEN Publishing Co., Ltd., Tokyo, through TOHAN CORPORATION, Tokyo. (BL7001)

HELLSING

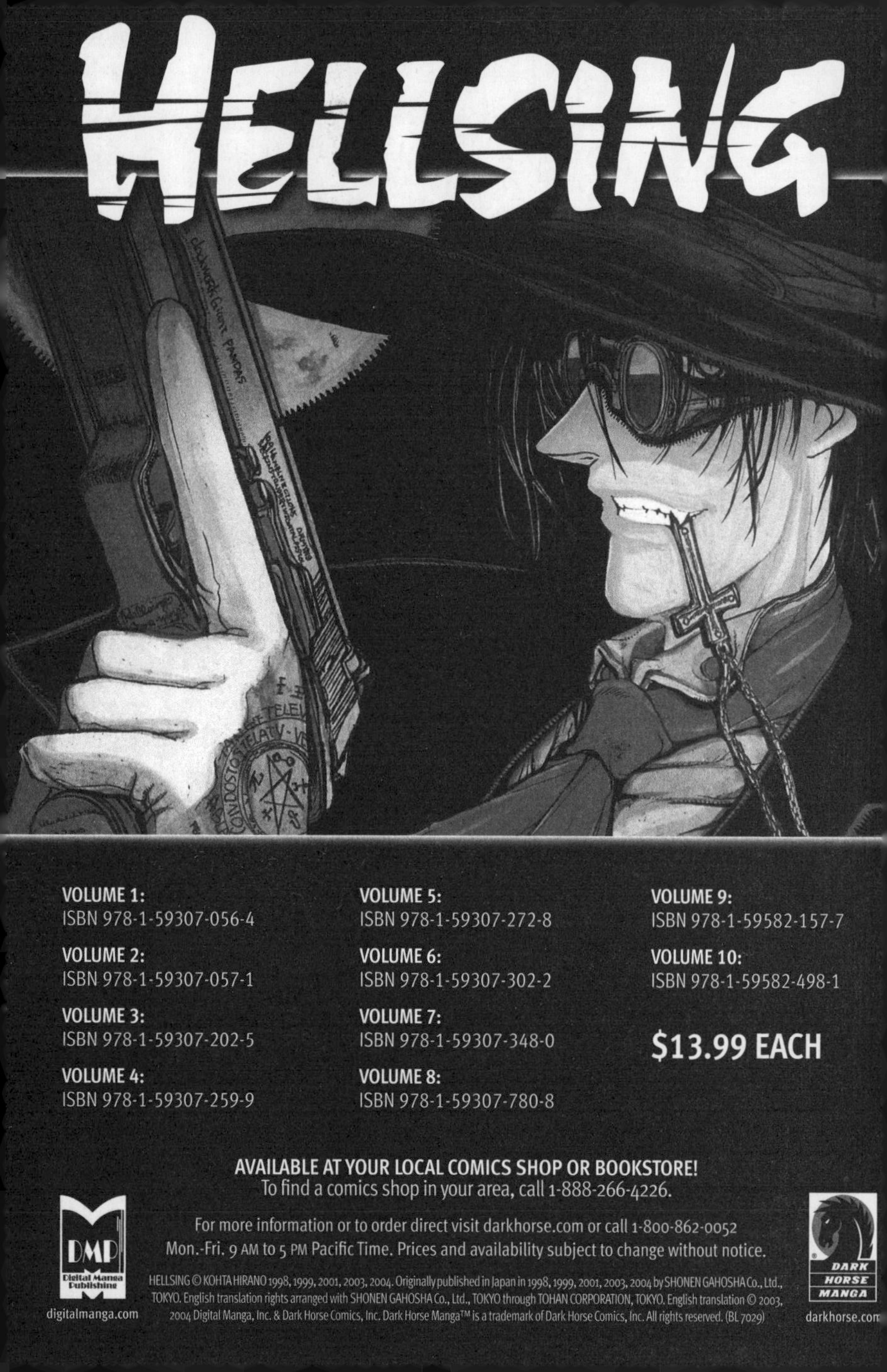

M P D - P S Y C H O

多　重　人　格　探　偵

田島昭宇 ✕ 大塚英志

SHO-U TAJIMA   EIJI OTSUKA

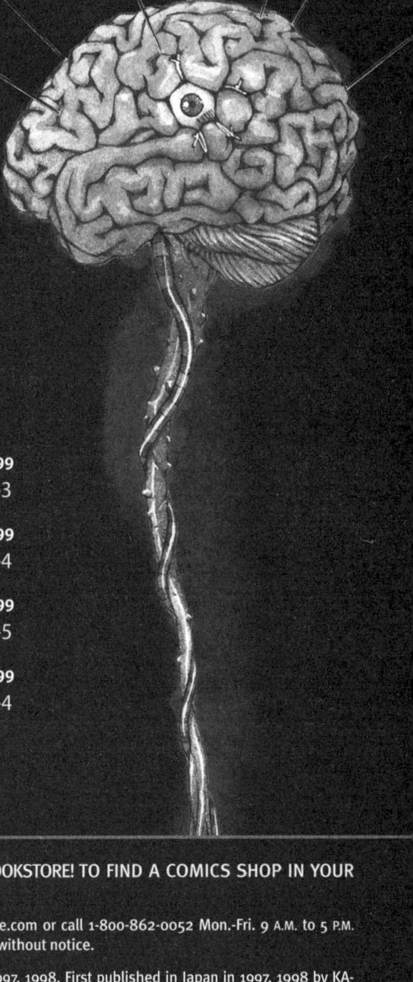

Police detective Yosuke Kobayashi's life is changed forever after a serial killer notices something "special" about him. That same killer mutilates Kobayashi's girlfriend and kick-starts a "multiple personality battle" within Kobayashi that pushes him into a complex tempest of interconnected deviants and evil forces.

Originally licensed by another U.S. publisher, *MPD-Psycho* was deemed too shocking for them to release, but Dark Horse is always prepared to give manga readers what they want and is proud to present *MPD-Psycho* uncensored, in all of its controversial and unflinchingly grotesque glory!

Volume 1	$10.99	**Volume 6**	$10.99
ISBN 978-1-59307-770-9		ISBN 978-1-59307-996-3	
Volume 2	$10.99	**Volume 7**	$12.99
ISBN 978-1-59307-840-9		ISBN 978-1-59582-202-4	
Volume 3	$10.99	**Volume 8**	$12.99
ISBN 978-1-59307-858-4		ISBN 978-1-59582-263-5	
Volume 4	$10.99	**Volume 9**	$12.99
ISBN 978-1-59307-897-3		ISBN 978-1-59582-330-4	
Volume 5	$10.99		
ISBN 978-1-59307-962-8			

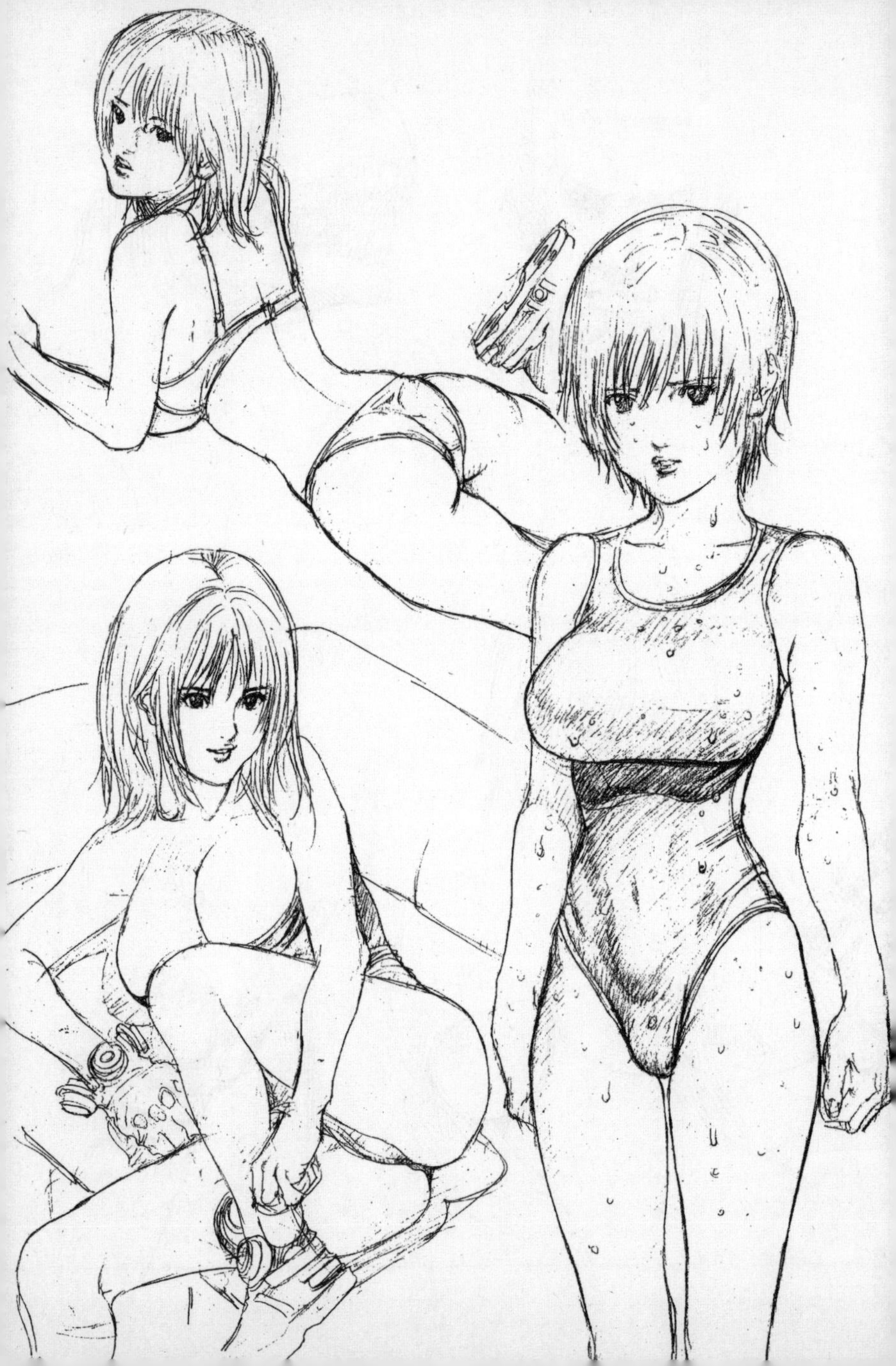

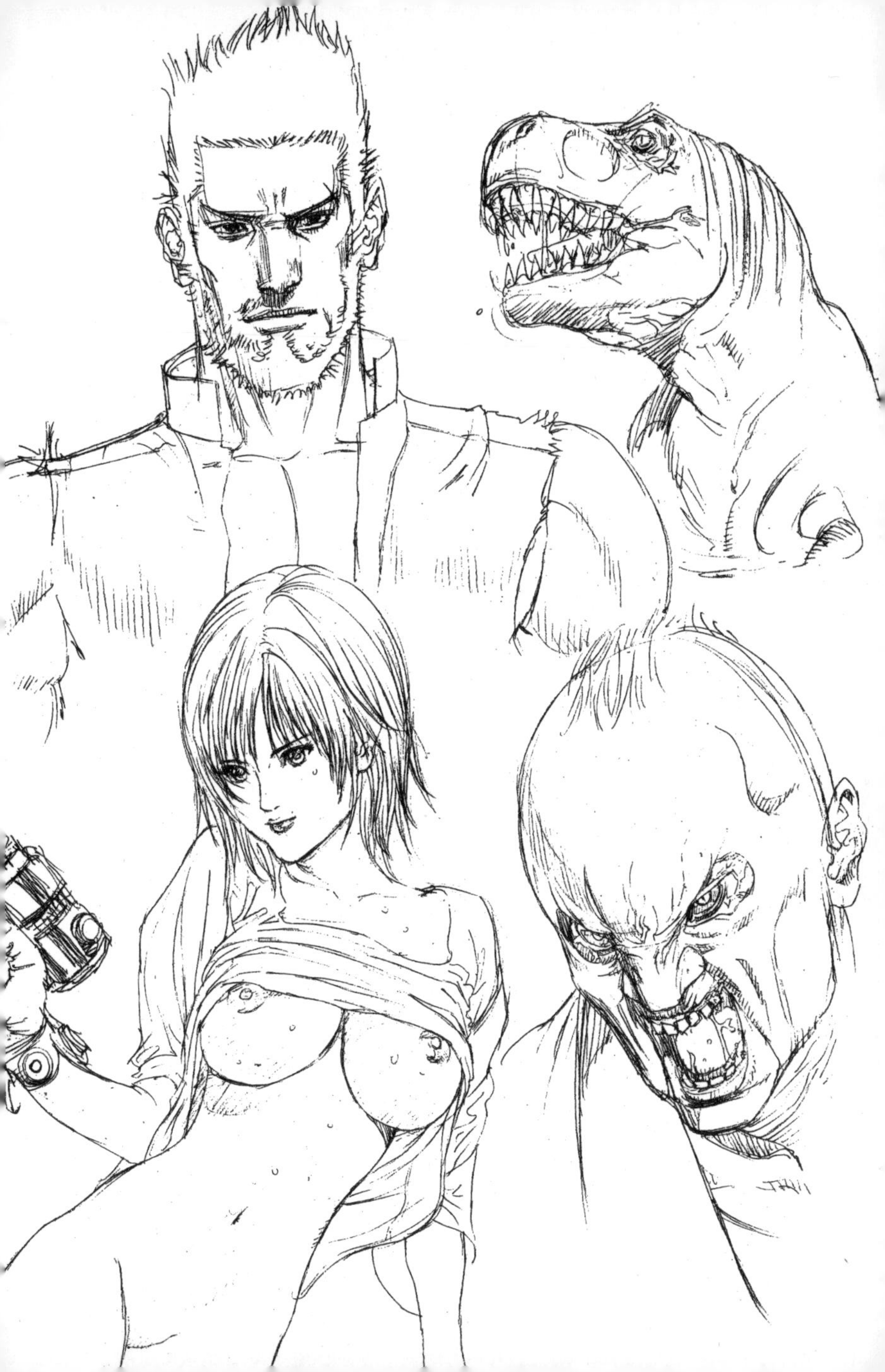

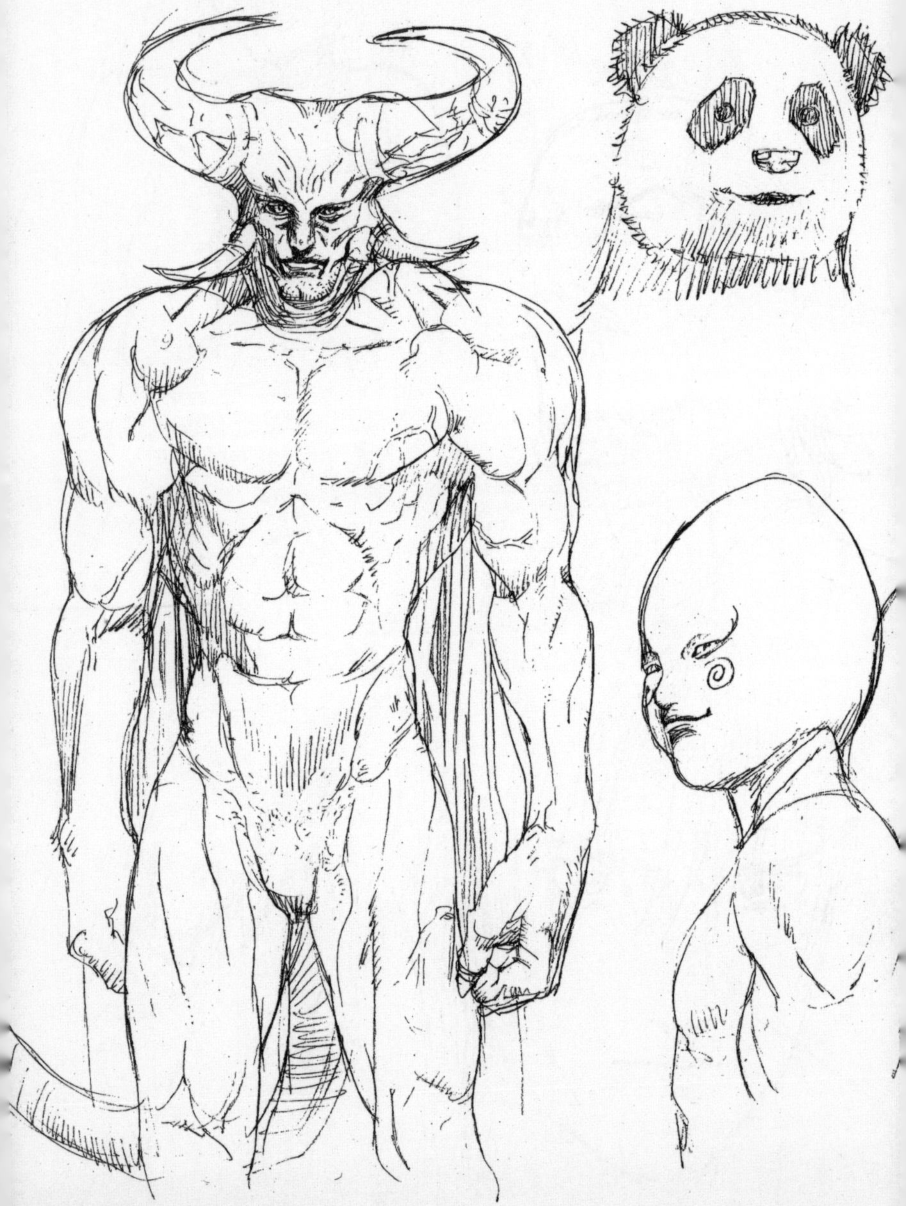

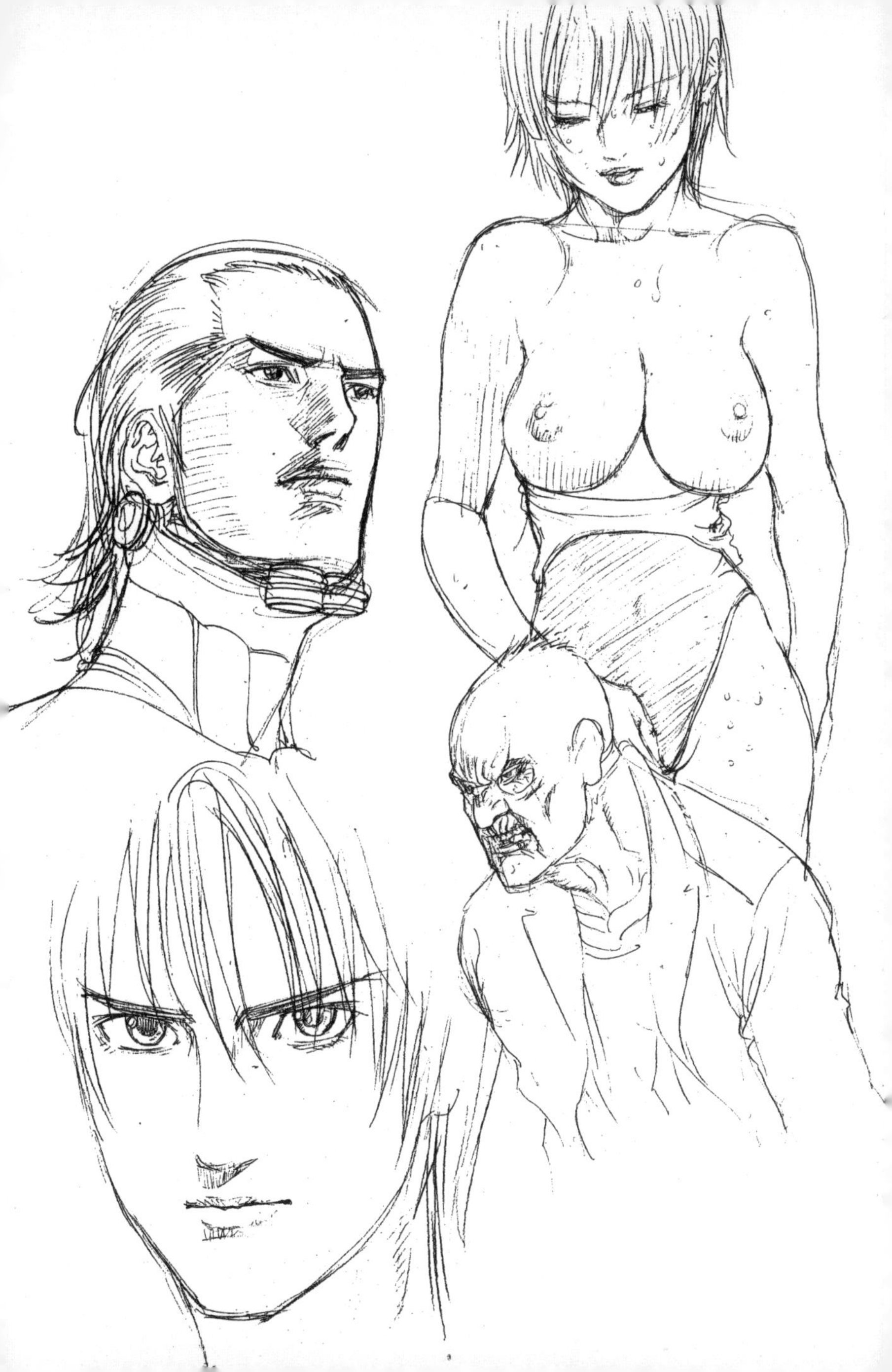

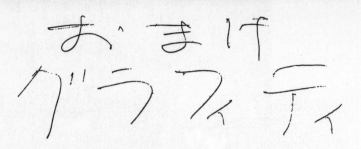

OMAKE GRAFFITI.
THESE ARE ACTUAL SKETCHES BY HIROYA OKU.

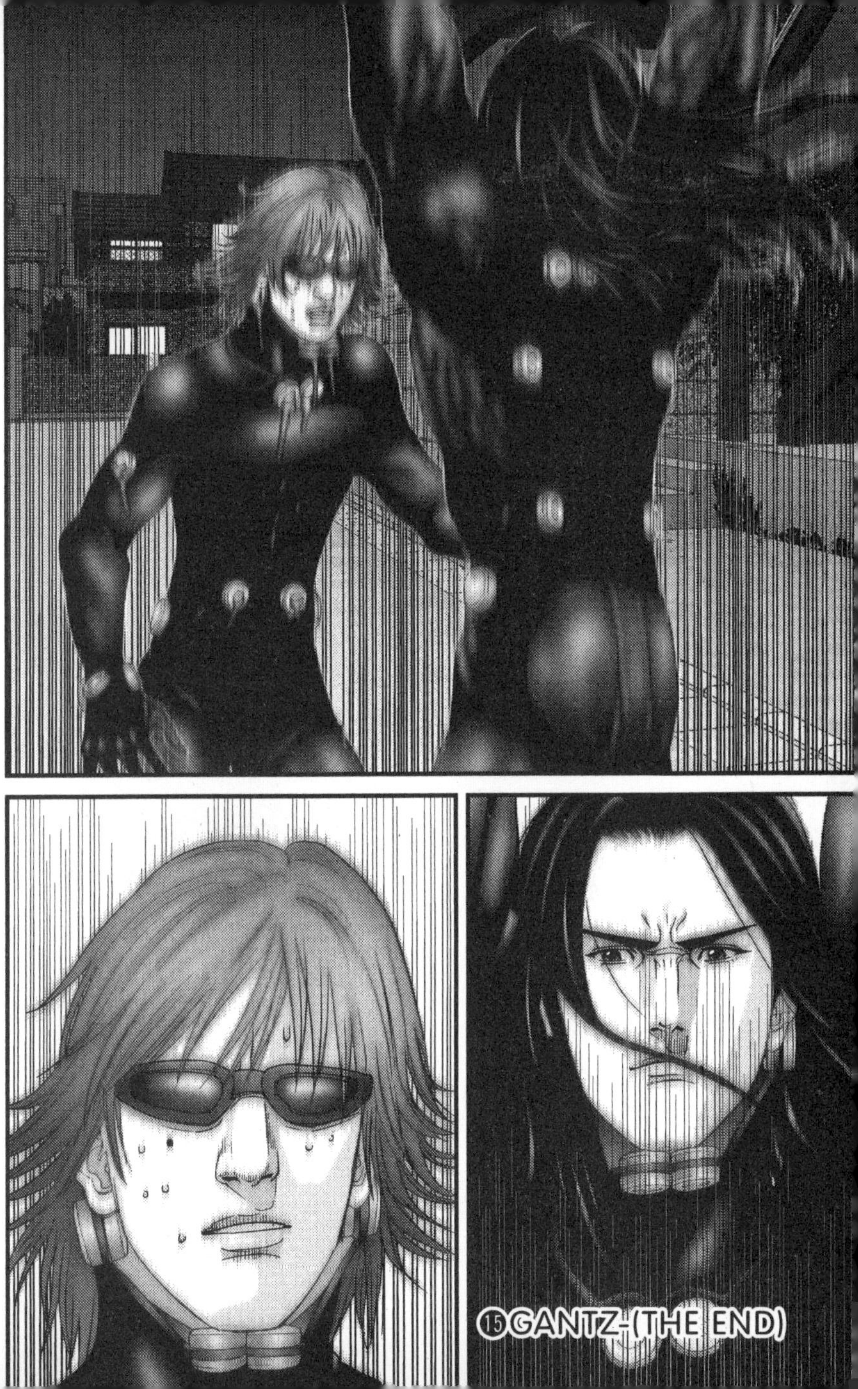
⑮GANTZ-(THE END)

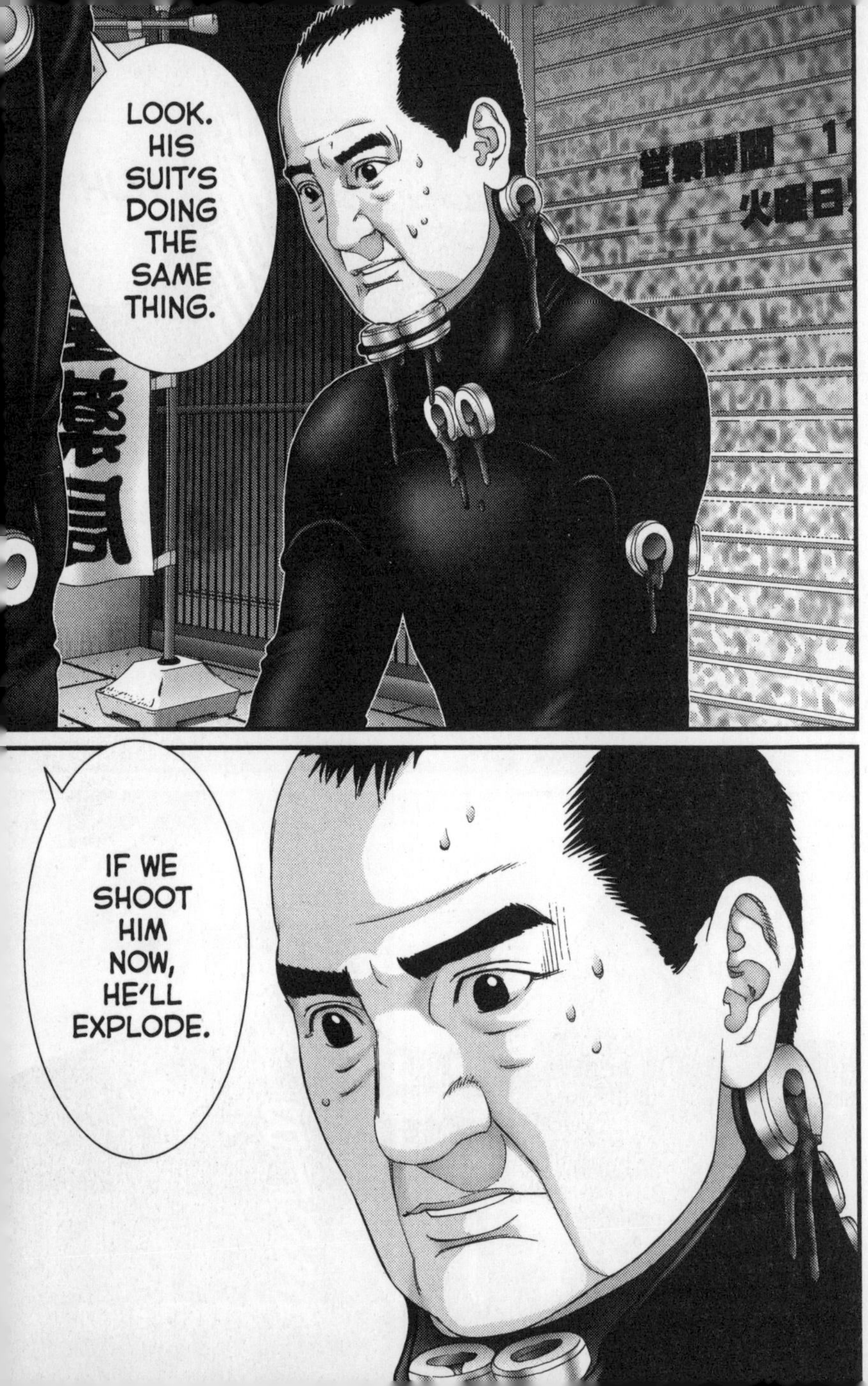
LOOK. HIS SUIT'S DOING THE SAME THING.
IF WE SHOOT HIM NOW, HE'LL EXPLODE.

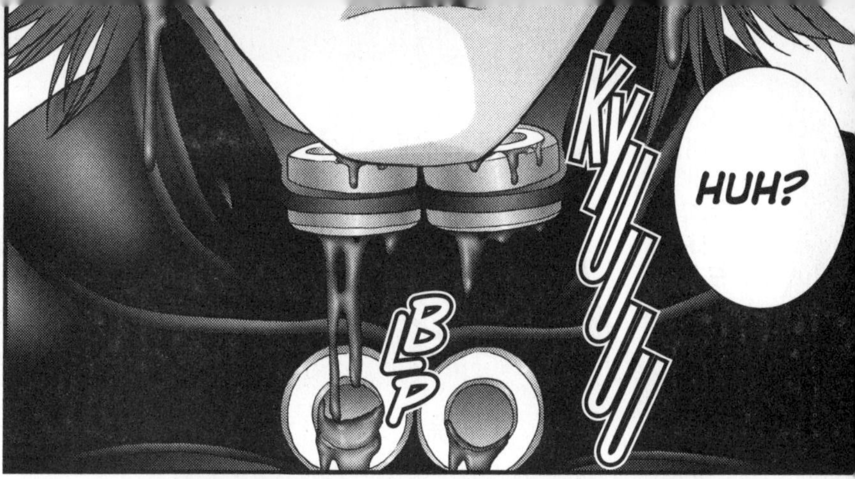
HUH?
KYUUUUU
BLP
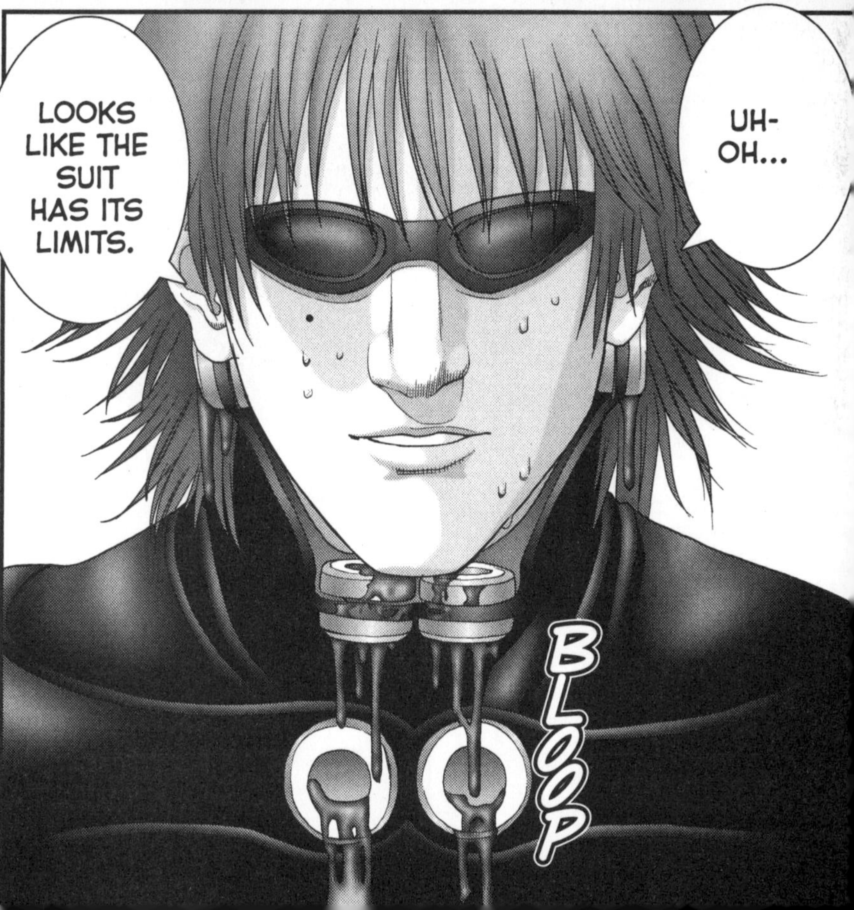
UH-OH...
LOOKS LIKE THE SUIT HAS ITS LIMITS.
BLOOP

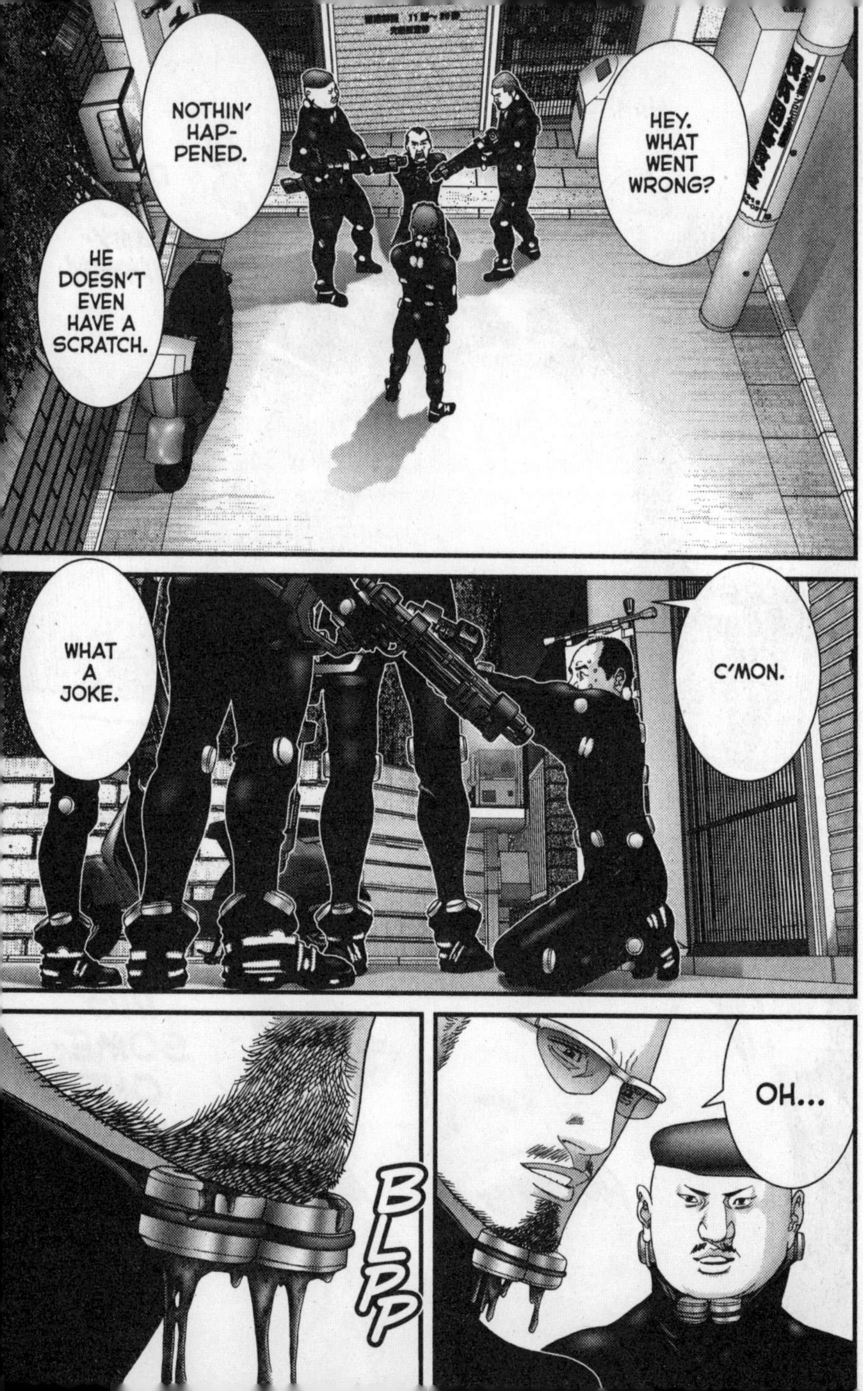
HEY. WHAT WENT WRONG?
NOTHIN' HAP-PENED.
HE DOESN'T EVEN HAVE A SCRATCH.
C'MON.
WHAT A JOKE.
OH...
BLPP

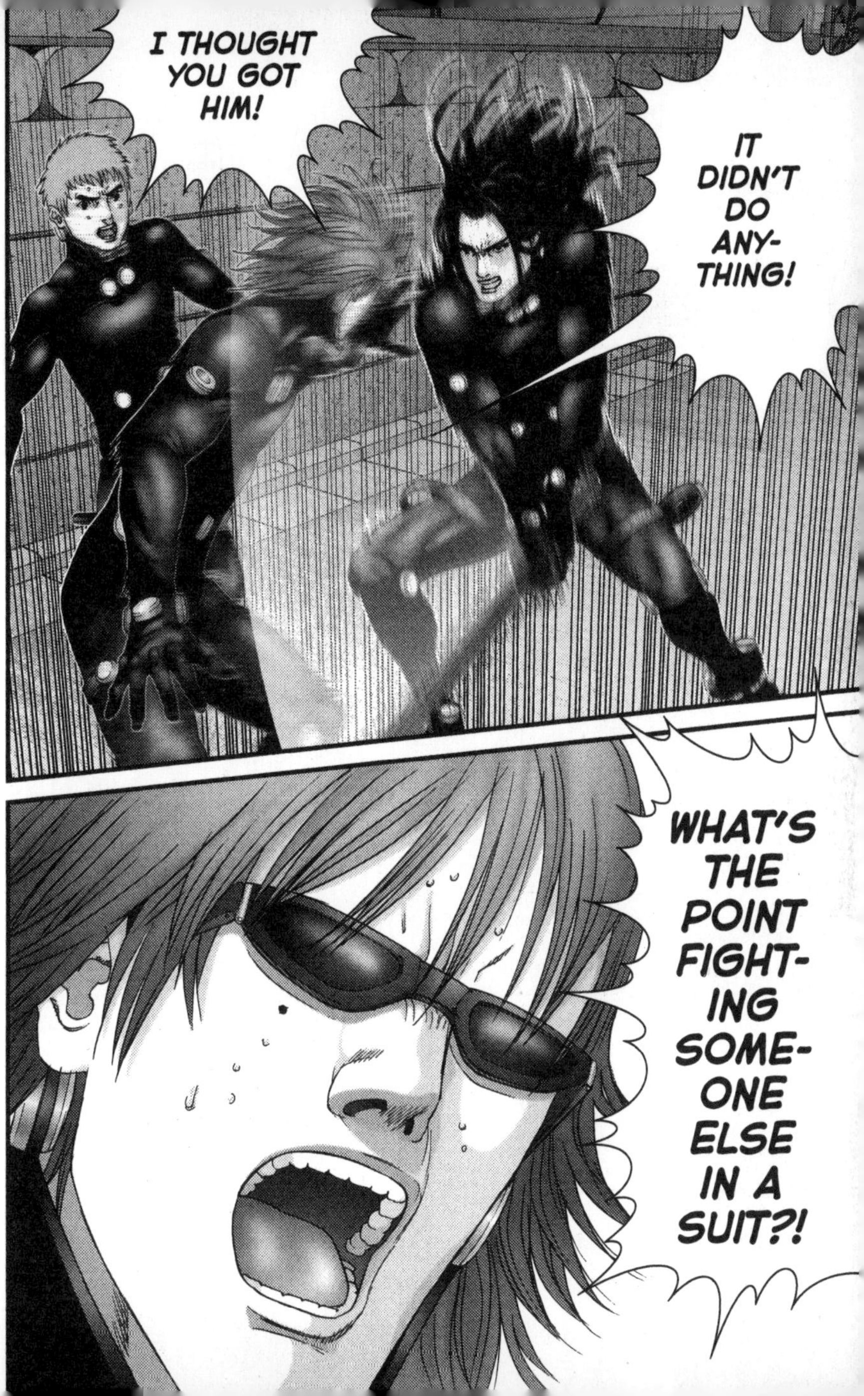
I THOUGHT YOU GOT HIM!
IT DIDN'T DO ANYTHING!
WHAT'S THE POINT FIGHTING SOMEONE ELSE IN A SUIT?!

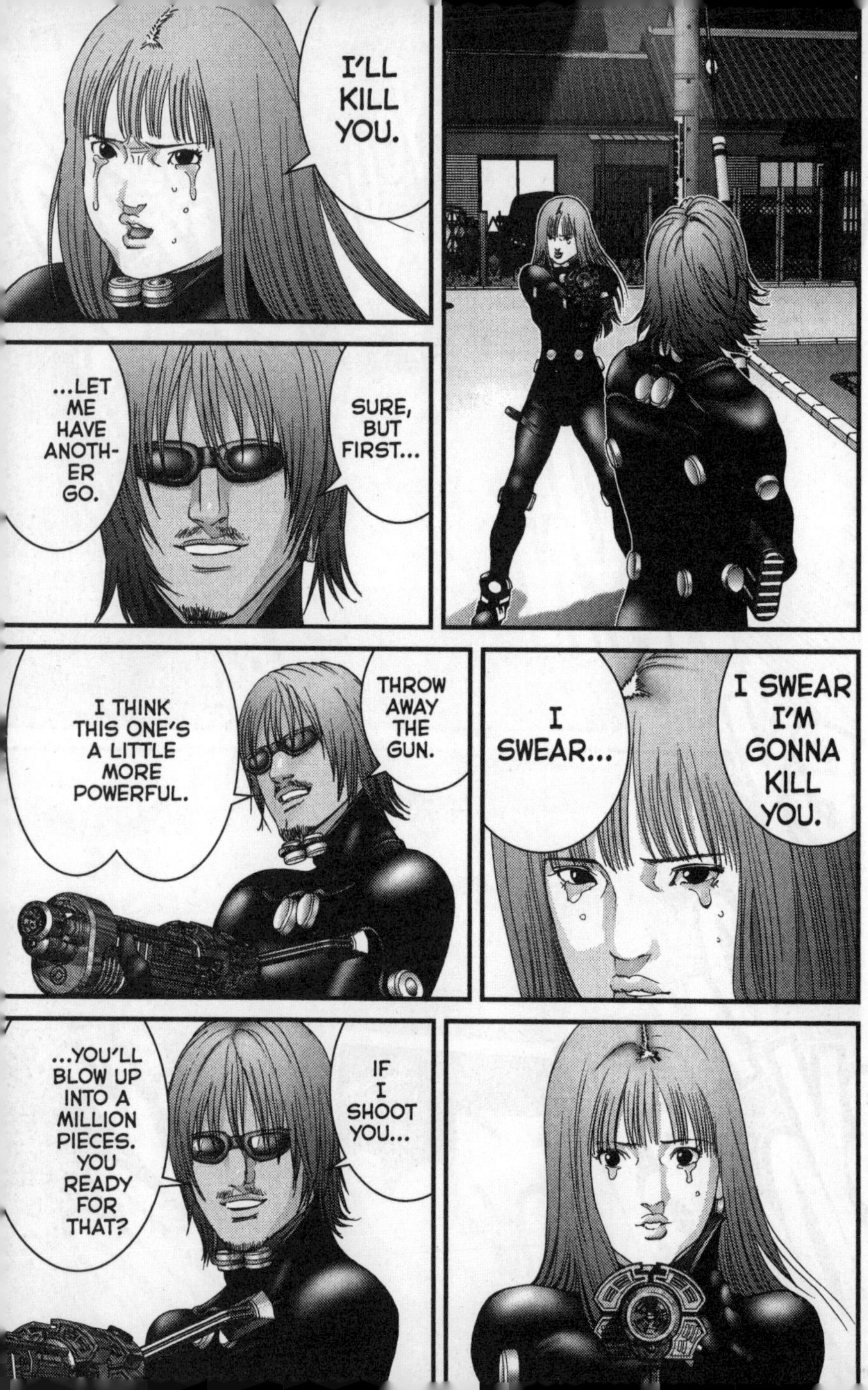
I'LL KILL YOU.
SURE, BUT FIRST...
...LET ME HAVE ANOTH-ER GO.
I SWEAR I'M GONNA KILL YOU.
I SWEAR...
THROW AWAY THE GUN.
I THINK THIS ONE'S A LITTLE MORE POWERFUL.
IF I SHOOT YOU...
...YOU'LL BLOW UP INTO A MILLION PIECES. YOU READY FOR THAT?

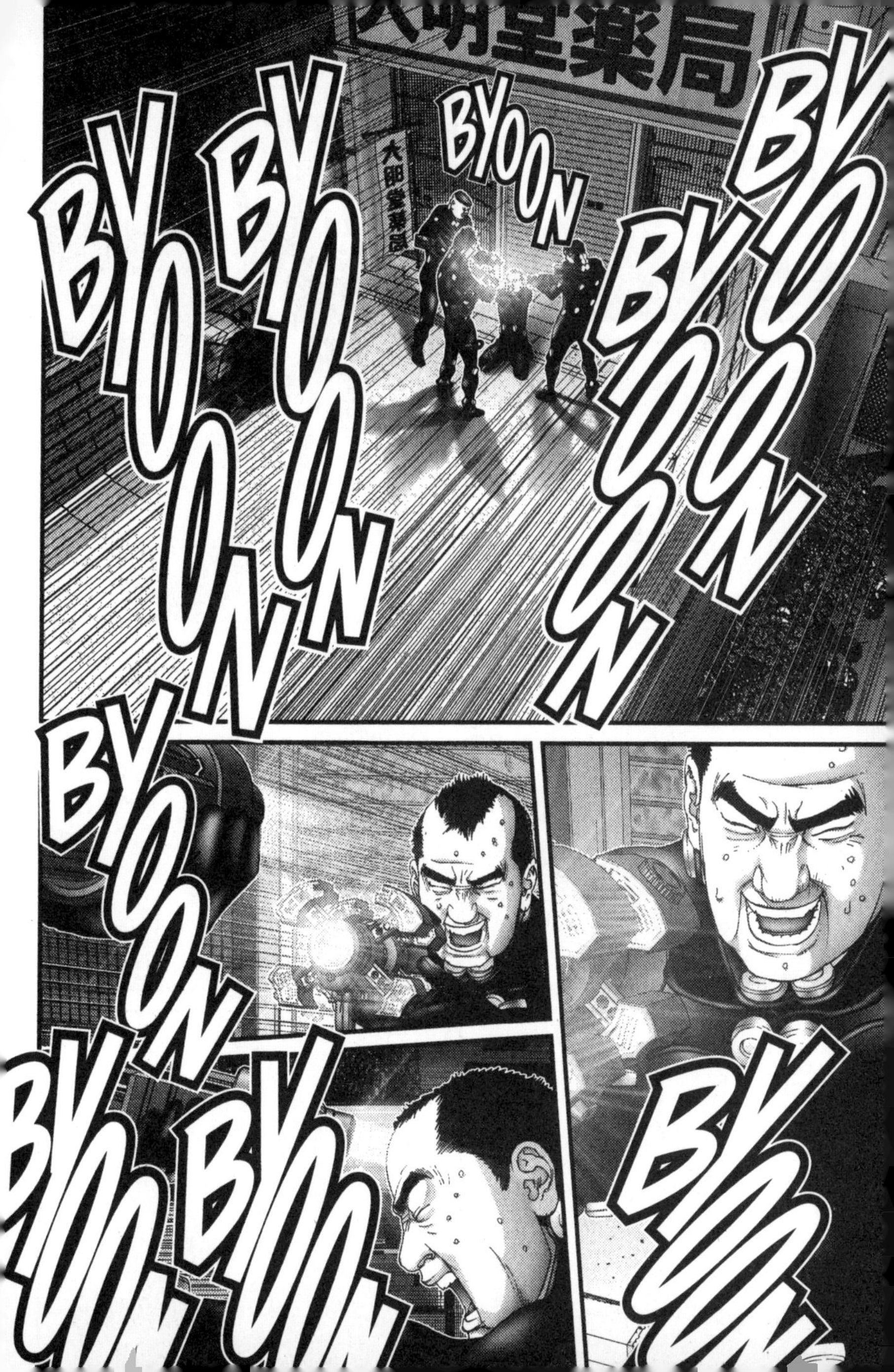
明堂薬局
BYOON
BYOON
BYOON
BYOON
BYOON
BYOON
BYOON
BYOON
BYOON

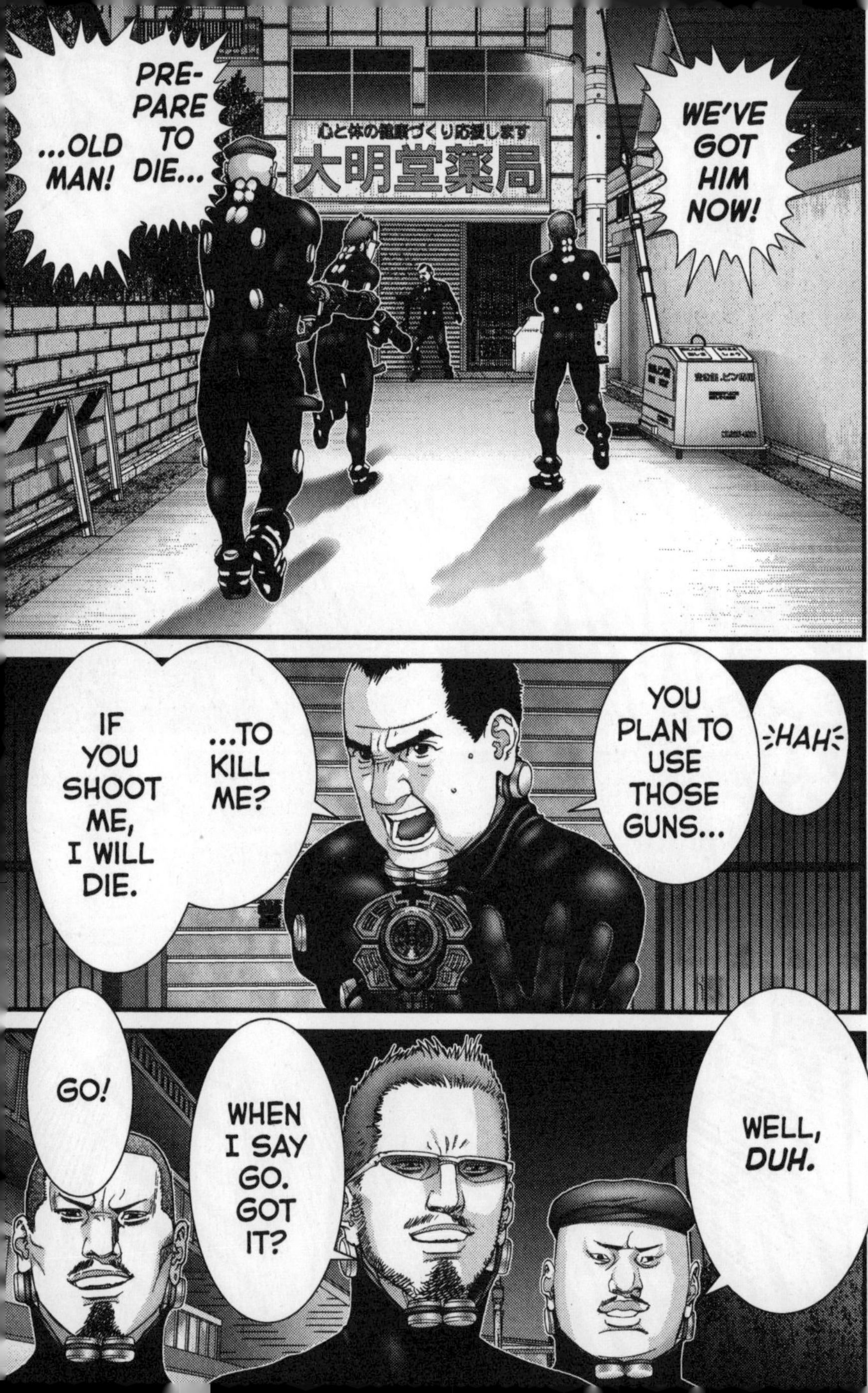
心と体の健康づくり応援します
大明堂薬局
WE'VE GOT HIM NOW!
PRE-PARE TO DIE...
...OLD MAN!
HAH
YOU PLAN TO USE THOSE GUNS...
...TO KILL ME?
IF YOU SHOOT ME, I WILL DIE.
WELL, DUH.
WHEN I SAY GO. GOT IT?
GO!

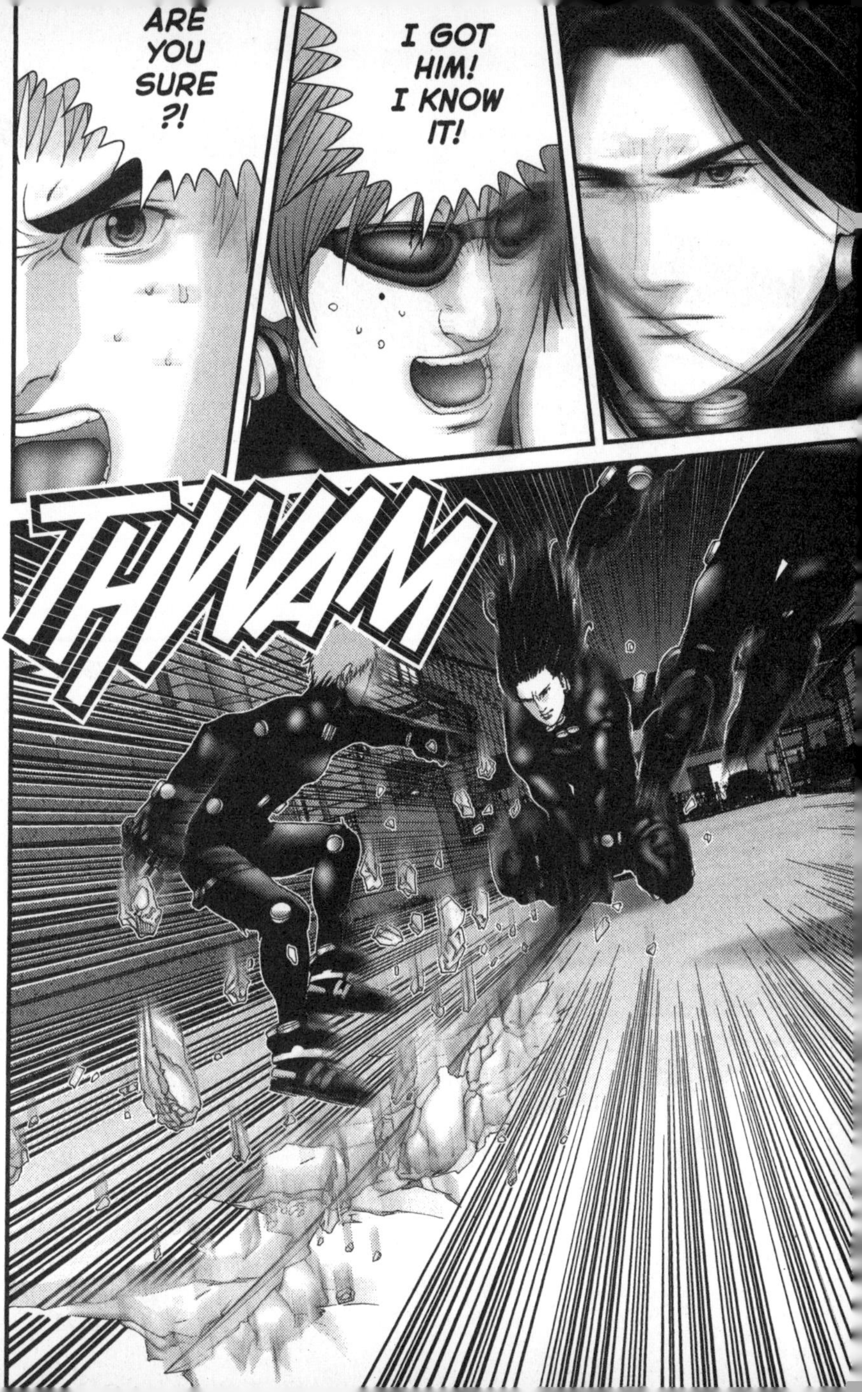
I GOT HIM! I KNOW IT!
ARE YOU SURE ?!
THWAM

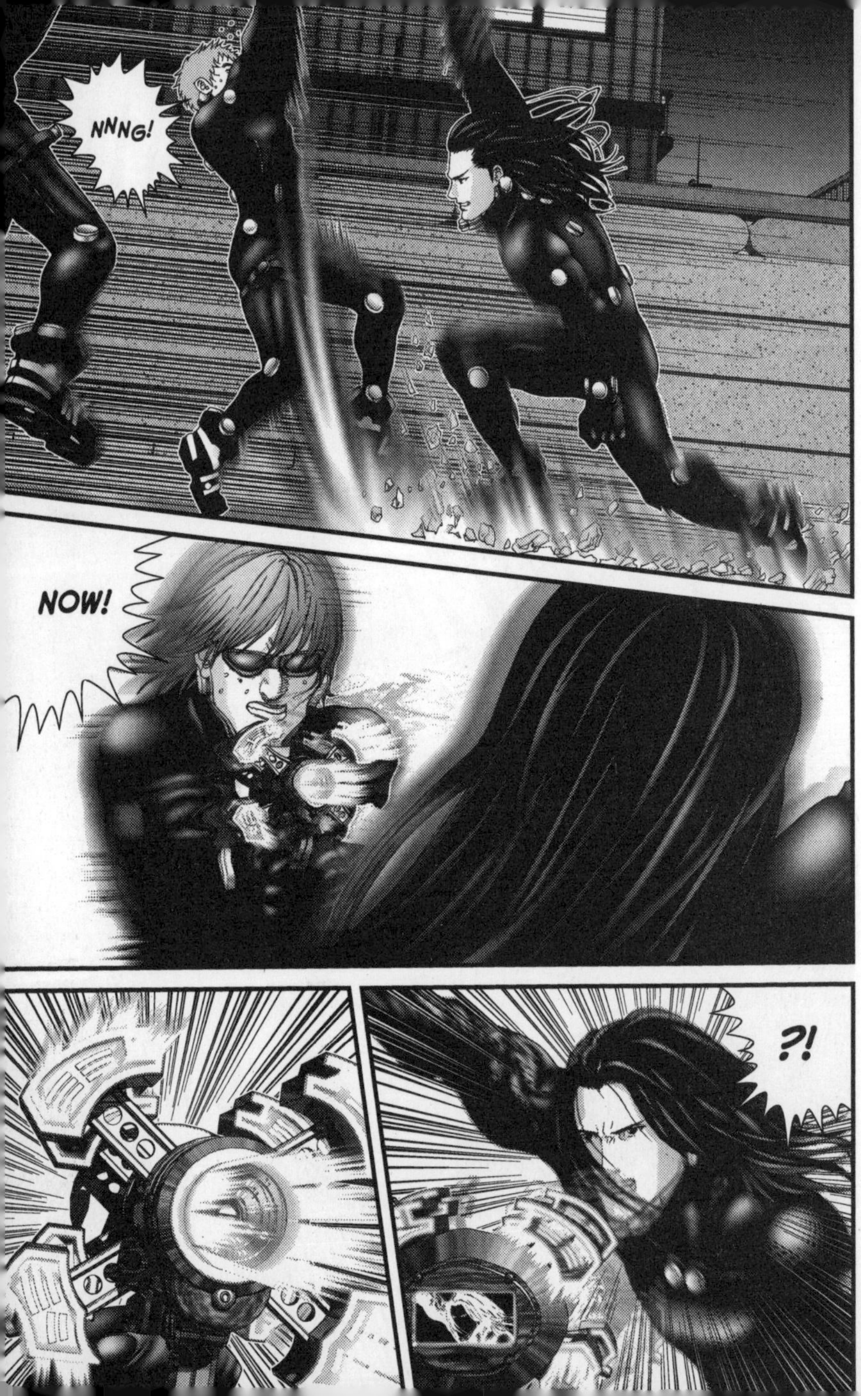
NNNG!
NOW!
?!

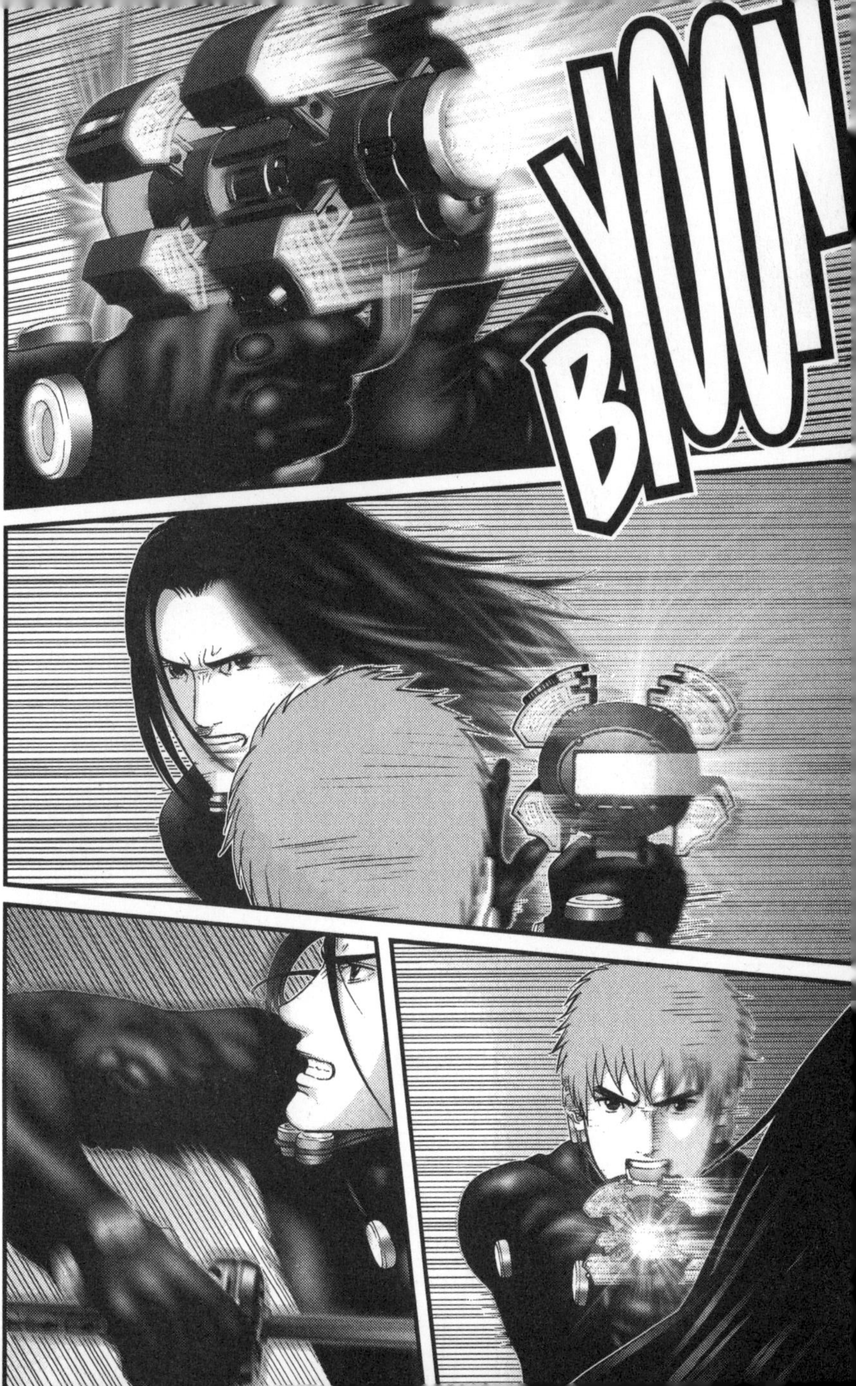
BYOOON!

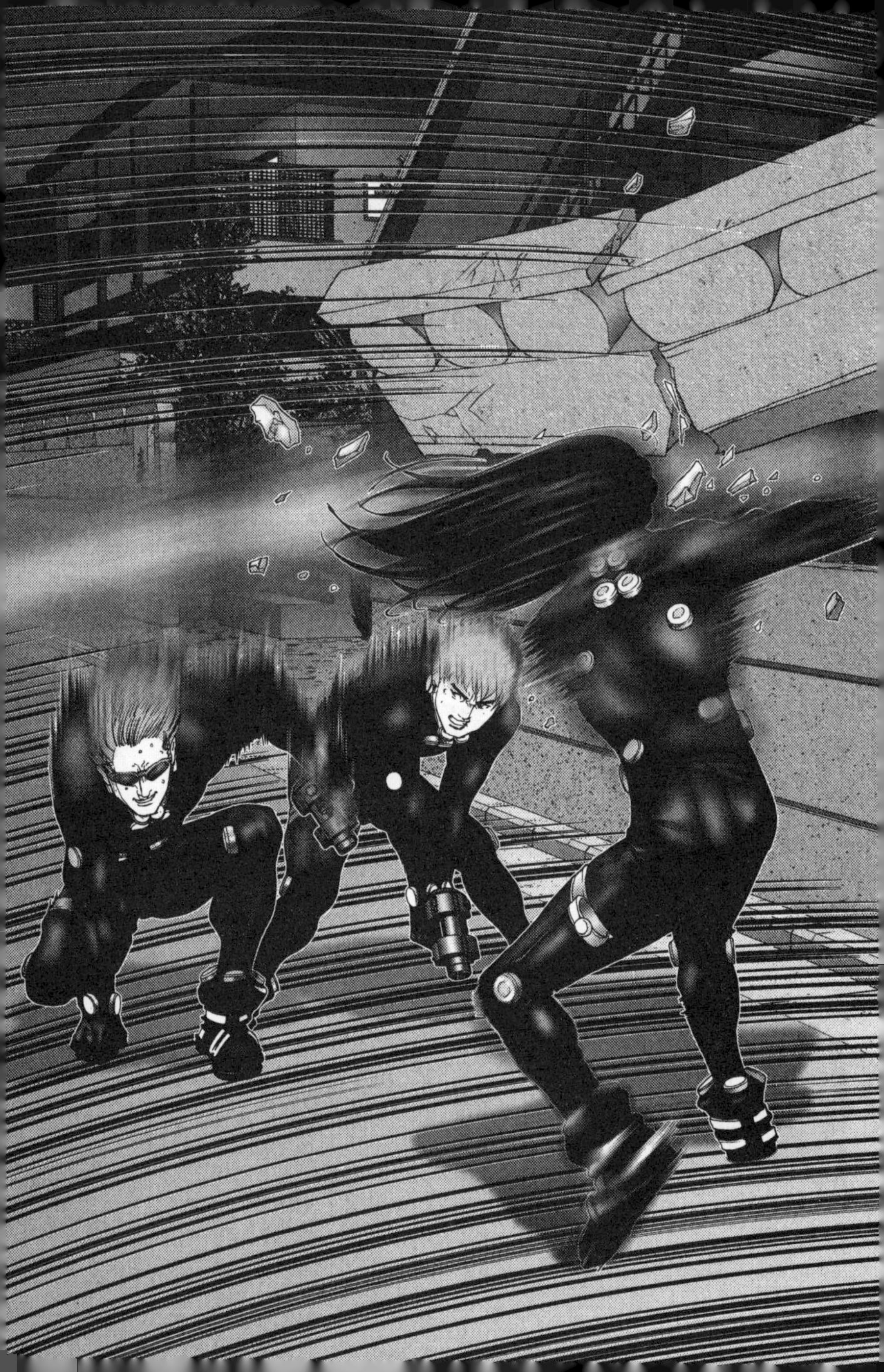

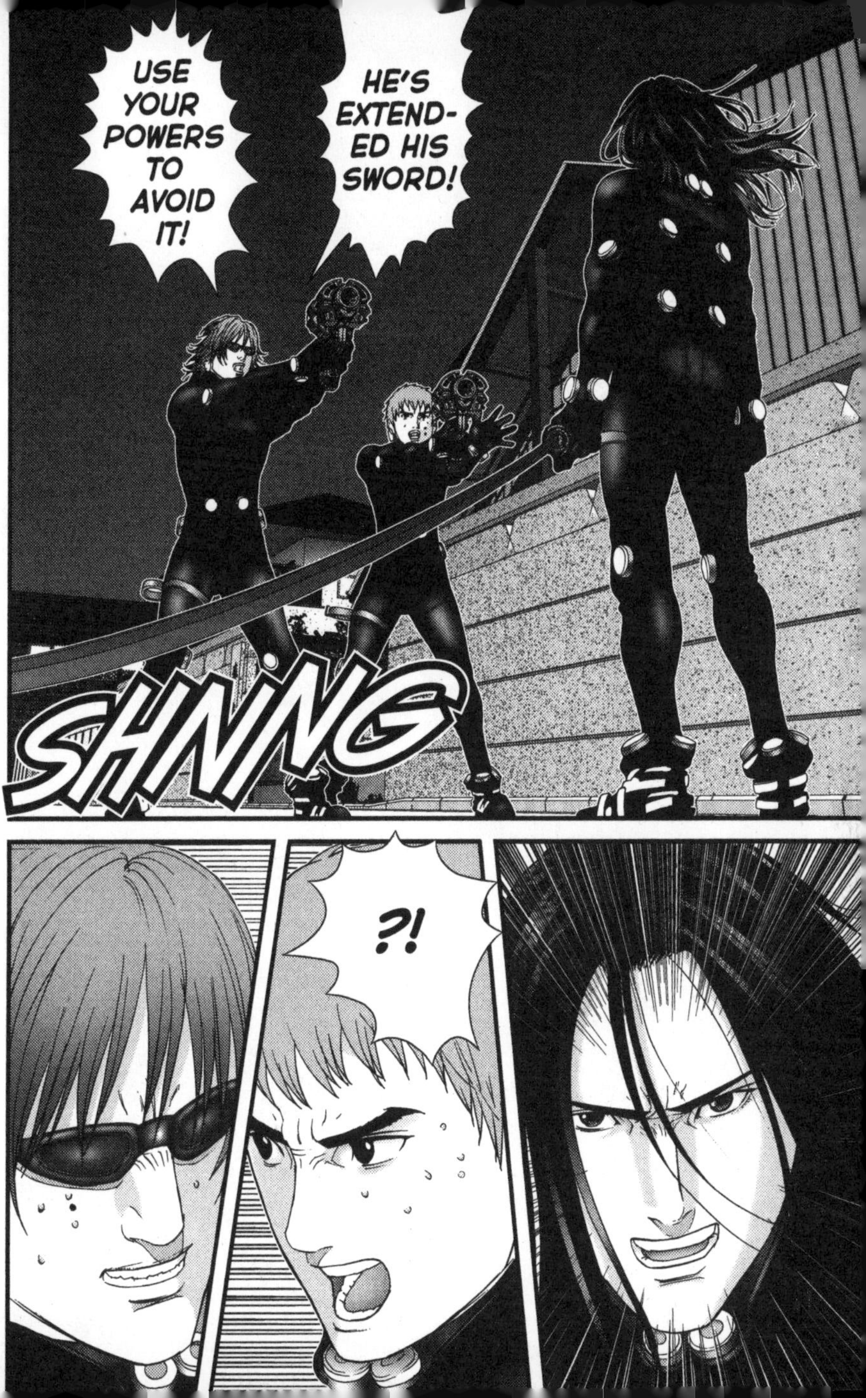
HE'S EXTENDED HIS SWORD!
USE YOUR POWERS TO AVOID IT!
SHING
?!

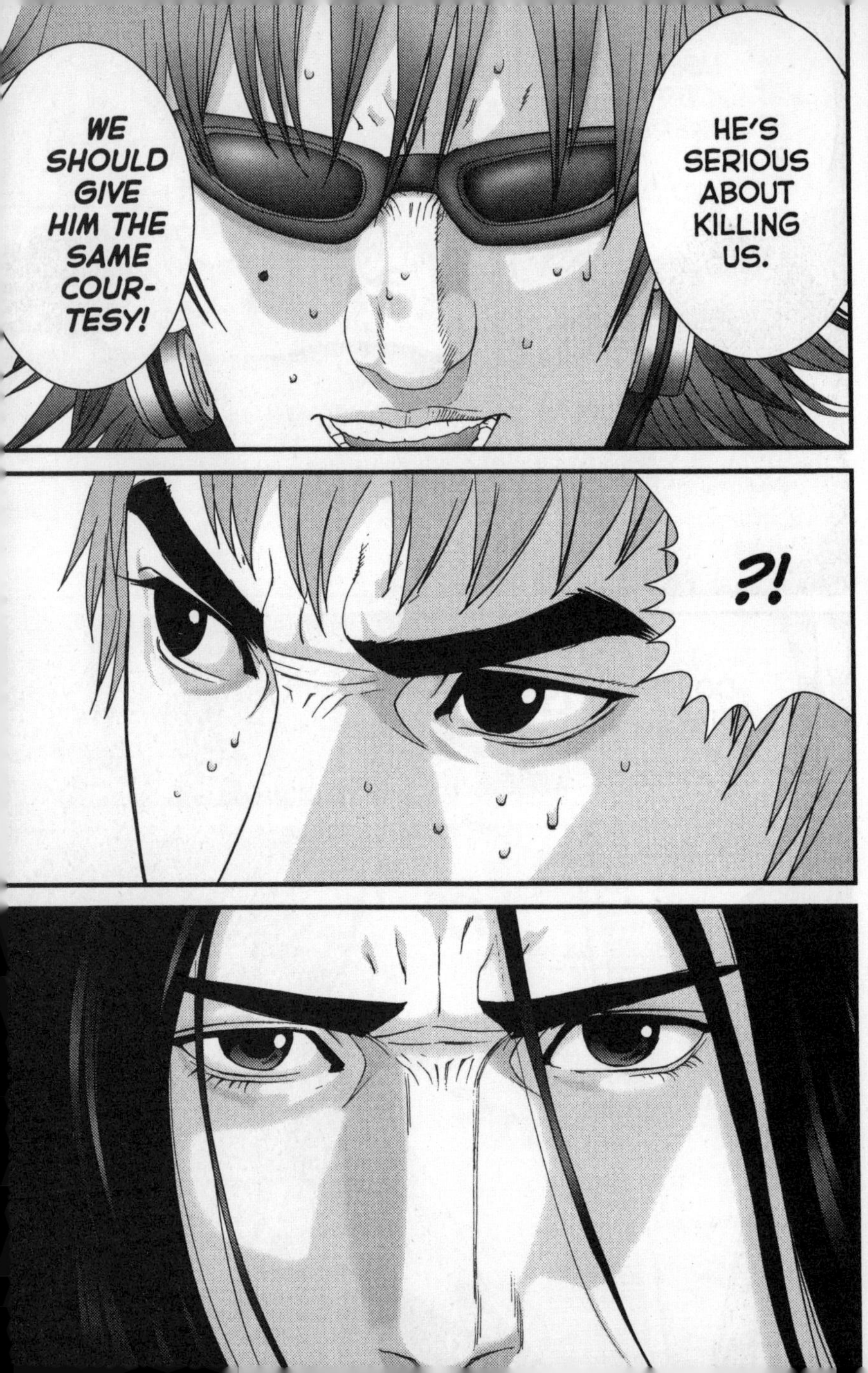
HE'S SERIOUS ABOUT KILLING US.
WE SHOULD GIVE HIM THE SAME COUR-TESY!
?!

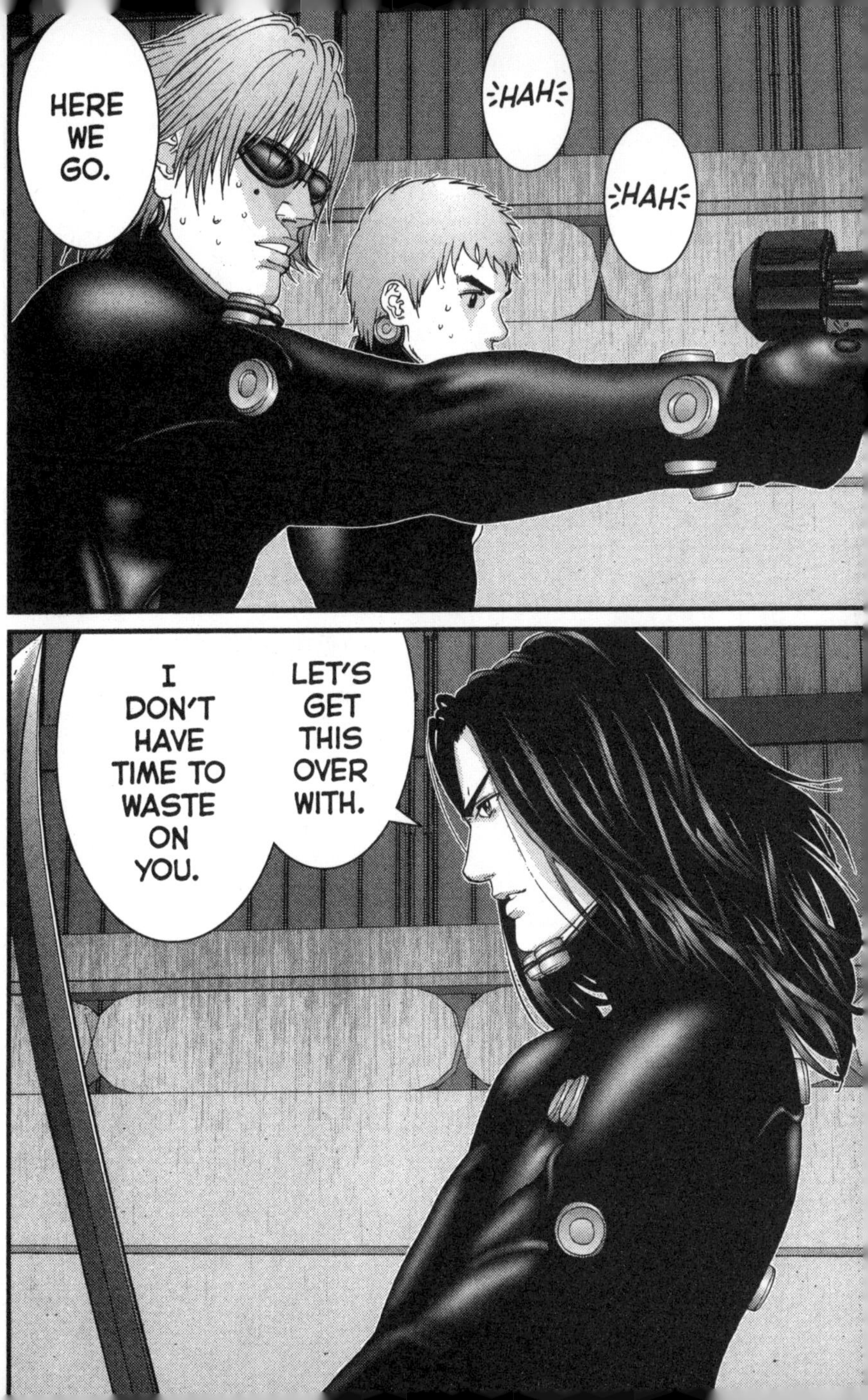
HAH
HAH
HERE WE GO.
LET'S GET THIS OVER WITH.
I DON'T HAVE TIME TO WASTE ON YOU.

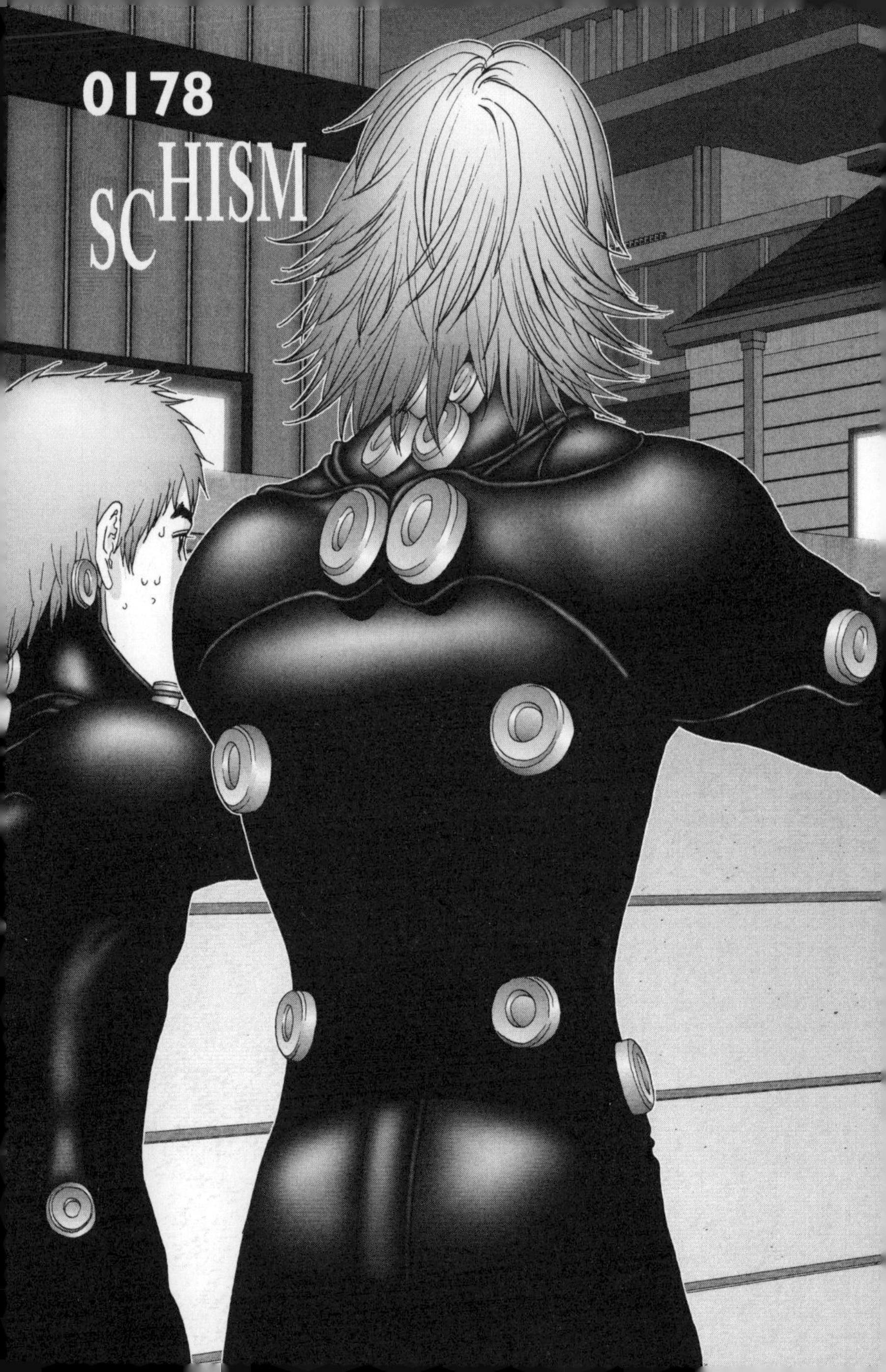
0178
SCHISM

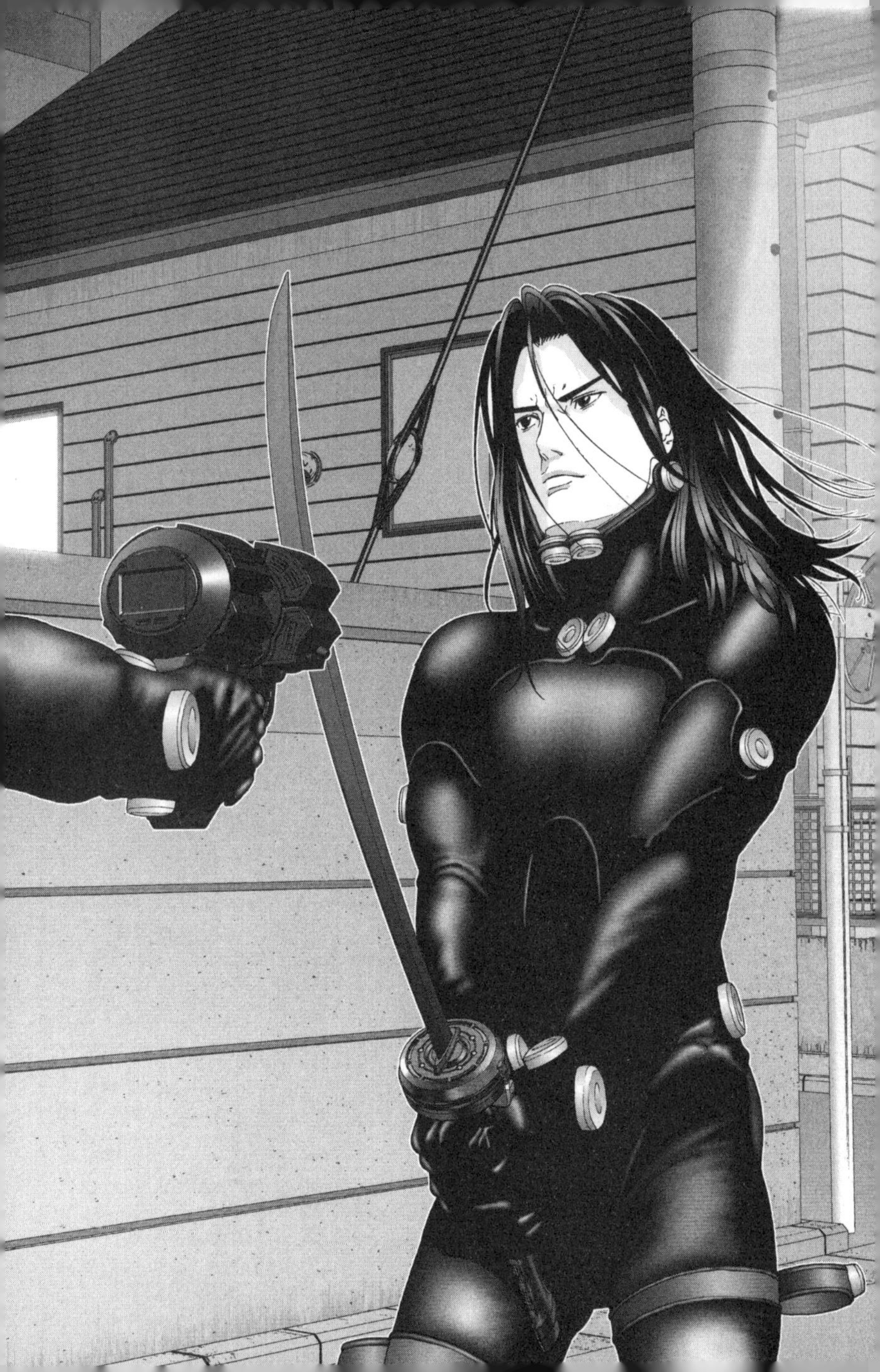

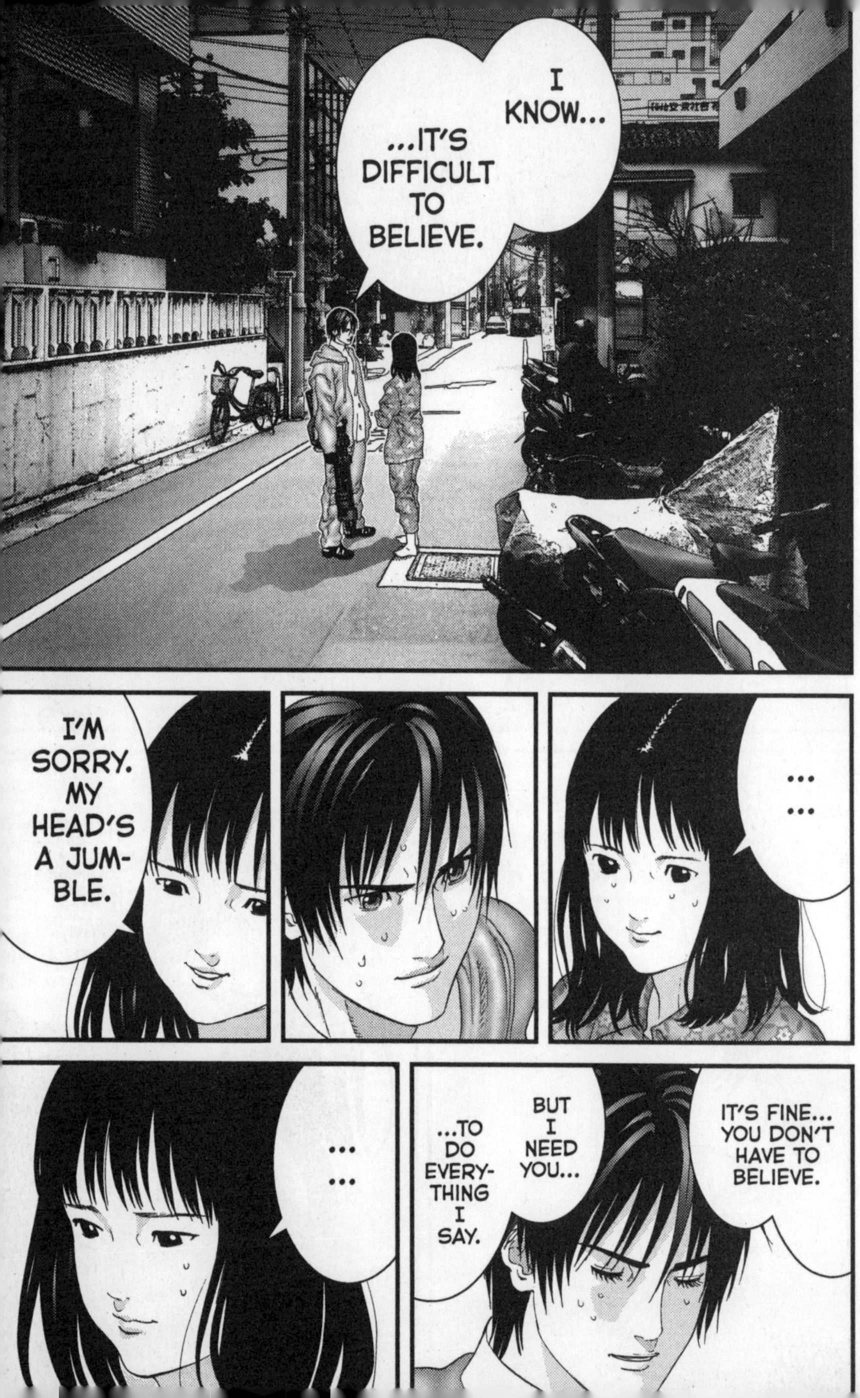
I KNOW... ...IT'S DIFFICULT TO BELIEVE.
... ...
I'M SORRY. MY HEAD'S A JUMBLE.
IT'S FINE... YOU DON'T HAVE TO BELIEVE.
BUT I NEED YOU...
...TO DO EVERYTHING I SAY.
... ...

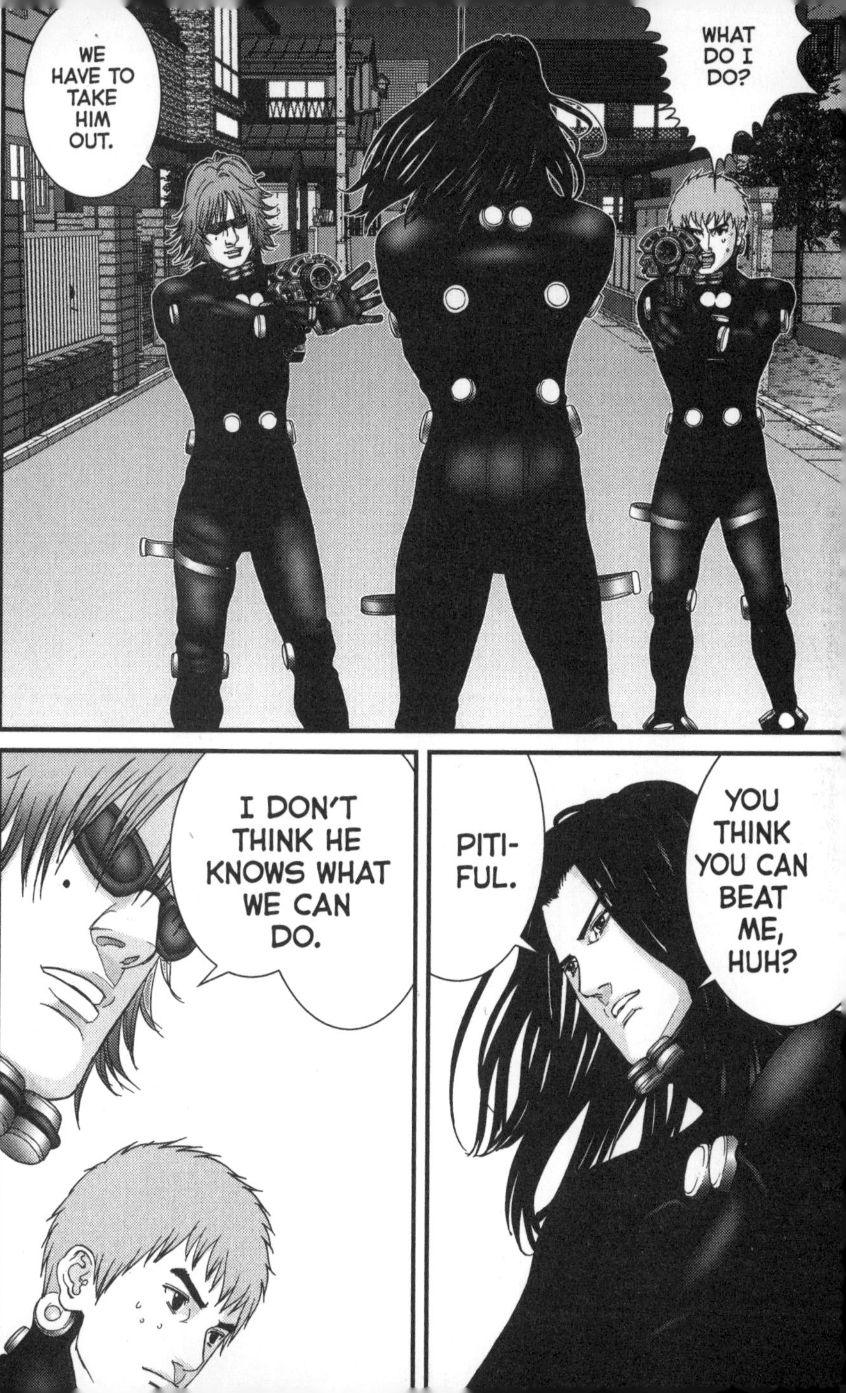
WHAT DO I DO?
WE HAVE TO TAKE HIM OUT.
YOU THINK YOU CAN BEAT ME, HUH?
PITI-FUL.
I DON'T THINK HE KNOWS WHAT WE CAN DO.

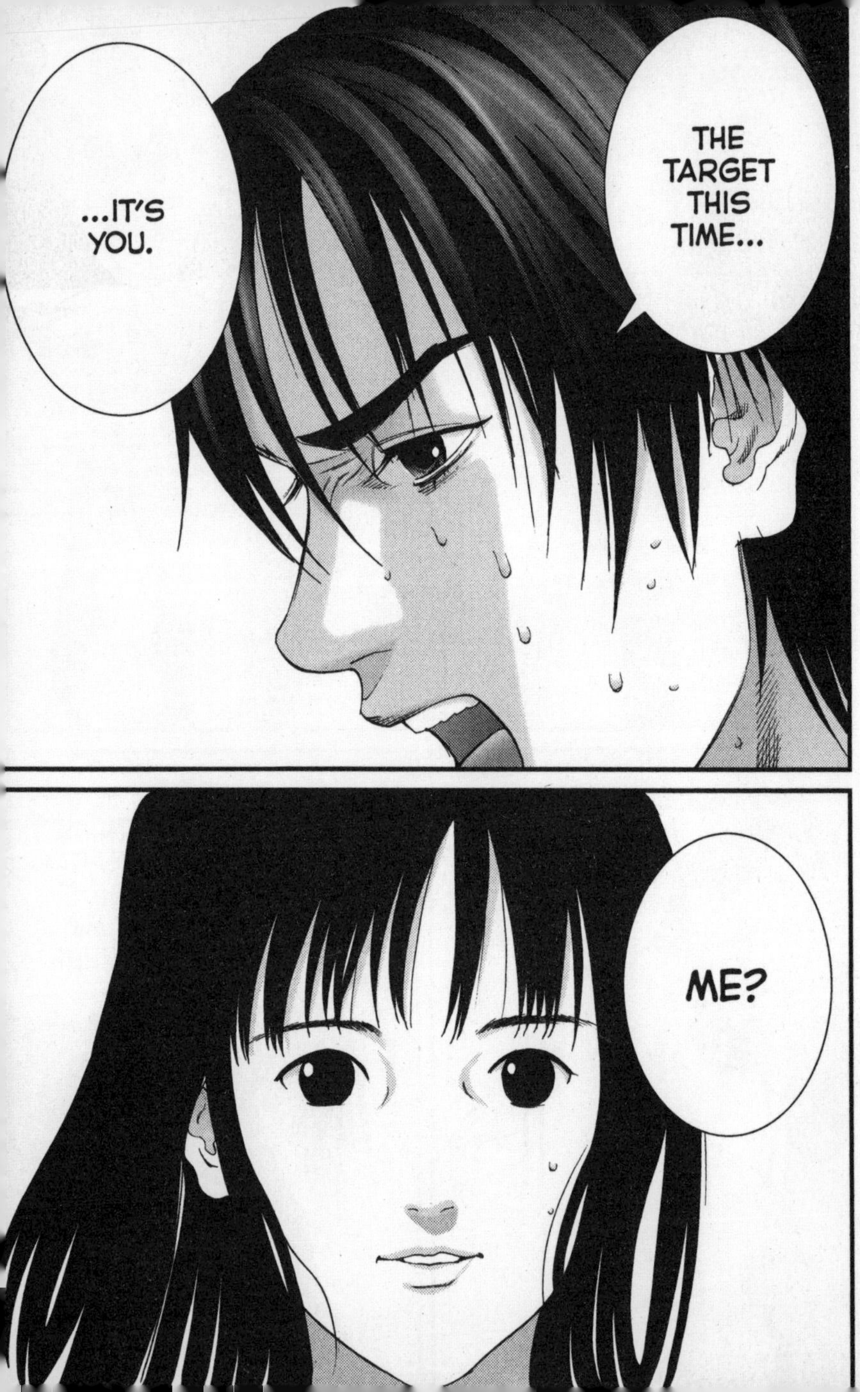
THE TARGET THIS TIME...
...IT'S YOU.
ME?

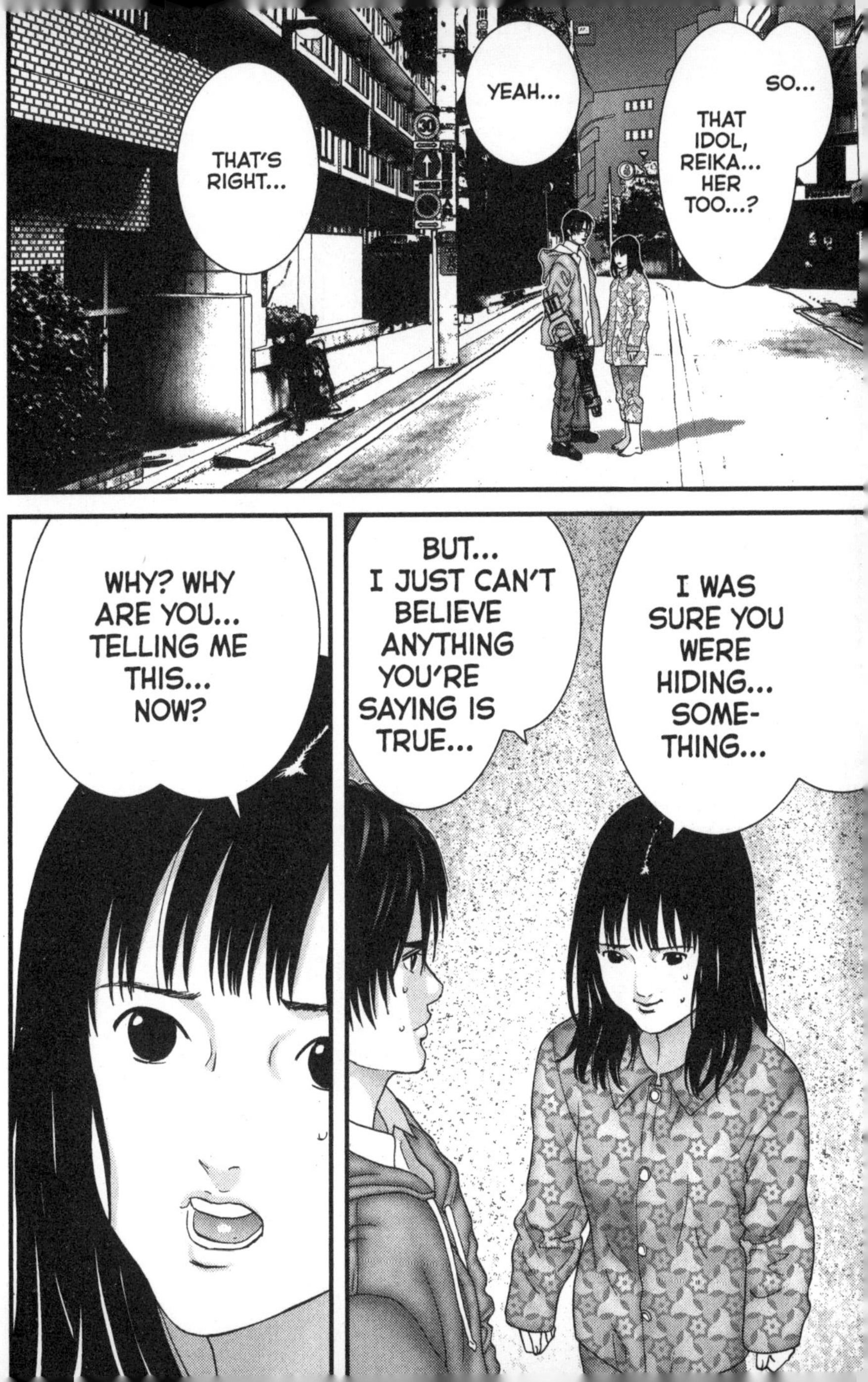
SO... THAT IDOL, REIKA... HER TOO...?
YEAH...
THAT'S RIGHT...
I WAS SURE YOU WERE HIDING... SOME-THING...
BUT... I JUST CAN'T BELIEVE ANYTHING YOU'RE SAYING IS TRUE...
WHY? WHY ARE YOU... TELLING ME THIS... NOW?

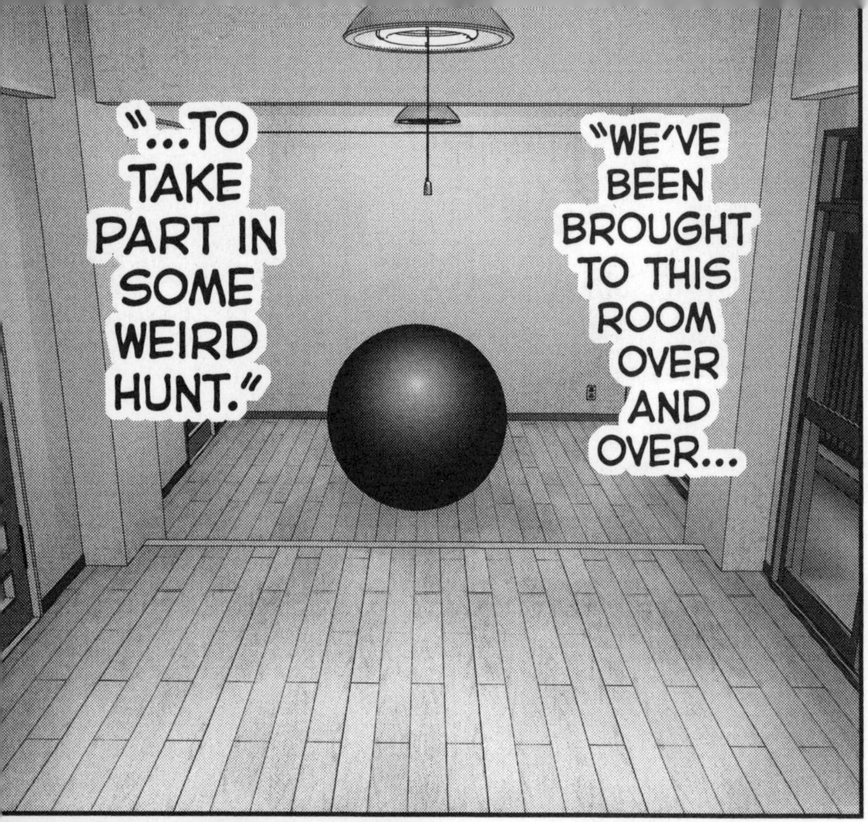
"WE'VE BEEN BROUGHT TO THIS ROOM OVER AND OVER...
"...TO TAKE PART IN SOME WEIRD HUNT."
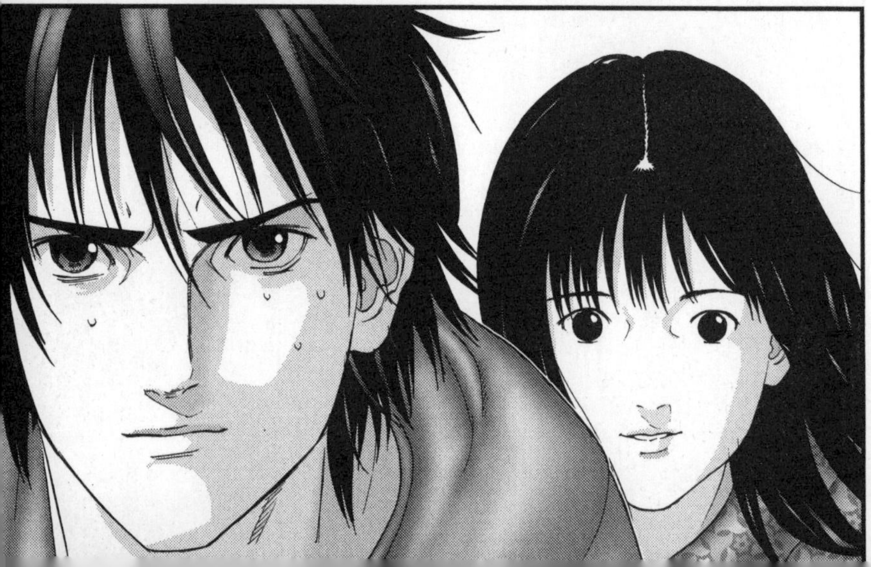

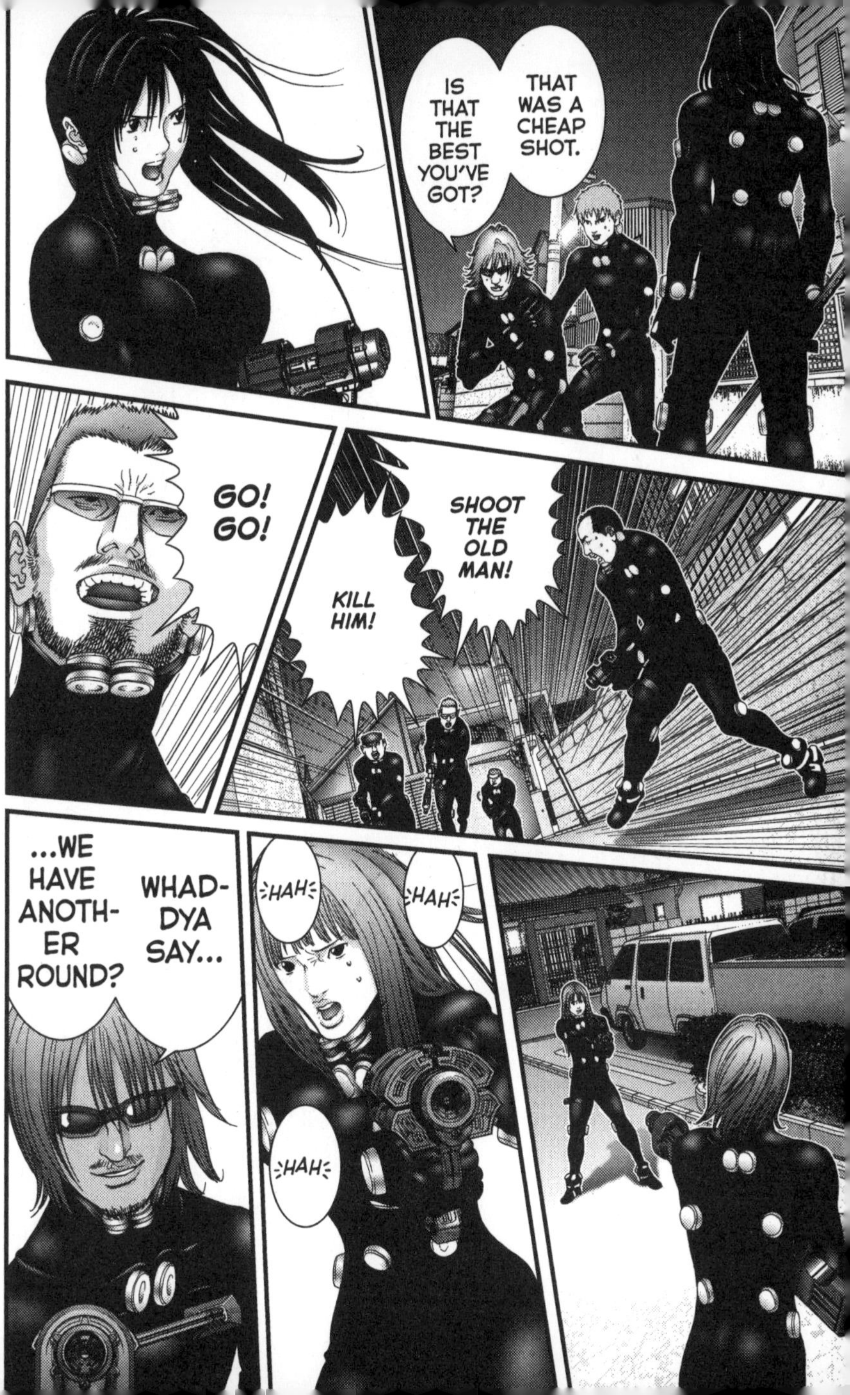
THAT WAS A CHEAP SHOT.
IS THAT THE BEST YOU'VE GOT?
SHOOT THE OLD MAN!
KILL HIM!
GO! GO!
HAH
HAH
HAH
WHAD-DYA SAY...
...WE HAVE ANOTH-ER ROUND?

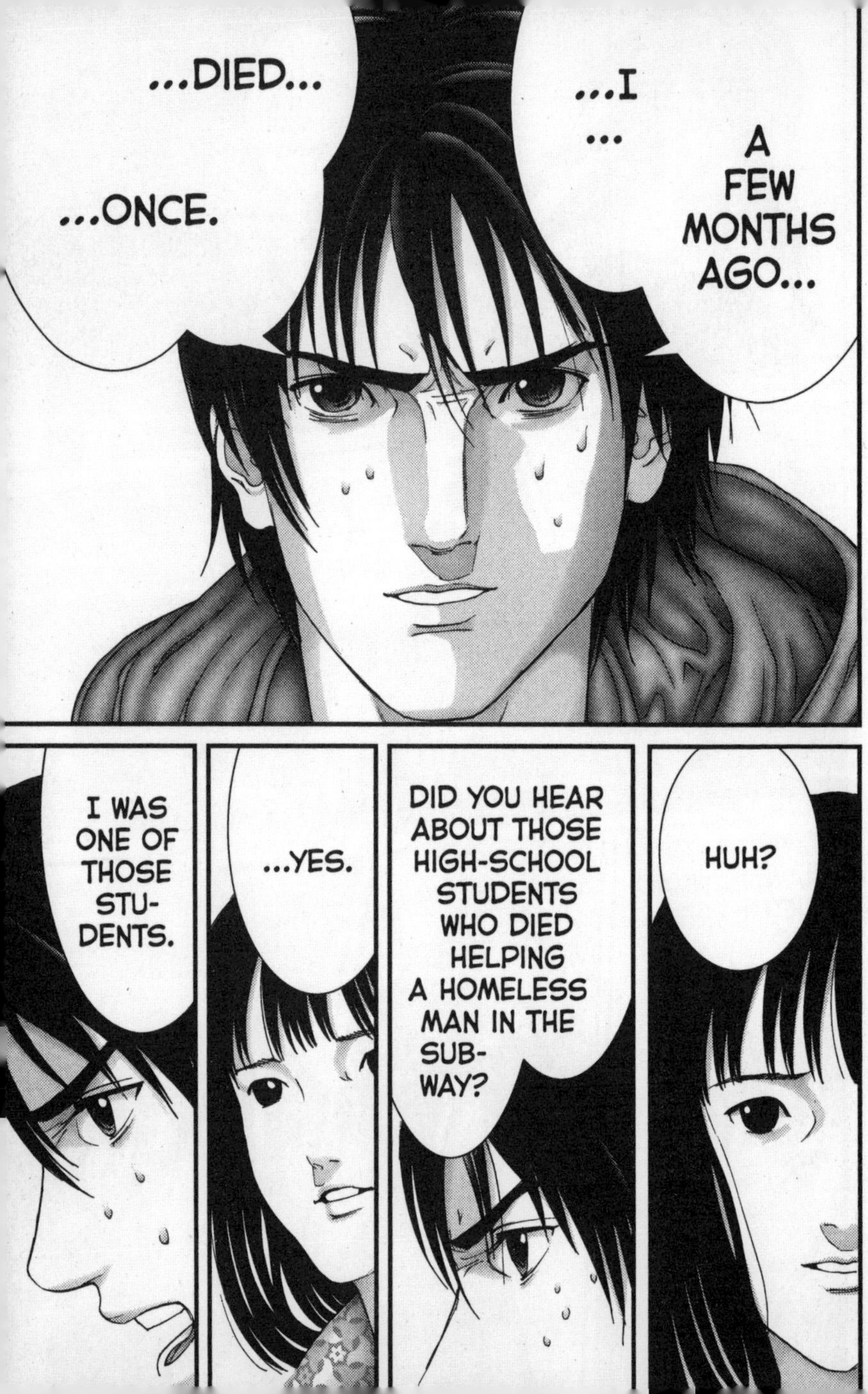
...I
...
A FEW MONTHS AGO...
...DIED...
...ONCE.
HUH?
DID YOU HEAR ABOUT THOSE HIGH-SCHOOL STUDENTS WHO DIED HELPING A HOMELESS MAN IN THE SUB-WAY?
...YES.
I WAS ONE OF THOSE STU-DENTS.

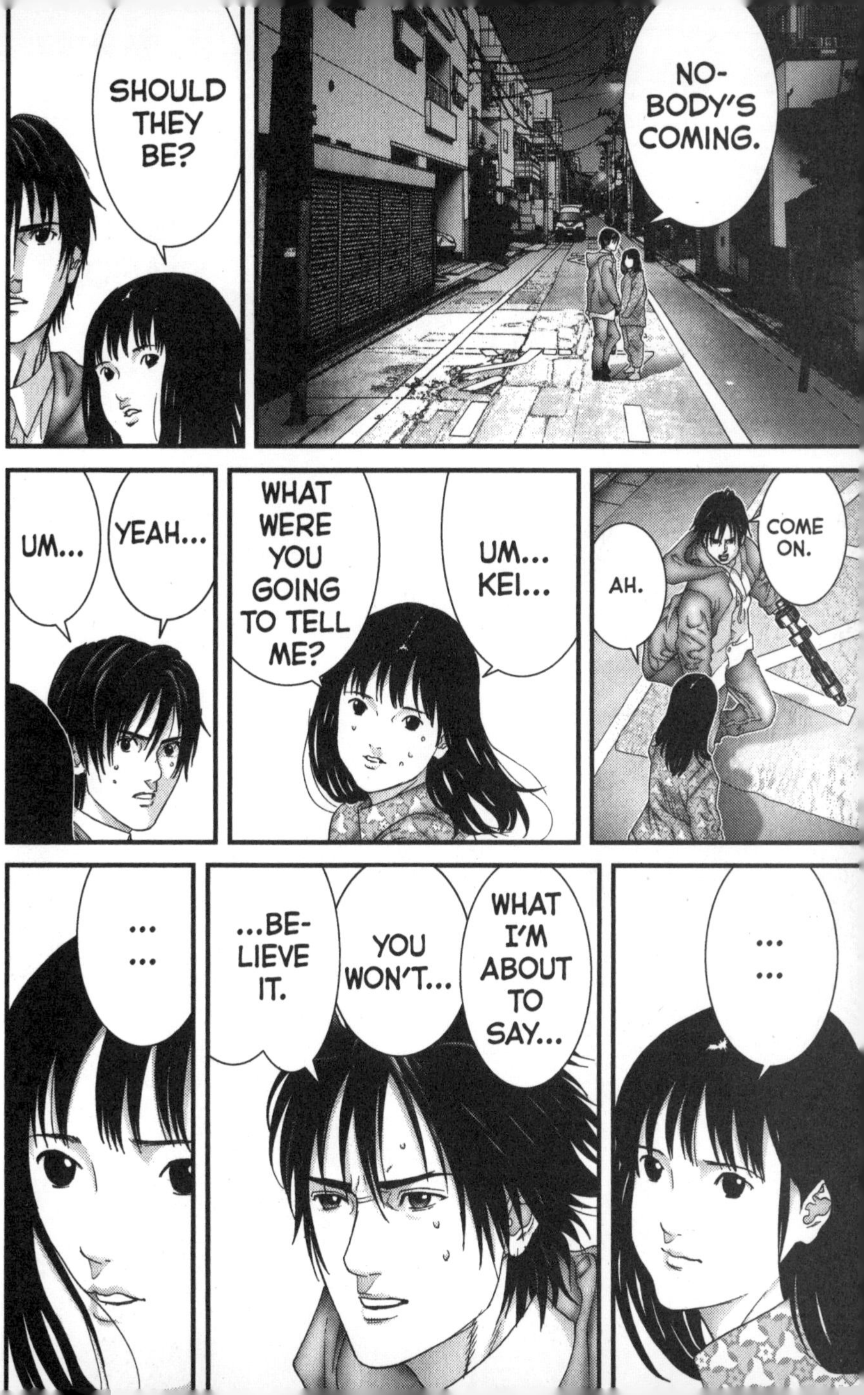
NO-BODY'S COMING.
SHOULD THEY BE?
COME ON.
AH.
UM... KEI...
WHAT WERE YOU GOING TO TELL ME?
YEAH...
UM...
... ...
WHAT I'M ABOUT TO SAY...
YOU WON'T...
...BE-LIEVE IT.
... ...

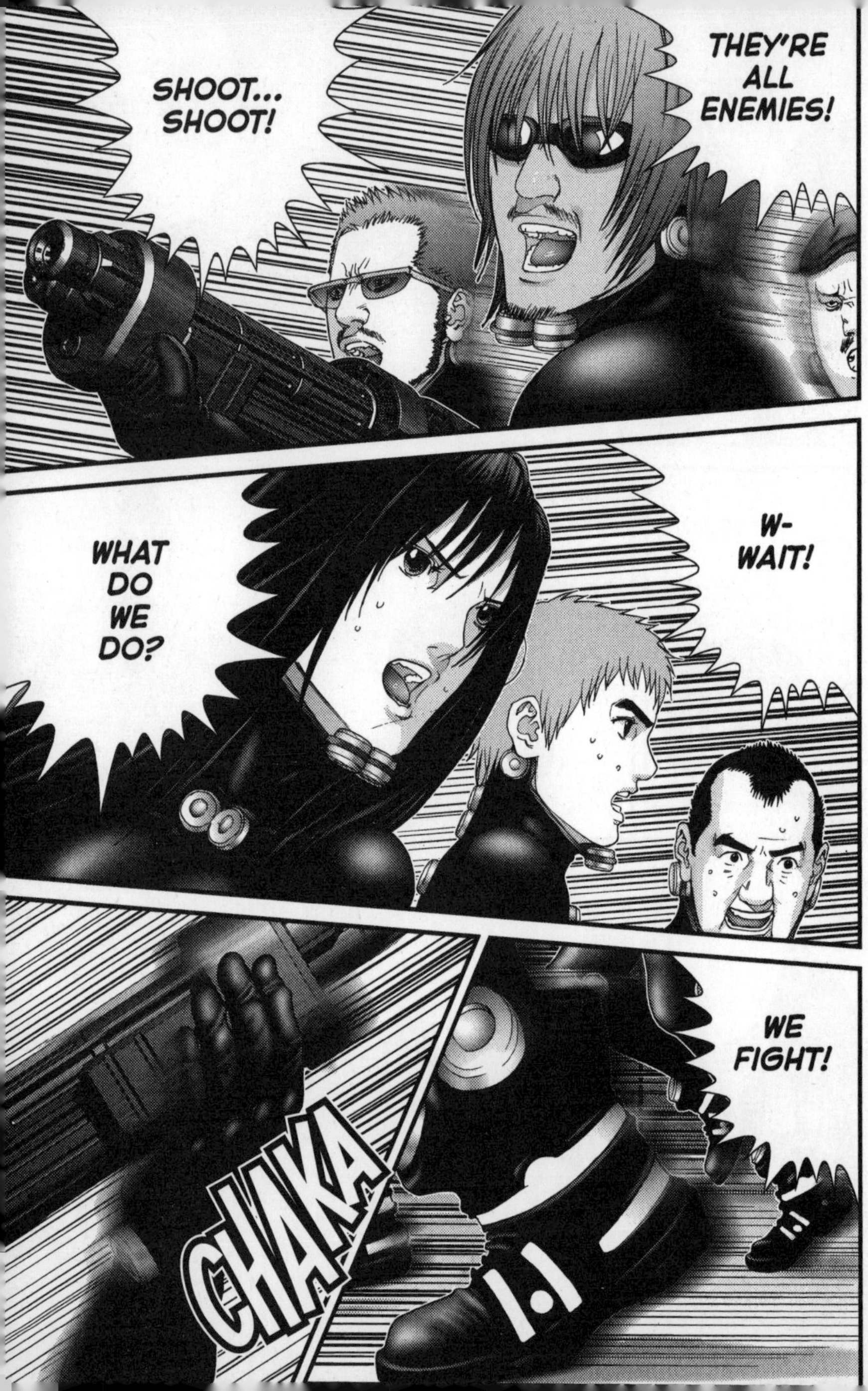
THEY'RE ALL ENEMIES!
SHOOT... SHOOT!
W-WAIT!
WHAT DO WE DO?
WE FIGHT!
CHAKA

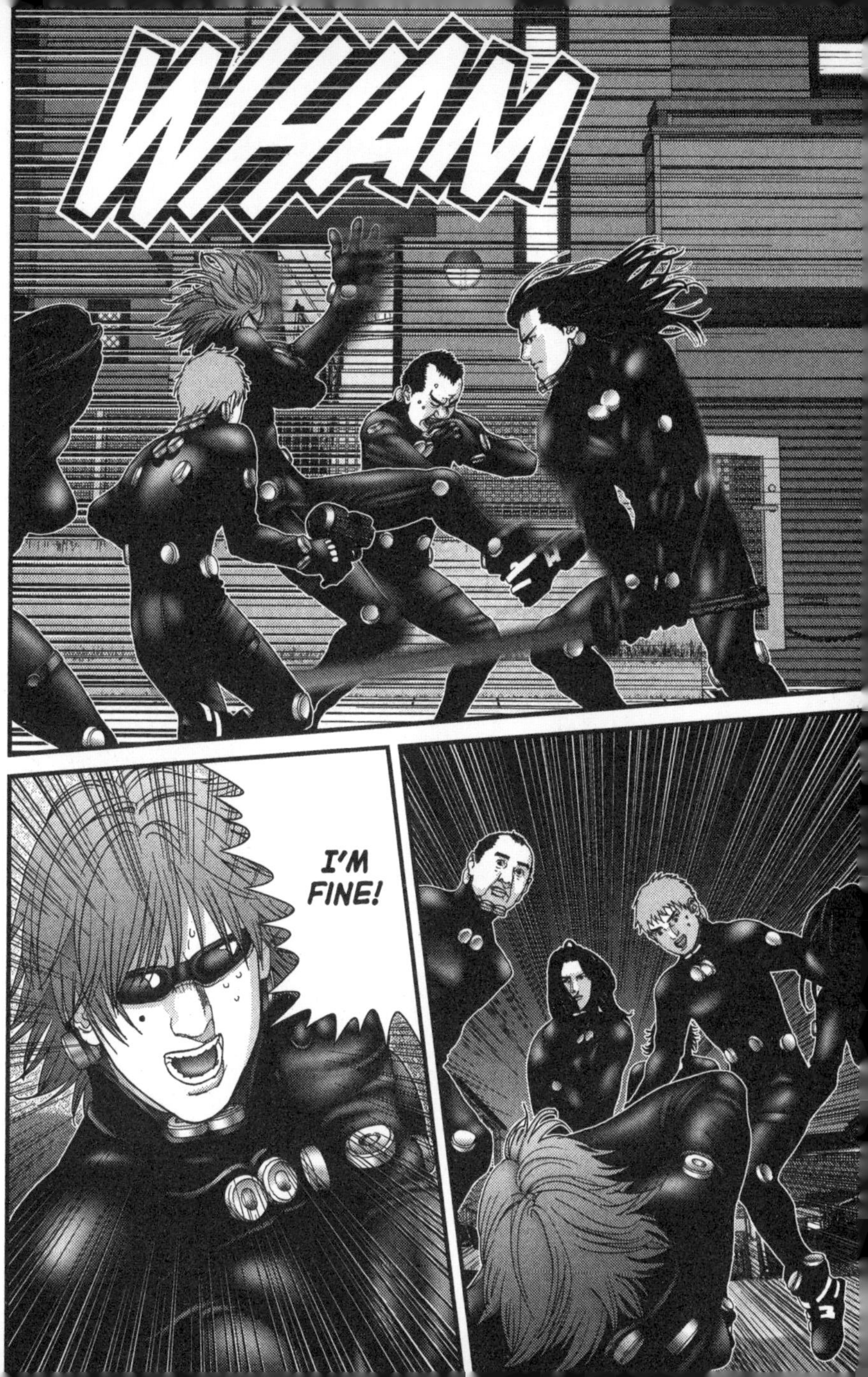
WHAM
I'M FINE!

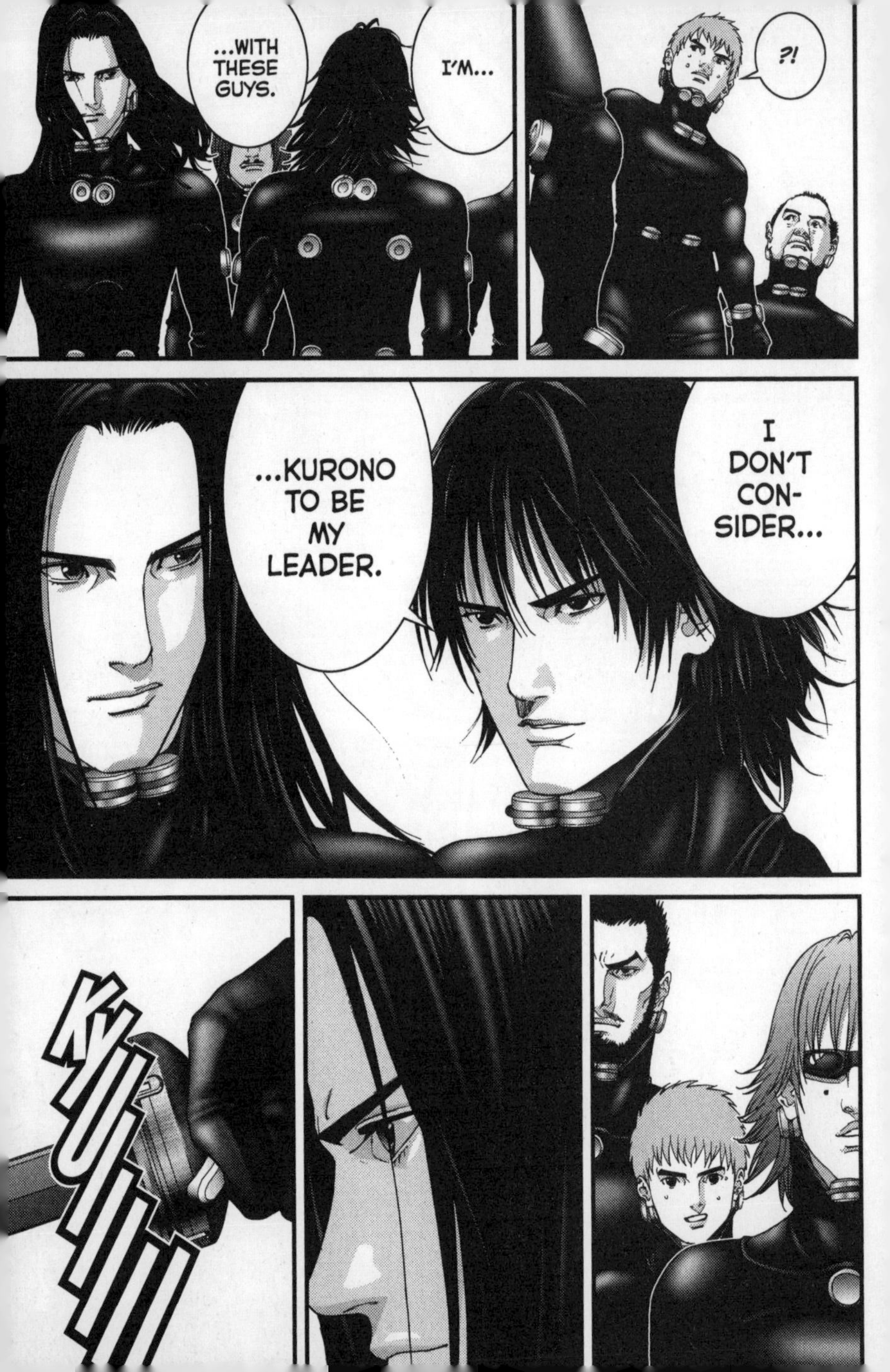
?!
I'M...
...WITH THESE GUYS.
I DON'T CON-SIDER...
...KURONO TO BE MY LEADER.
KYUIIII

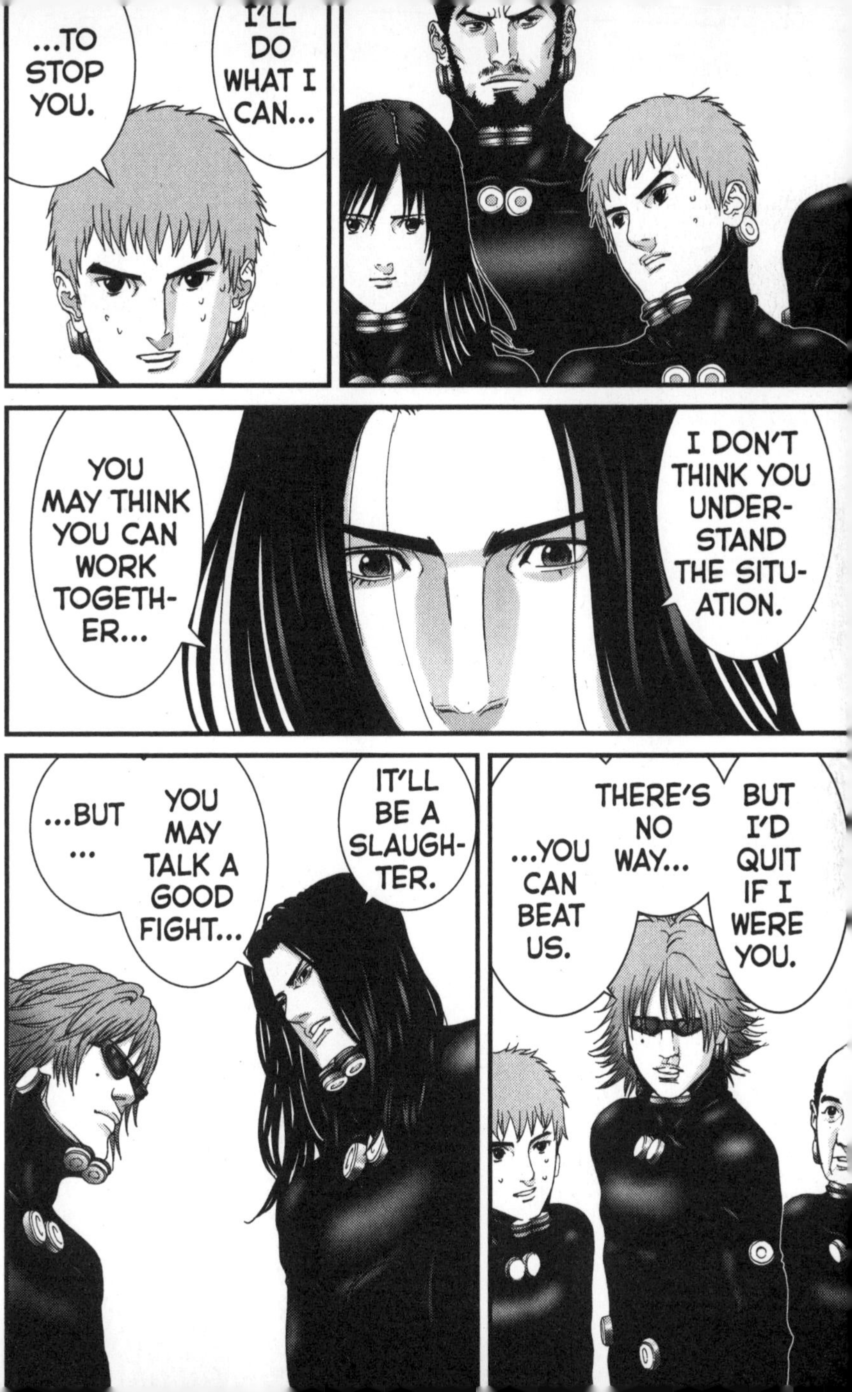
I'LL DO WHAT I CAN...
...TO STOP YOU.
I DON'T THINK YOU UNDERSTAND THE SITUATION.
YOU MAY THINK YOU CAN WORK TOGETHER...
BUT I'D QUIT IF I WERE YOU.
THERE'S NO WAY...
...YOU CAN BEAT US.
IT'LL BE A SLAUGHTER.
YOU MAY TALK A GOOD FIGHT...
...BUT ...

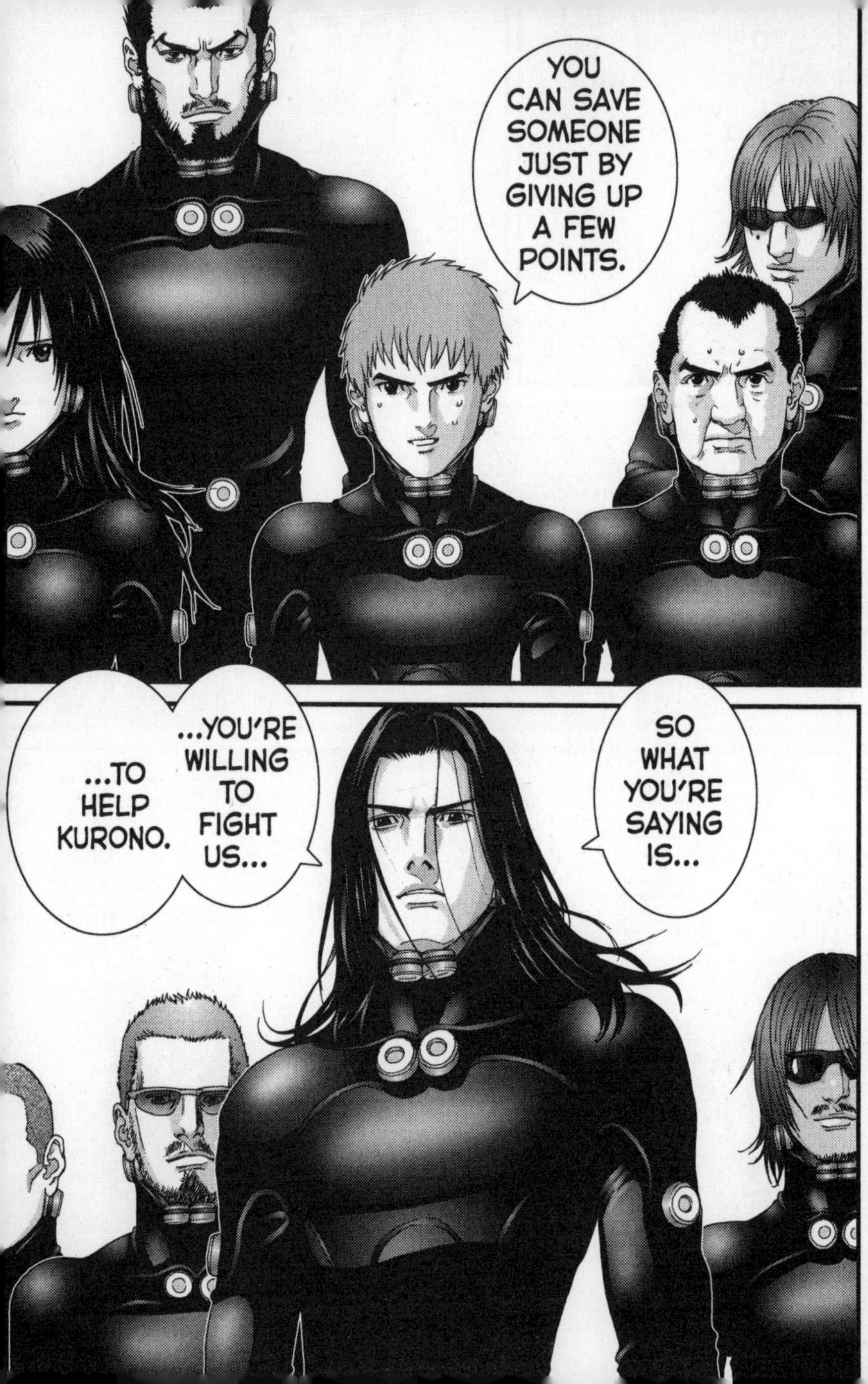
YOU CAN SAVE SOMEONE JUST BY GIVING UP A FEW POINTS.
SO WHAT YOU'RE SAYING IS...
...YOU'RE WILLING TO FIGHT US...
...TO HELP KURONO.

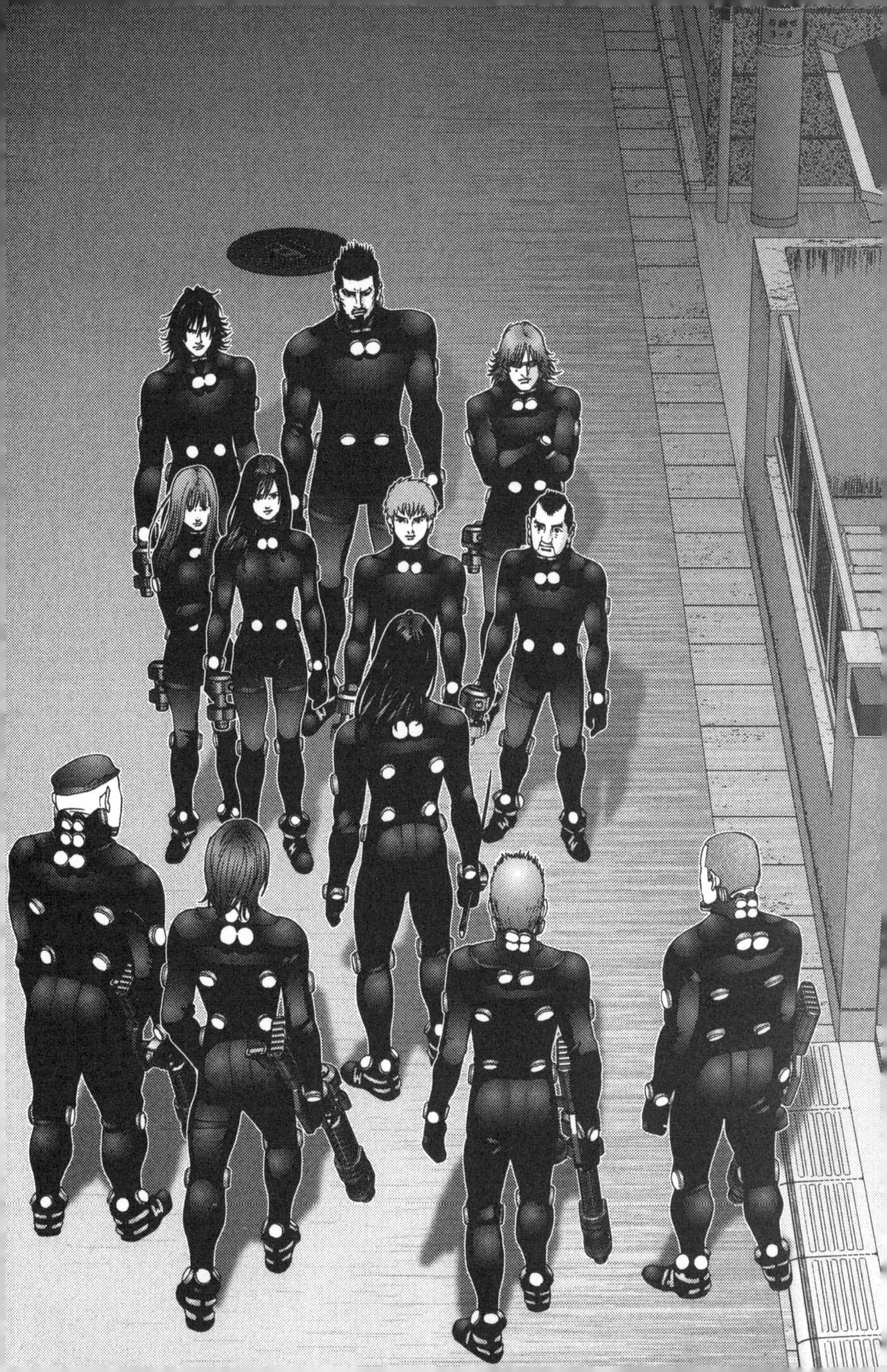

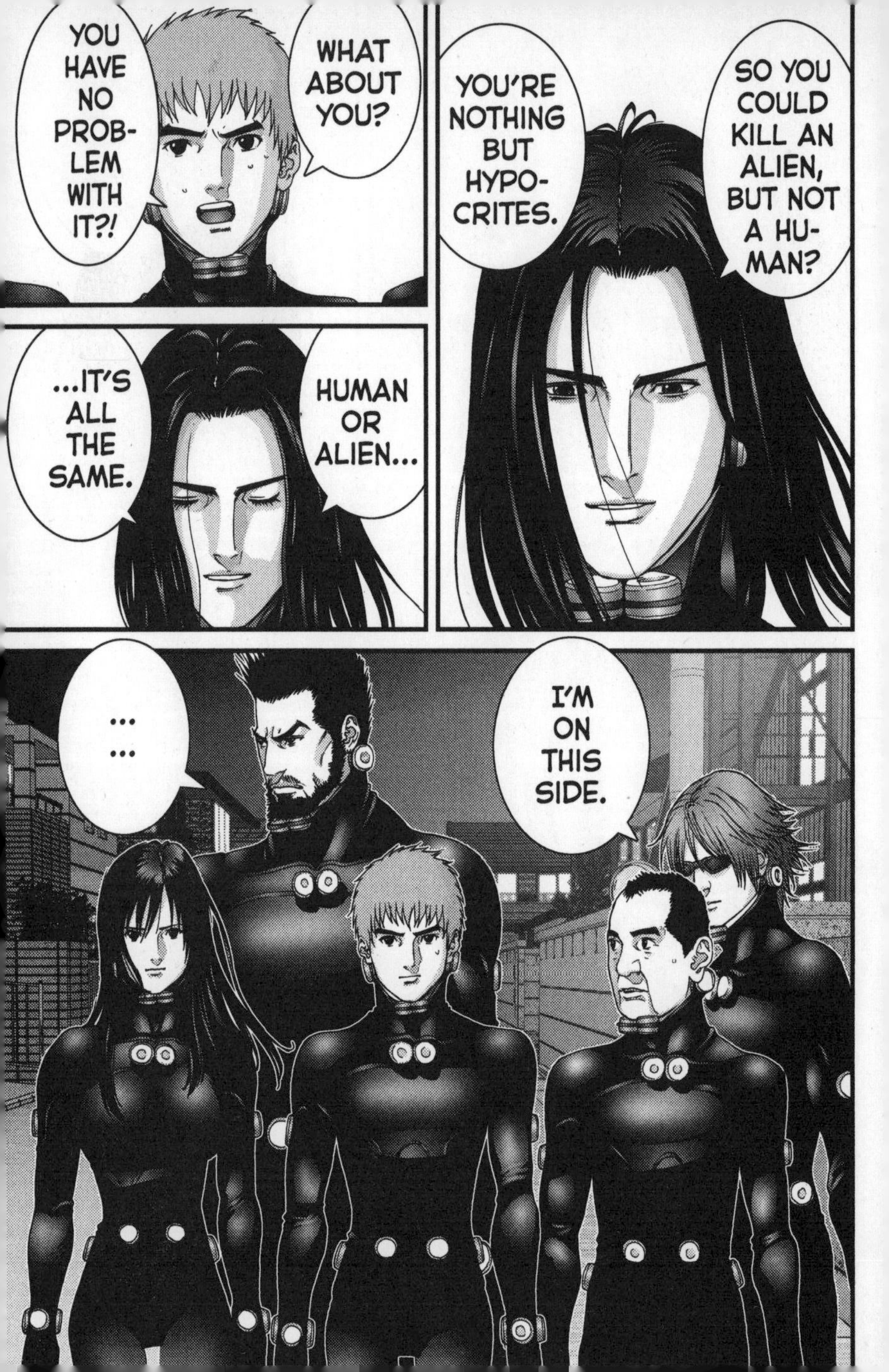
WHAT ABOUT YOU?
YOU HAVE NO PROB-LEM WITH IT?!
HUMAN OR ALIEN...
...IT'S ALL THE SAME.
SO YOU COULD KILL AN ALIEN, BUT NOT A HU-MAN?
YOU'RE NOTHING BUT HYPO-CRITES.
I'M ON THIS SIDE.
... ...

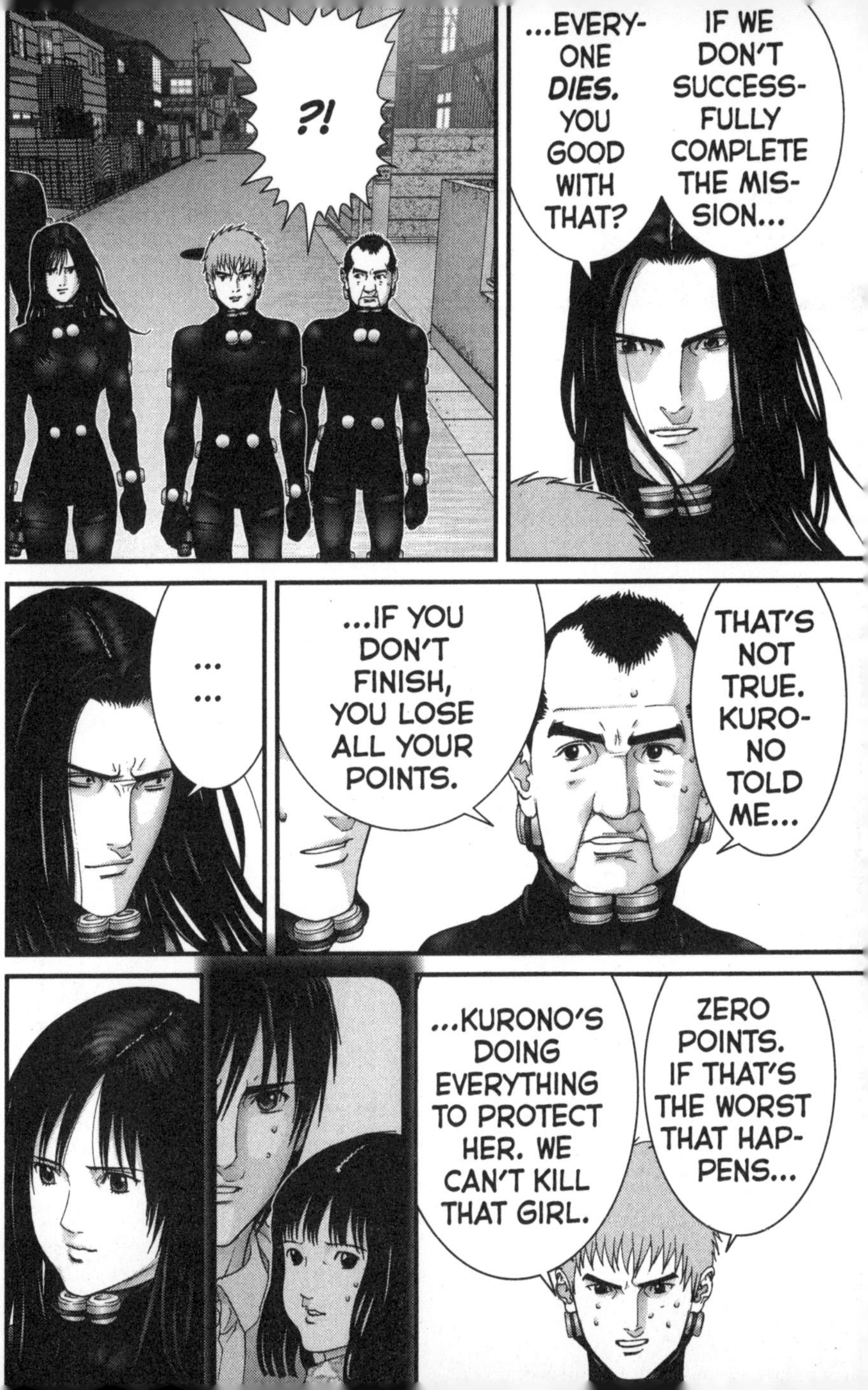
IF WE DON'T SUCCESSFULLY COMPLETE THE MISSION...
...EVERYONE *DIES.* YOU GOOD WITH THAT?
?!
THAT'S NOT TRUE. KURONO TOLD ME...
...IF YOU DON'T FINISH, YOU LOSE ALL YOUR POINTS.
......
ZERO POINTS. IF THAT'S THE WORST THAT HAPPENS...
...KURONO'S DOING EVERYTHING TO PROTECT HER. WE CAN'T KILL THAT GIRL.

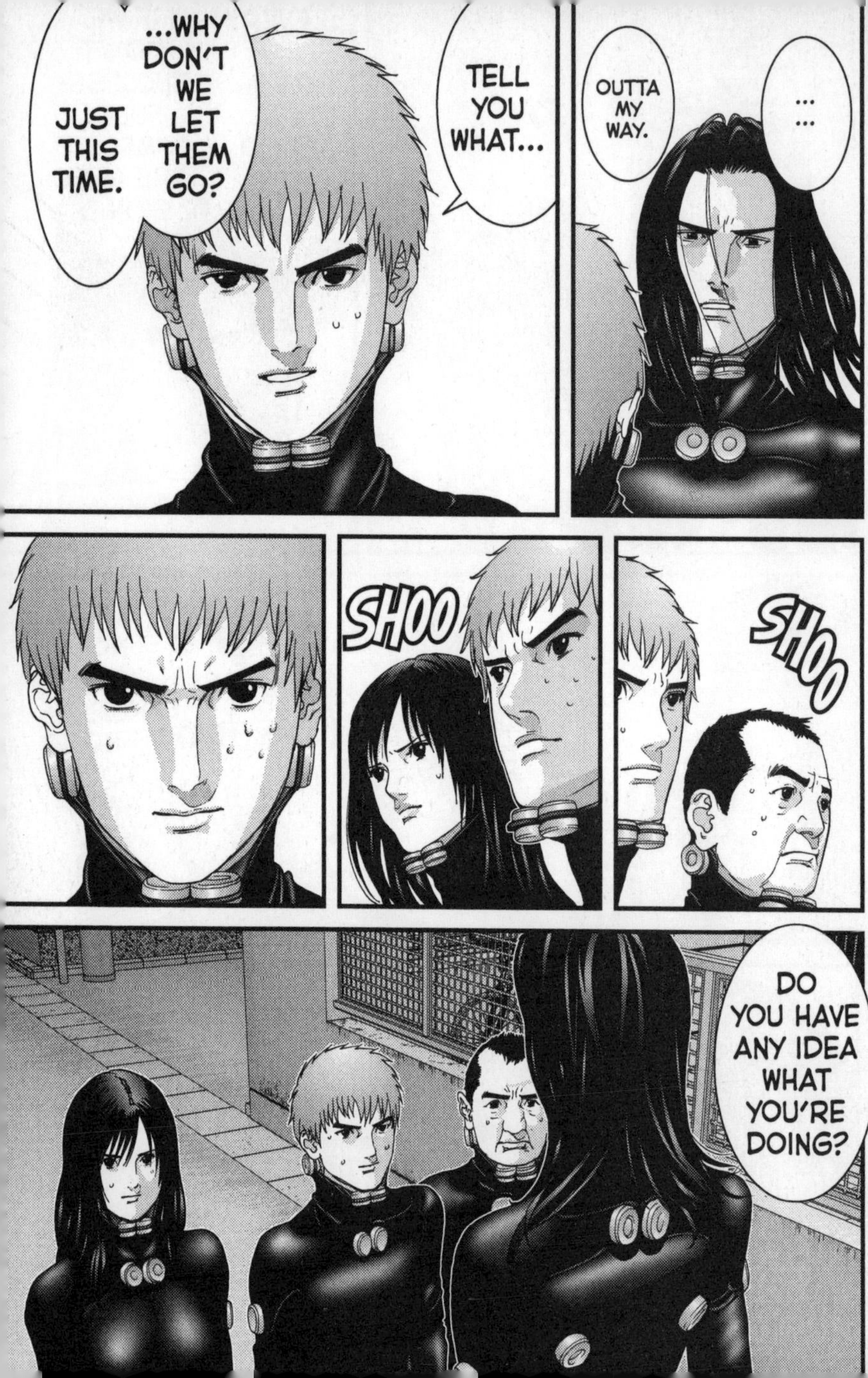
……
OUTTA MY WAY.
TELL YOU WHAT...
...WHY DON'T WE LET THEM GO?
JUST THIS TIME.
SHOO
SHOO
DO YOU HAVE ANY IDEA WHAT YOU'RE DOING?

0177 TRUE FEELINGS

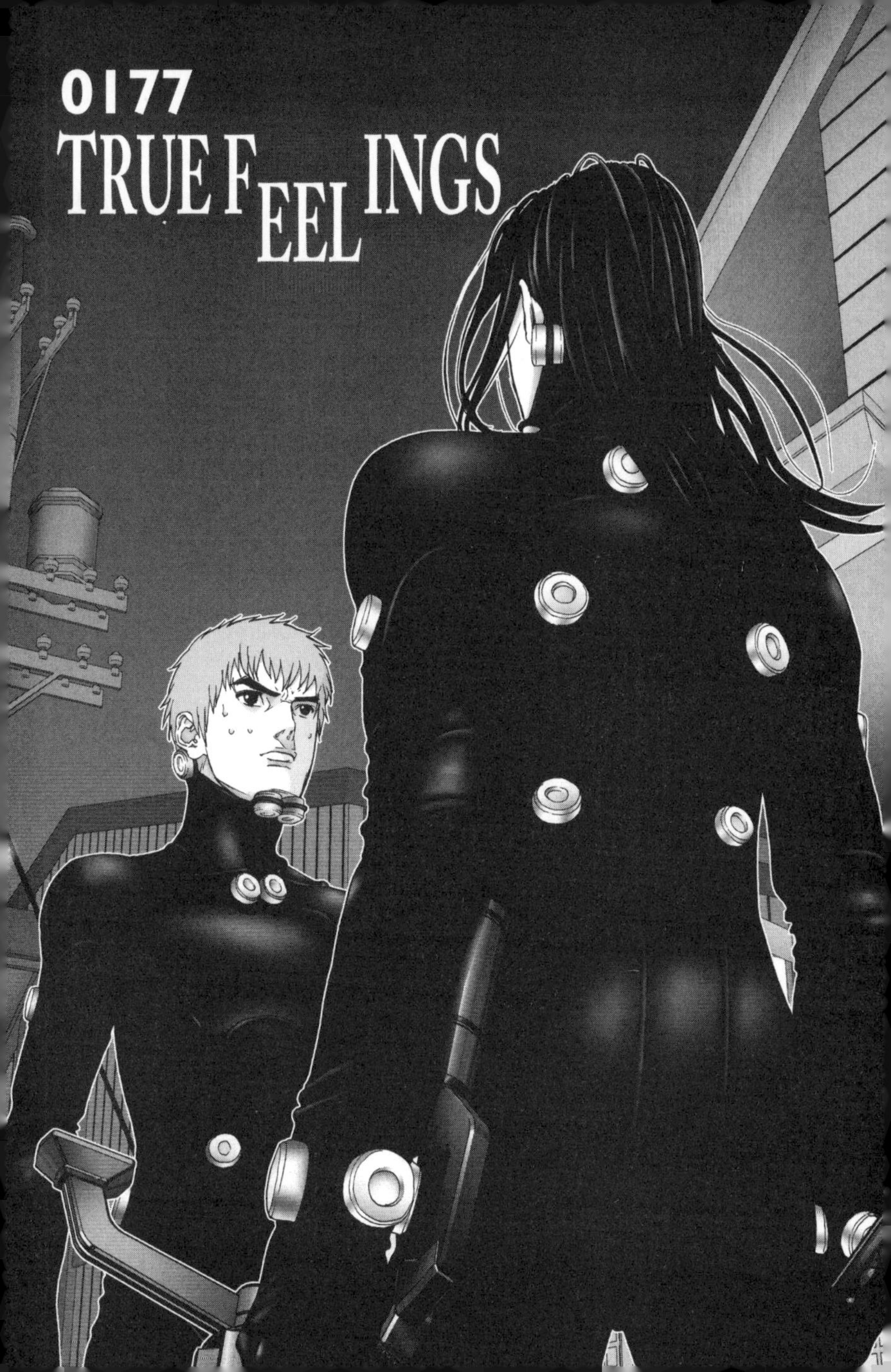

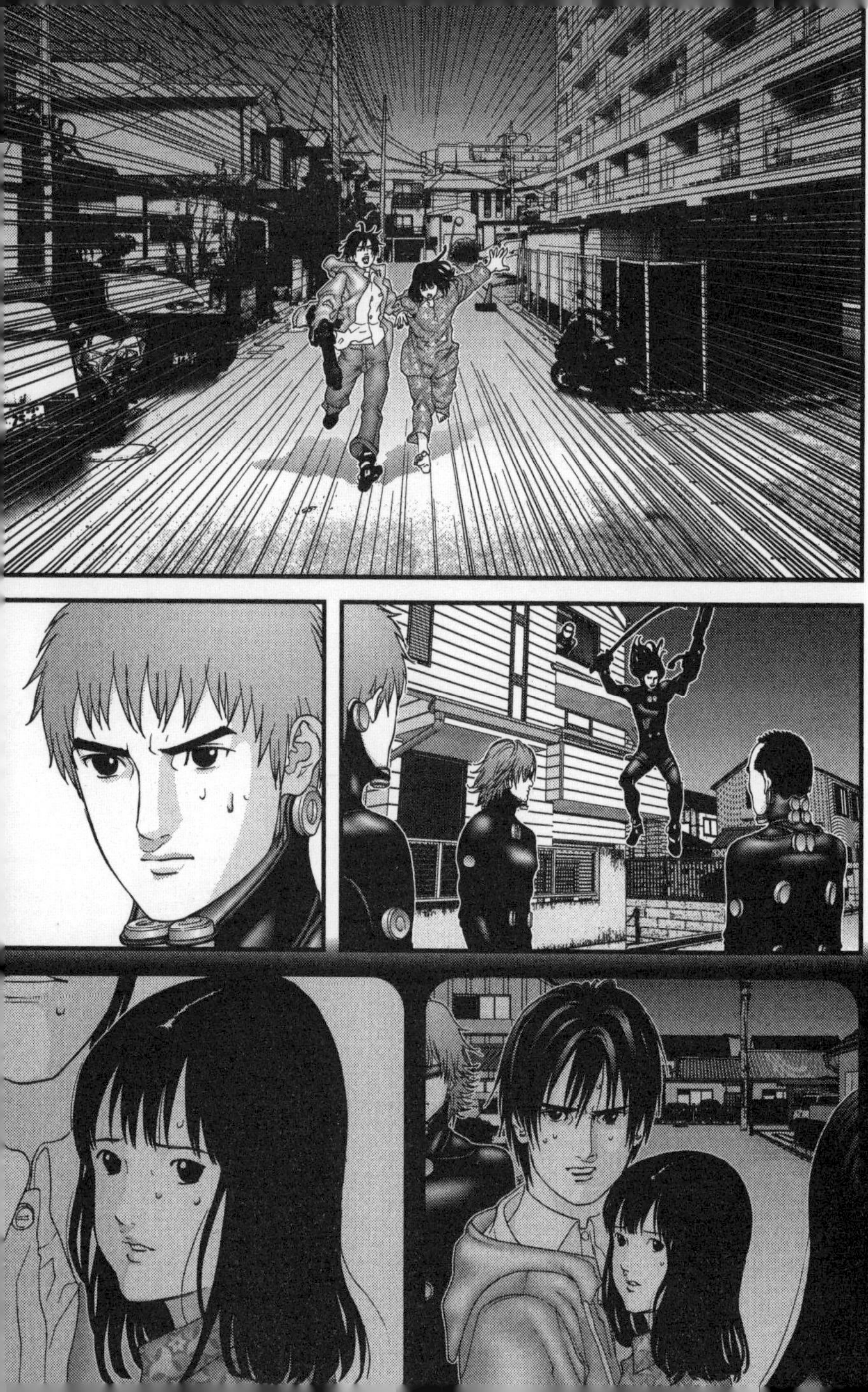

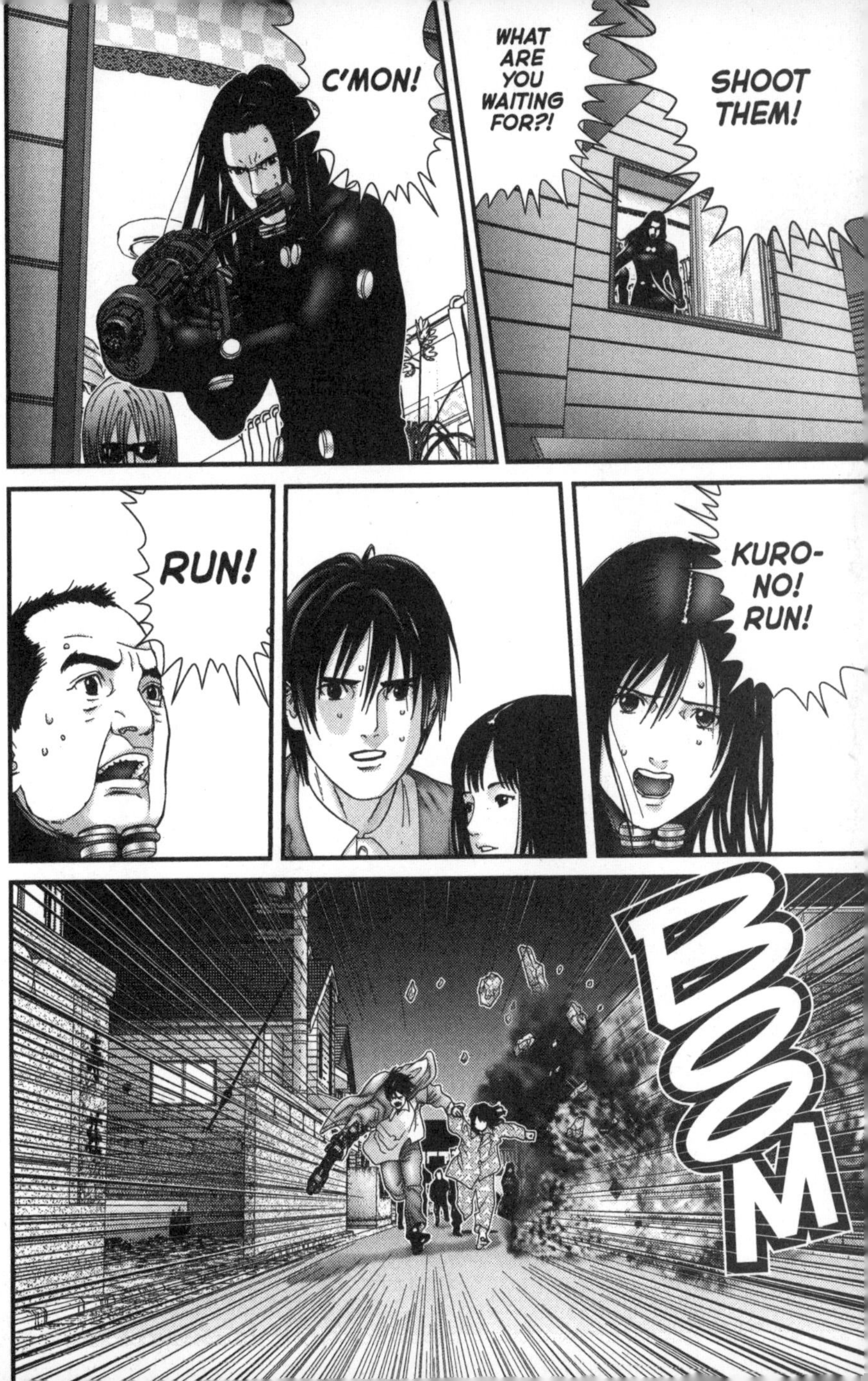
WHAT ARE YOU WAITING FOR?!
SHOOT THEM!
C'MON!
KURO-NO! RUN!
RUN!
BOOM

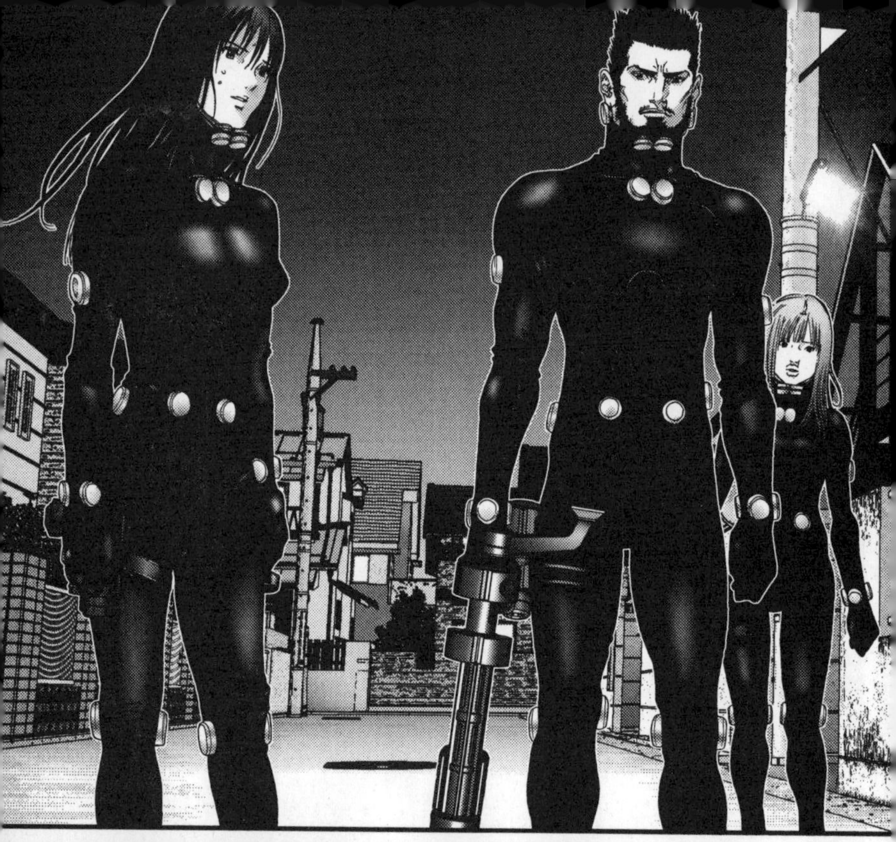

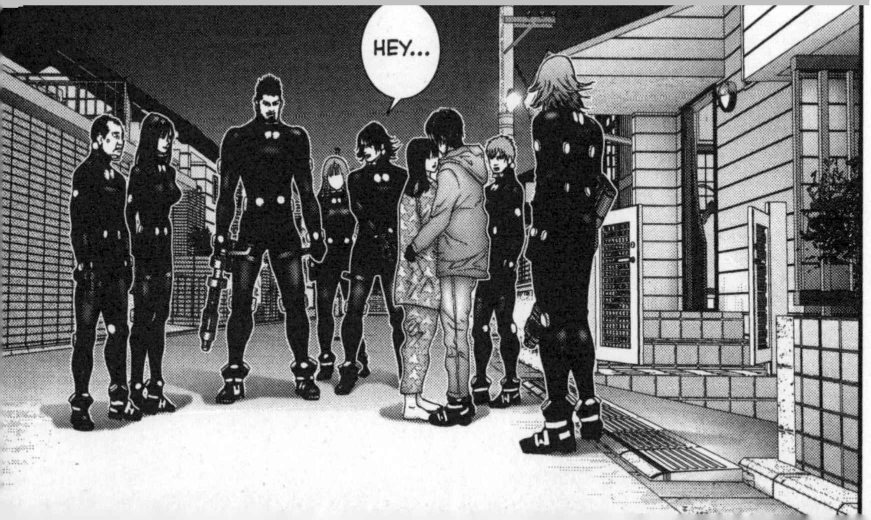
HEY...

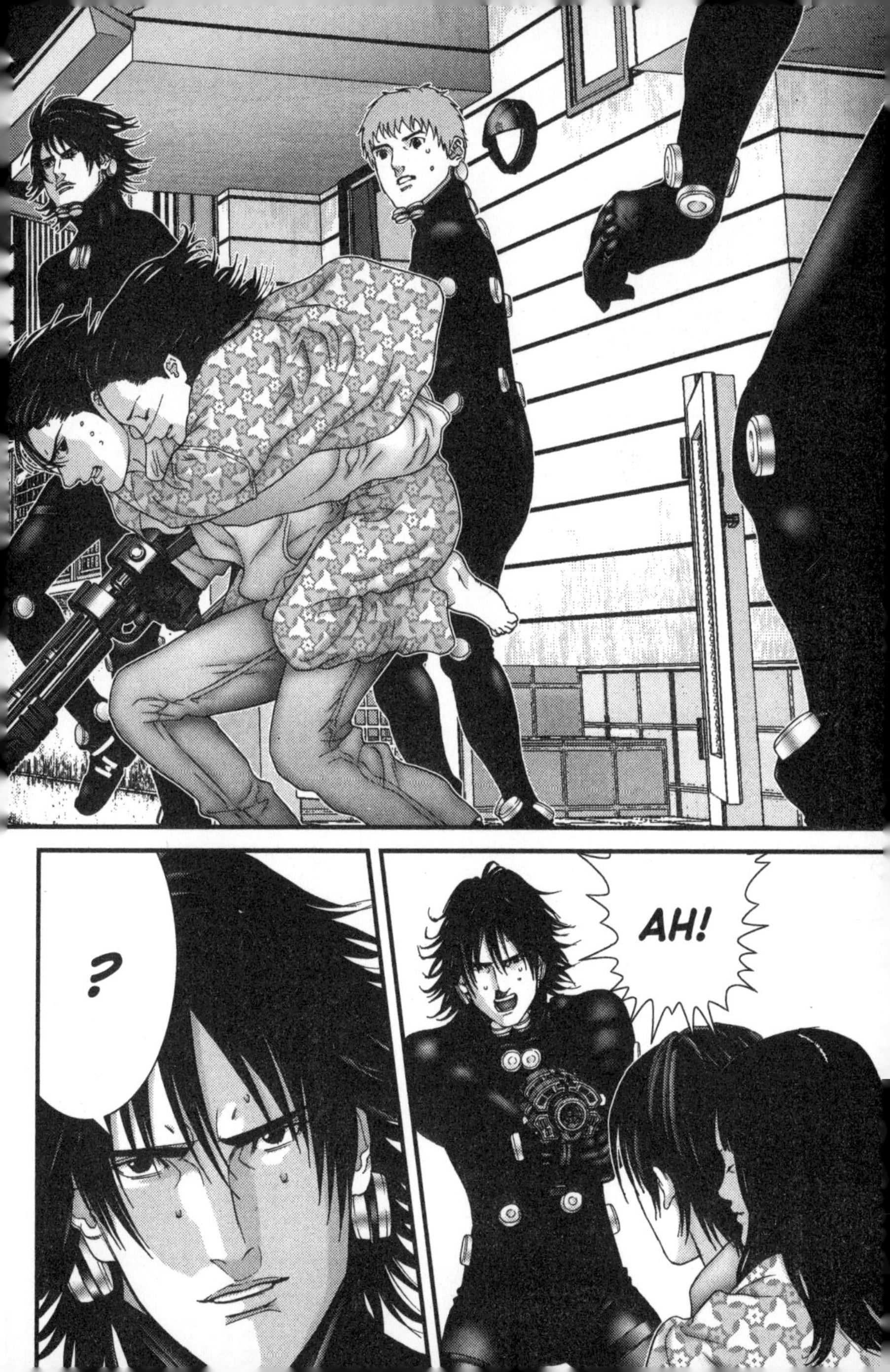
AH!
?

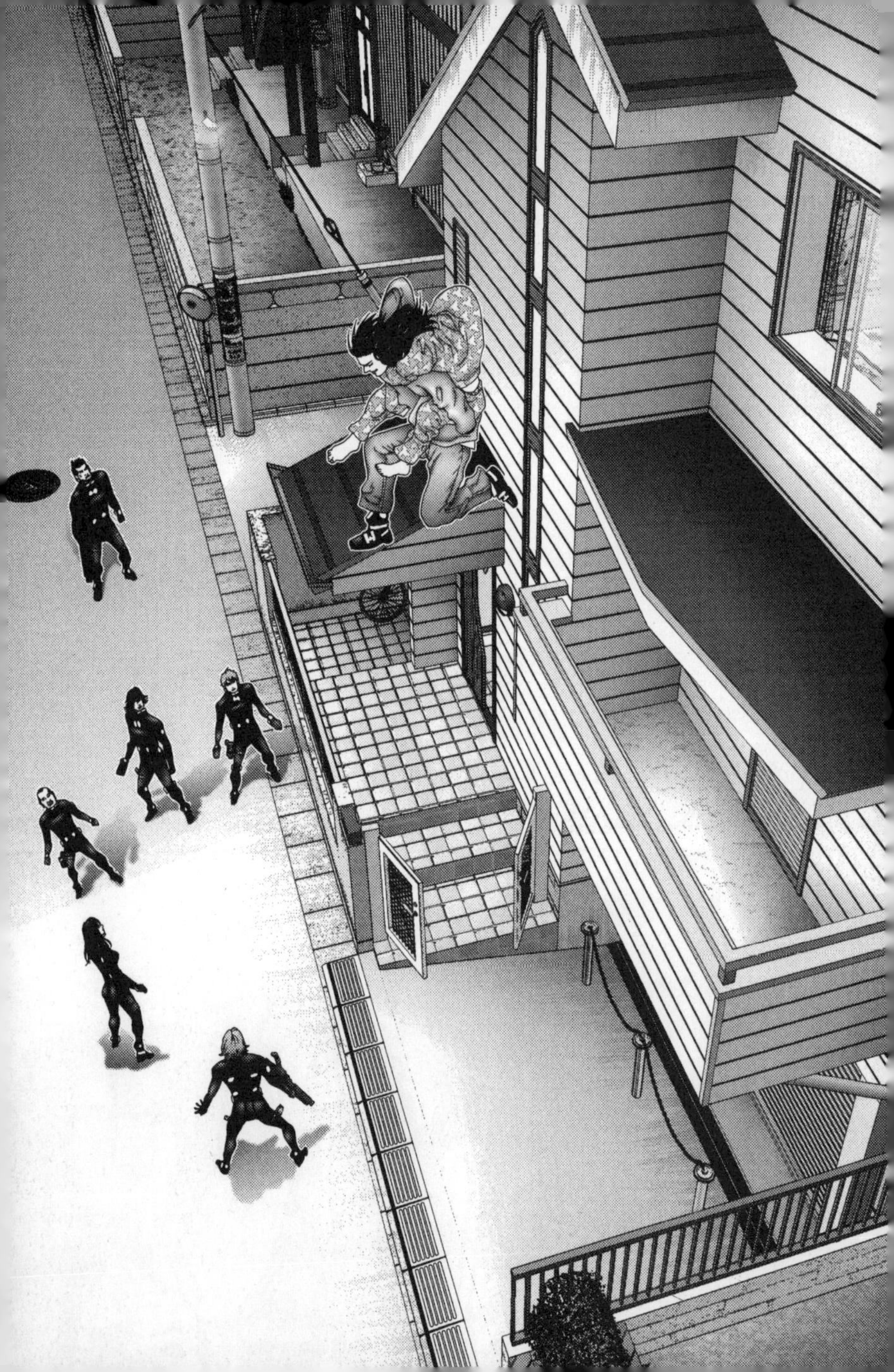

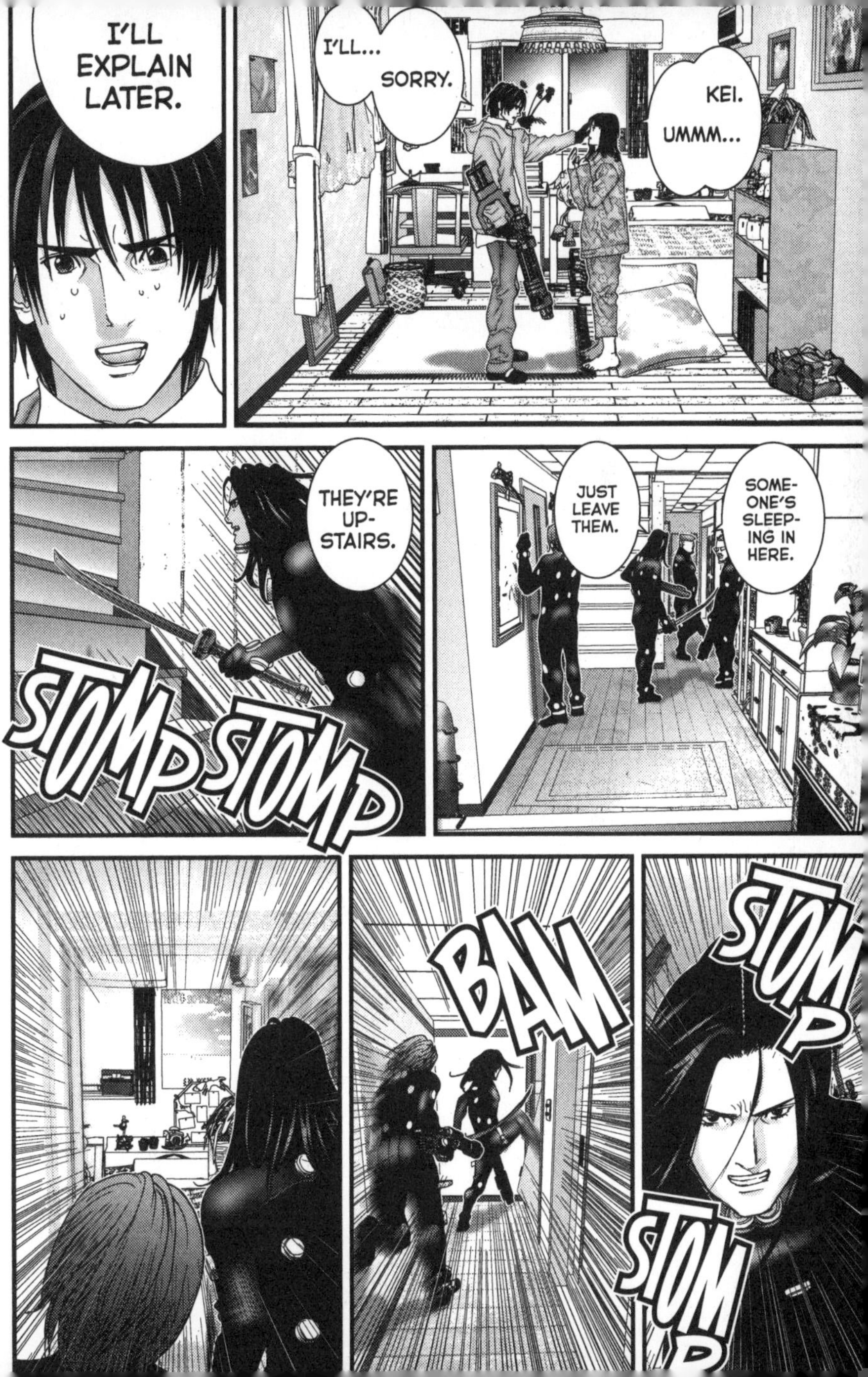
KEI. UMMM...
I'LL... SORRY.
I'LL EXPLAIN LATER.
SOME-ONE'S SLEEP-ING IN HERE.
JUST LEAVE THEM.
THEY'RE UP-STAIRS.
STOMP STOMP
STOMP
STOMP
BAM

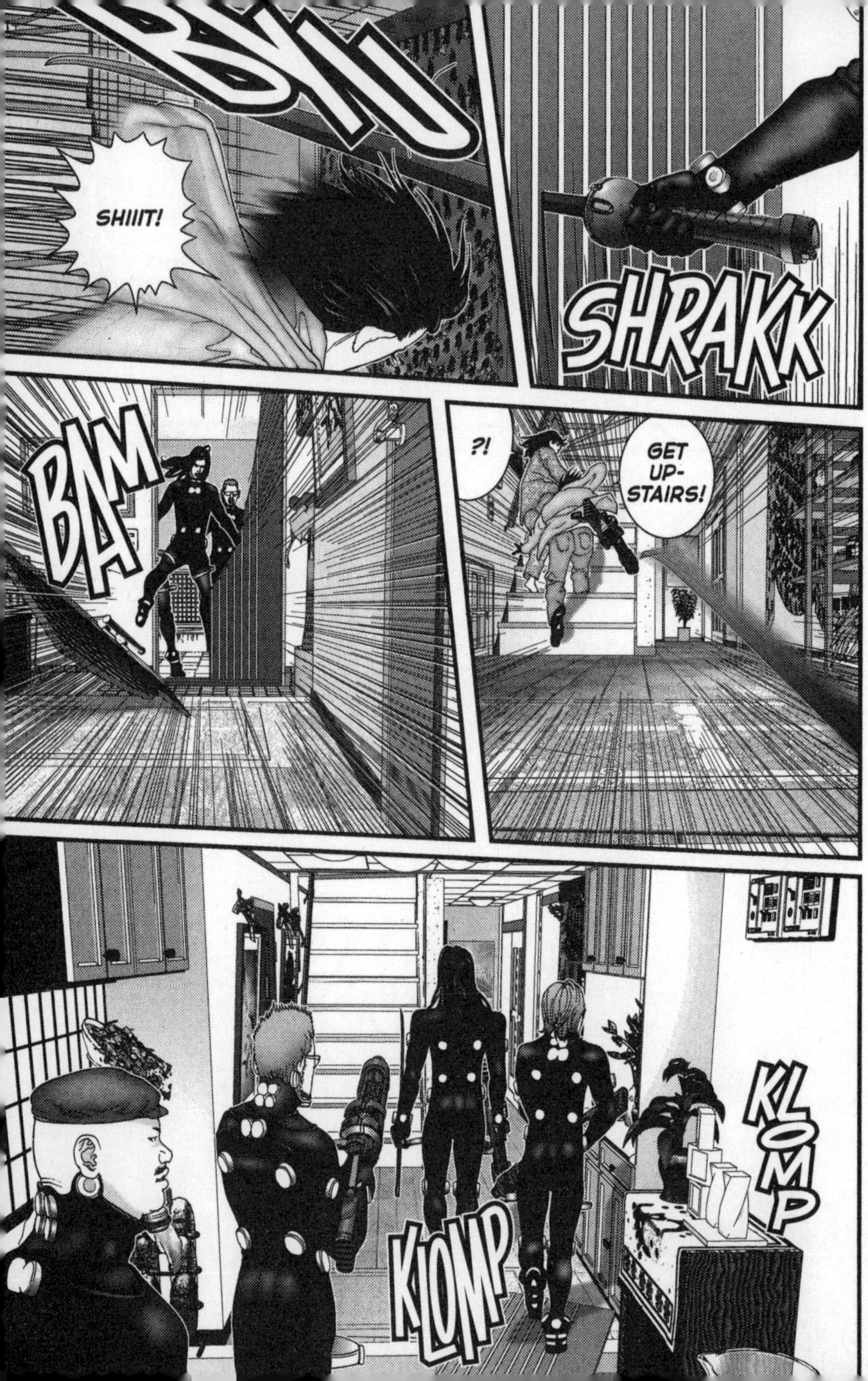
SHRAKK
BYU
SHIIIT!
?!
GET UP-STAIRS!
BAM
KLOMP
KLOMP

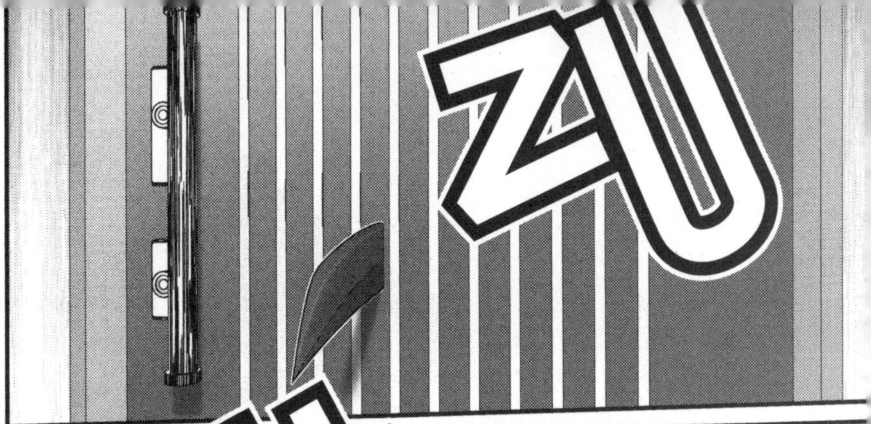
ZU
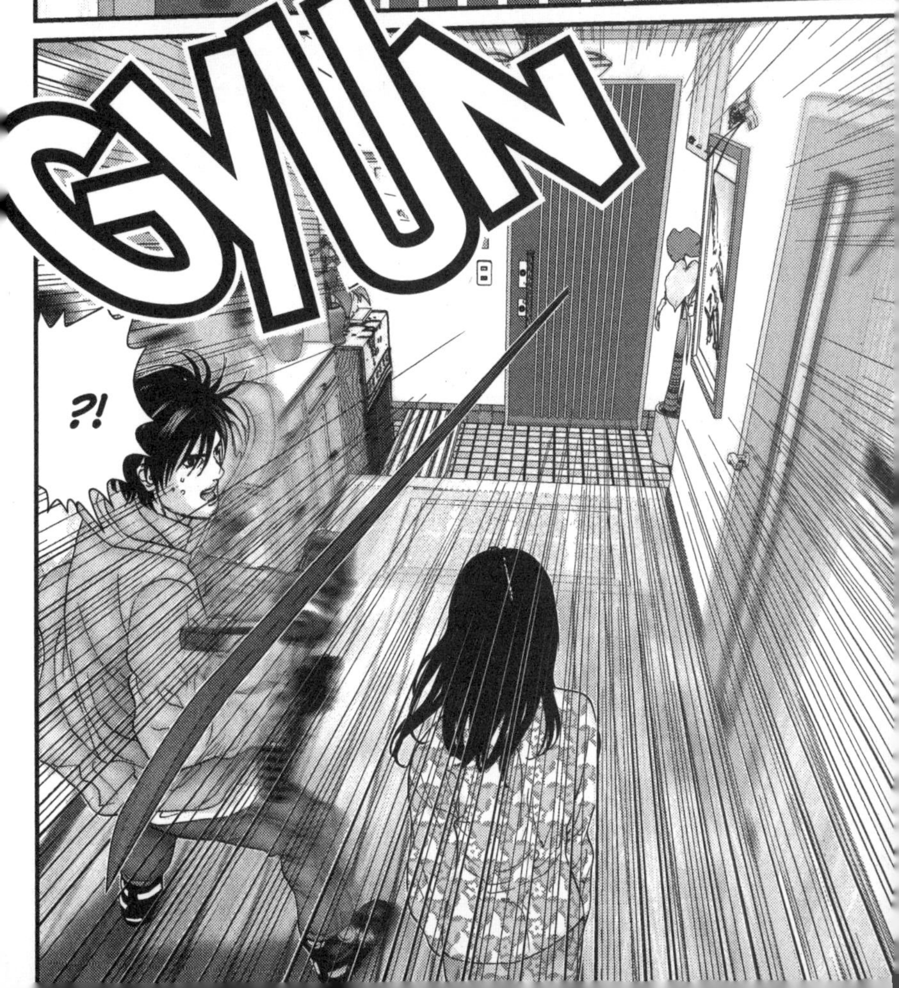
GYUN
?!

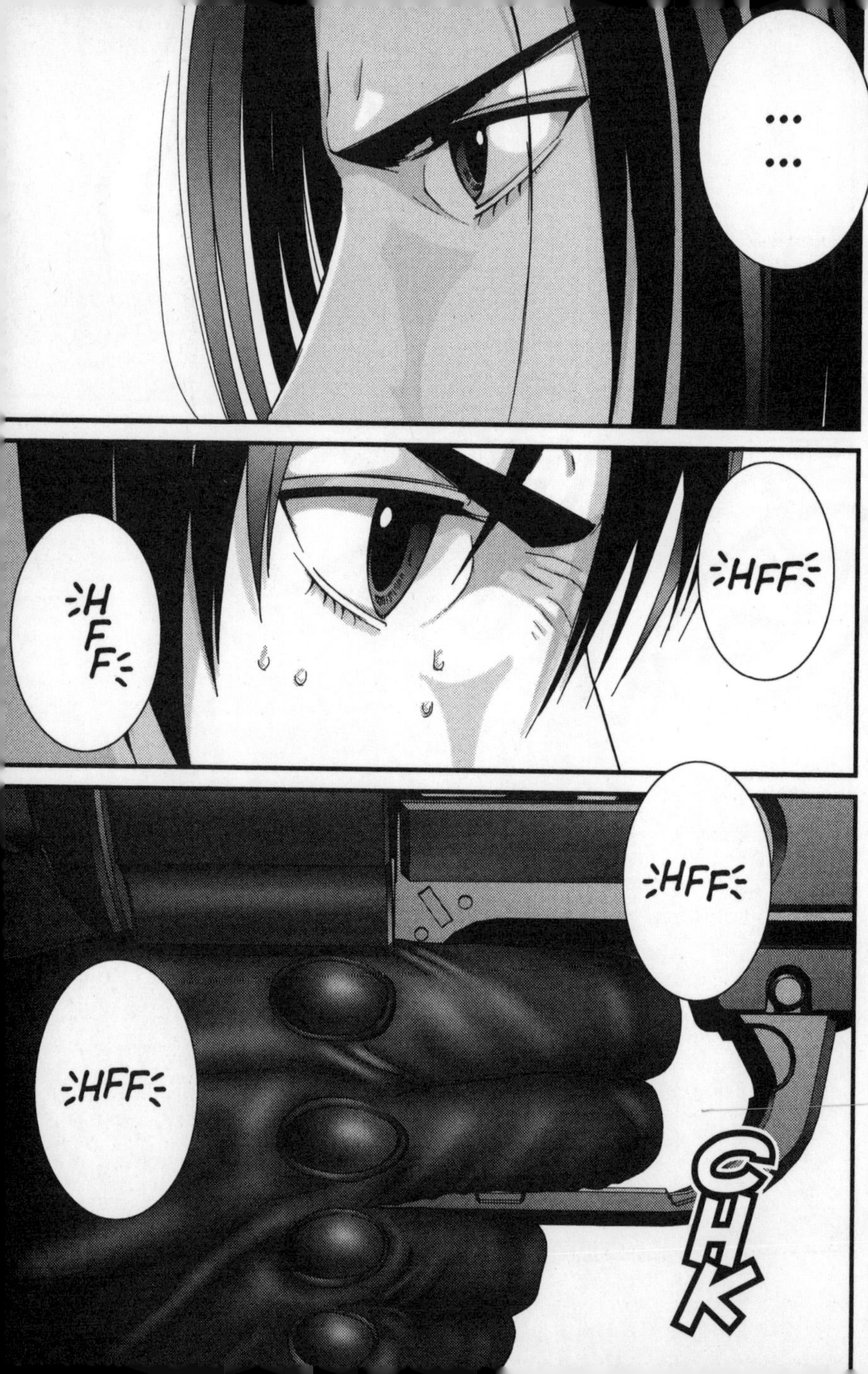
…
…
HFF
HFF
HFF
HFF
CHK

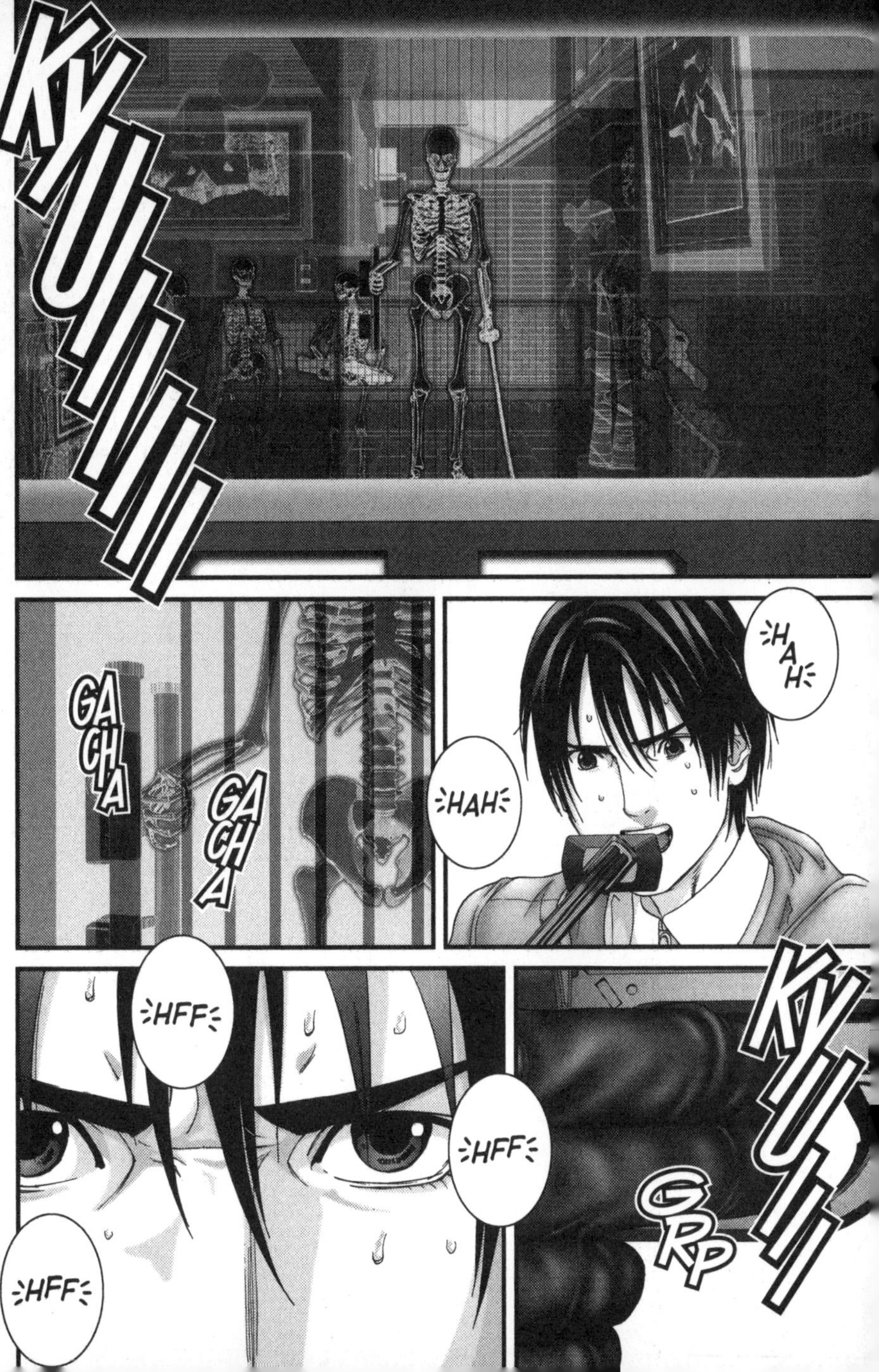
KYUIIIIIII
HAH
HAH
GACHA
GACHA
KYUIII
GRP
HFF
HFF
HFF

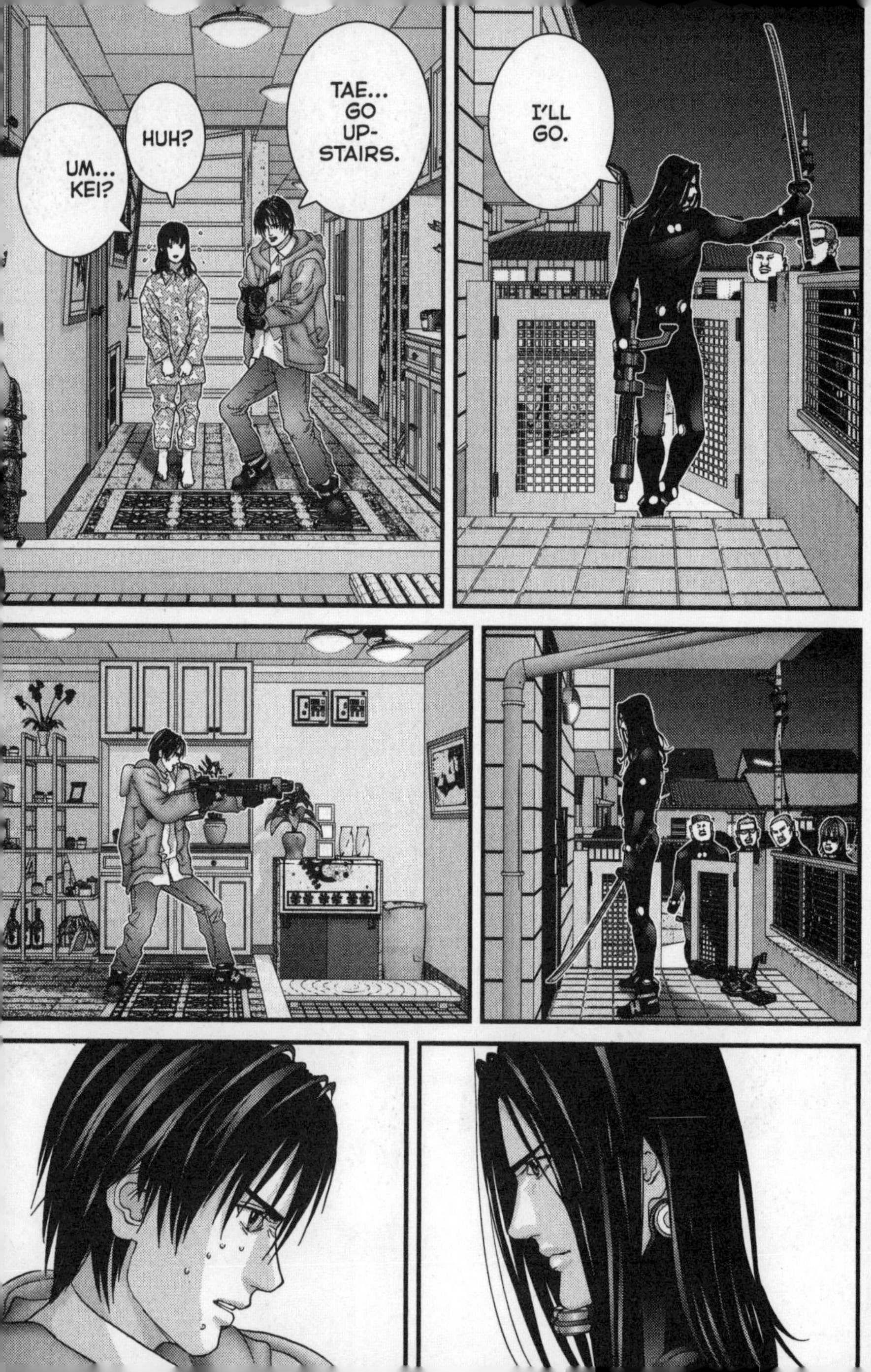
I'LL GO.
TAE... GO UP-STAIRS.
HUH?
UM... KEI?

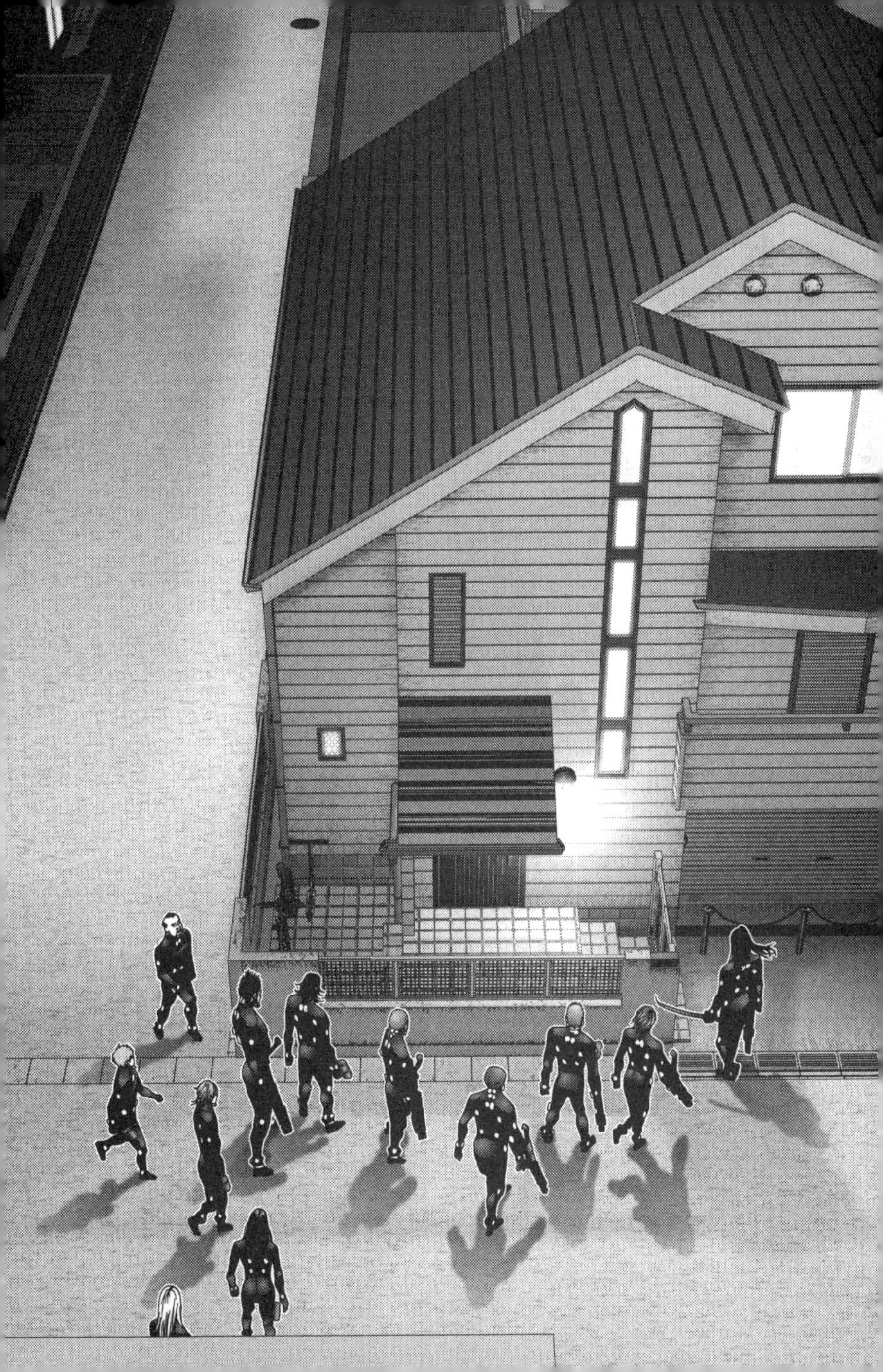

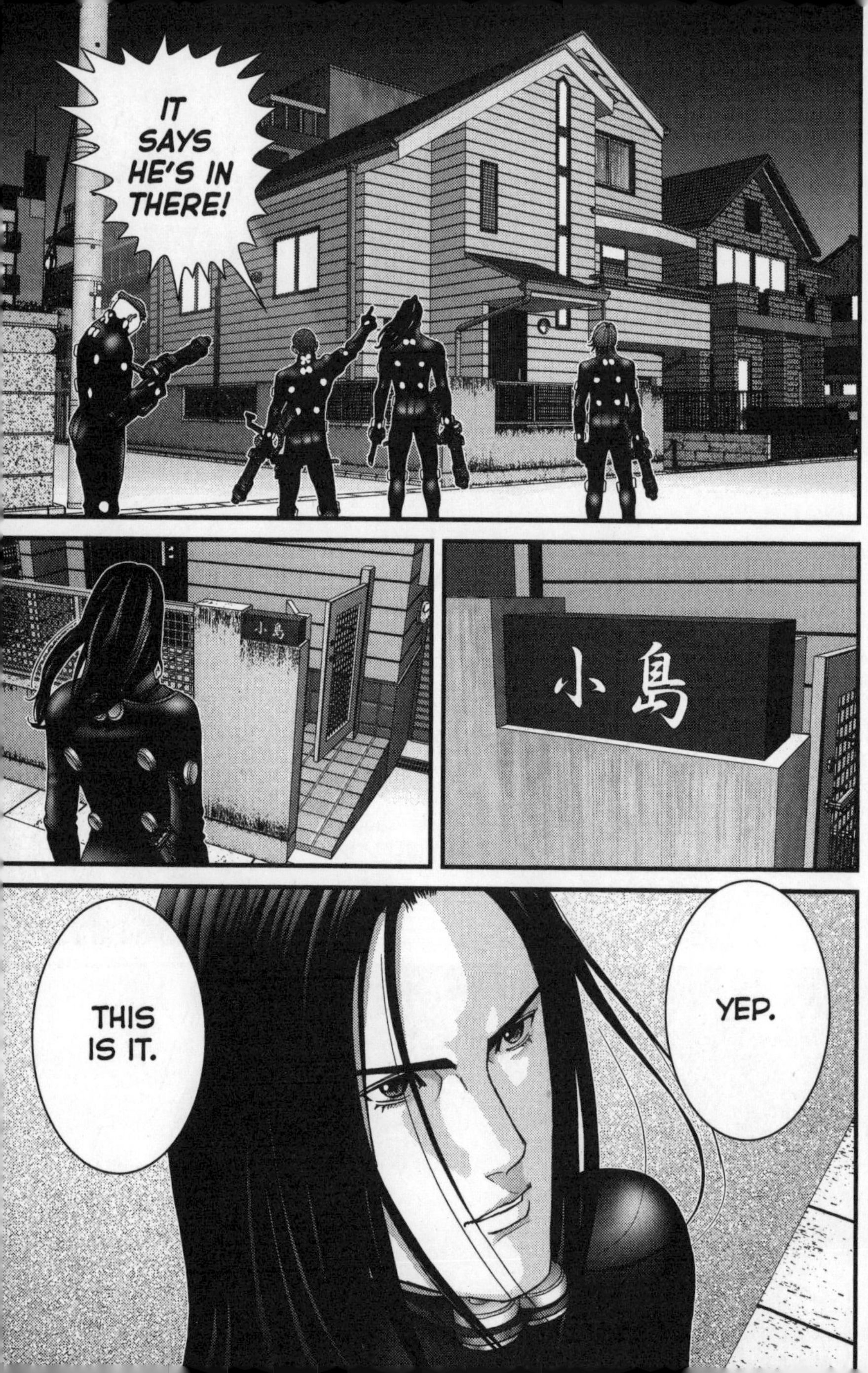
IT SAYS HE'S IN THERE!
小島
小島
THIS IS IT.
YEP.

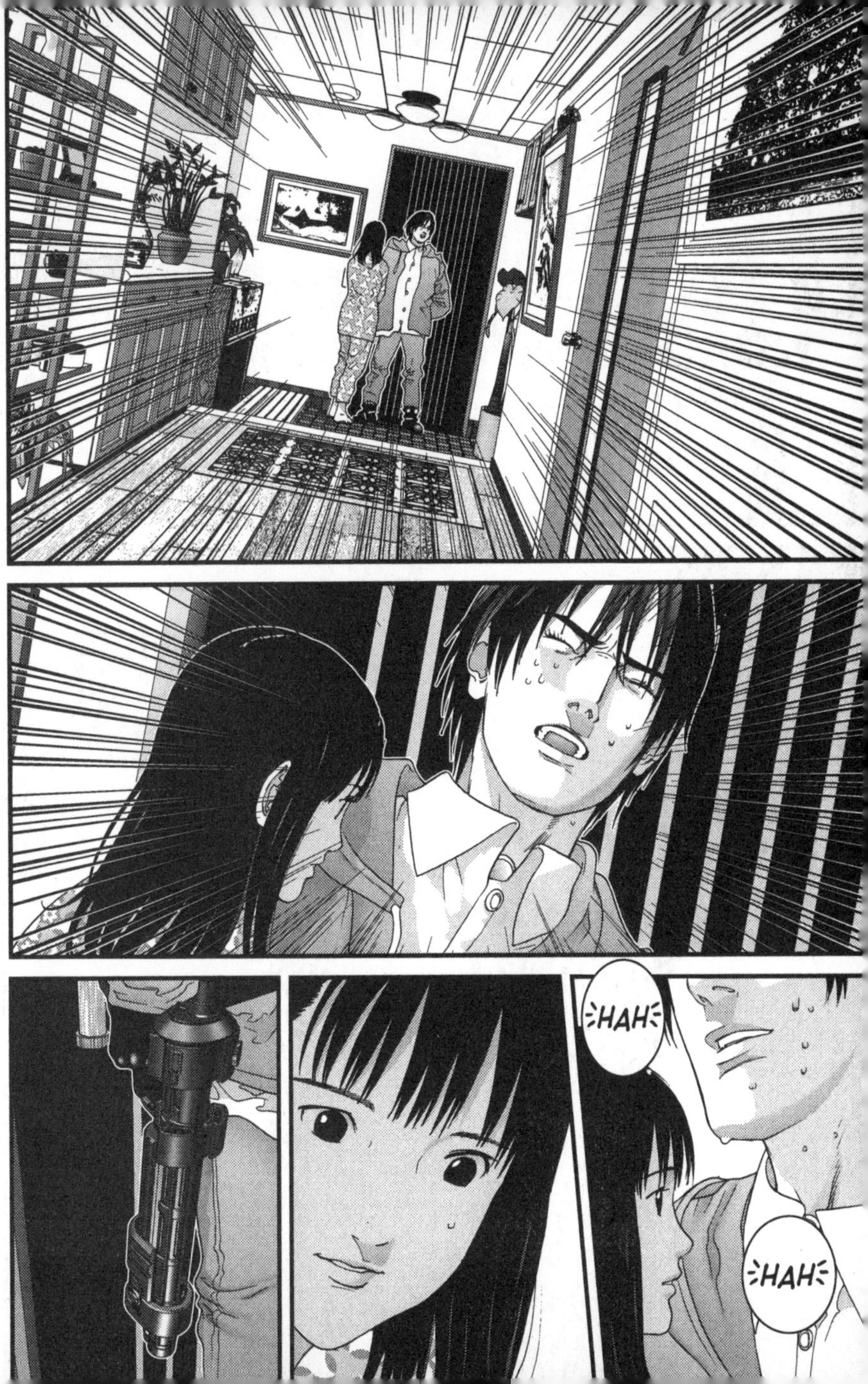
HAH
HAH

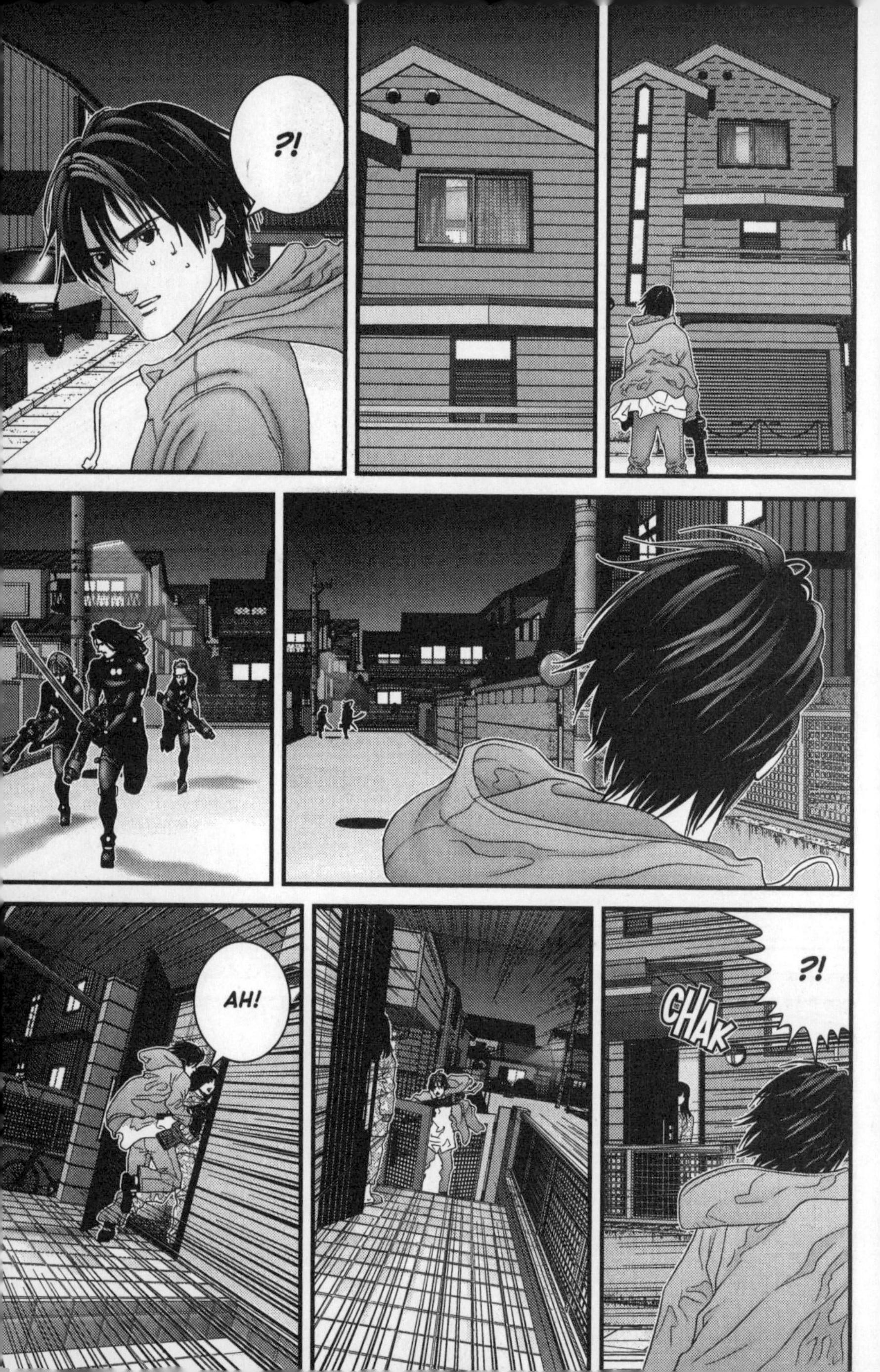
?!
?!
CHAK
AH!

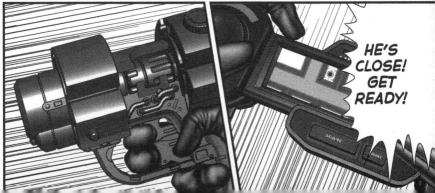

HE'S
CLOSE!
GET
READY!

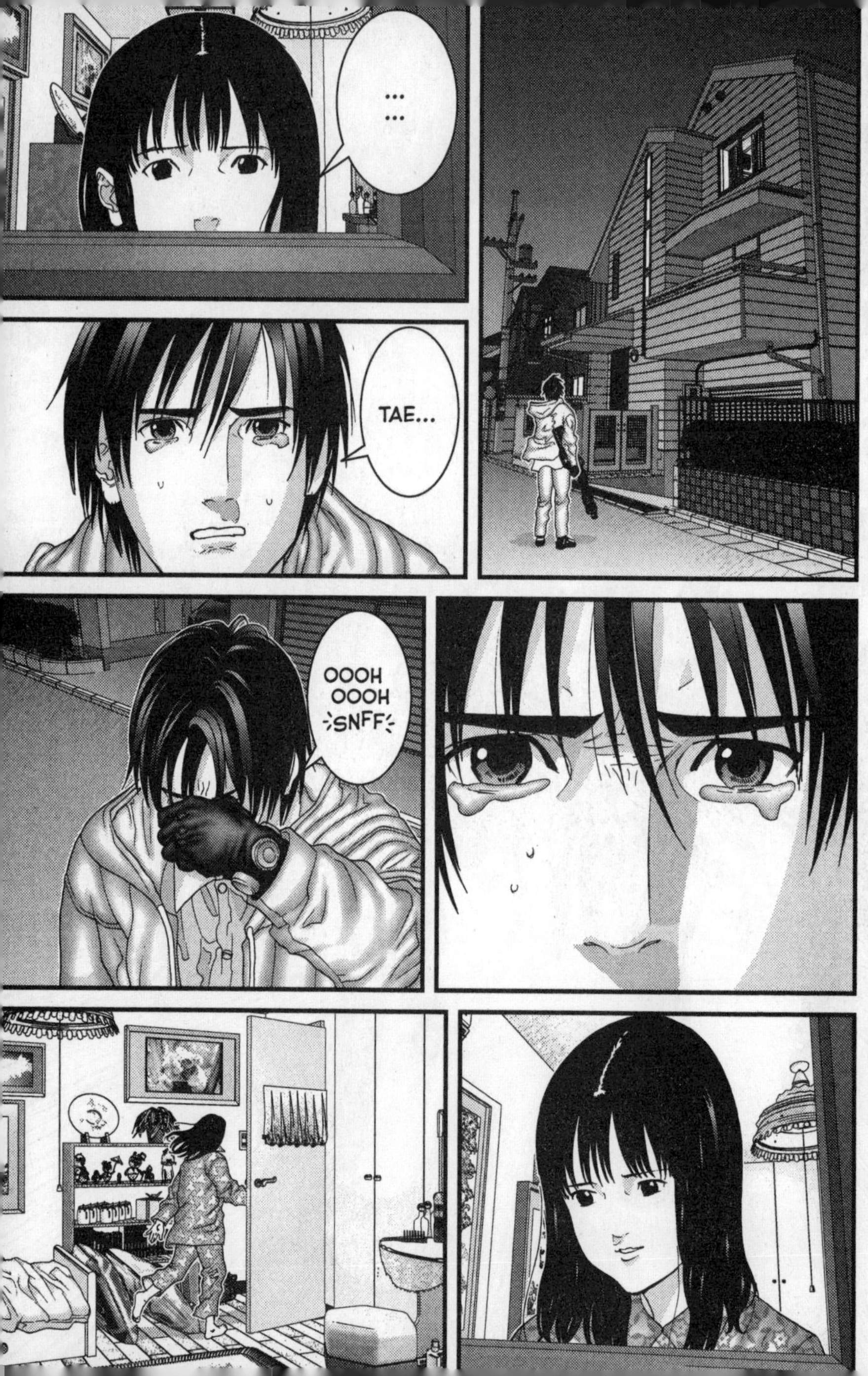

......
TAE...
OOOH
OOOH
SNFF

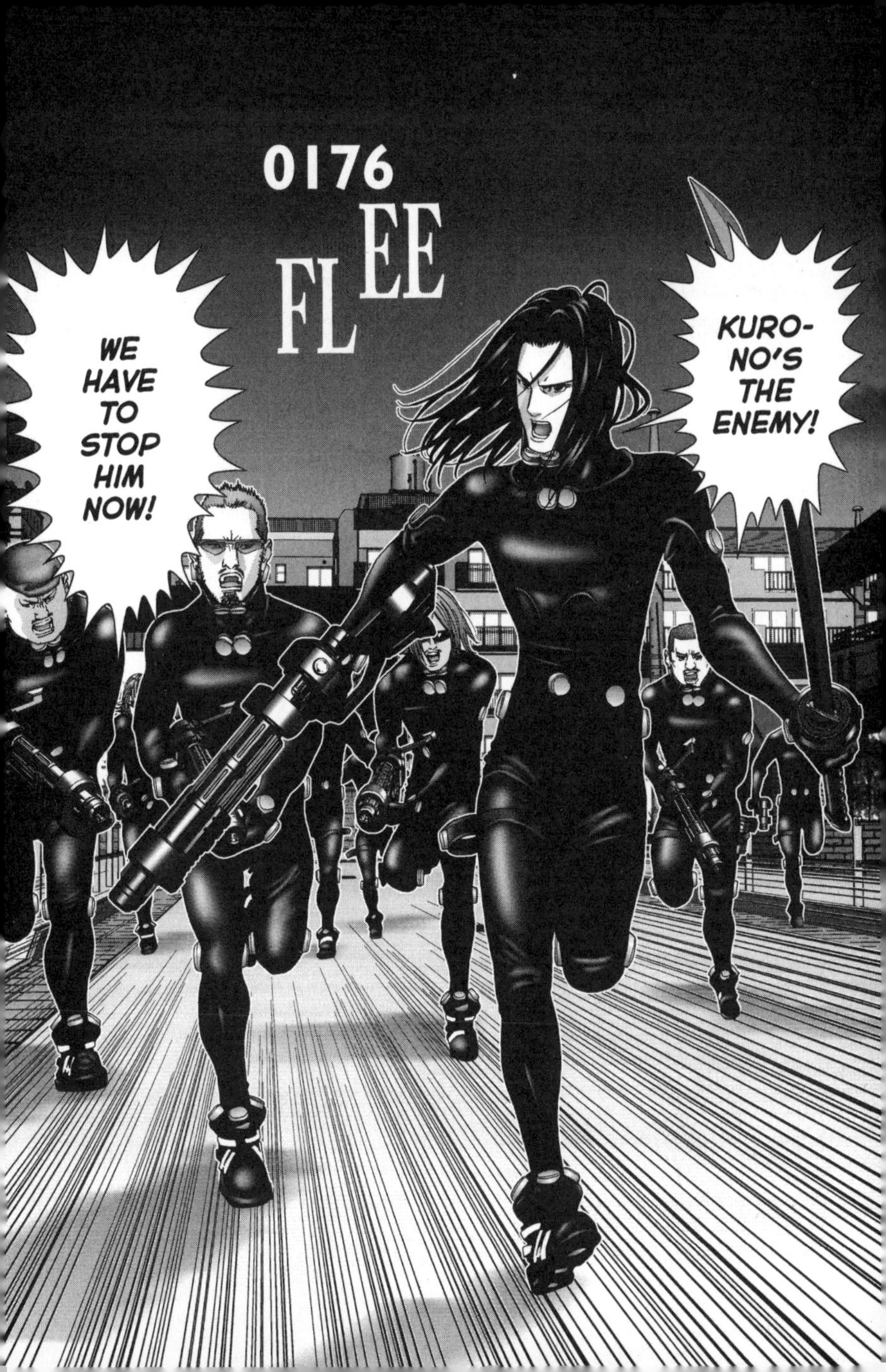
0176
FLEE
KURO-NO'S THE ENEMY!
WE HAVE TO STOP HIM NOW!

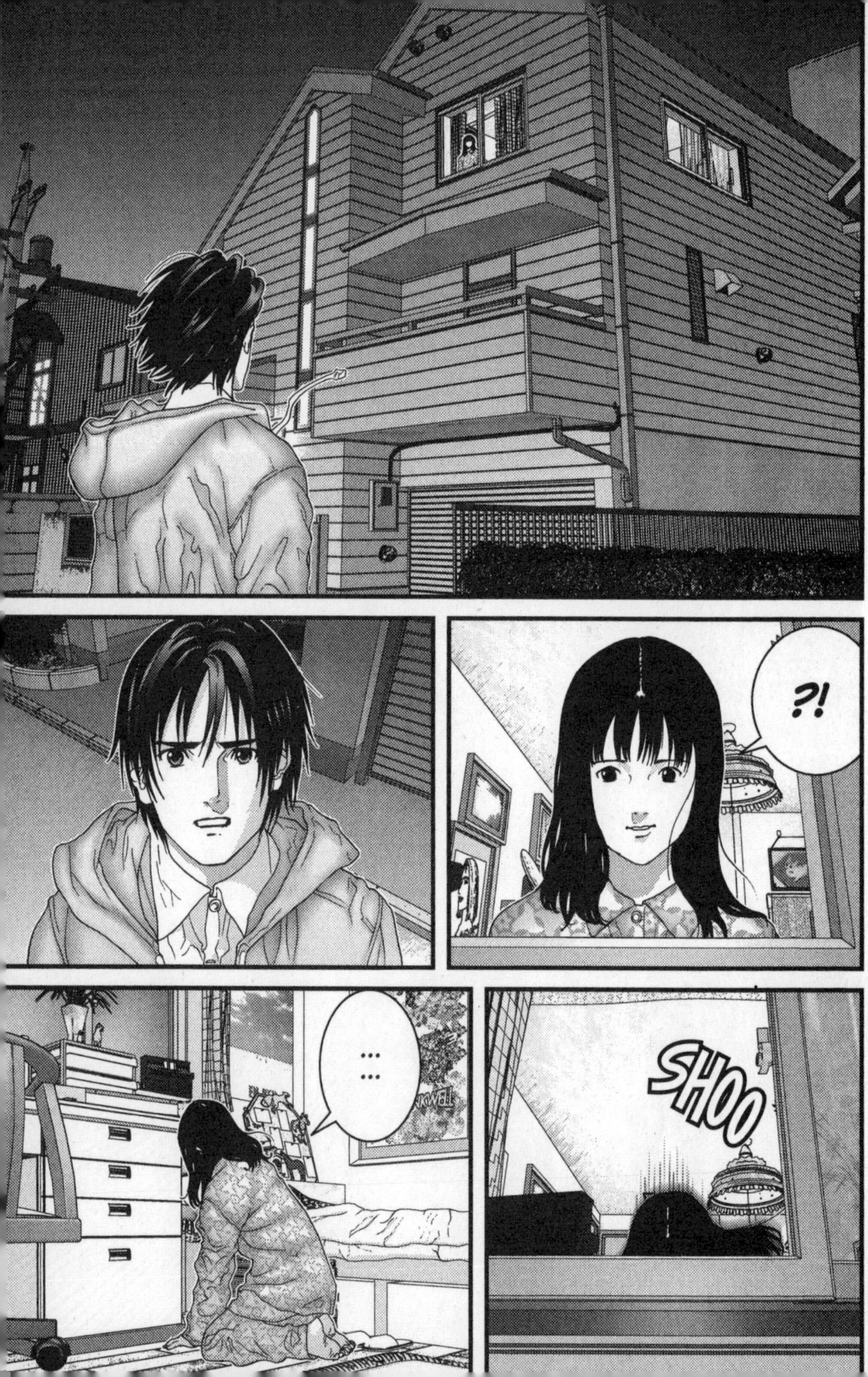
?!
...
...
SHOO

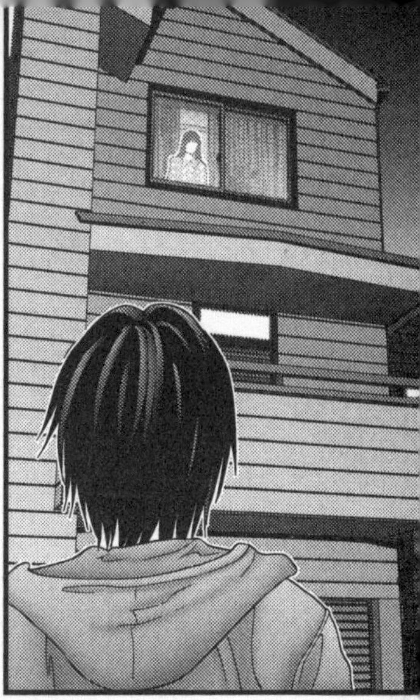
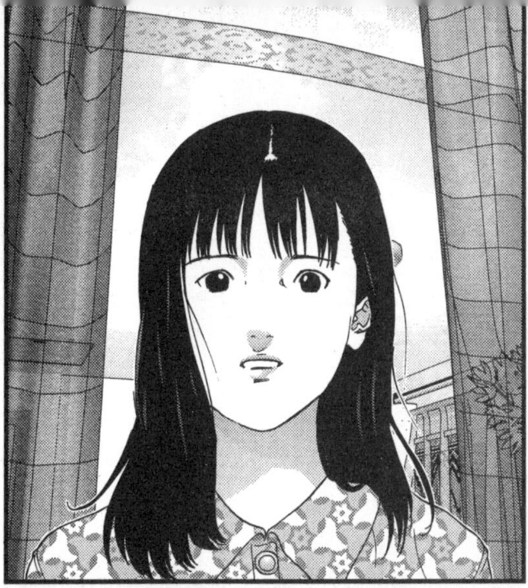
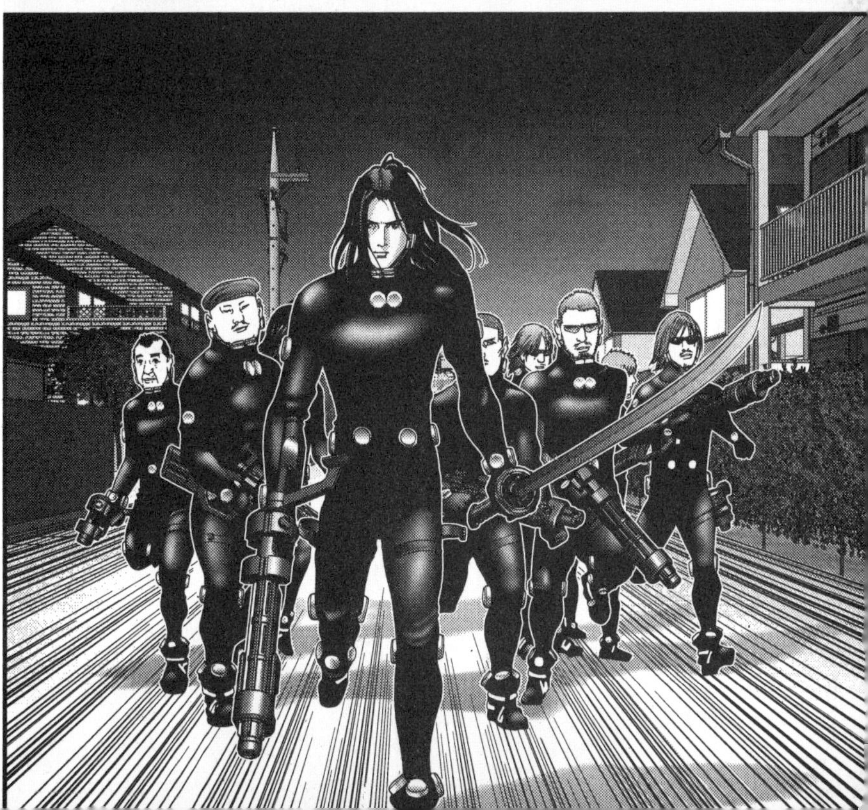

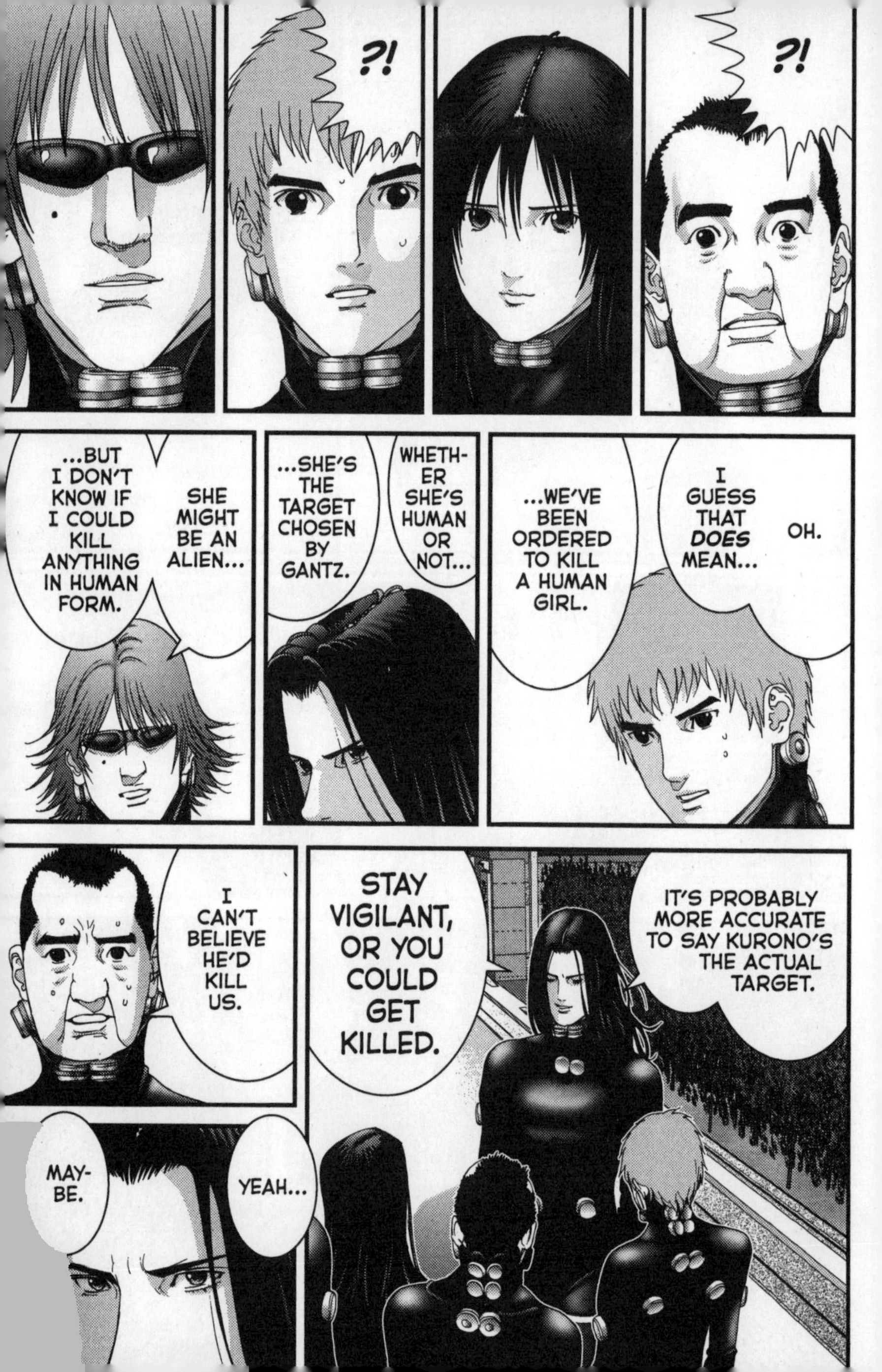
?!
?!
OH.
I GUESS THAT *DOES* MEAN...
...WE'VE BEEN ORDERED TO KILL A HUMAN GIRL.
WHETH-ER SHE'S HUMAN OR NOT...
...SHE'S THE TARGET CHOSEN BY GANTZ.
SHE MIGHT BE AN ALIEN...
...BUT I DON'T KNOW IF I COULD KILL ANYTHING IN HUMAN FORM.
IT'S PROBABLY MORE ACCURATE TO SAY KURONO'S THE ACTUAL TARGET.
STAY VIGILANT, OR YOU COULD GET KILLED.
I CAN'T BELIEVE HE'D KILL US.
YEAH...
MAY-BE.

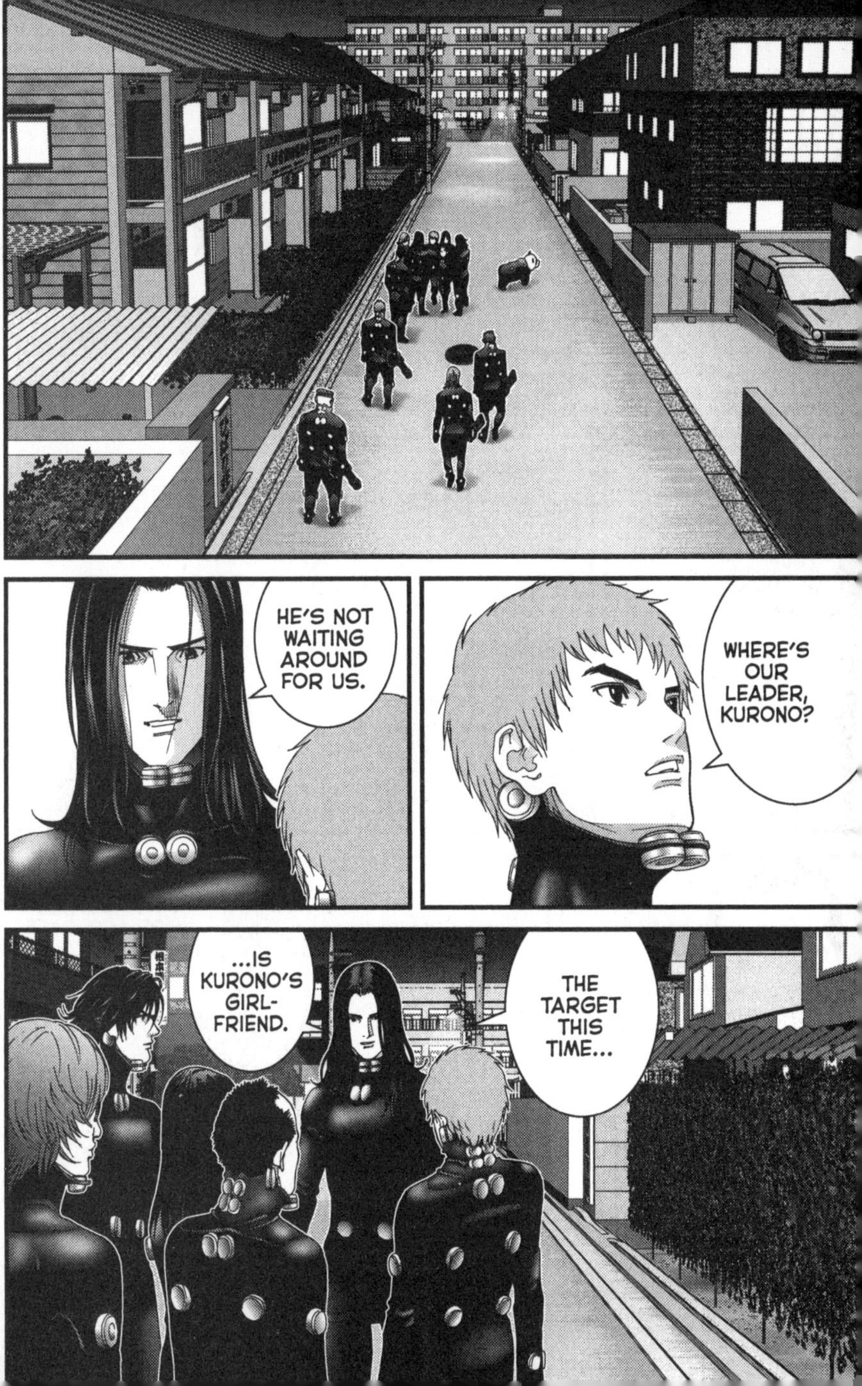
WHERE'S OUR LEADER, KURONO?
HE'S NOT WAITING AROUND FOR US.
THE TARGET THIS TIME...
...IS KURONO'S GIRL-FRIEND.

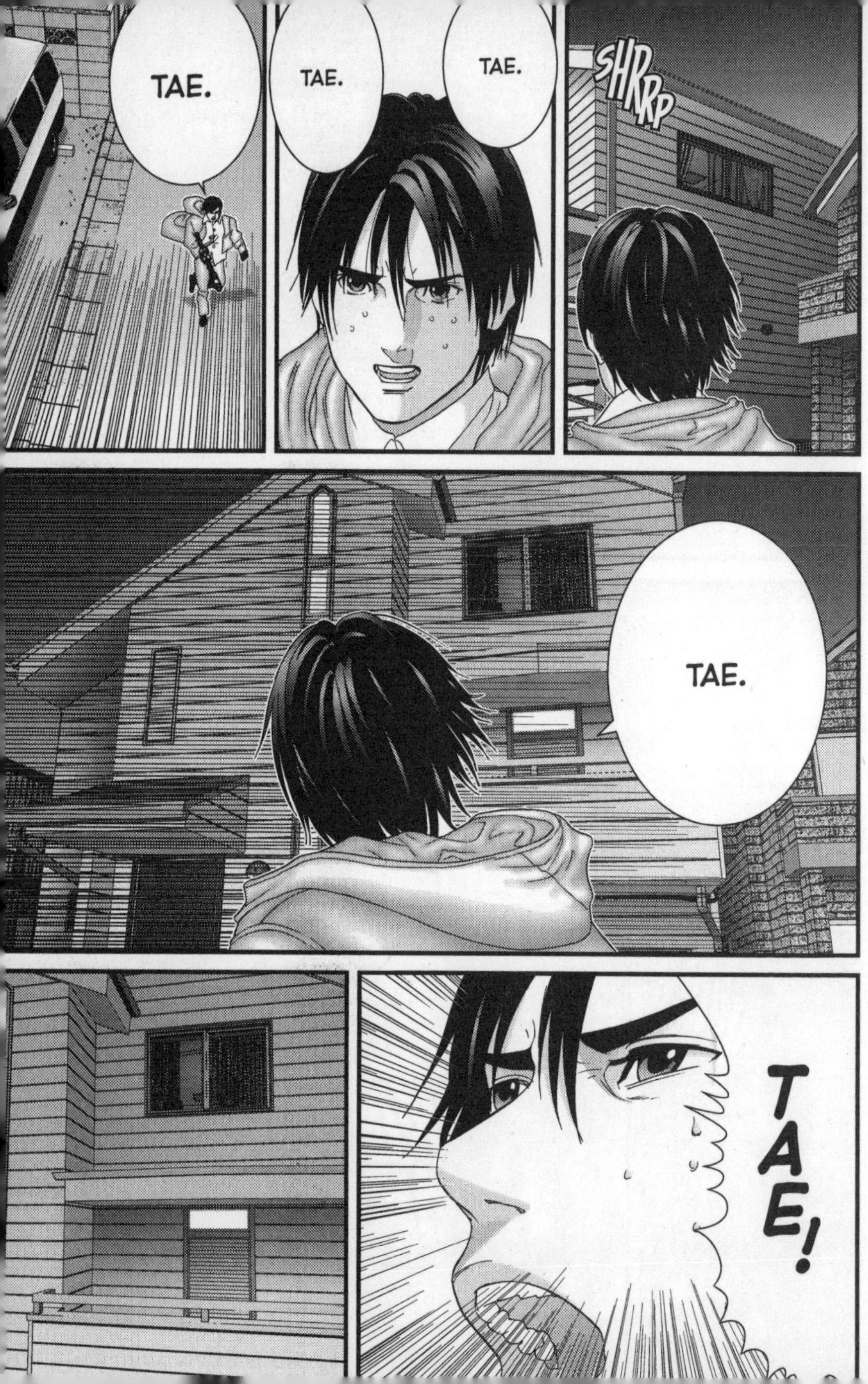
SHRRP
TAE.
TAE.
TAE.
TAE.
TAE!

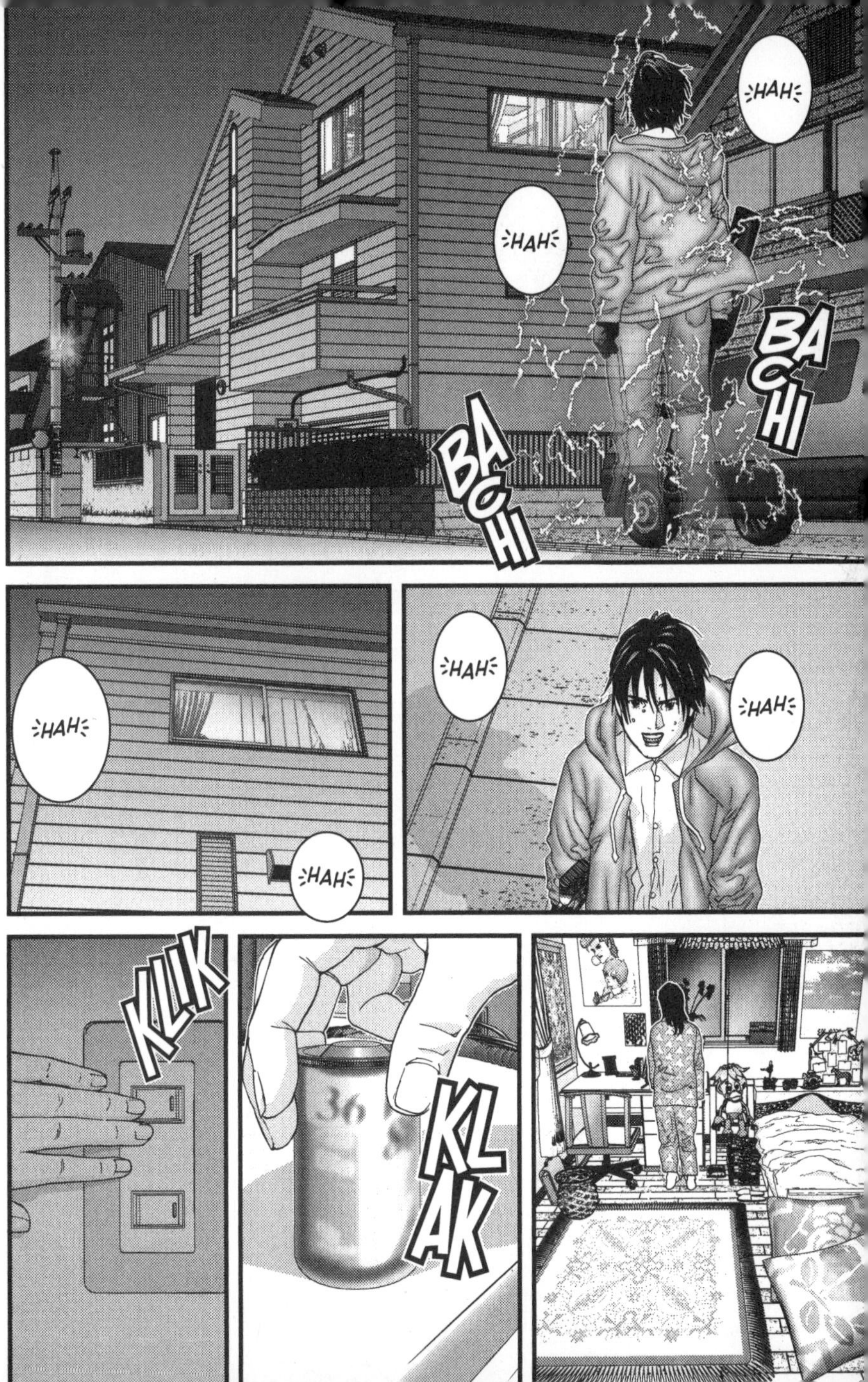
HAH
BACHI
HAH
BACHI
HAH
HAH
HAH
HAH
KLAK
KLIK

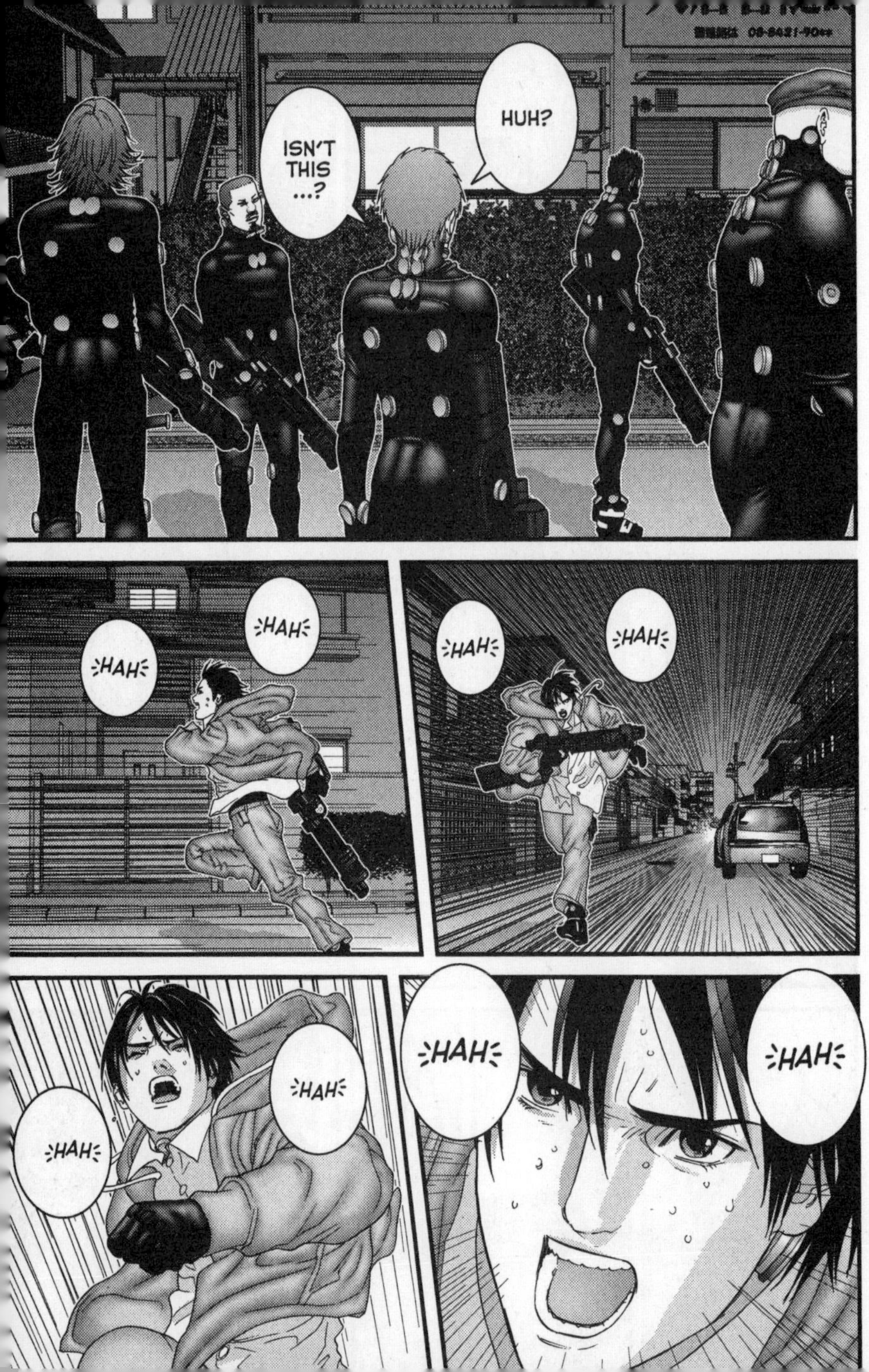
HUH?
ISN'T THIS ...?
HAH
HAH
HAH
HAH
HAH
HAH
HAH
HAH

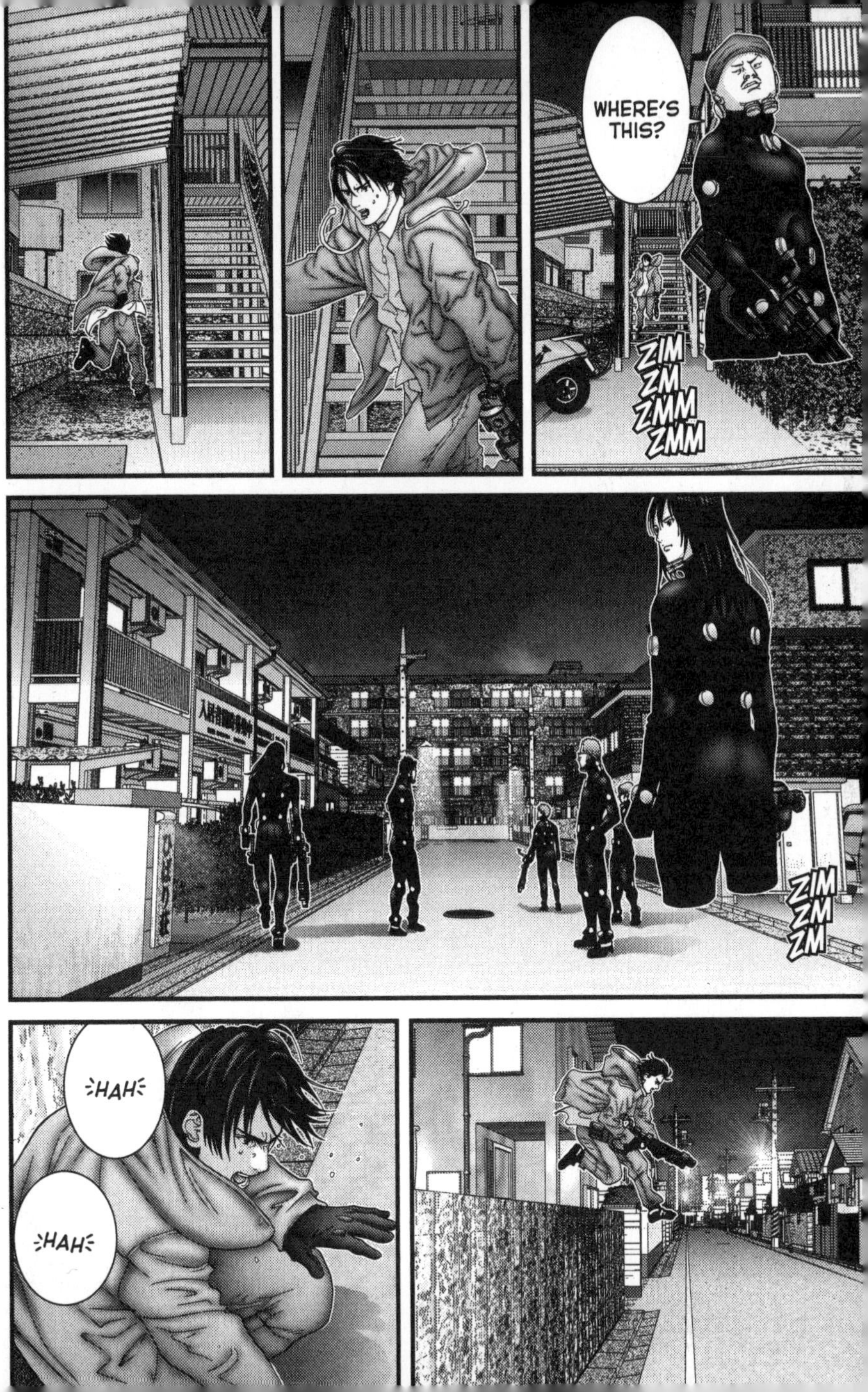
WHERE'S THIS?
ZIM ZM ZMM ZMM
ZIM ZM ZM
HAH
HAH

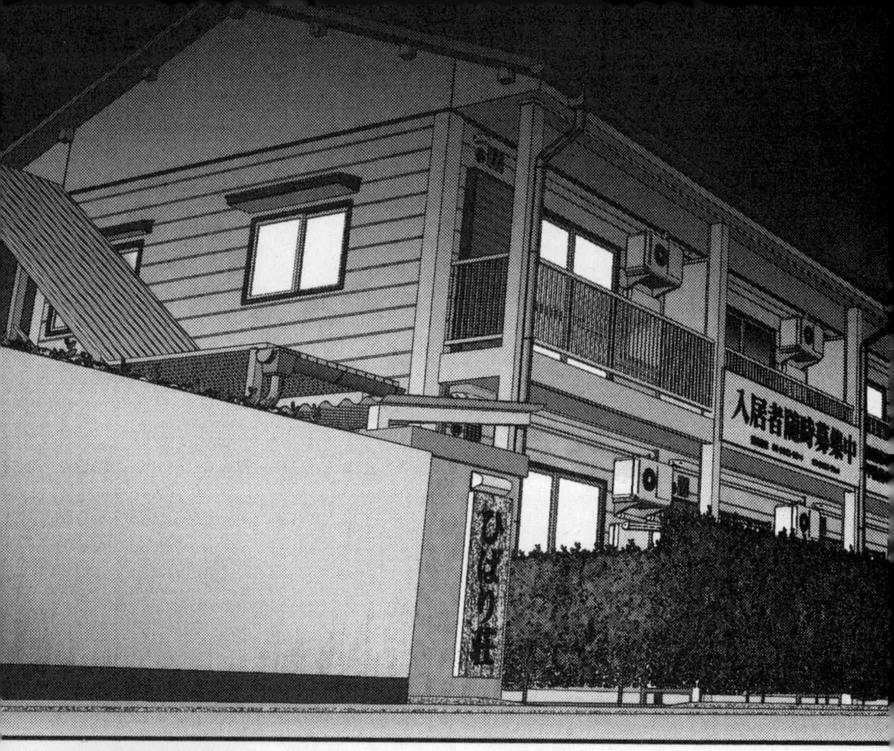
入居者随時募集中
ひばり荘
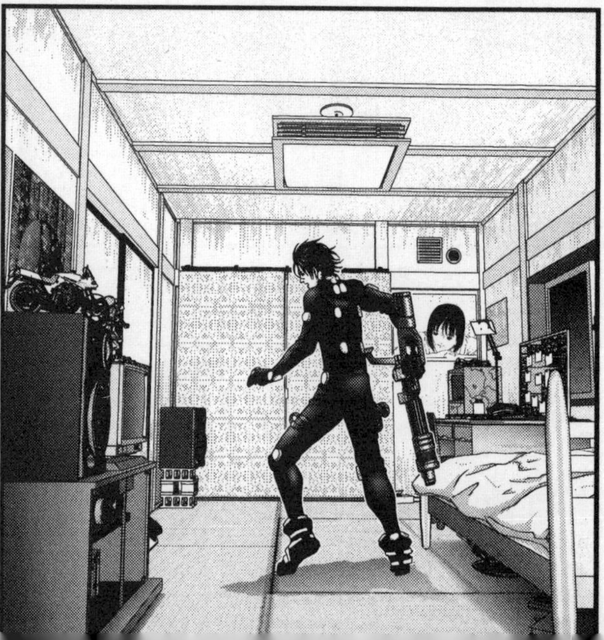
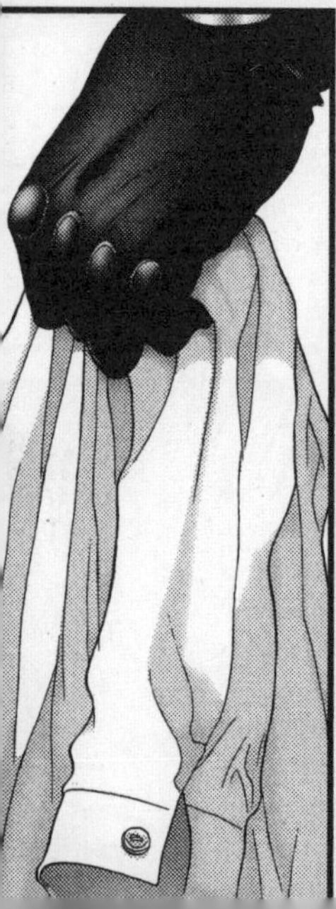

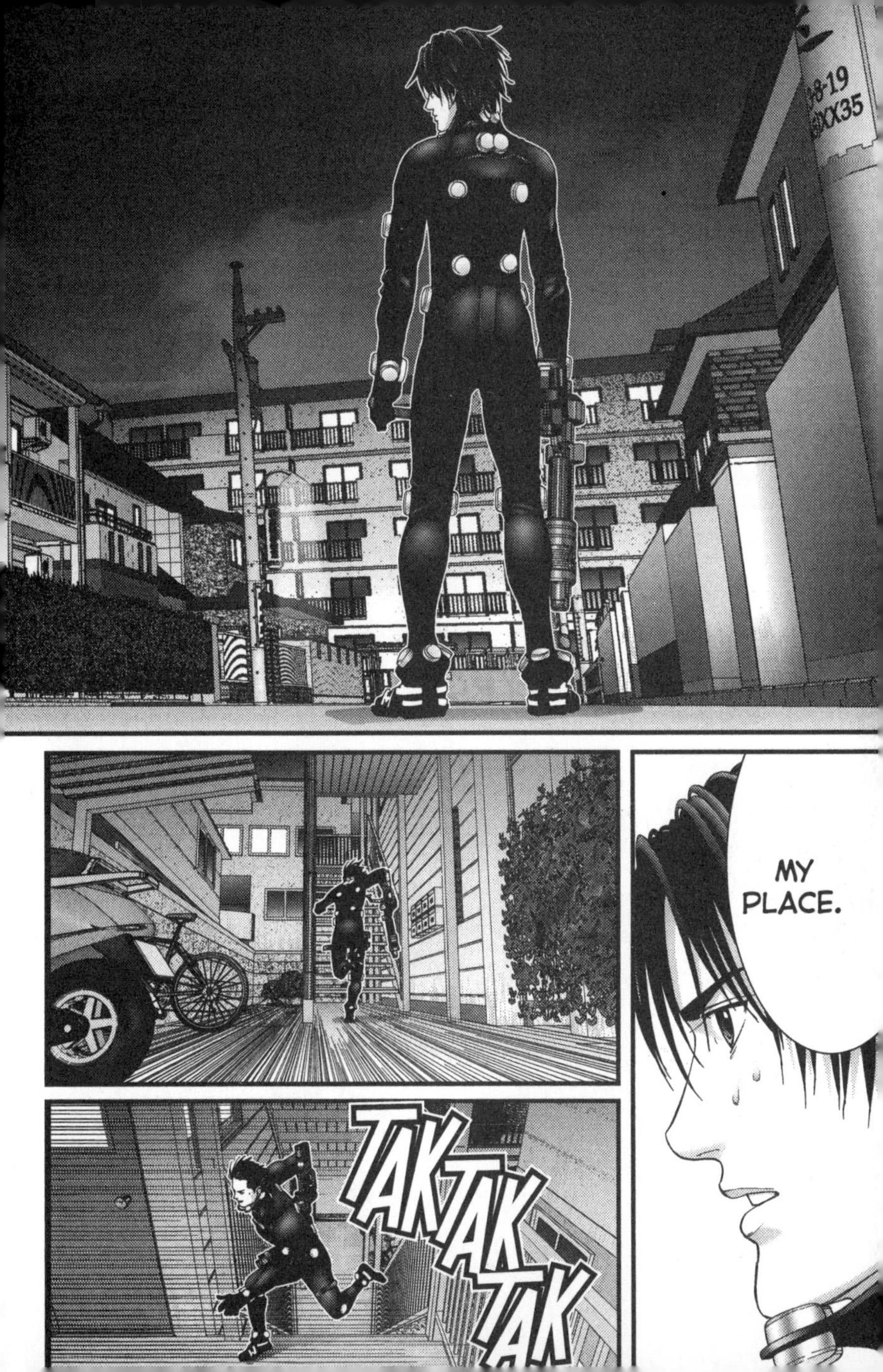
MY PLACE.
TAK TAK TAK

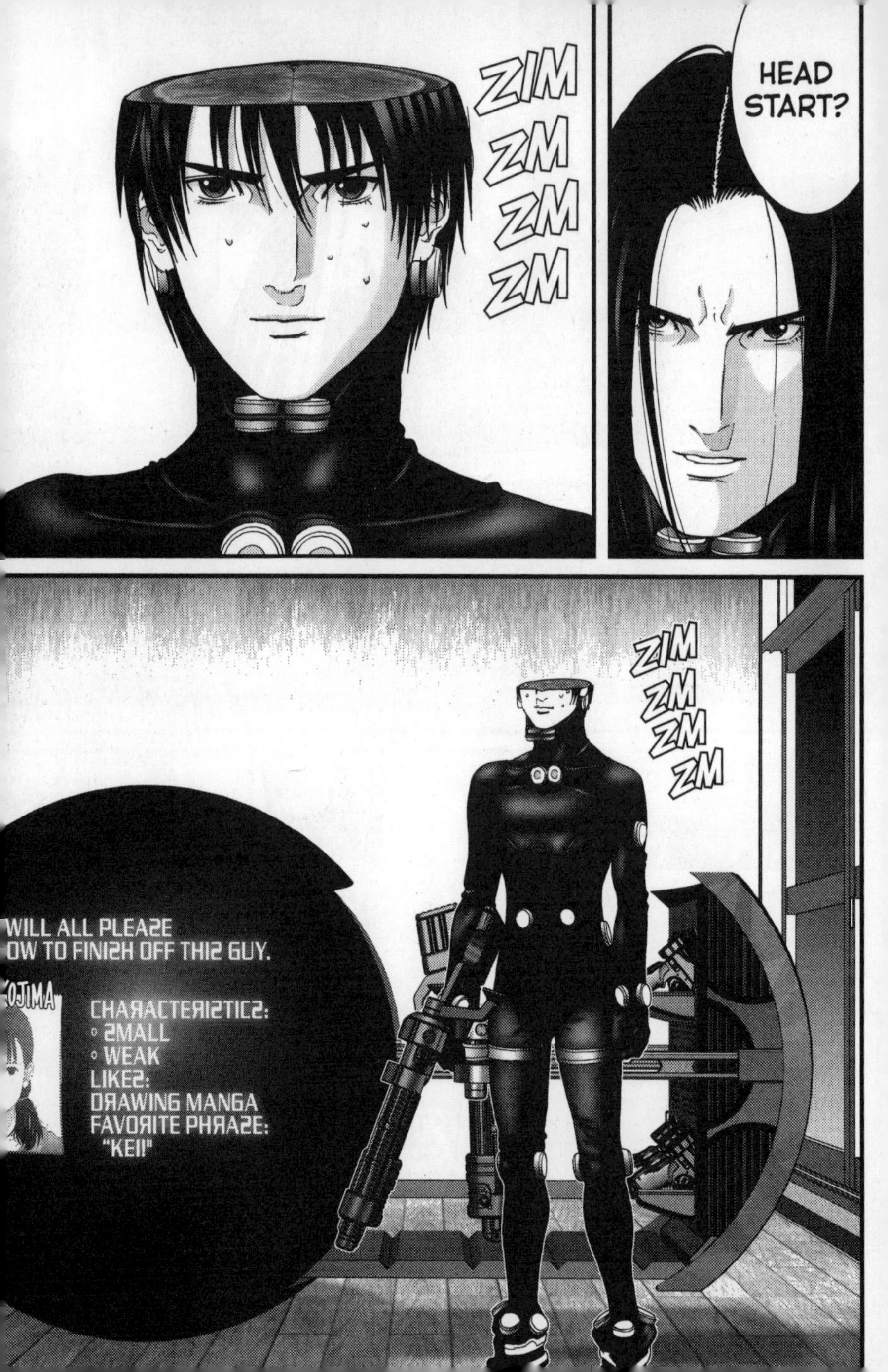
HEAD START?
ZIM ZM ZM ZM
ZIM ZM ZM ZM
WILL ALL PLEASE
OW TO FINISH OFF THIS GUY.
OJIMA
CHARACTERISTICS:
◦ SMALL
◦ WEAK
LIKES:
DRAWING MANGA
FAVORITE PHRASE:
"KEI!"

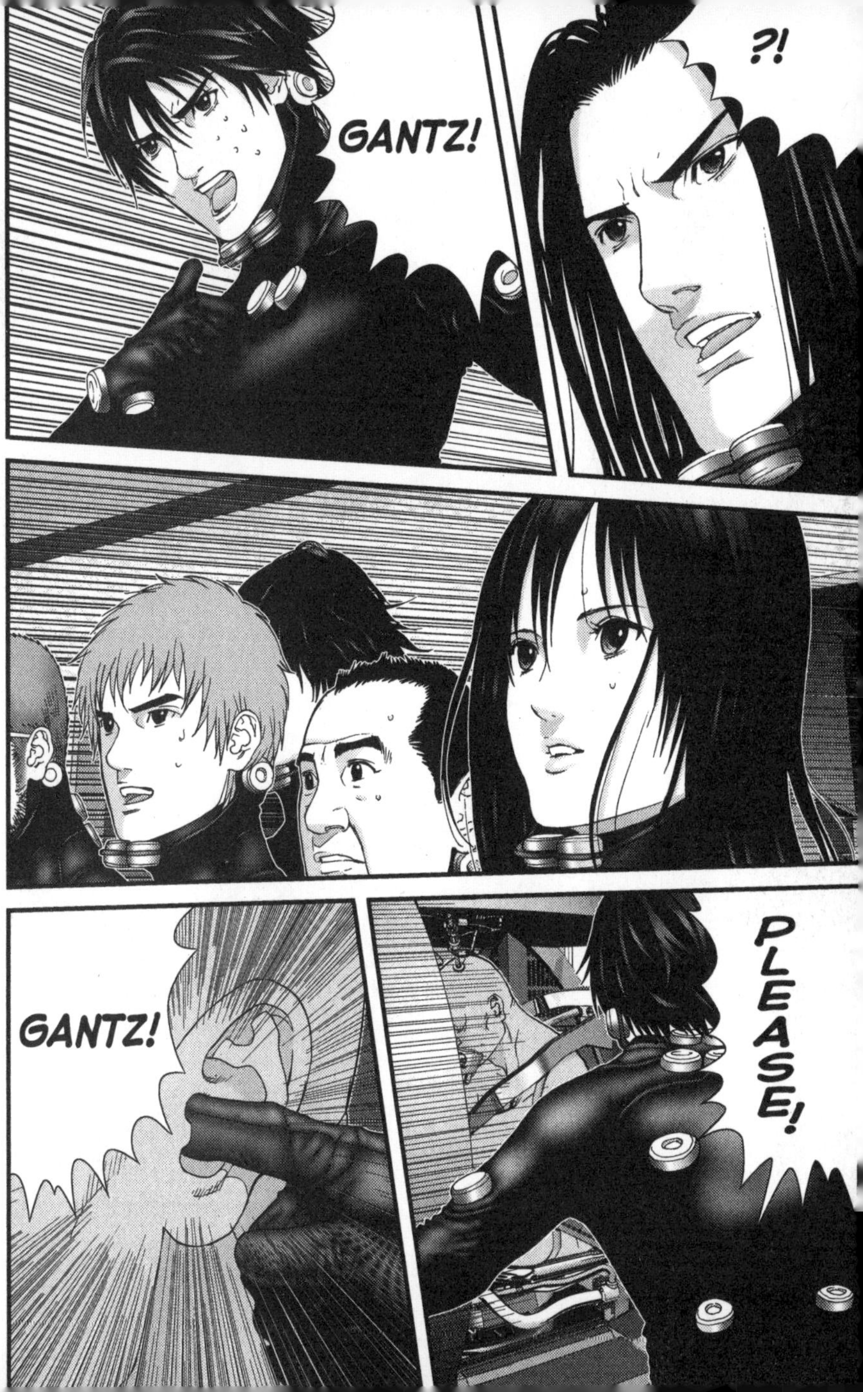
GANTZ!
?!
GANTZ!
PLEASE!

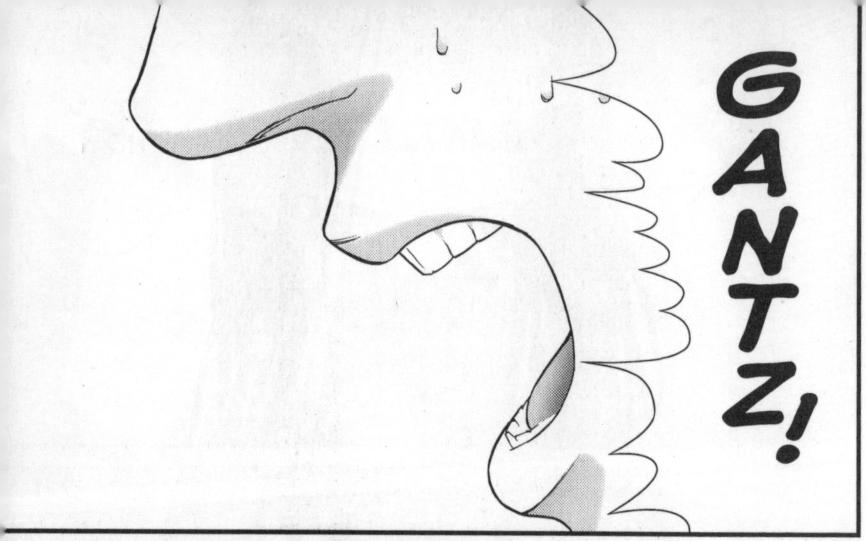
GANTZ!
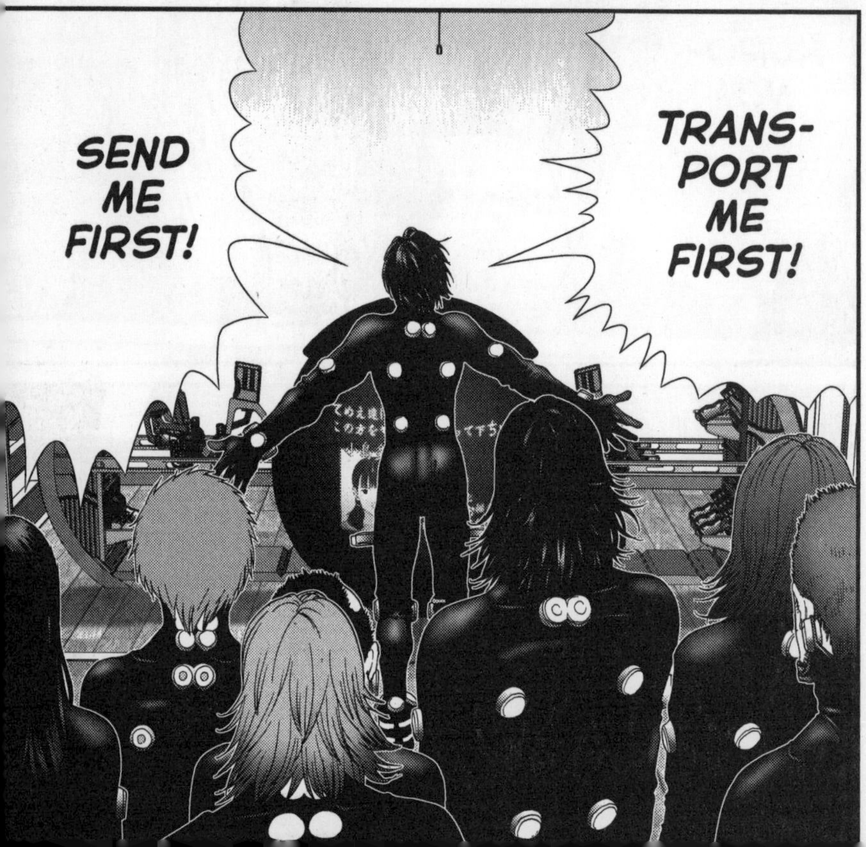
TRANS-PORT ME FIRST!
SEND ME FIRST!

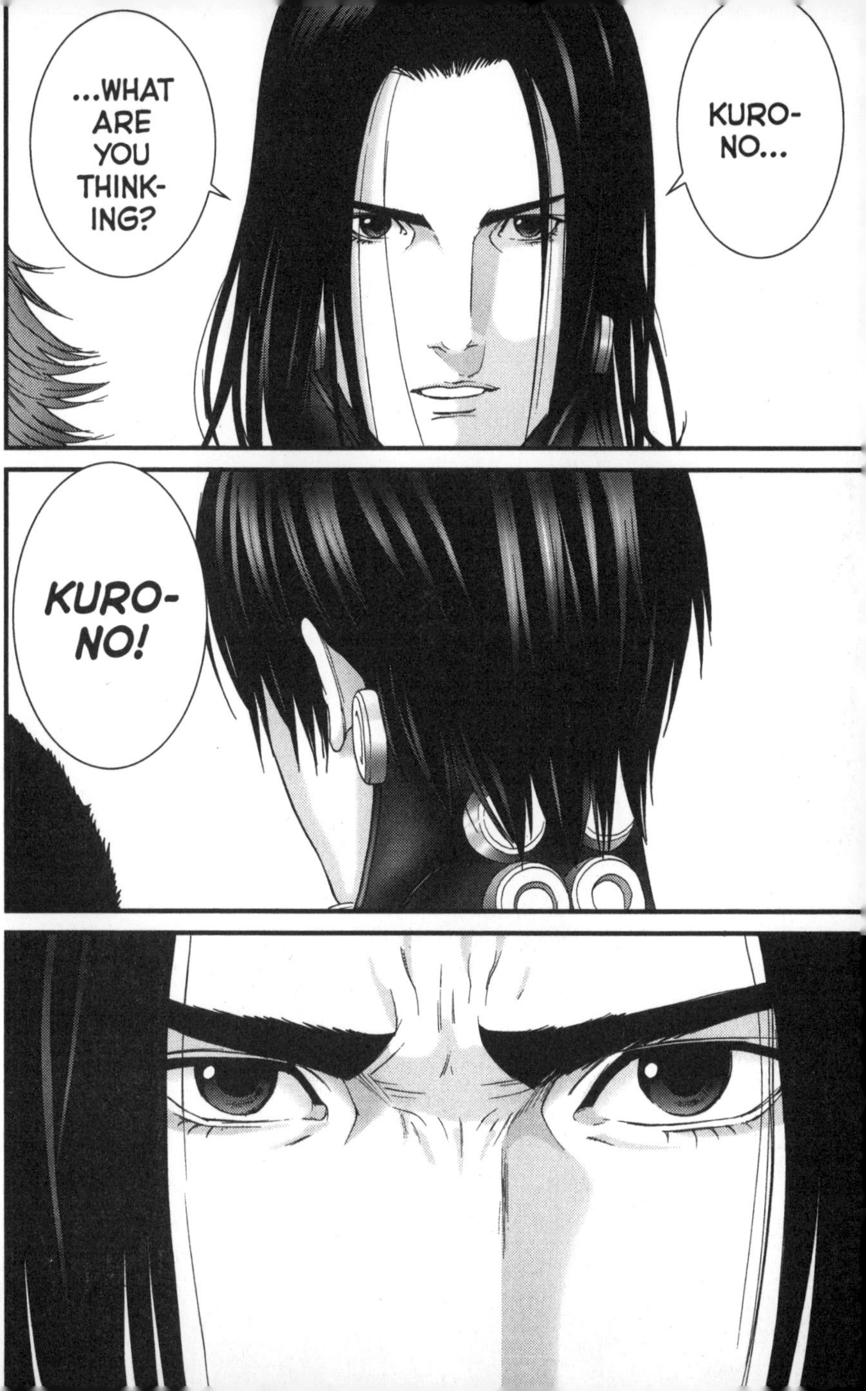
KURO-NO...
...WHAT ARE YOU THINKING?
KURO-NO!

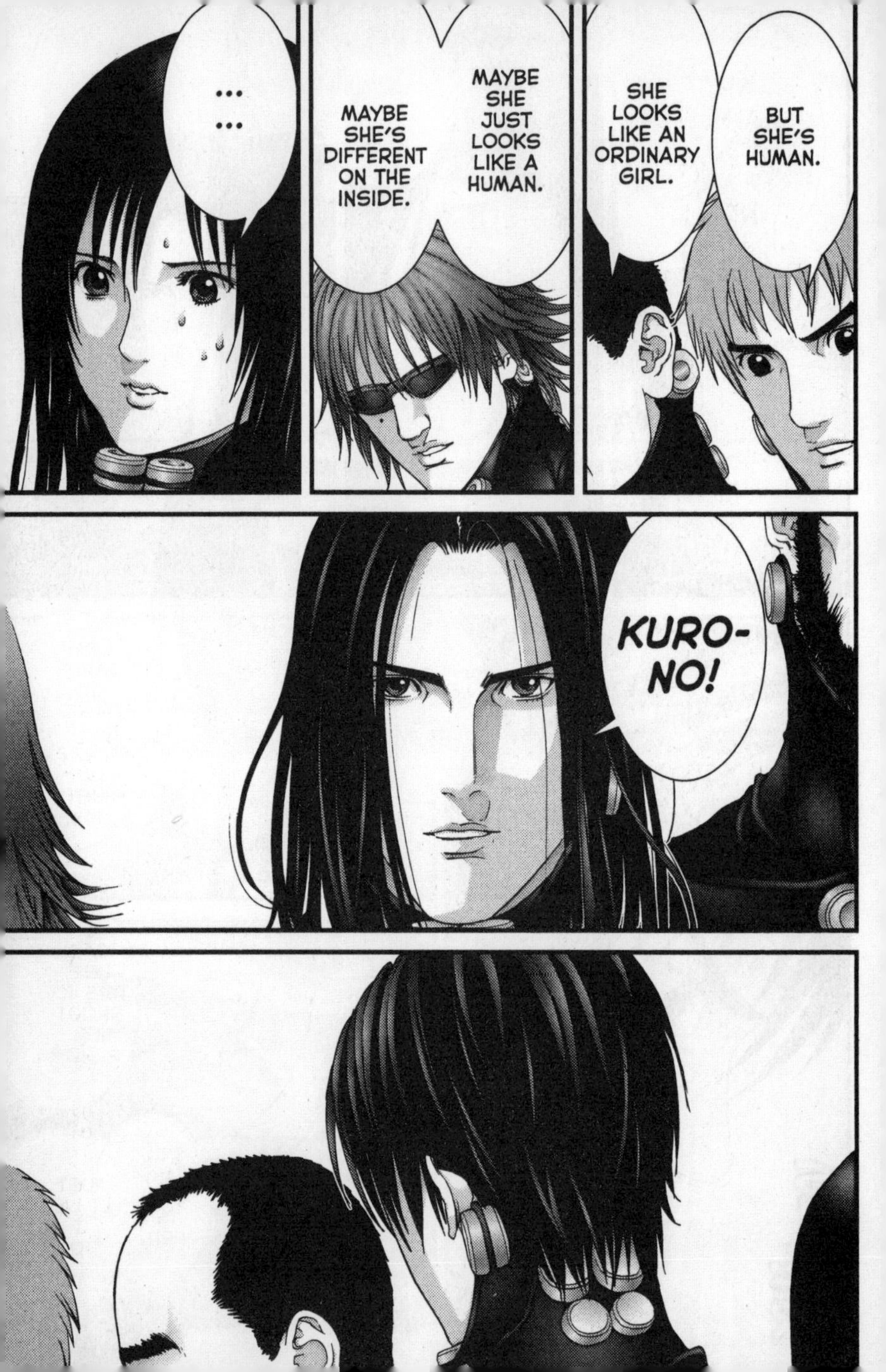
BUT SHE'S HUMAN.
SHE LOOKS LIKE AN ORDINARY GIRL.
MAYBE SHE JUST LOOKS LIKE A HUMAN.
MAYBE SHE'S DIFFERENT ON THE INSIDE.
... ...
KURO-NO!

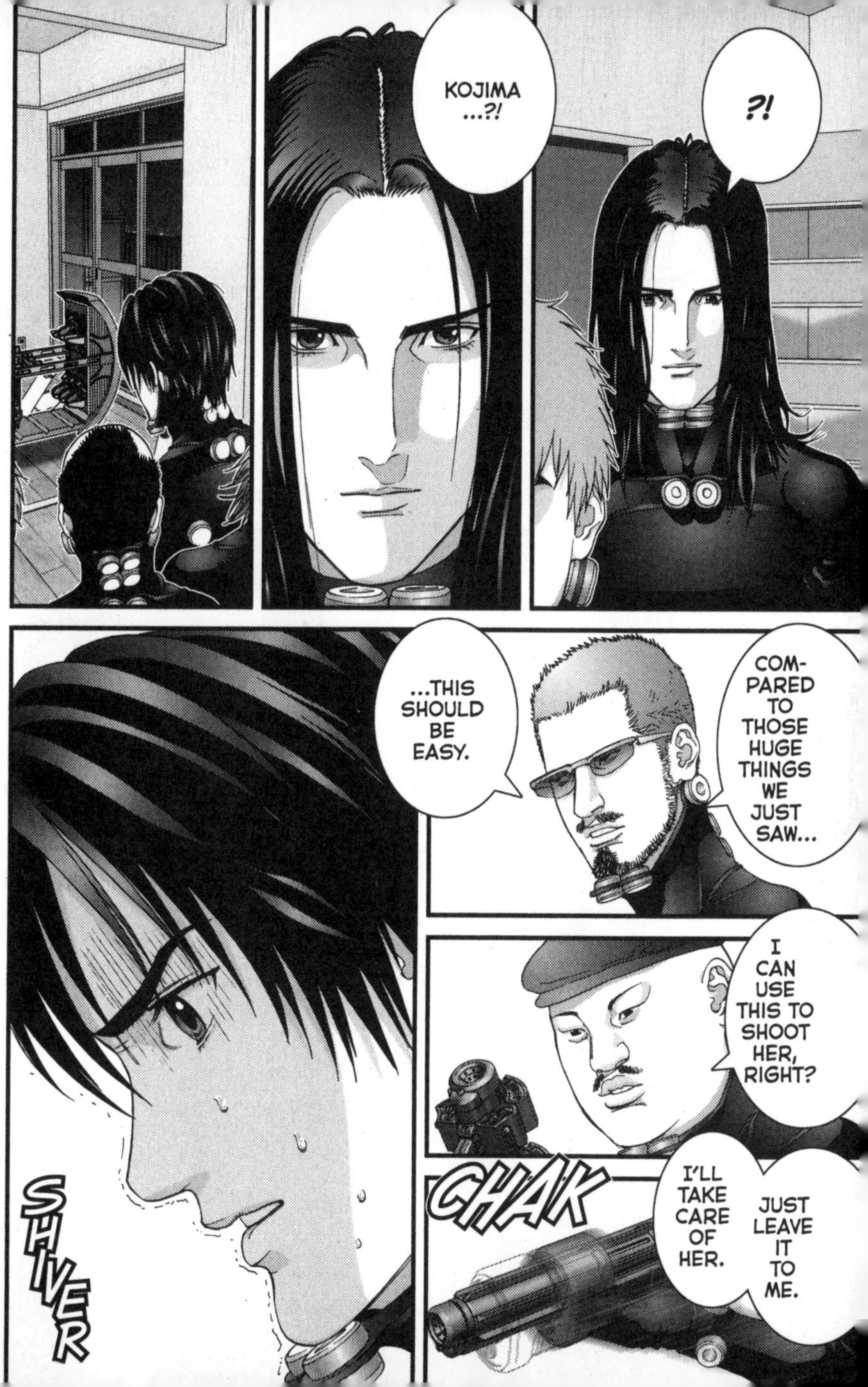
?!
KOJIMA ...?!
COM-PARED TO THOSE HUGE THINGS WE JUST SAW...
...THIS SHOULD BE EASY.
I CAN USE THIS TO SHOOT HER, RIGHT?
CHAK
JUST LEAVE IT TO ME.
I'LL TAKE CARE OF HER.
SHIVER

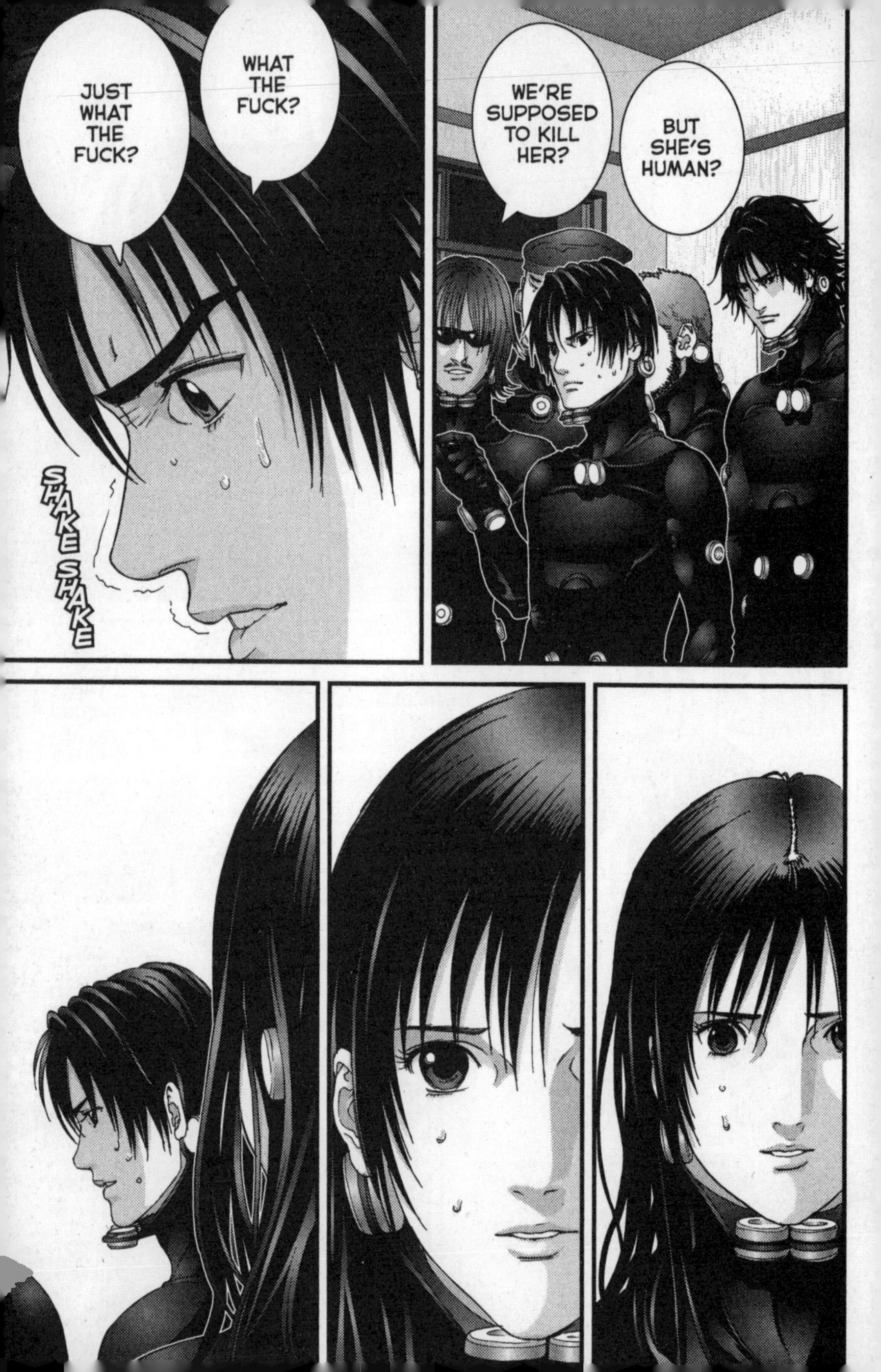
BUT SHE'S HUMAN?
WE'RE SUPPOSED TO KILL HER?
WHAT THE FUCK?
JUST WHAT THE FUCK?
SHAKE SHAKE

RE UNION

YOU WILL ALL PLEASE
GO NOW TO FINISH OFF THIS GUY.

TAE KOJIMA

CHARACTERISTICS:
○ SMALL
○ WEAK
LIKES:
DRAWING MANGA
FAVORITE PHRASE:
 "KEI!"

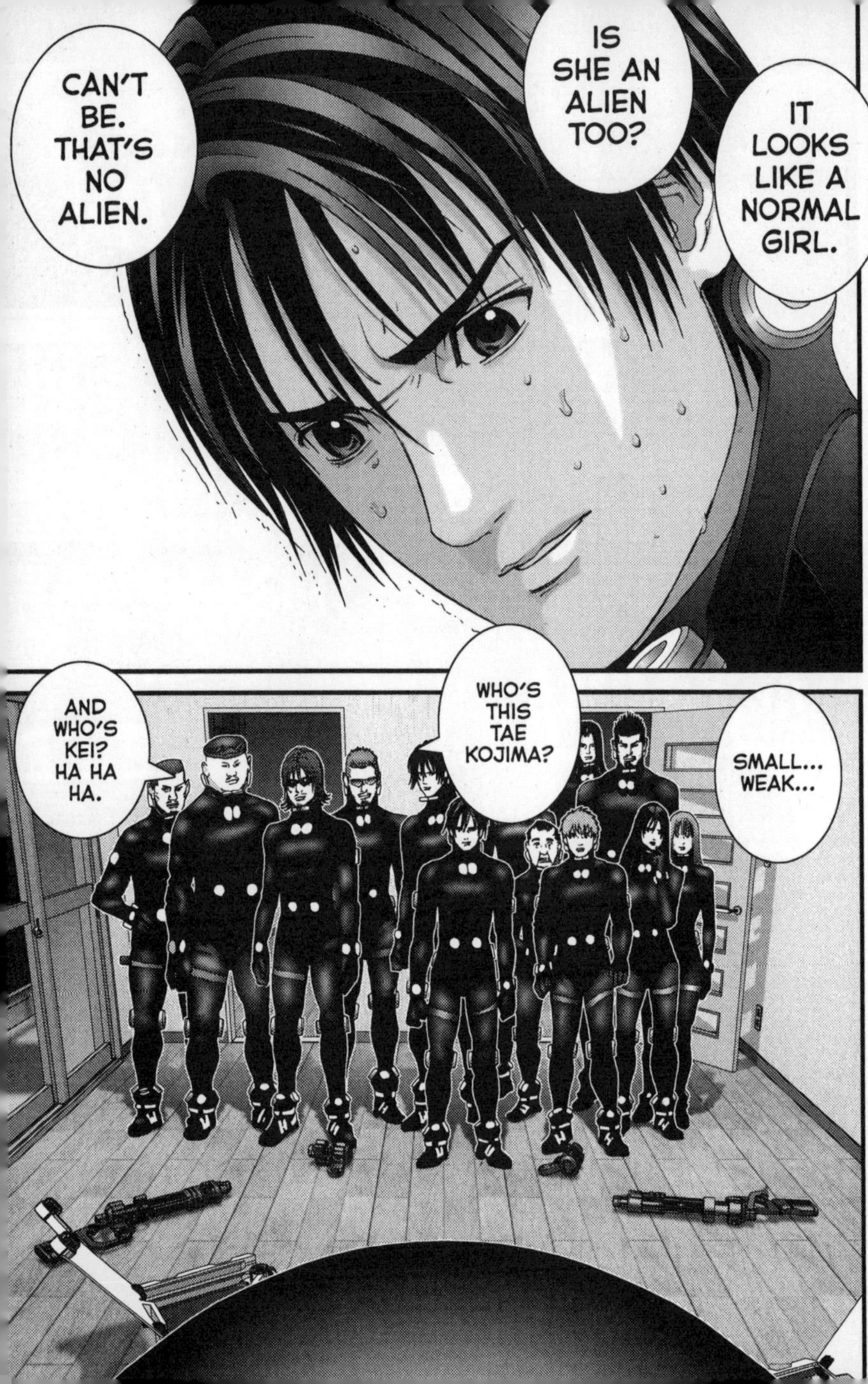
IS SHE AN ALIEN TOO?
IT LOOKS LIKE A NORMAL GIRL.
CAN'T BE. THAT'S NO ALIEN.
SMALL... WEAK...
WHO'S THIS TAE KOJIMA?
AND WHO'S KEI? HA HA HA.

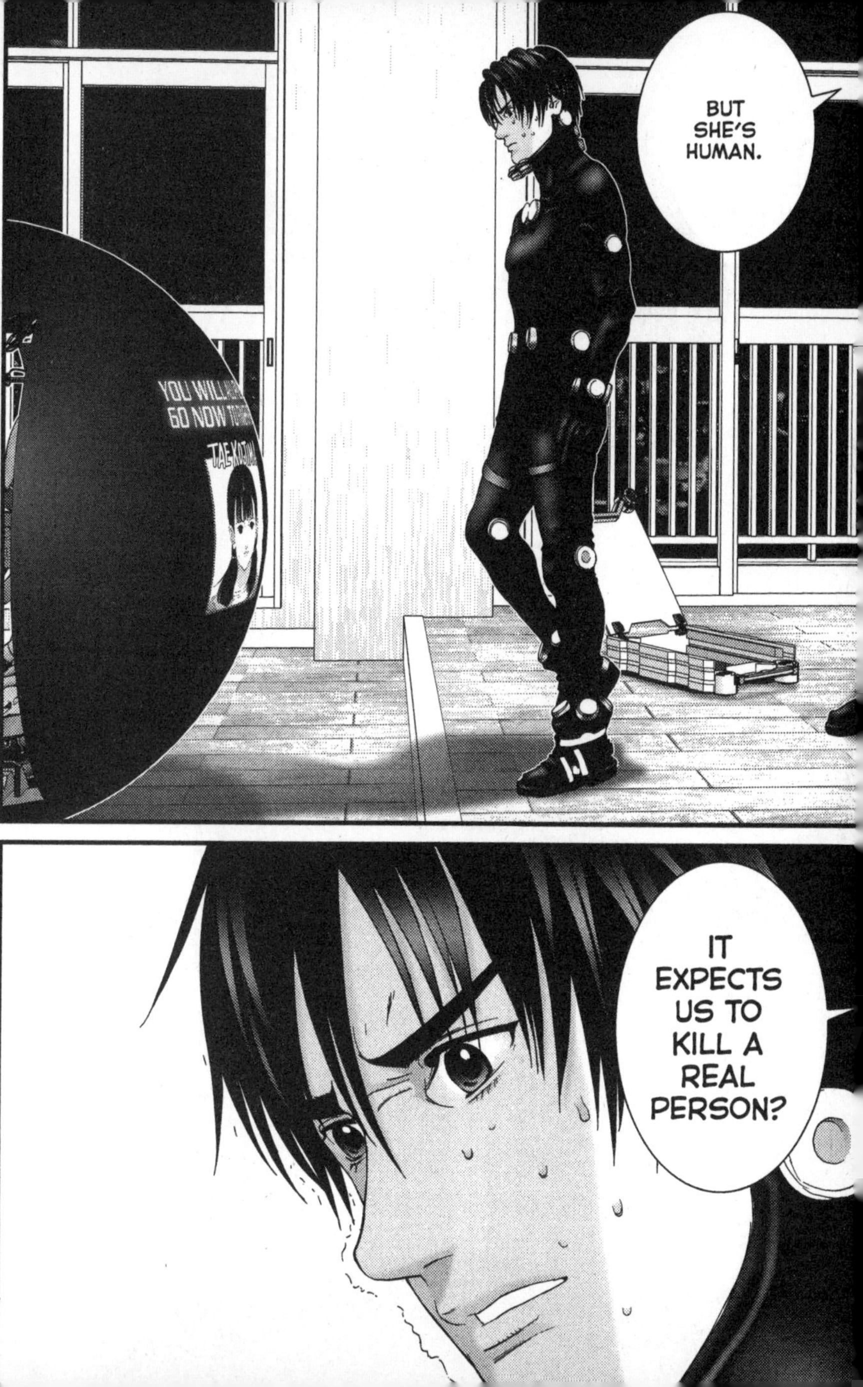
BUT SHE'S HUMAN.
IT EXPECTS US TO KILL A REAL PERSON?

YOU WILL ALL PLE
GO NOW TO FINI2H

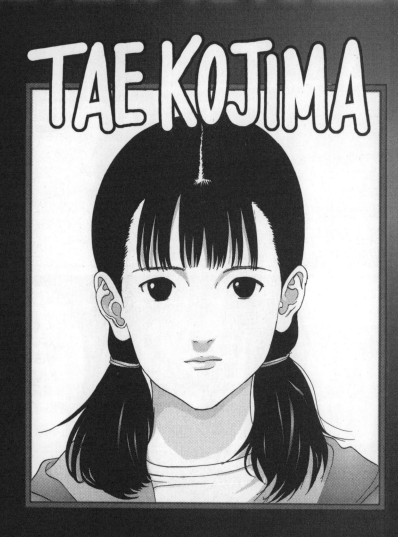

TAE KOJIMA

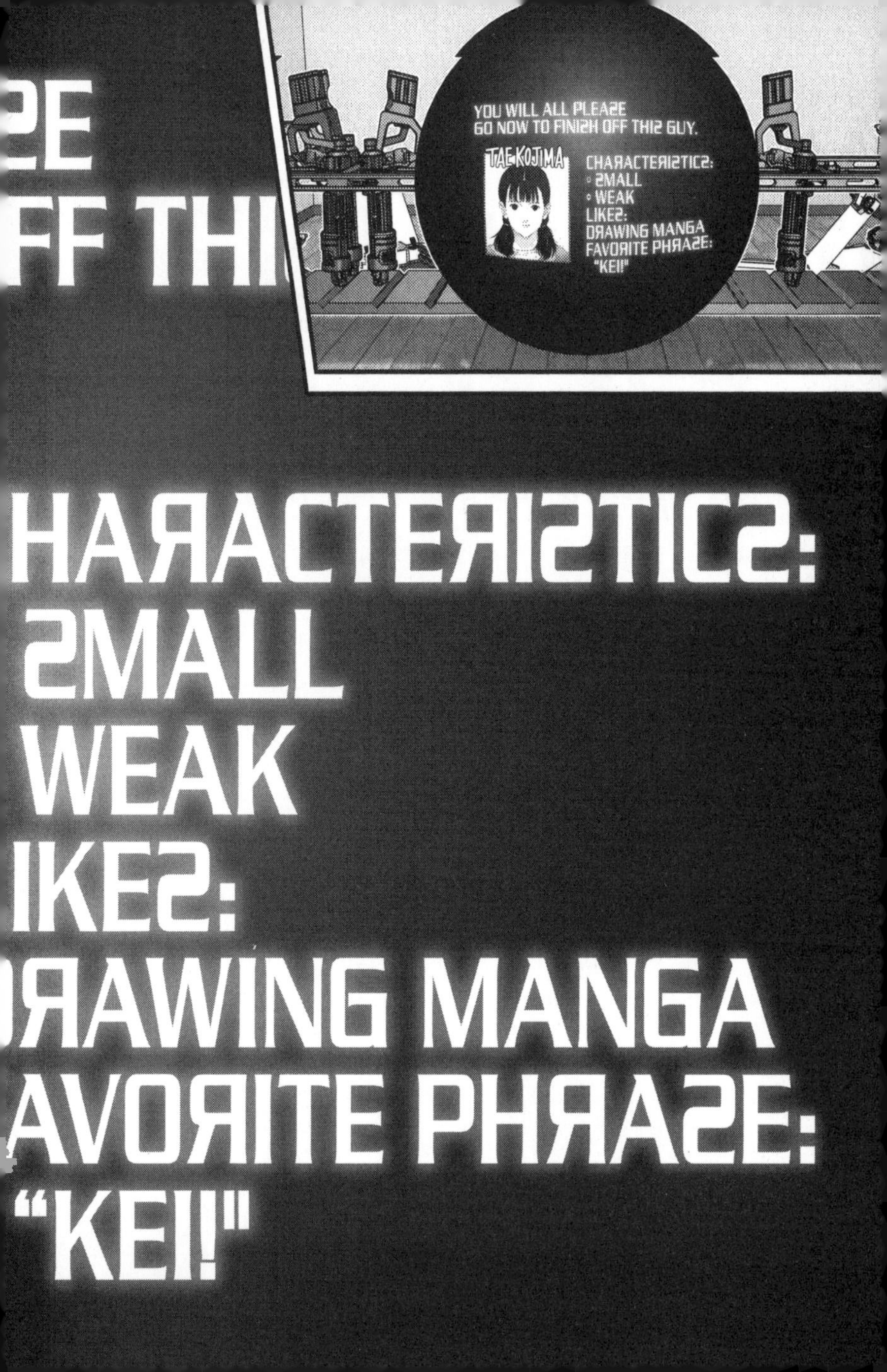
YOU WILL ALL PLEASE
GO NOW TO FINISH OFF THIS GUY.
TAE KOJIMA
CHARACTERISTICS:
◦ SMALL
◦ WEAK
LIKES:
DRAWING MANGA
FAVORITE PHRASE:
"KEI!"
SE
FF THI
HARACTERISTICS:
SMALL
WEAK
IKES:
RAWING MANGA
AVORITE PHRASE:
“KEI!”

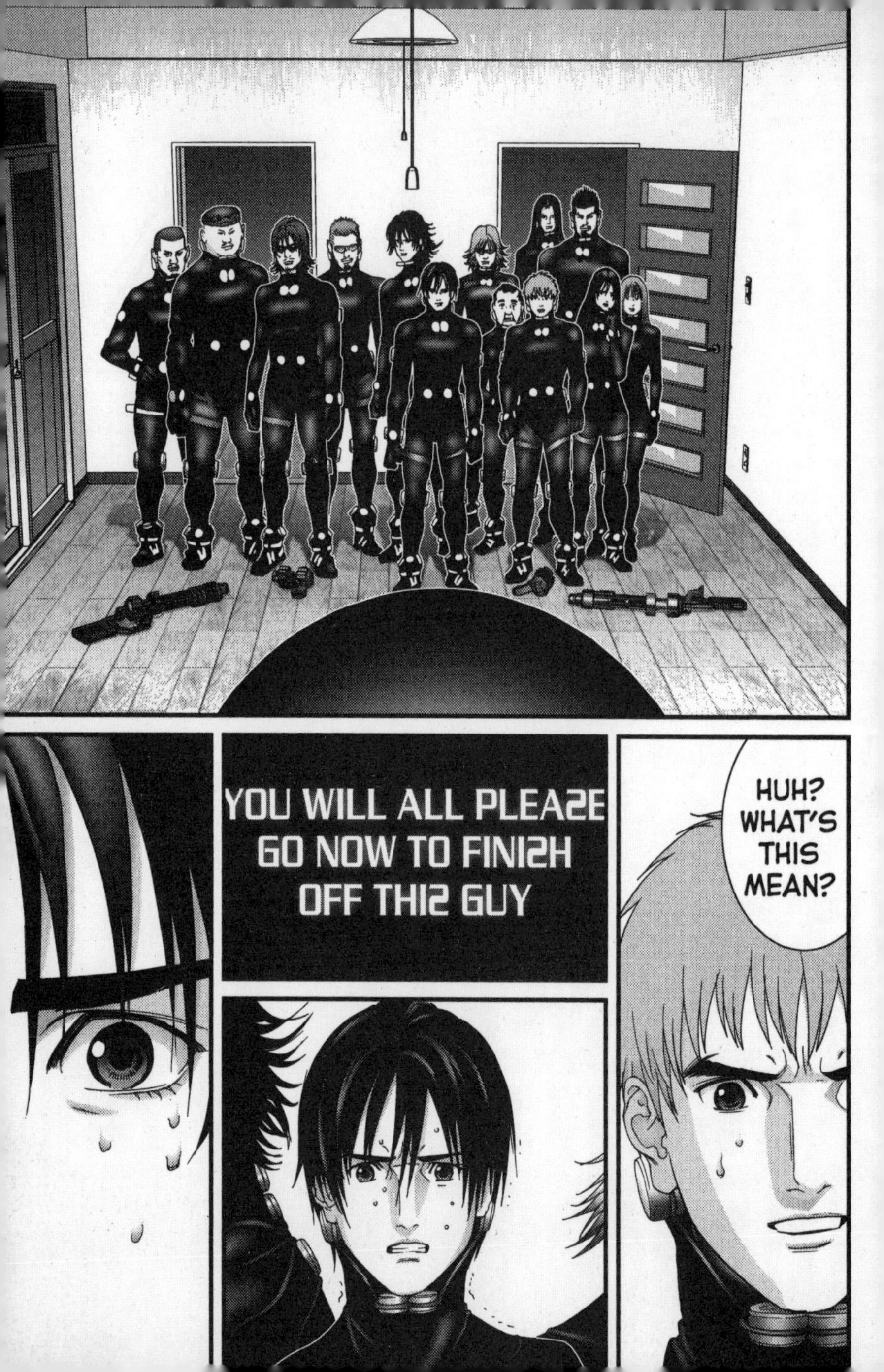
YOU WILL ALL PLEAZE GO NOW TO FINIZH OFF THIZ GUY
HUH? WHAT'S THIS MEAN?

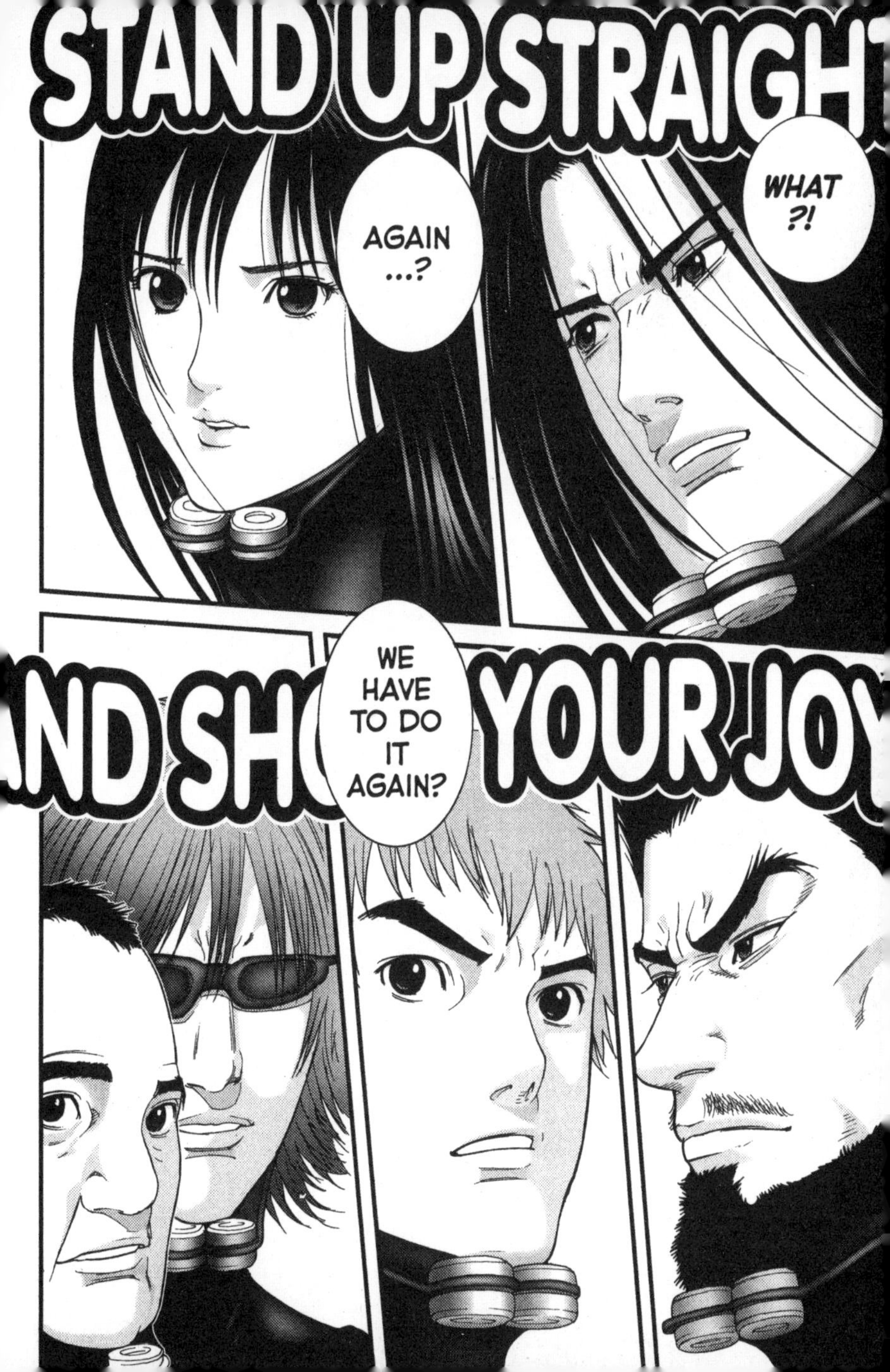
STAND UP STRAIGH
WHAT ?!
AGAIN ...?
ND SHO
WE HAVE TO DO IT AGAIN?
YOUR JO

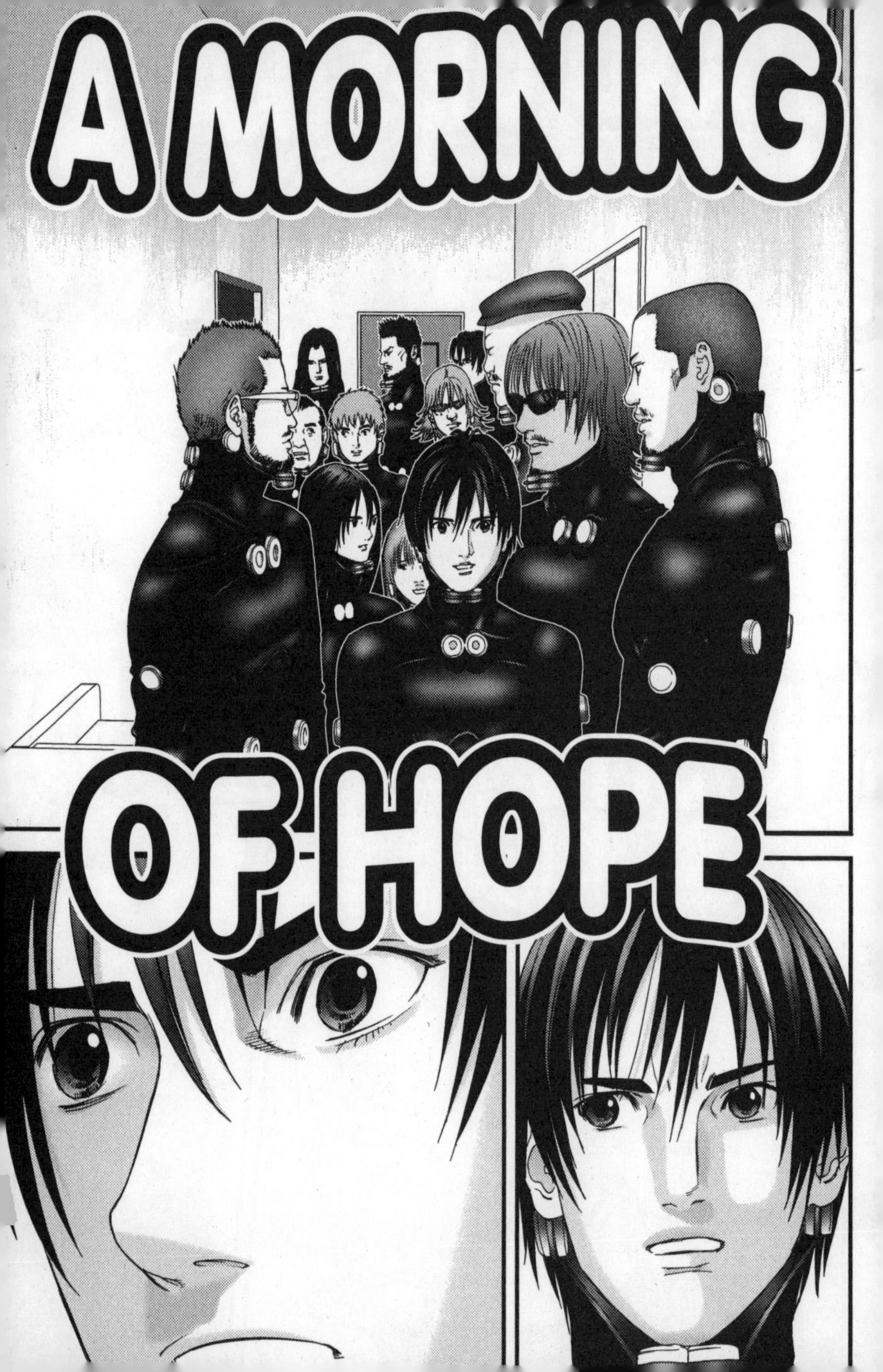
A MORNING
OF HOPE

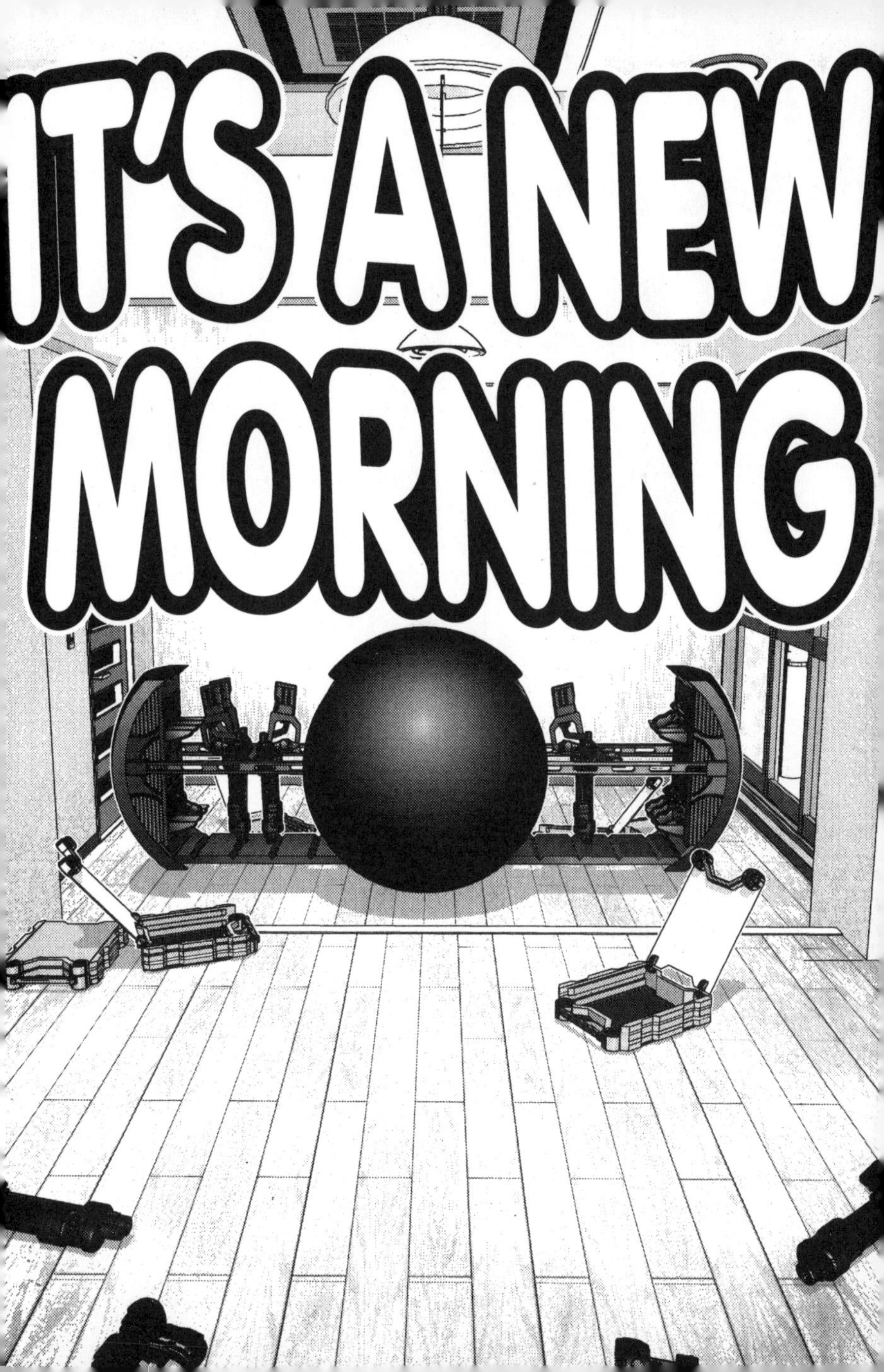
IT'S A NEW MORNING

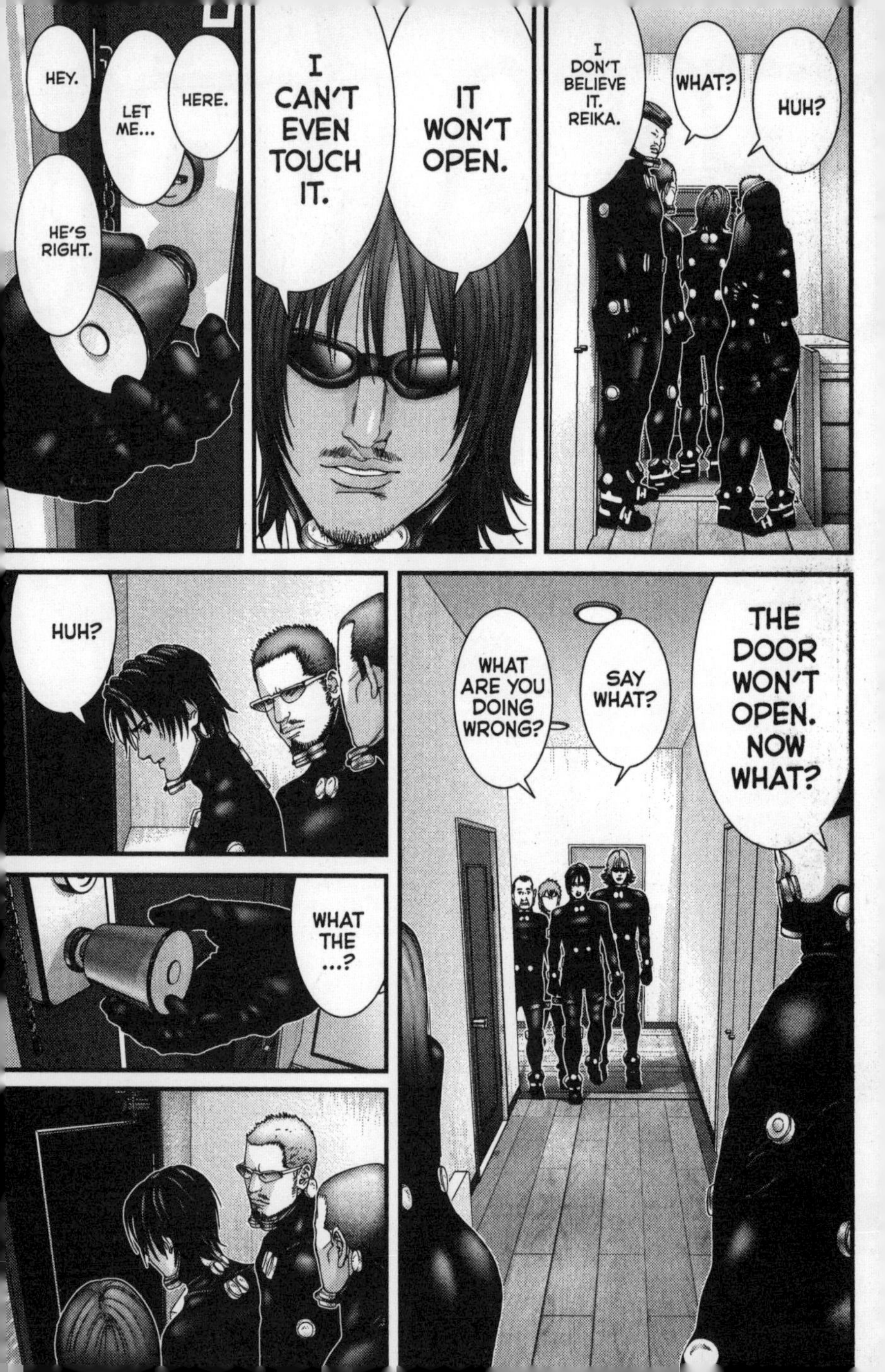
HUH?
WHAT?
I DON'T BELIEVE IT. REIKA.
IT WON'T OPEN.
I CAN'T EVEN TOUCH IT.
HERE.
LET ME...
HEY.
HE'S RIGHT.
THE DOOR WON'T OPEN. NOW WHAT?
SAY WHAT?
WHAT ARE YOU DOING WRONG?
HUH?
WHAT THE ...?

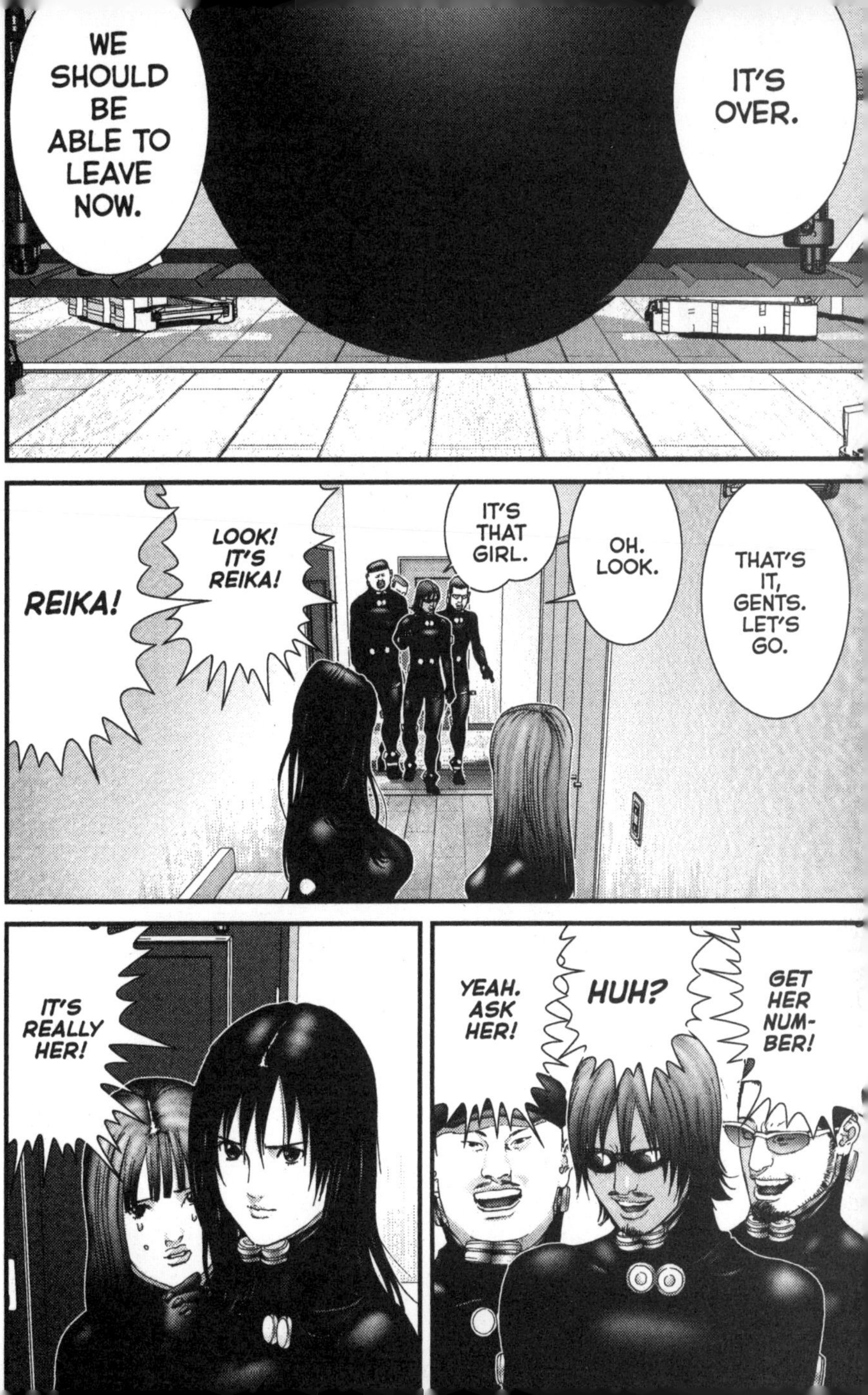
IT'S OVER.
WE SHOULD BE ABLE TO LEAVE NOW.
THAT'S IT, GENTS. LET'S GO.
OH. LOOK.
IT'S THAT GIRL.
LOOK! IT'S REIKA!
REIKA!
GET HER NUM-BER!
HUH?
YEAH. ASK HER!
IT'S REALLY HER!

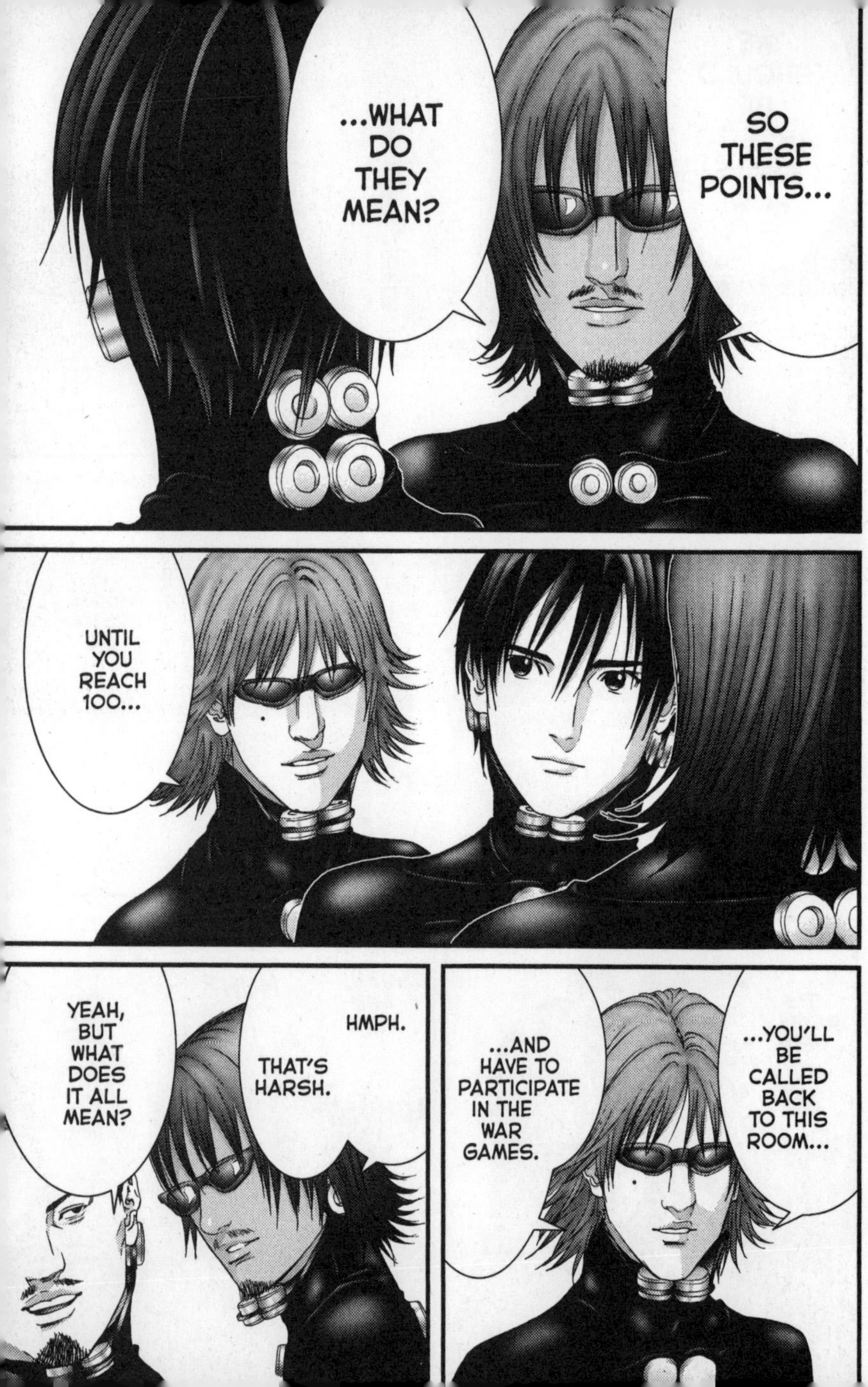
SO THESE POINTS...
...WHAT DO THEY MEAN?
UNTIL YOU REACH 100...
...YOU'LL BE CALLED BACK TO THIS ROOM...
...AND HAVE TO PARTICIPATE IN THE WAR GAMES.
HMPH.
THAT'S HARSH.
YEAH, BUT WHAT DOES IT ALL MEAN?

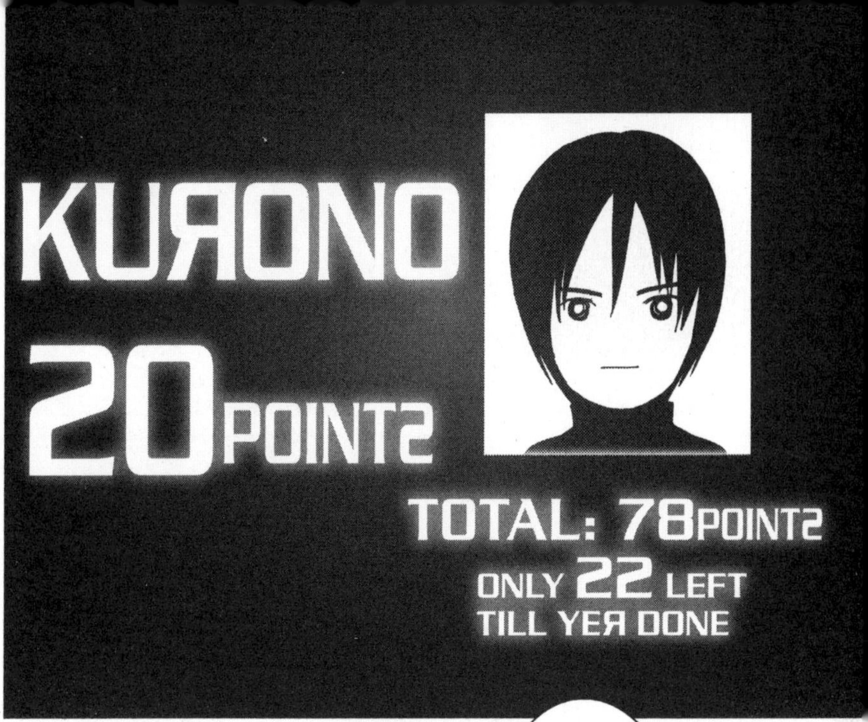
KURONO
20 POINTS
TOTAL: 78 POINTS
ONLY 22 LEFT
TILL YER DONE

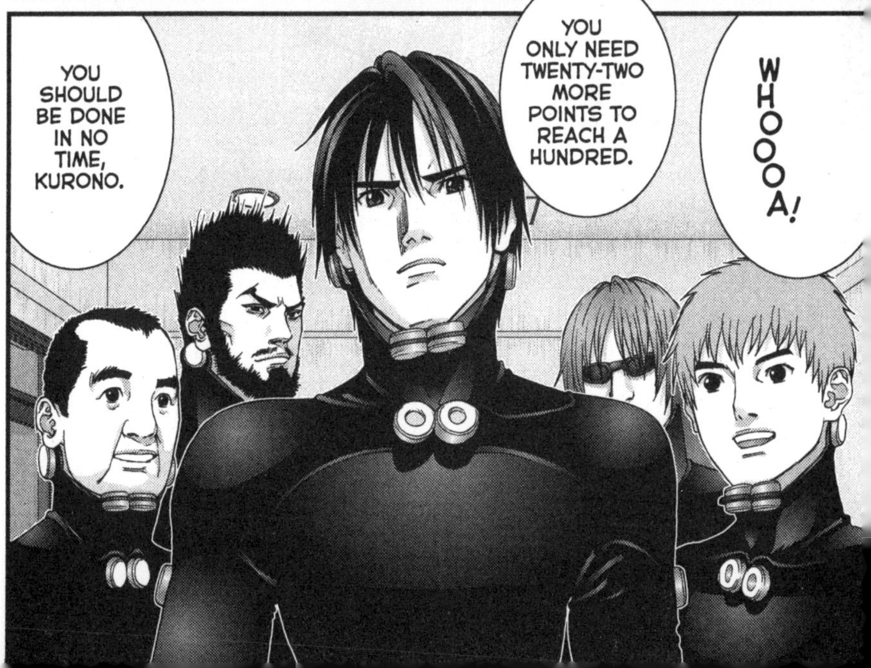
WHOOOA!
YOU ONLY NEED TWENTY-TWO MORE POINTS TO REACH A HUNDRED.
YOU SHOULD BE DONE IN NO TIME, KURONO.

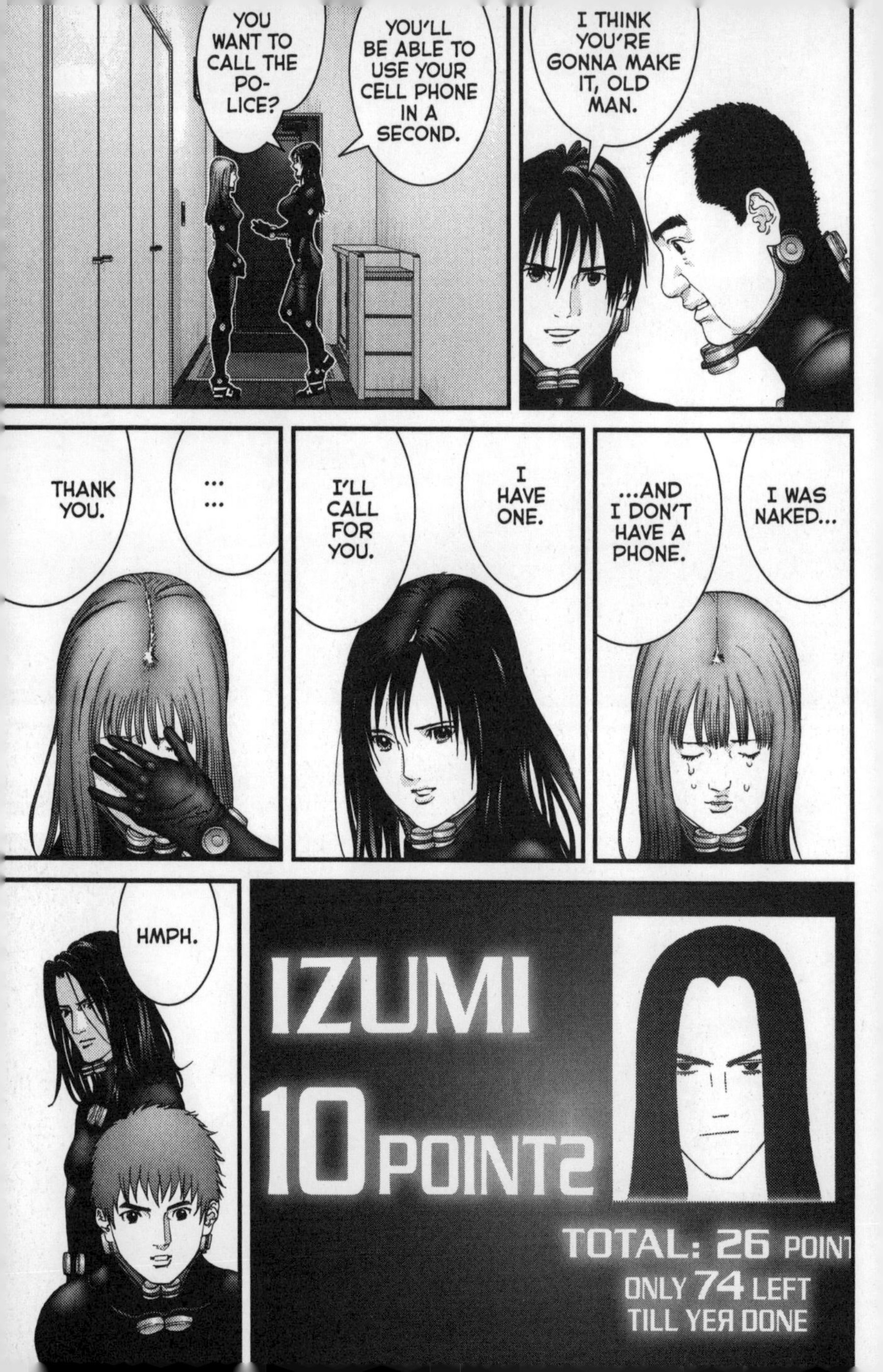
I THINK YOU'RE GONNA MAKE IT, OLD MAN.
YOU'LL BE ABLE TO USE YOUR CELL PHONE IN A SECOND.
YOU WANT TO CALL THE PO-LICE?
I WAS NAKED...
...AND I DON'T HAVE A PHONE.
I HAVE ONE.
I'LL CALL FOR YOU.
... ...
THANK YOU.
IZUMI
10 POINTS
TOTAL: 26 POINT
ONLY 74 LEFT
TILL YER DONE
HMPH.

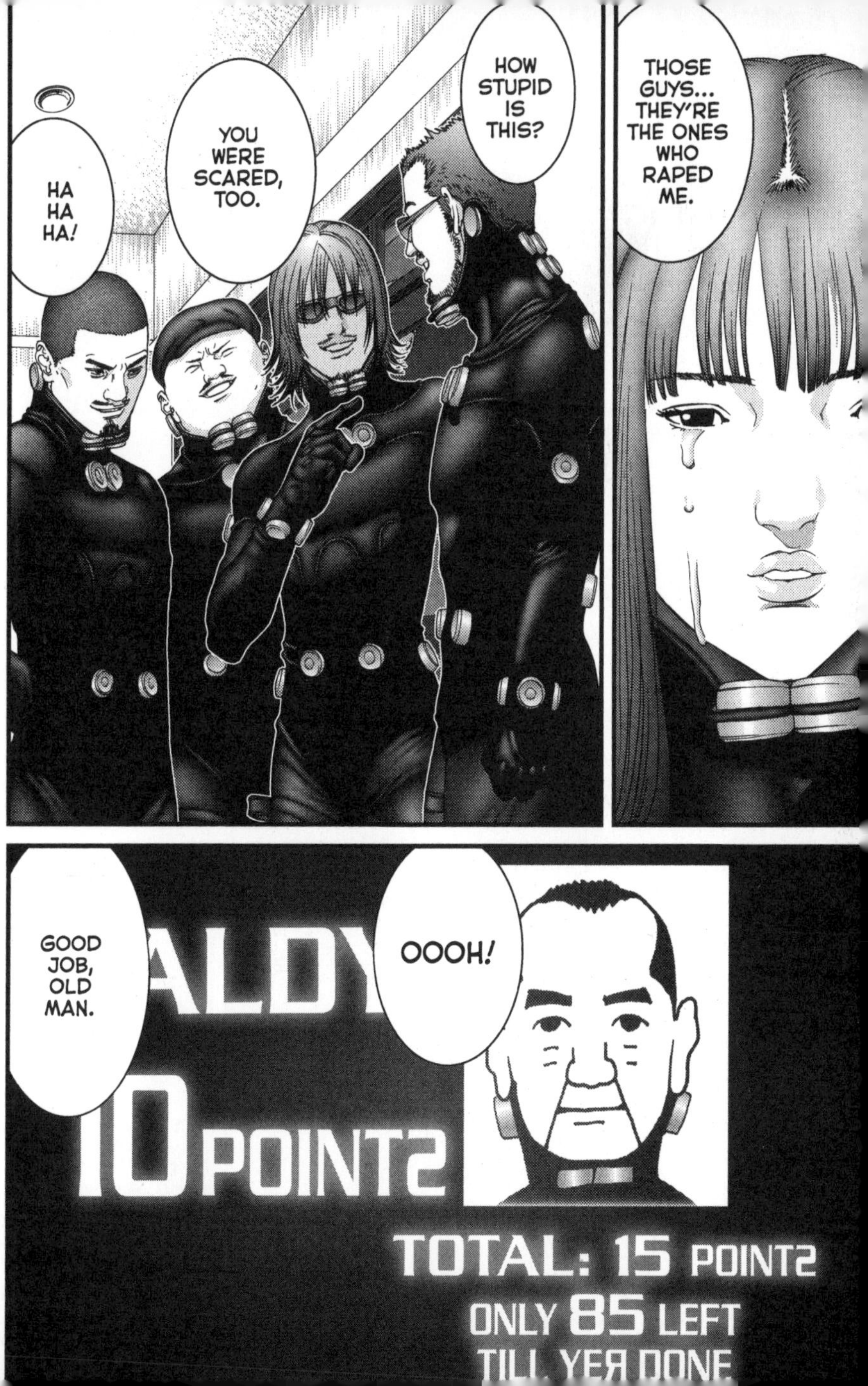
THOSE GUYS... THEY'RE THE ONES WHO RAPED ME.
HOW STUPID IS THIS?
YOU WERE SCARED, TOO.
HA HA HA!
OOOH!
GOOD JOB, OLD MAN.
10 POINTS
TOTAL: 15 POINTS
ONLY 85 LEFT
TILL YER DONE

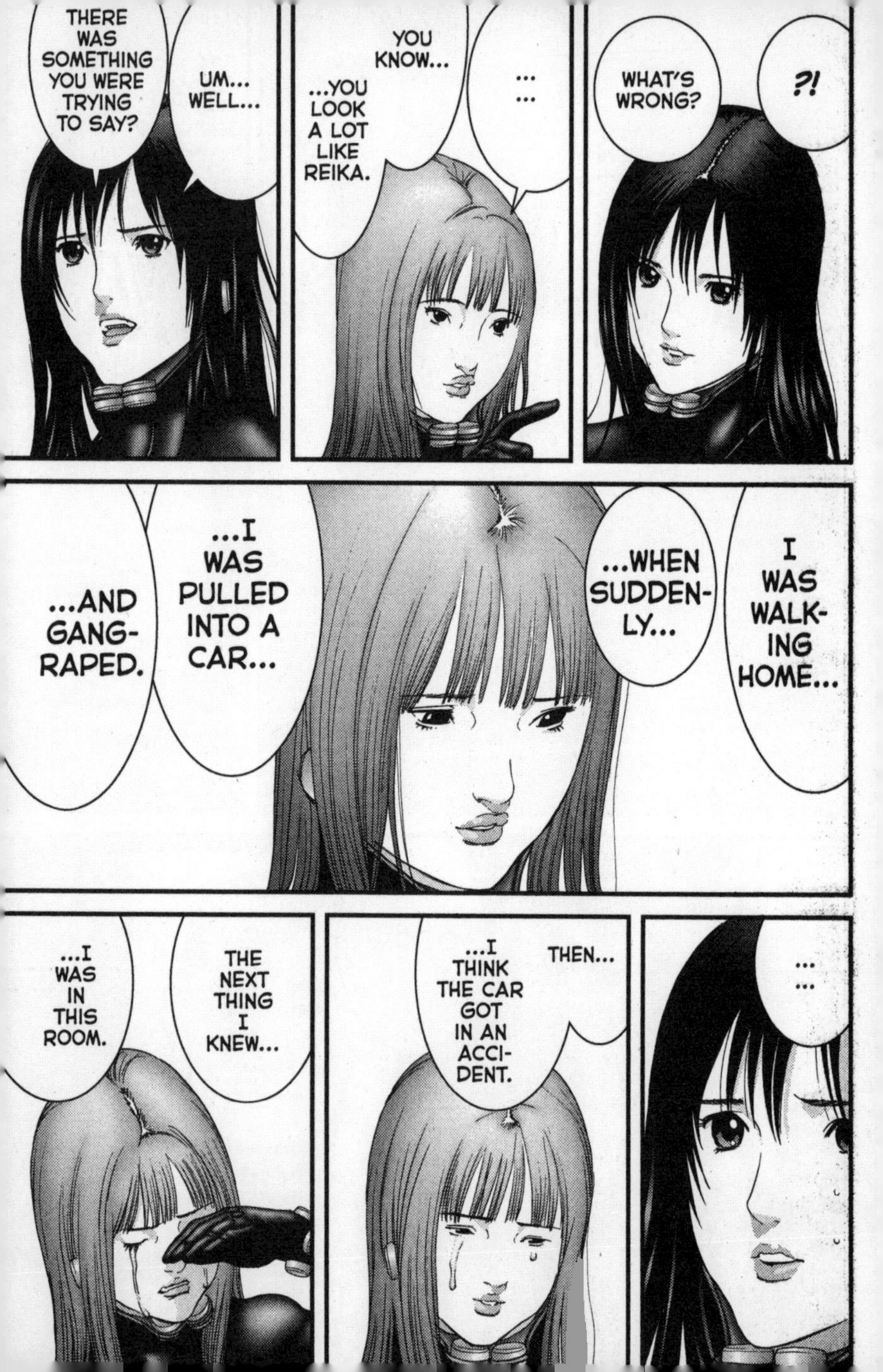
?!
WHAT'S WRONG?
……
YOU KNOW...
...YOU LOOK A LOT LIKE REIKA.
UM... WELL...
THERE WAS SOMETHING YOU WERE TRYING TO SAY?
I WAS WALK-ING HOME...
...WHEN SUDDEN-LY...
...I WAS PULLED INTO A CAR...
...AND GANG-RAPED.
……
THEN...
...I THINK THE CAR GOT IN AN ACCI-DENT.
THE NEXT THING I KNEW...
...I WAS IN THIS ROOM.

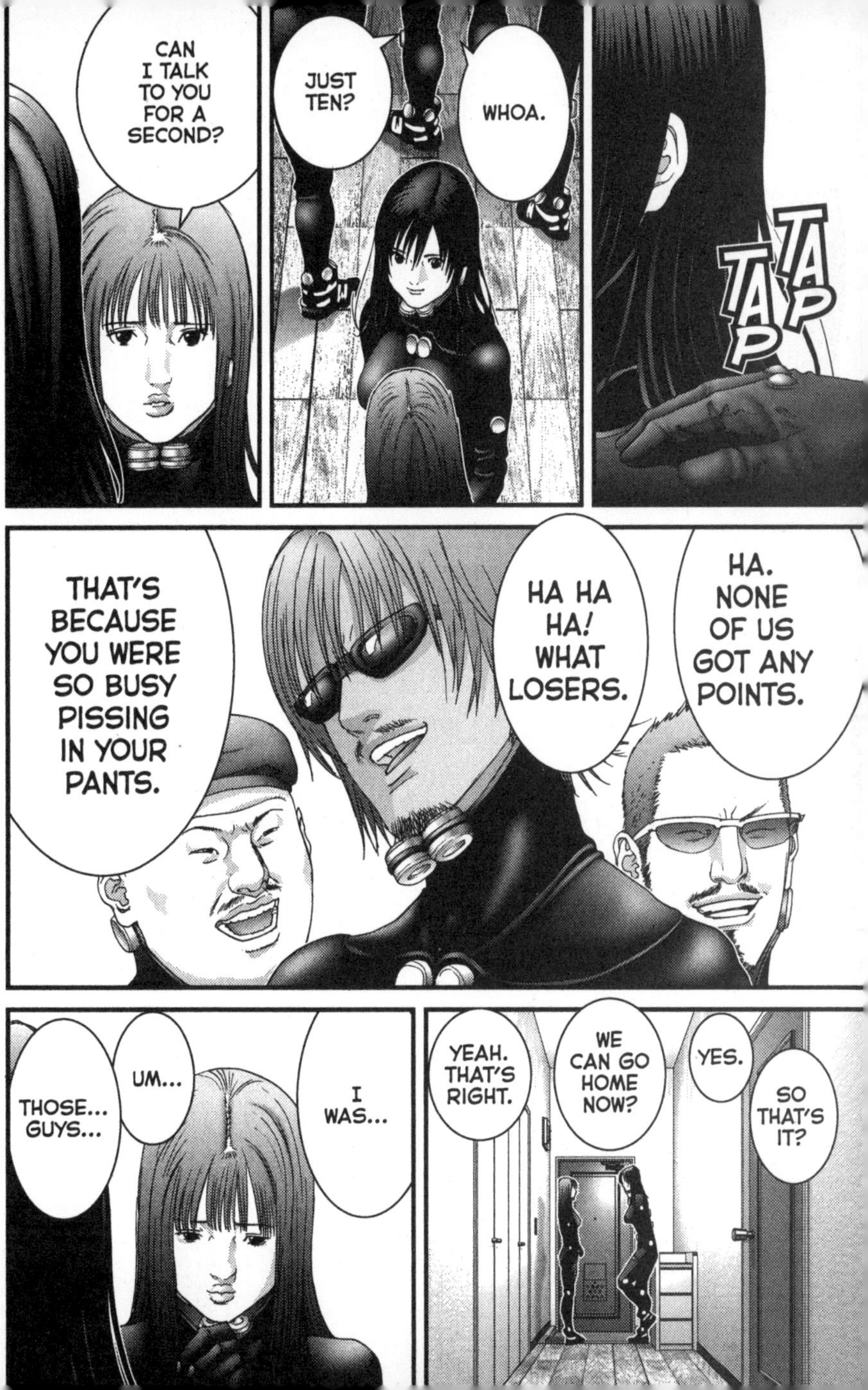
TAP TAP
WHOA.
JUST TEN?
CAN I TALK TO YOU FOR A SECOND?
HA. NONE OF US GOT ANY POINTS.
HA HA HA! WHAT LOSERS.
THAT'S BECAUSE YOU WERE SO BUSY PISSING IN YOUR PANTS.
SO THAT'S IT?
YES.
WE CAN GO HOME NOW?
YEAH. THAT'S RIGHT.
I WAS...
UM...
THOSE... GUYS...

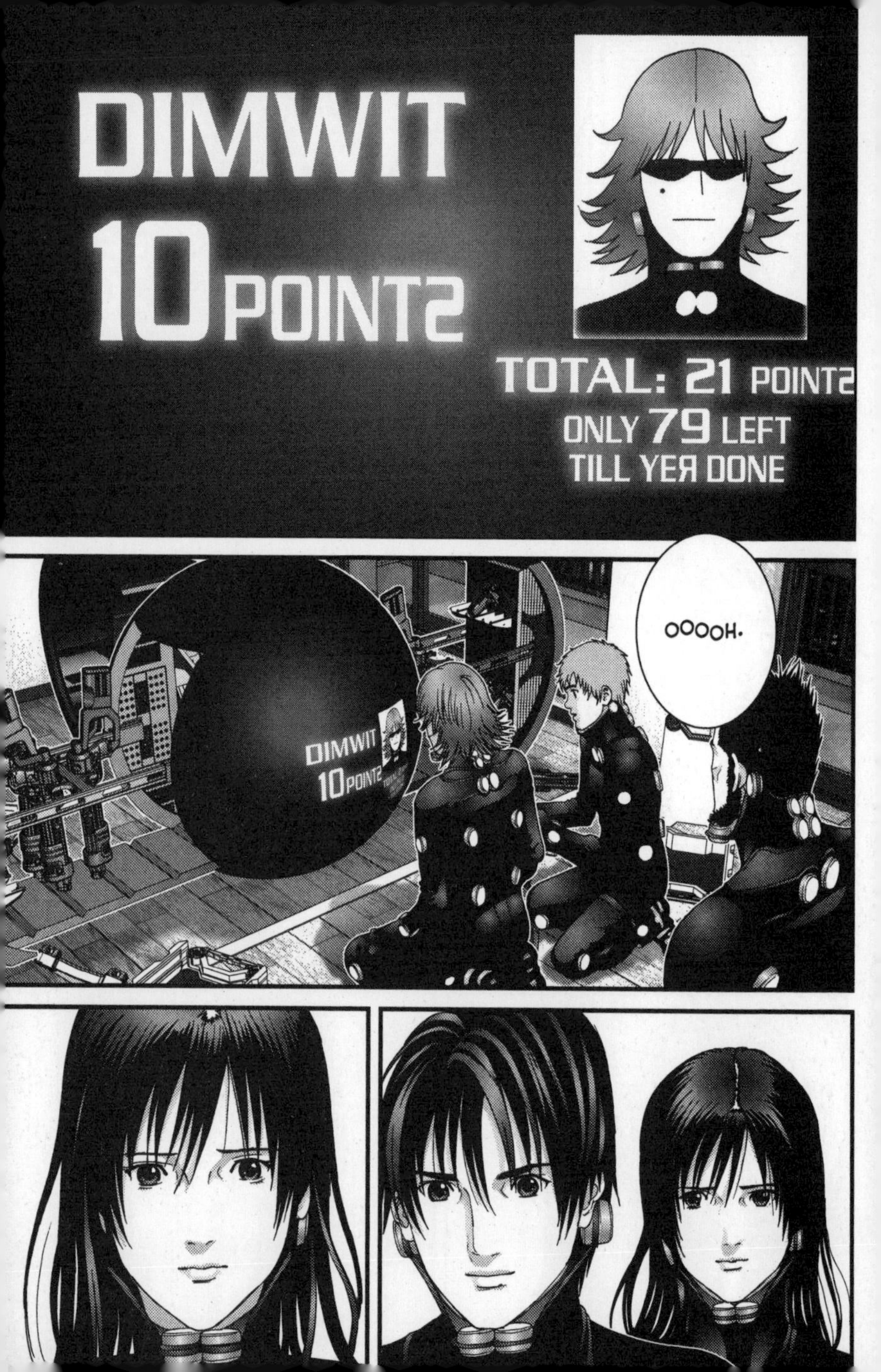
DIMWIT
10 POINTZ
TOTAL: 21 POINTZ
ONLY 79 LEFT
TILL YEЯ DONE
OOOOH.
DIMWIT
10 POINTZ

0174 TARGET DIIING

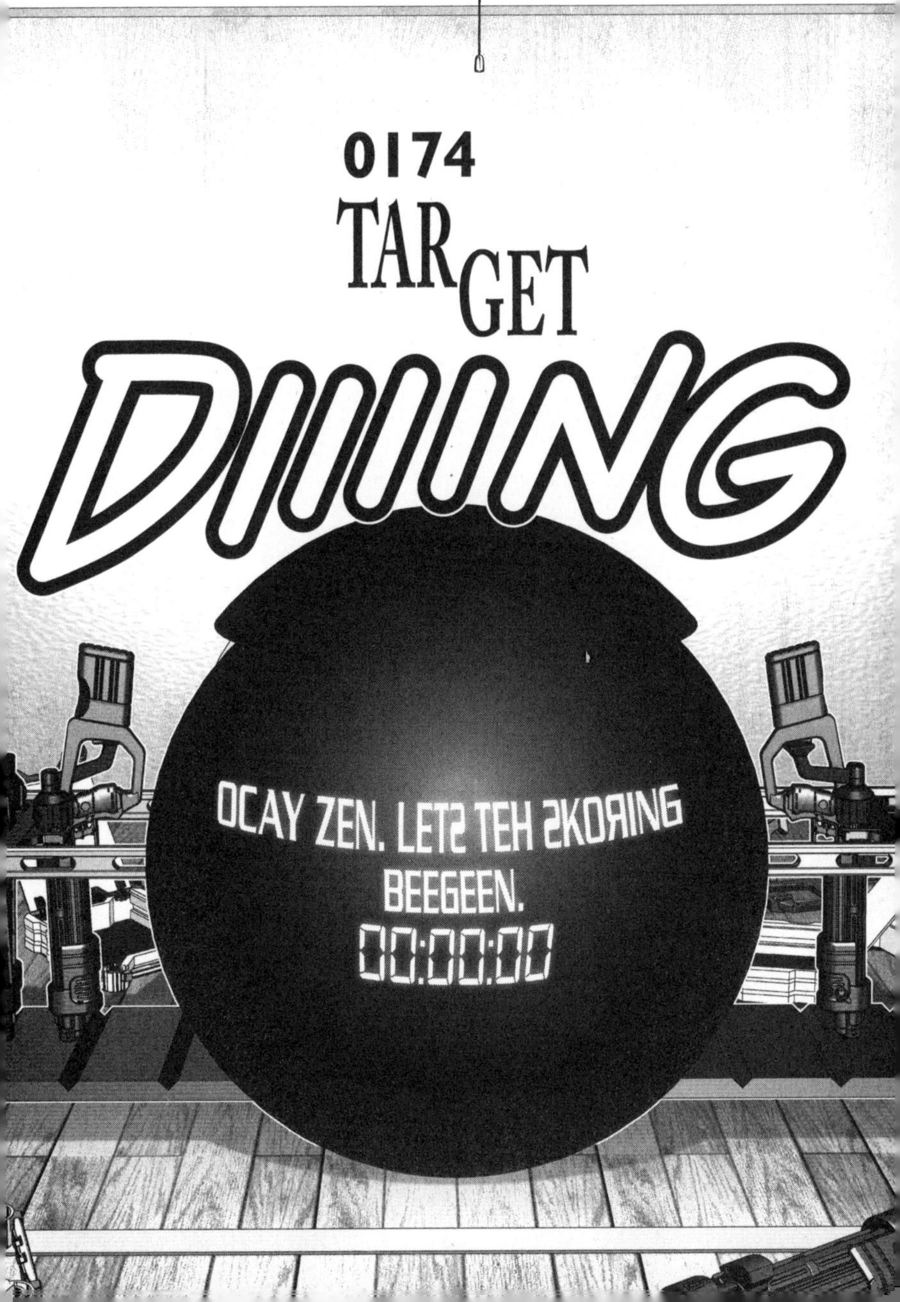
OCAY ZEN. LETS TEH SKORING
BEEGEEN.
00:00:00

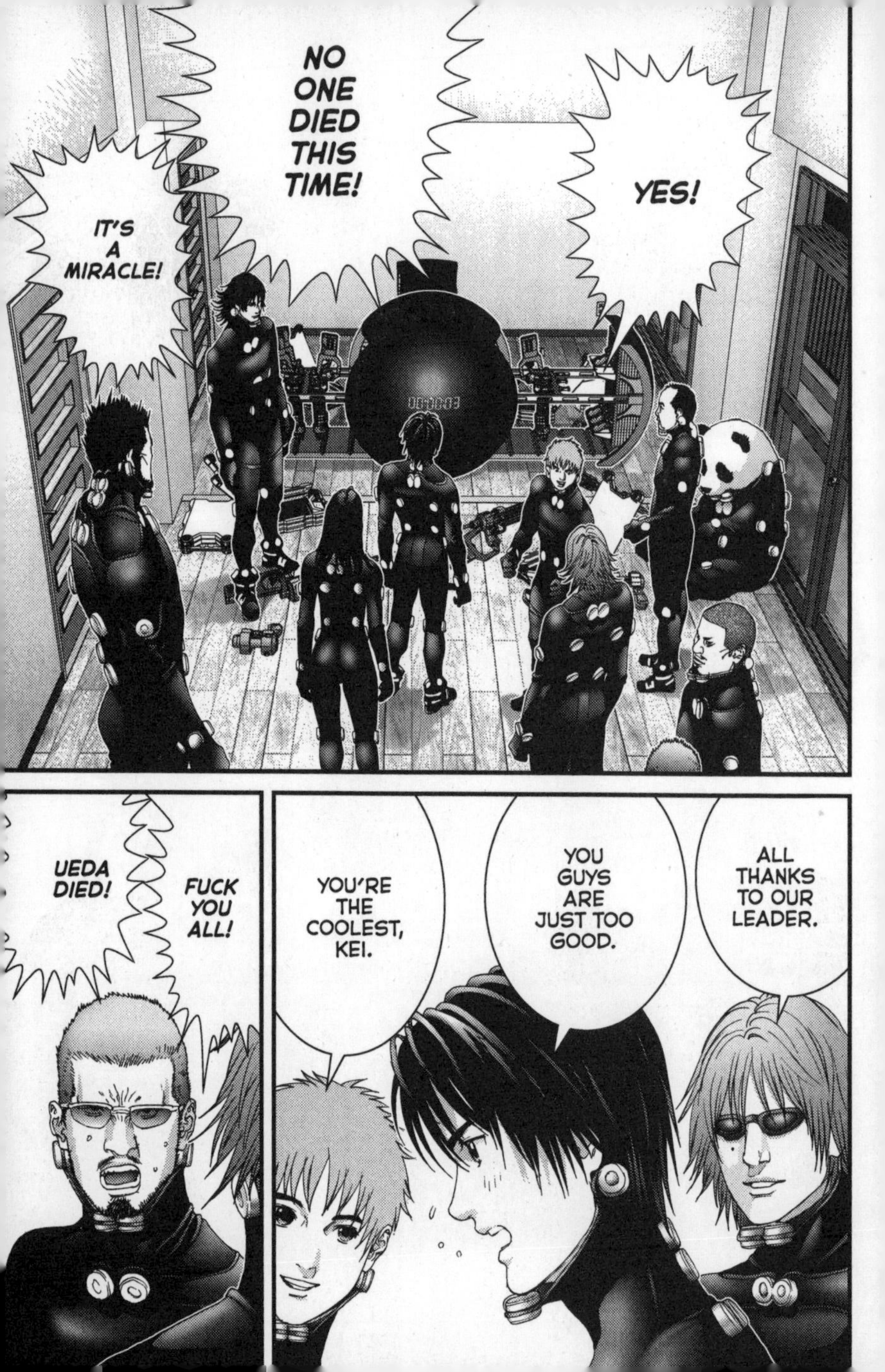
YES!
NO ONE DIED THIS TIME!
IT'S A MIRACLE!
ALL THANKS TO OUR LEADER.
YOU GUYS ARE JUST TOO GOOD.
YOU'RE THE COOLEST, KEI.
FUCK YOU ALL!
UEDA DIED!

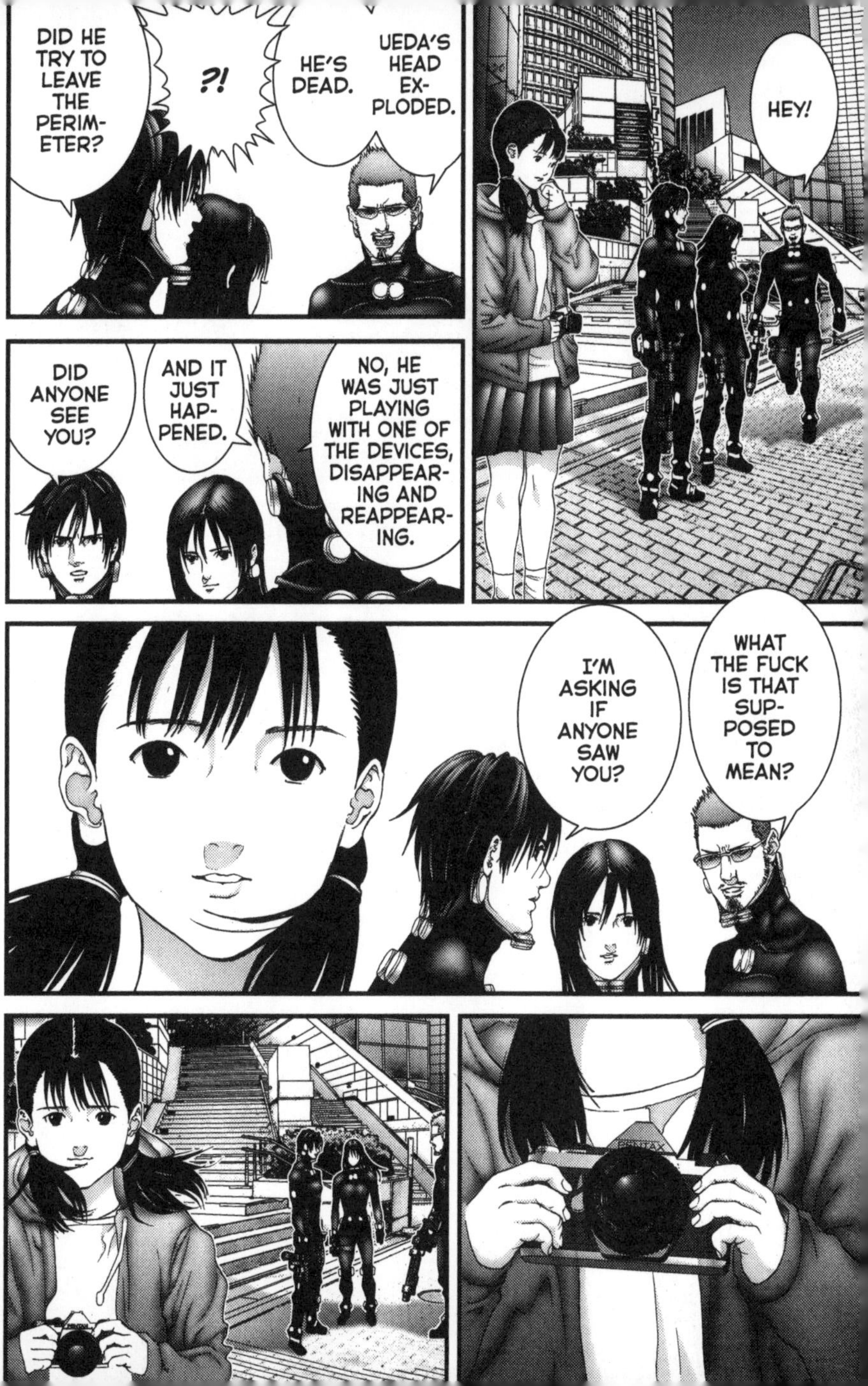
HEY!
UEDA'S HEAD EX-PLODED.
HE'S DEAD.
?!
DID HE TRY TO LEAVE THE PERIM-ETER?
NO, HE WAS JUST PLAYING WITH ONE OF THE DEVICES, DISAPPEAR-ING AND REAPPEAR-ING.
AND IT JUST HAP-PENED.
DID ANYONE SEE YOU?
WHAT THE FUCK IS THAT SUP-POSED TO MEAN?
I'M ASKING IF ANYONE SAW YOU?

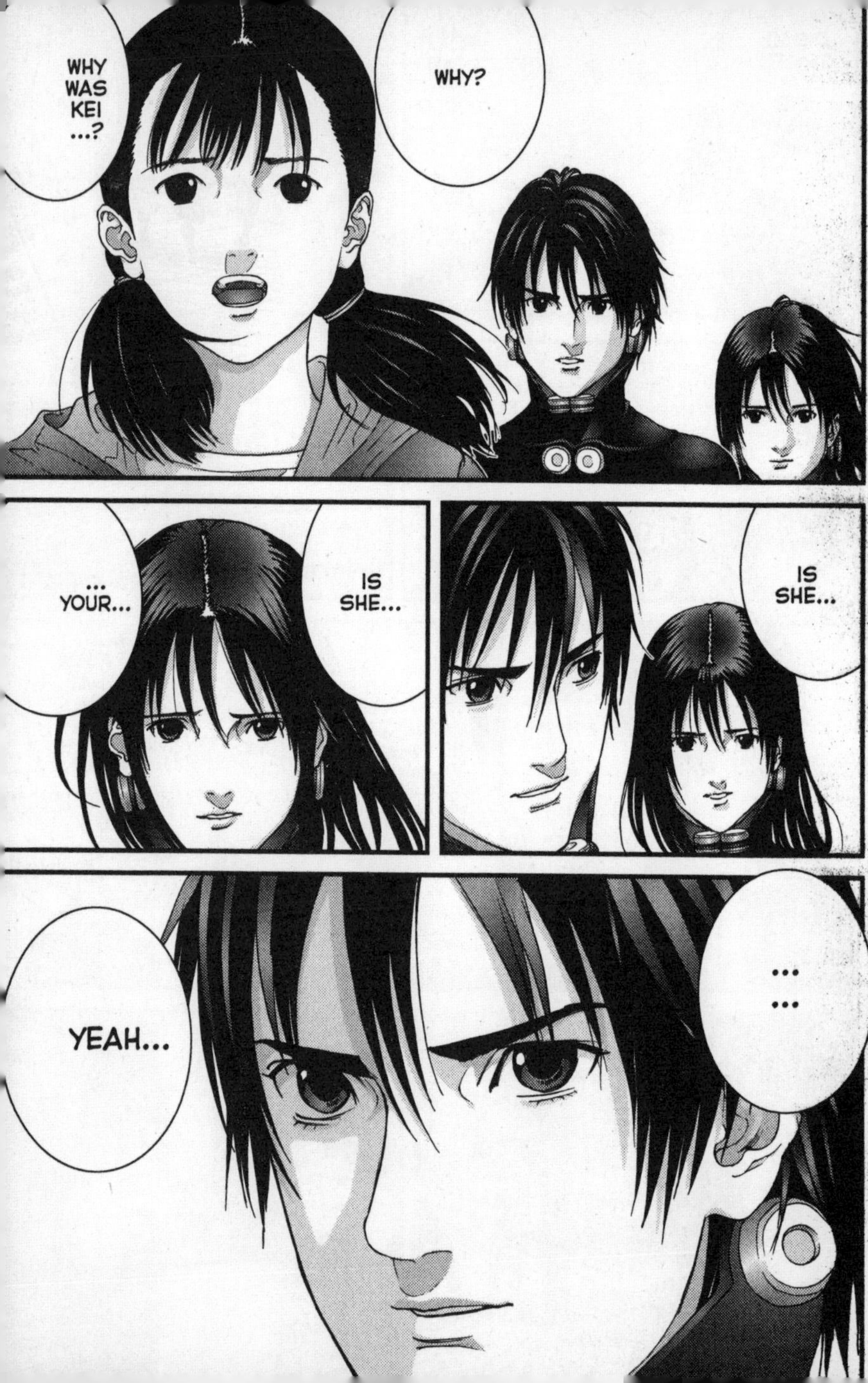
WHY?
WHY WAS KEI ...?
IS SHE...
IS SHE...
... YOUR...
... ...
YEAH...

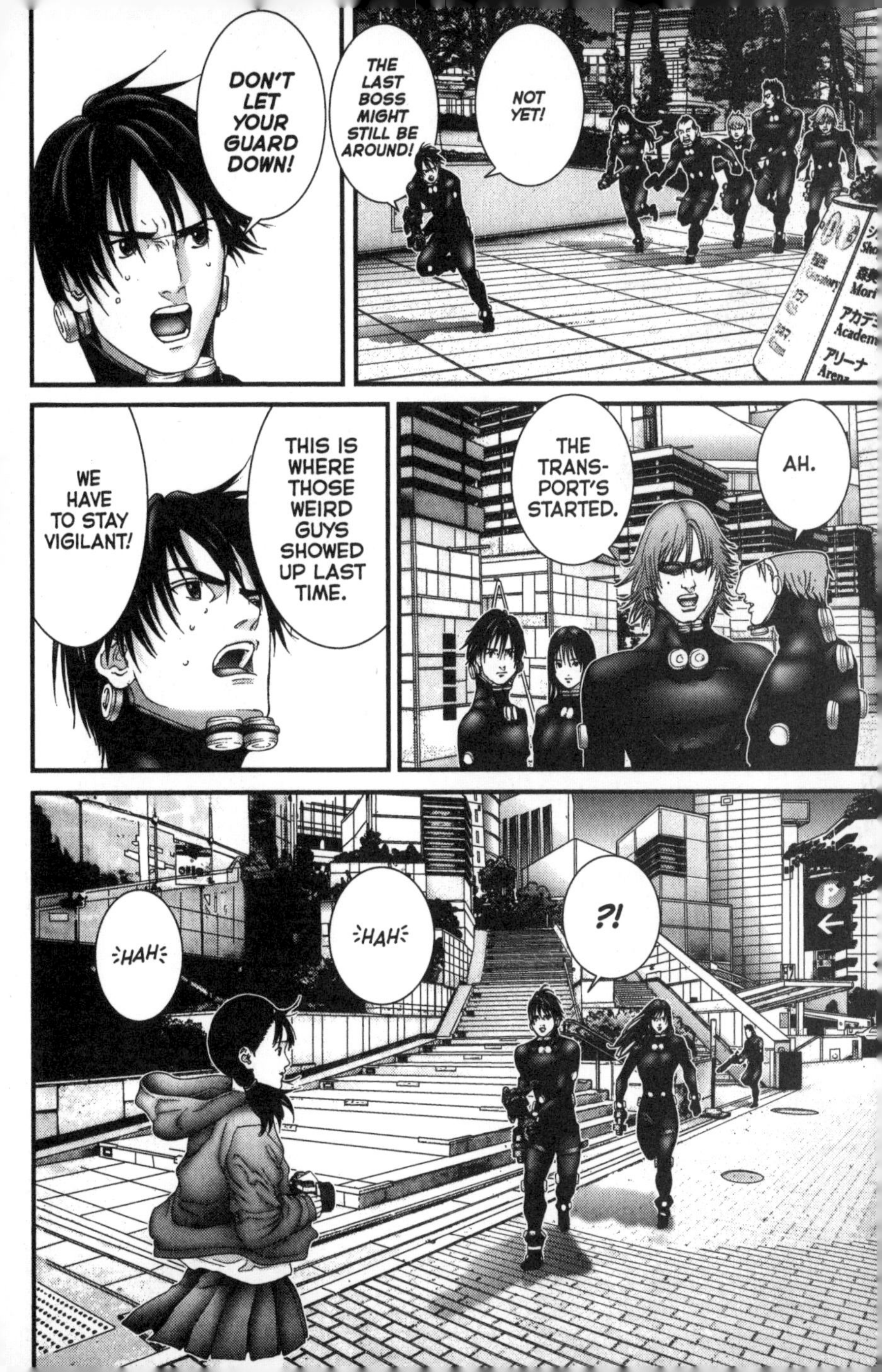
NOT YET!
THE LAST BOSS MIGHT STILL BE AROUND!
DON'T LET YOUR GUARD DOWN!
AH.
THE TRANS-PORT'S STARTED.
THIS IS WHERE THOSE WEIRD GUYS SHOWED UP LAST TIME.
WE HAVE TO STAY VIGILANT!
?!
HAH
HAH

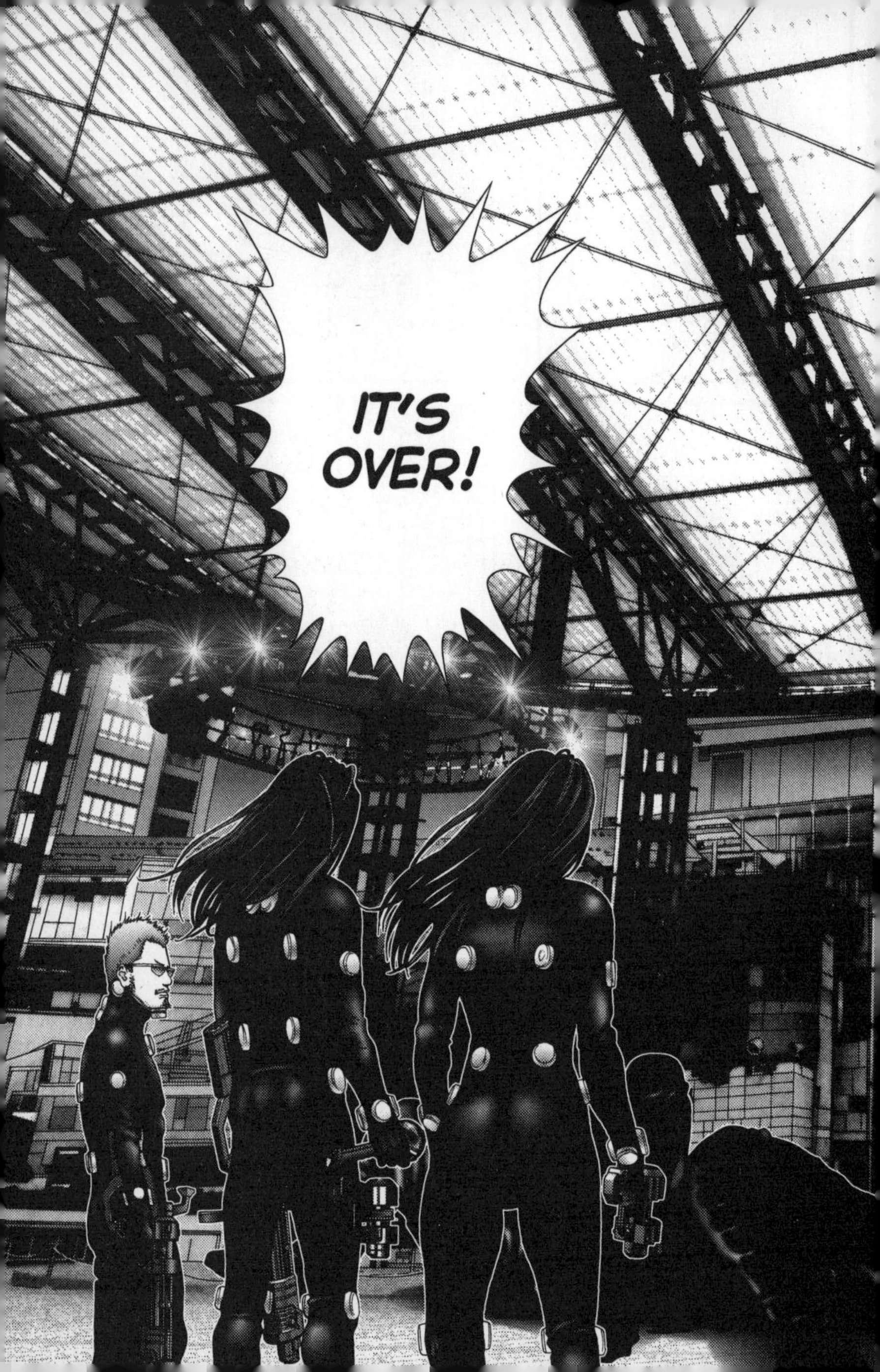
IT'S OVER!

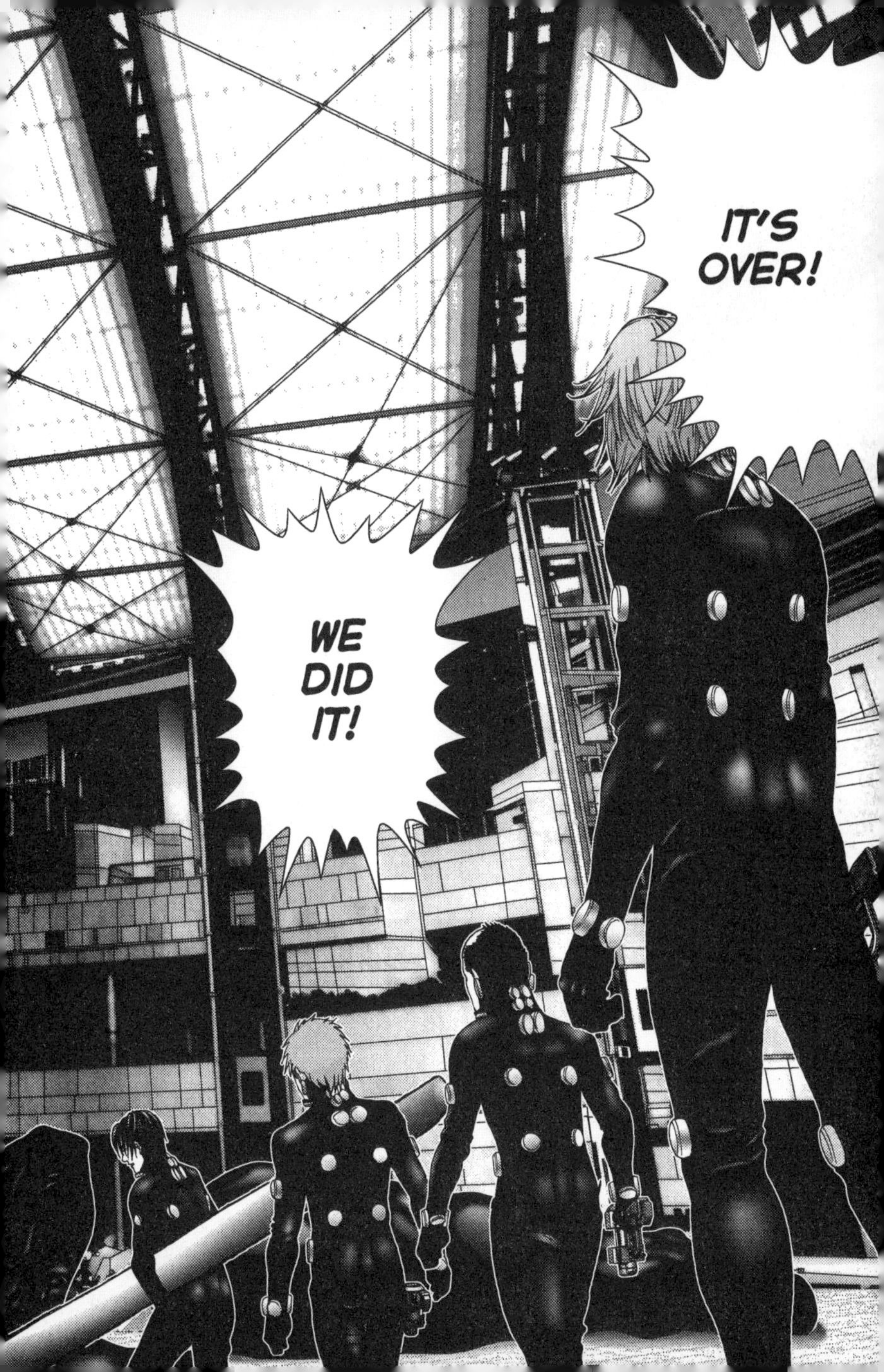
IT'S OVER!
WE DID IT!

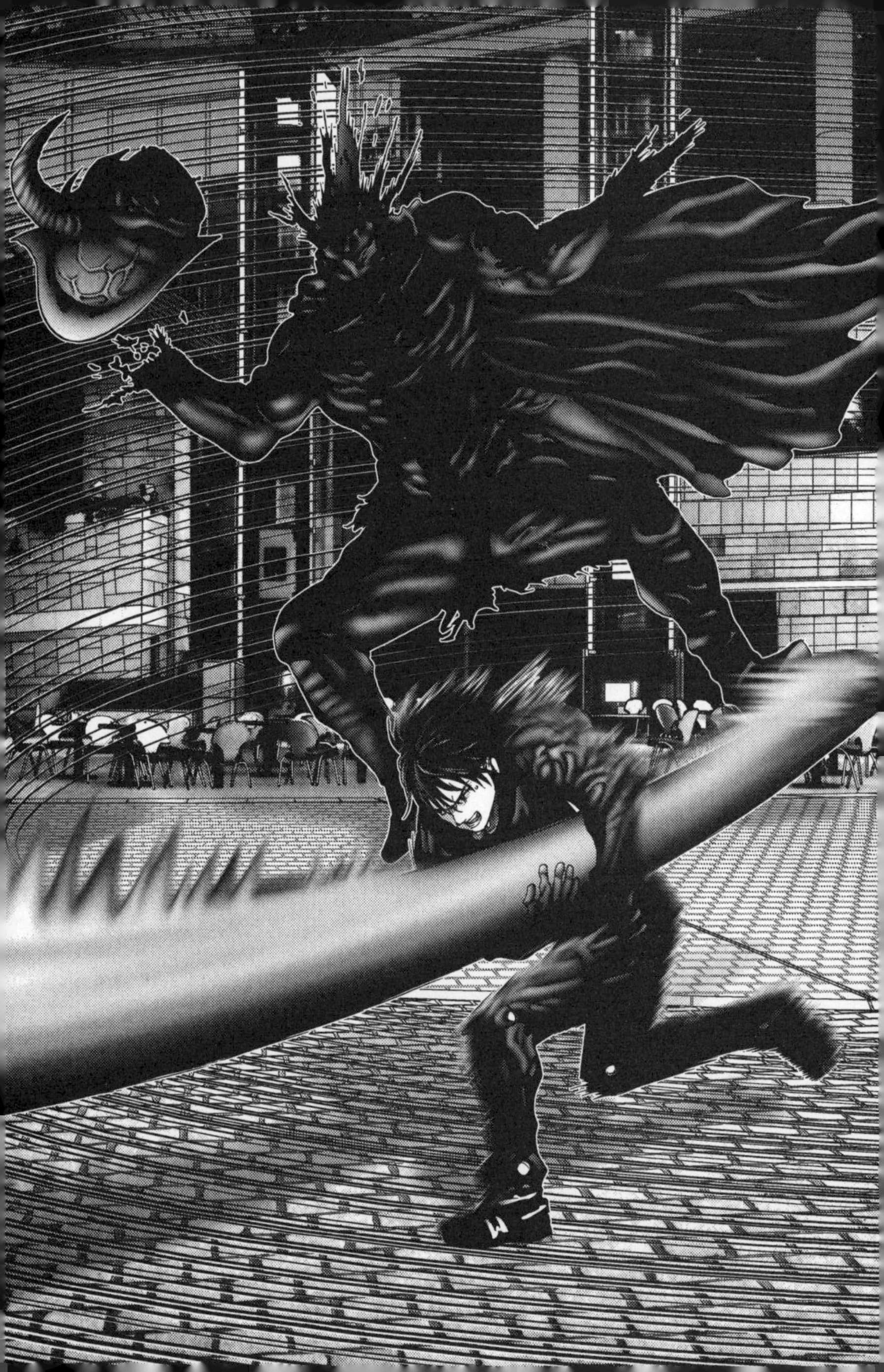

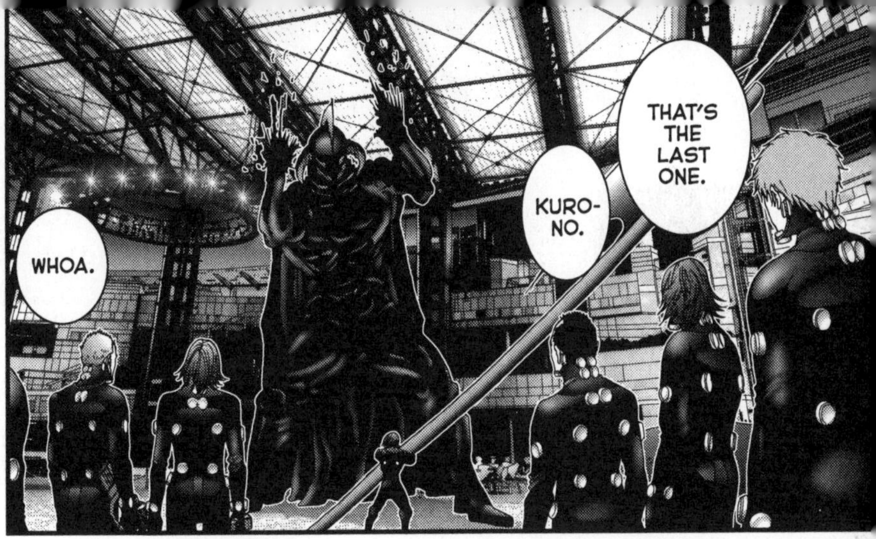
THAT'S THE LAST ONE.
KURO-NO.
WHOA.
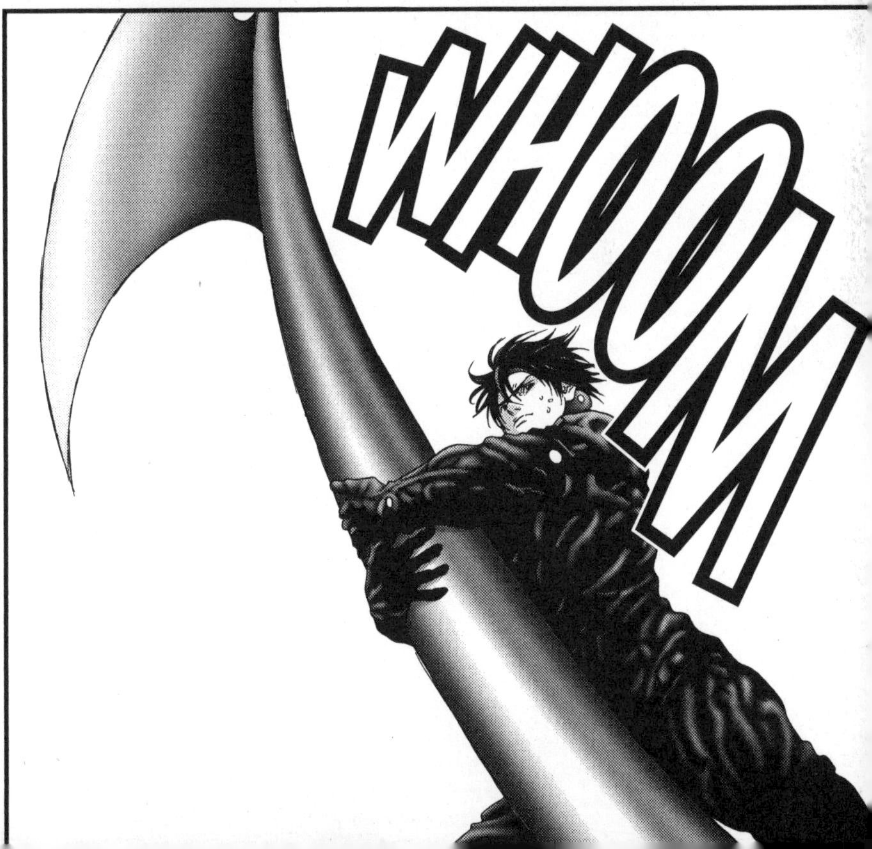
WHOOM

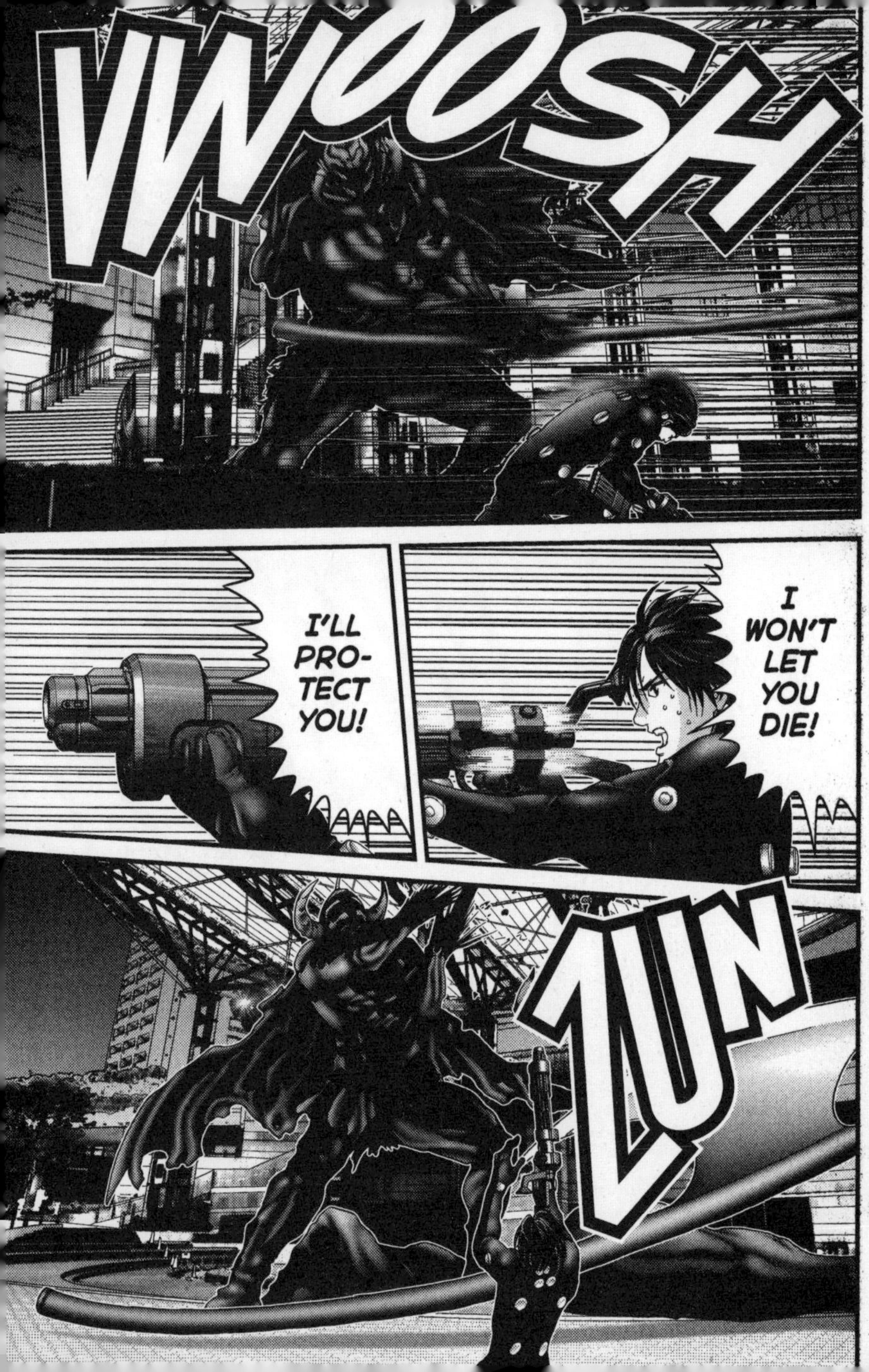
VWOOSH
I WON'T LET YOU DIE!
I'LL PRO-TECT YOU!
ZUN

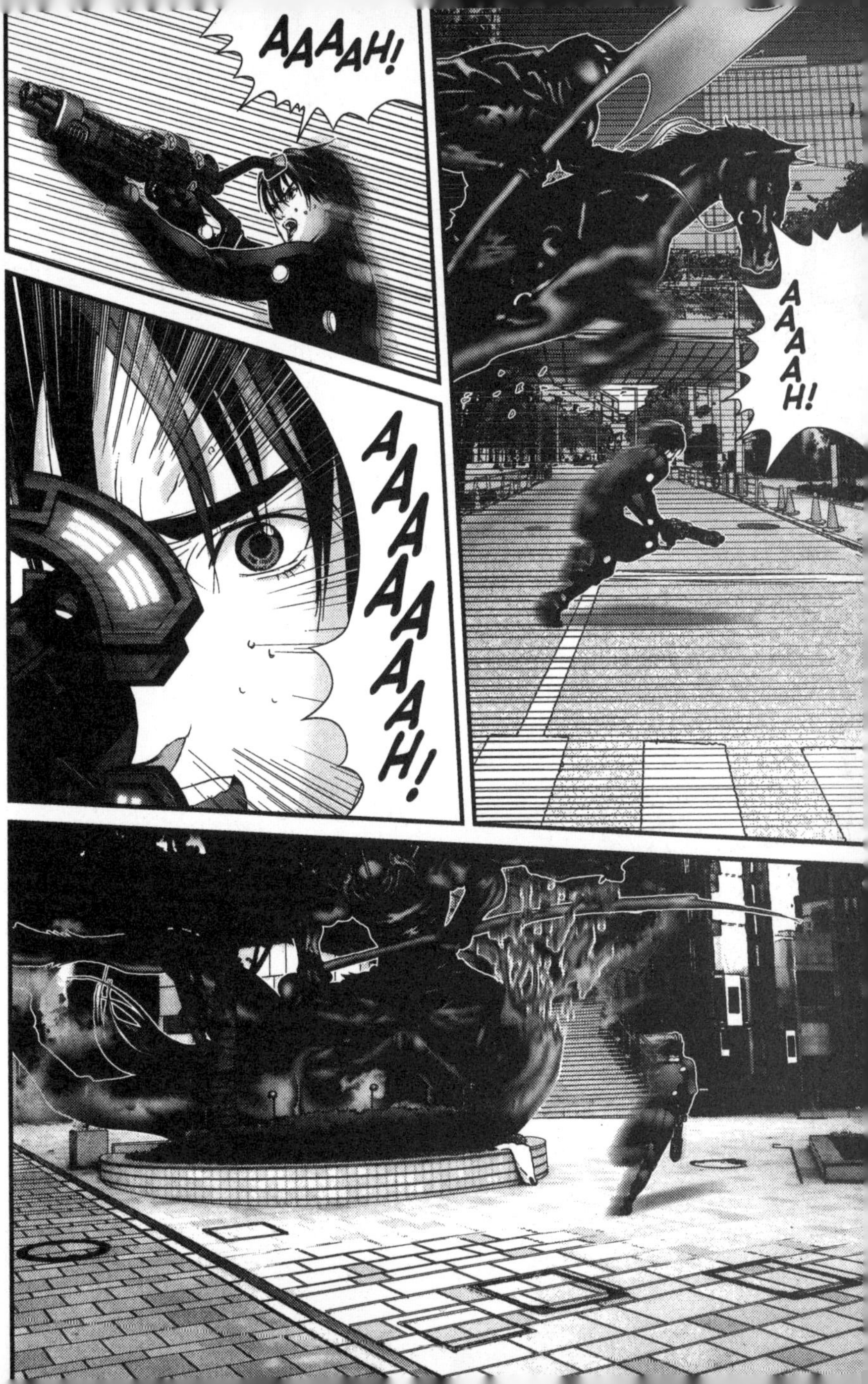
AAAAH!
AAAAH!
AAAAAAAH!

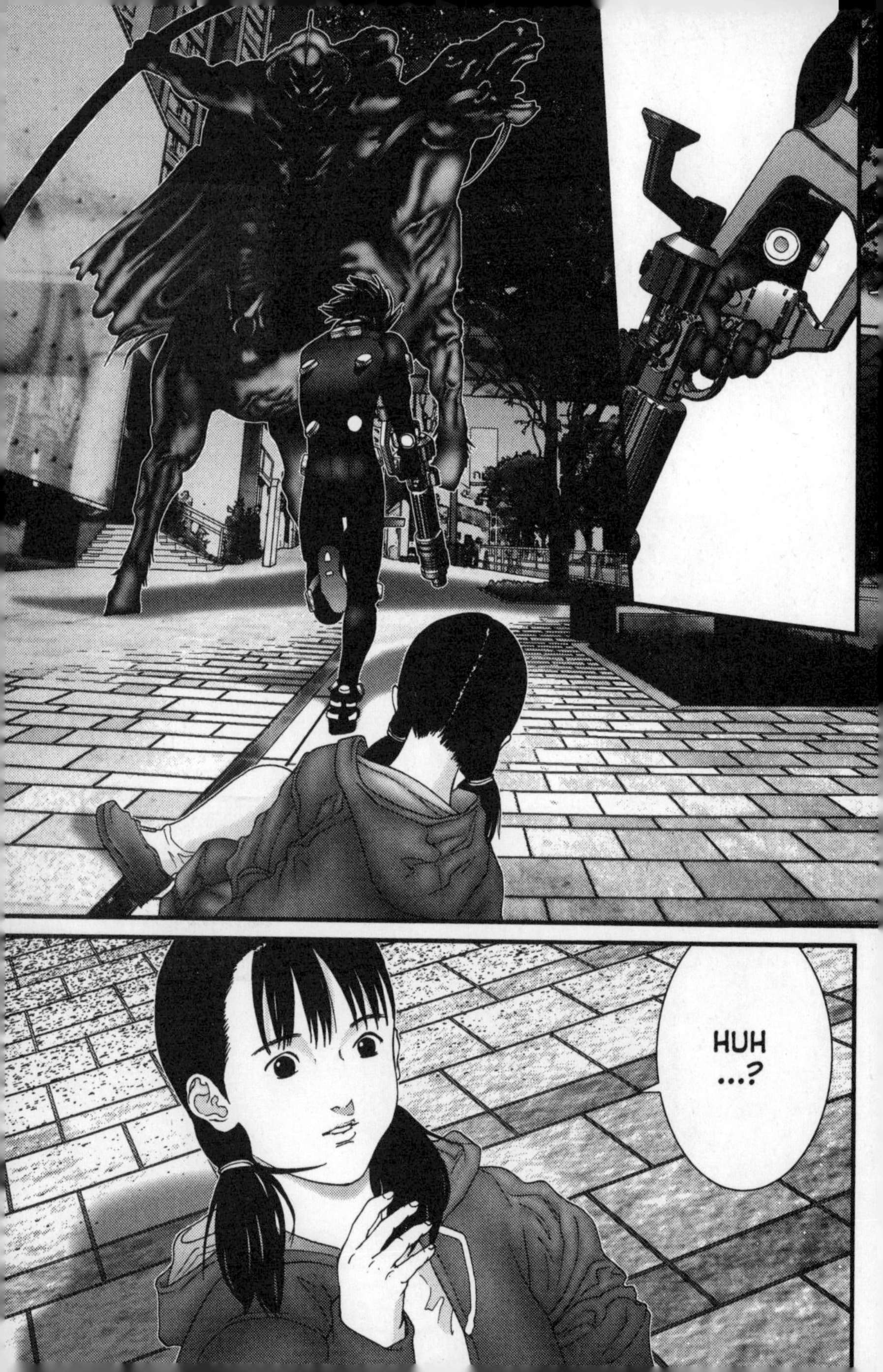
HUH ...?

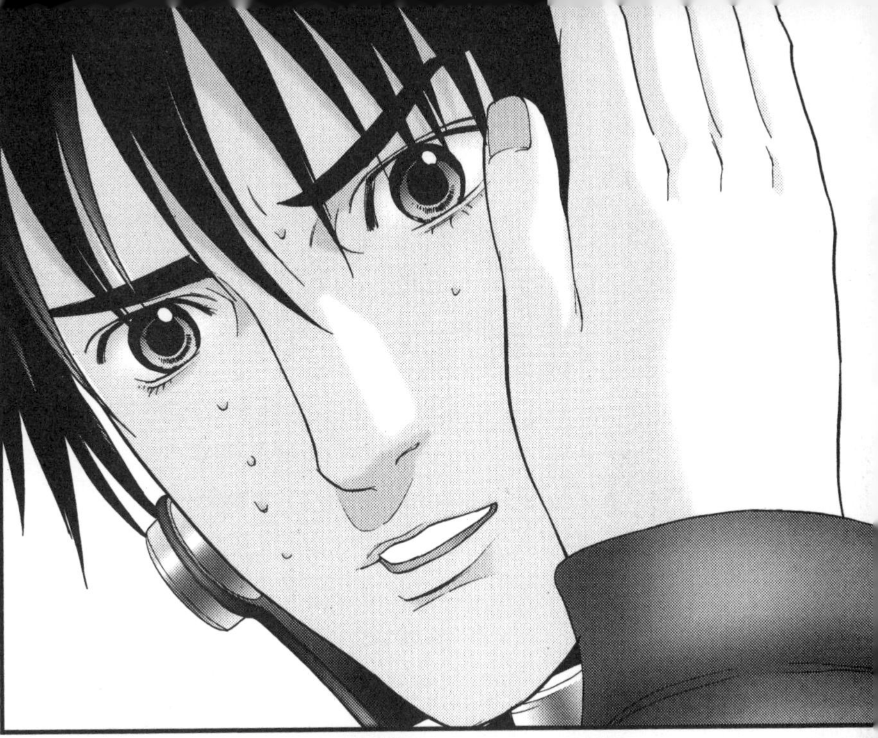
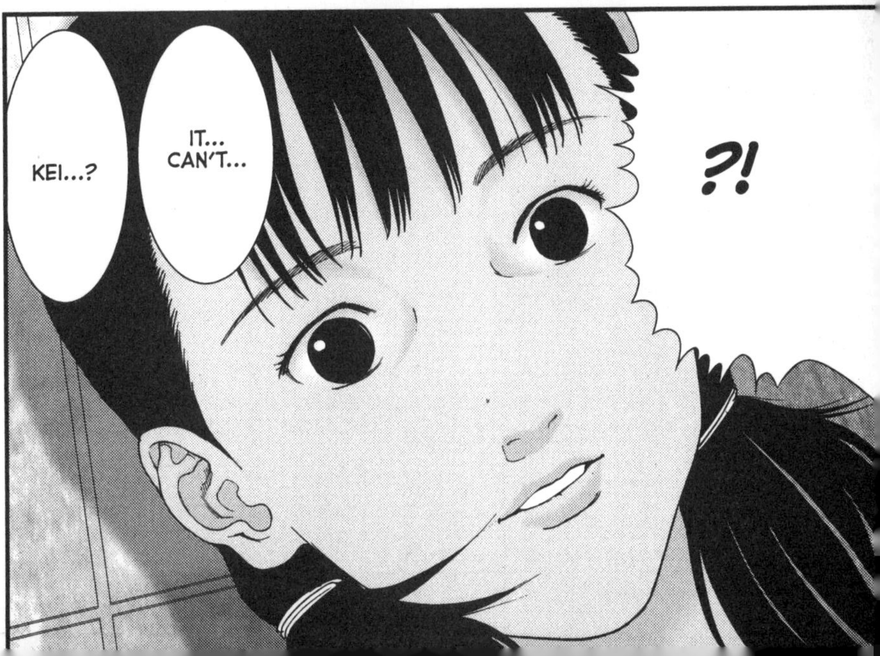
?!
IT... CAN'T...
KEI...?

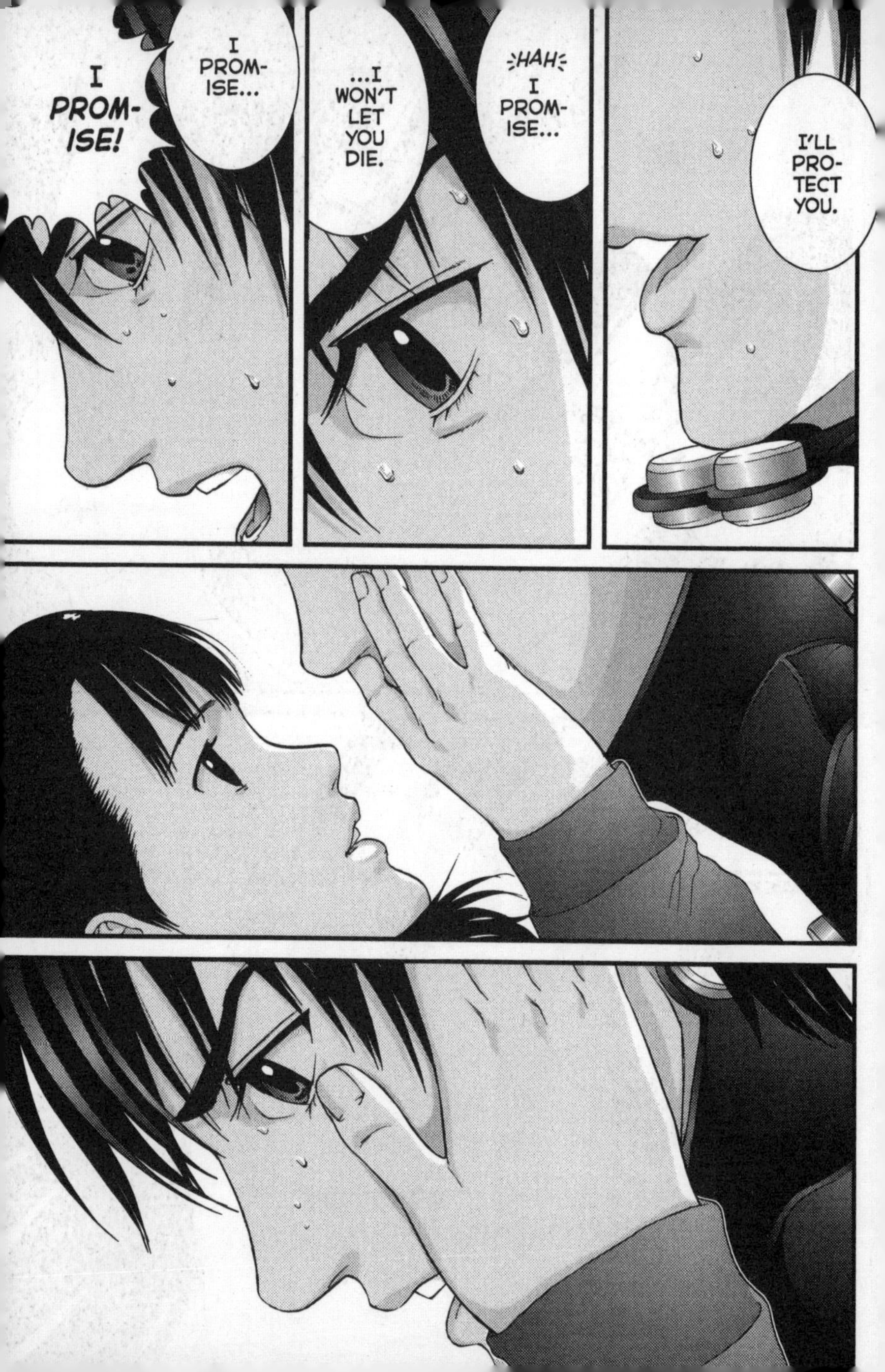
I'LL PROTECT YOU.
HAH
I PROMISE...
...I WON'T LET YOU DIE.
I PROMISE...
I PROMISE!

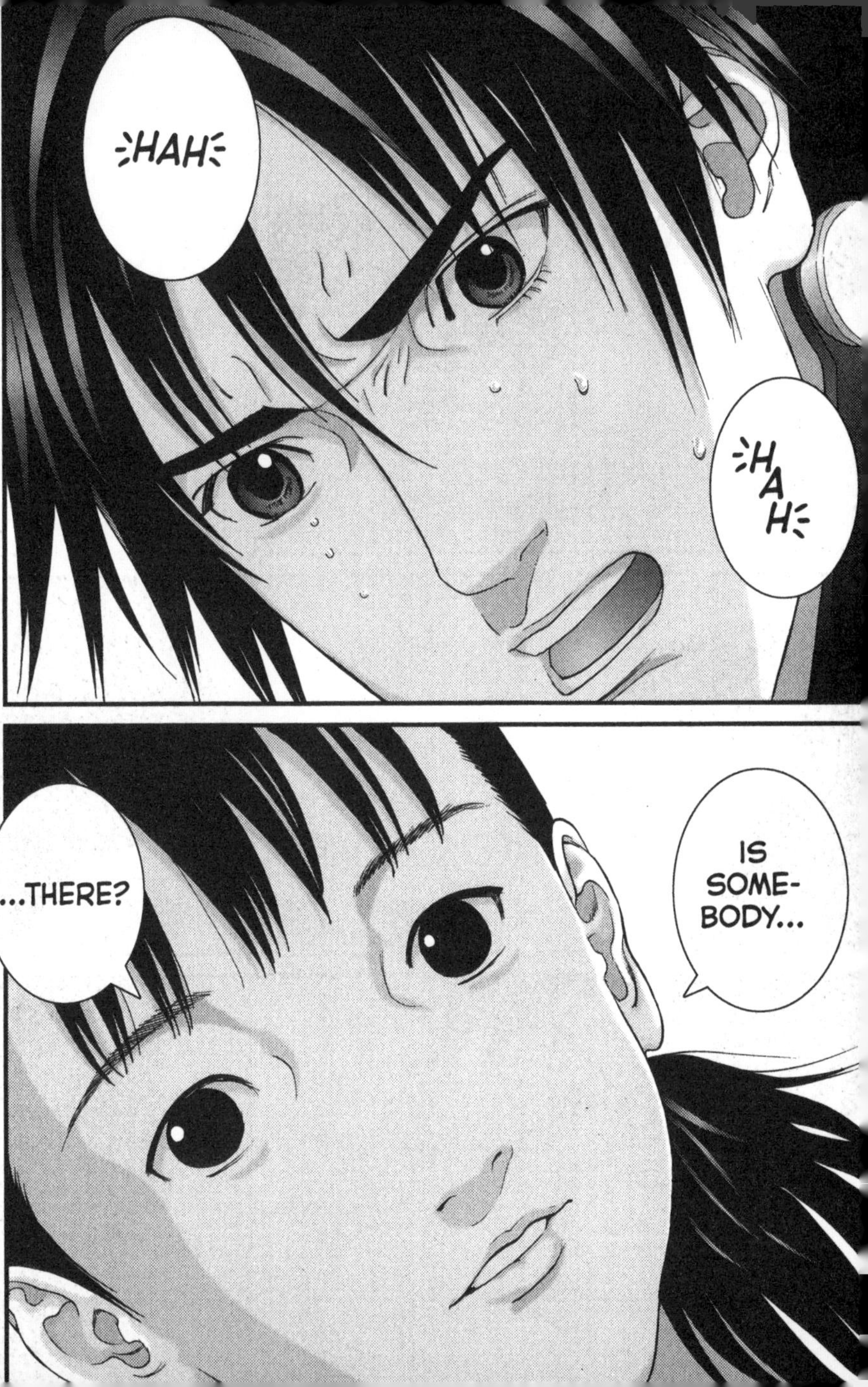
HAH
HAH
IS SOME-BODY...
...THERE?

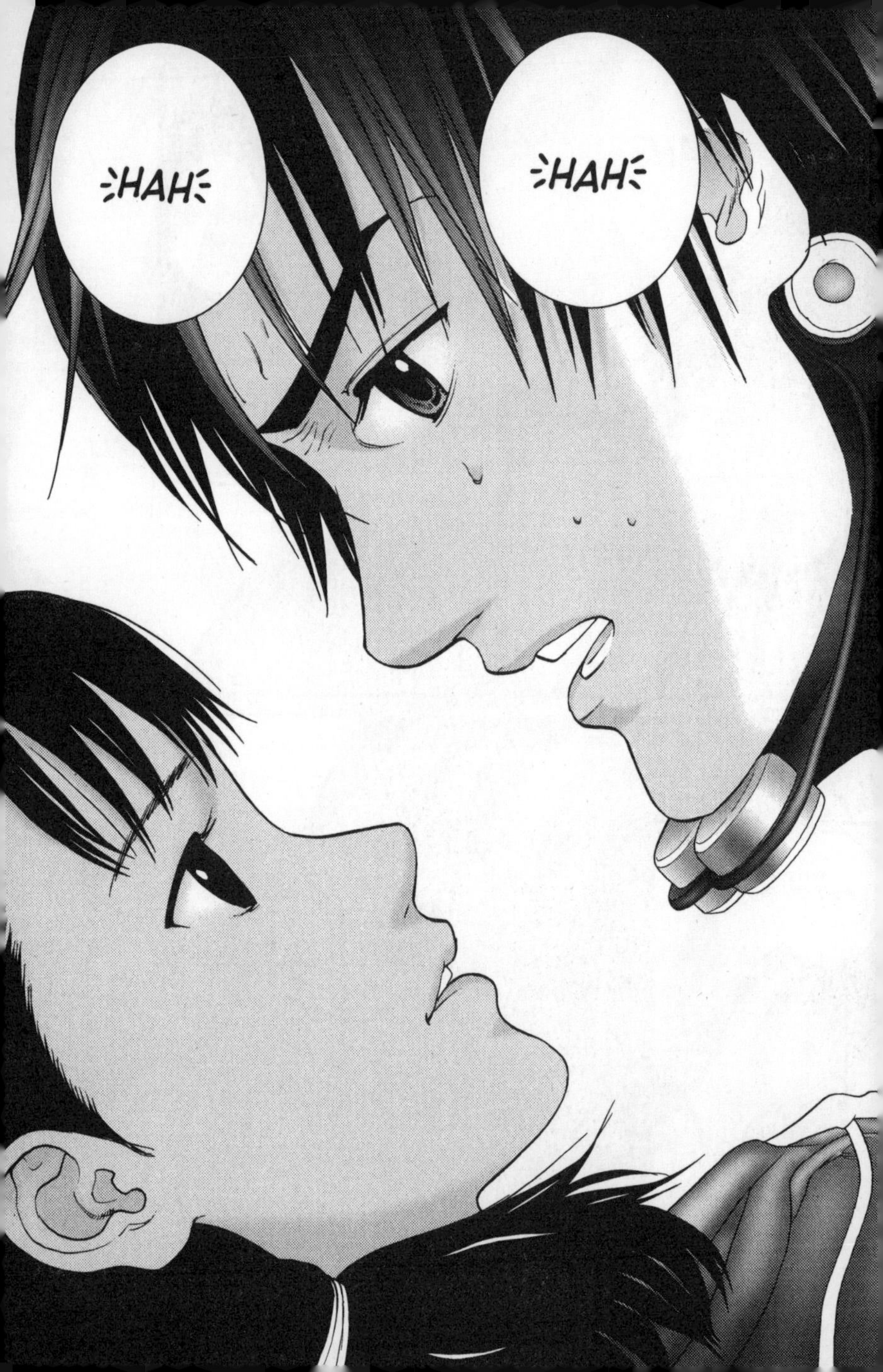
HAH
HAH

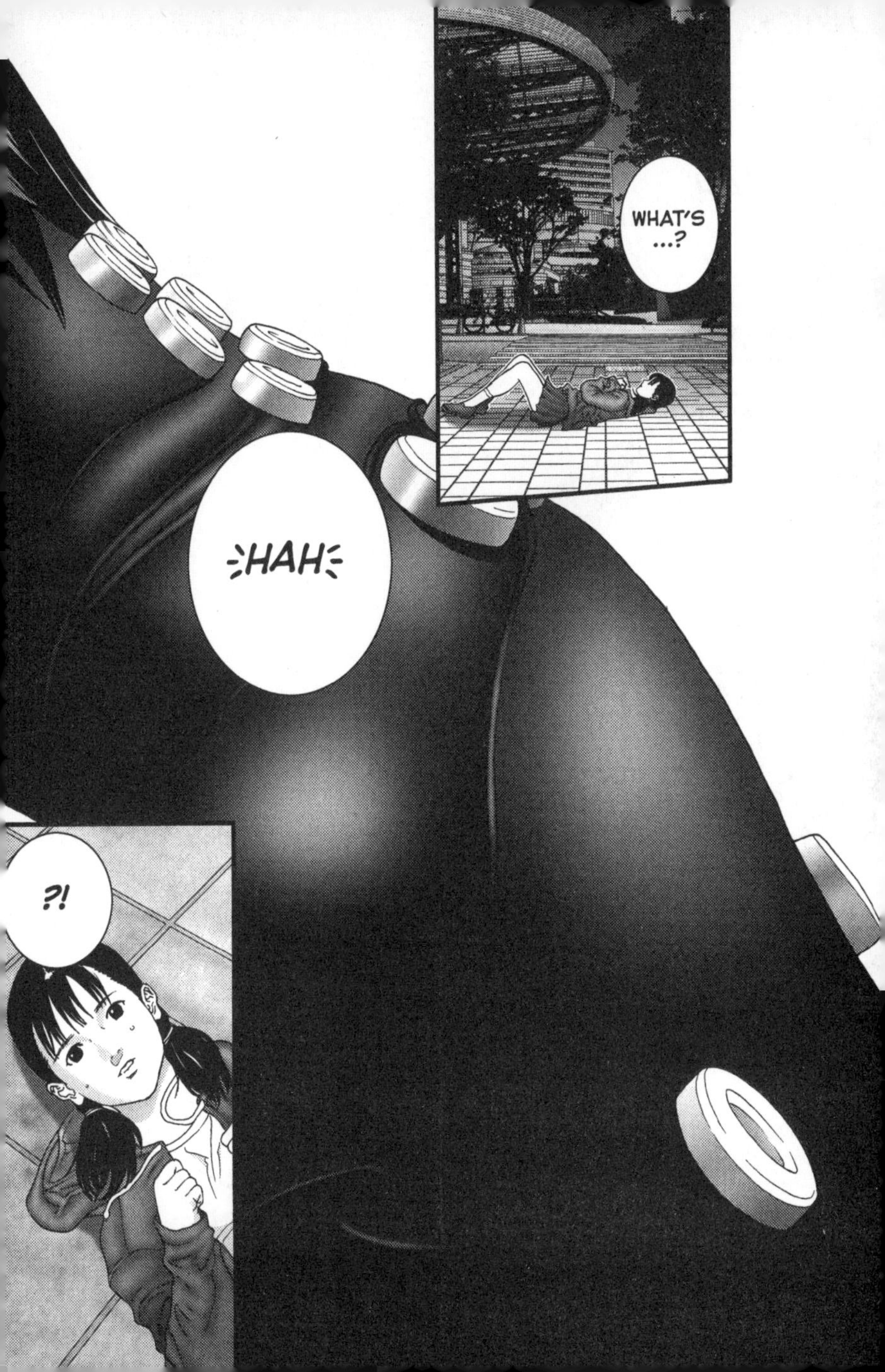
WHAT'S ...?
HAH
?!

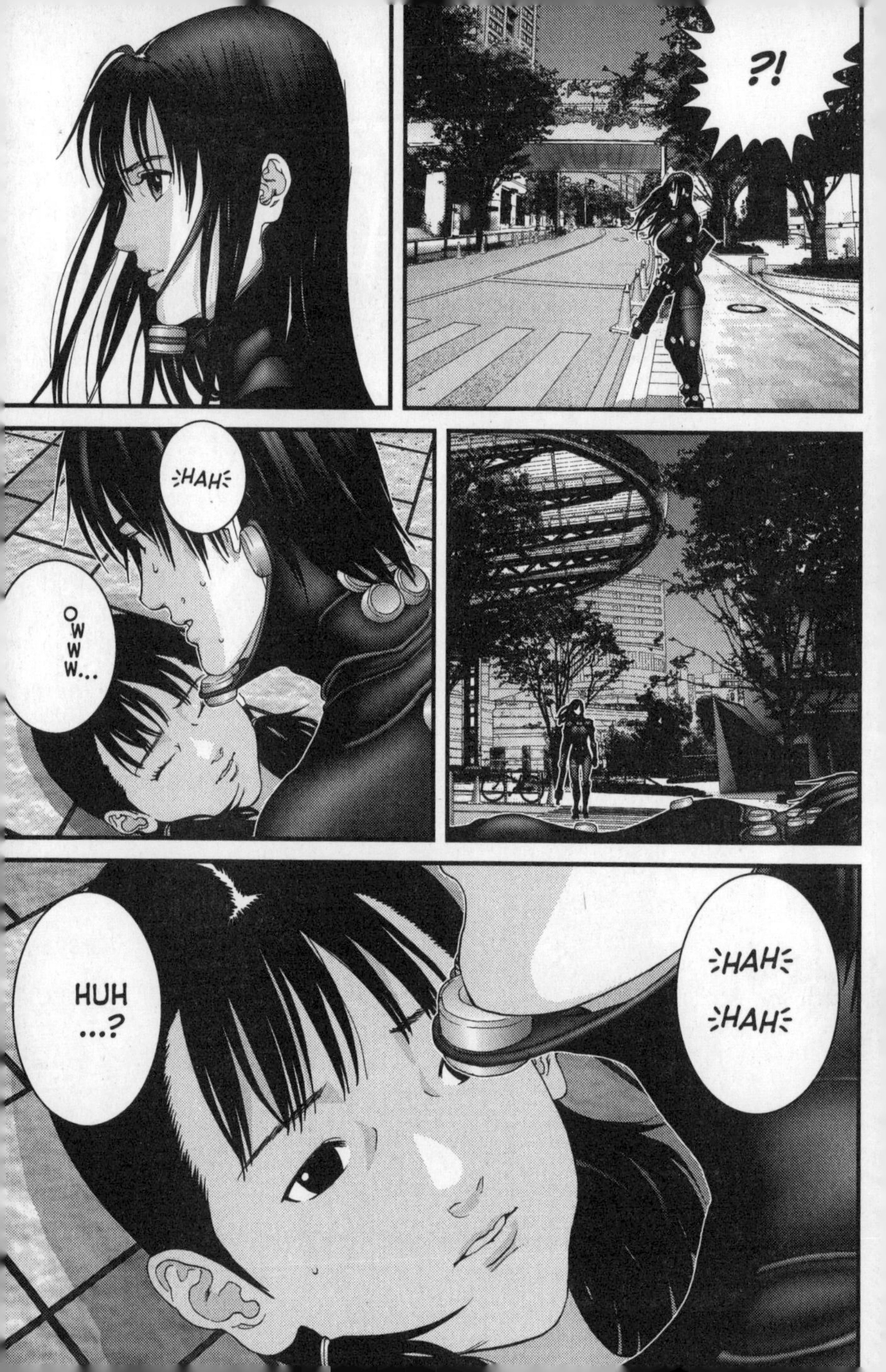
?!
HAH
OWWW...
HAH HAH
HUH ...?

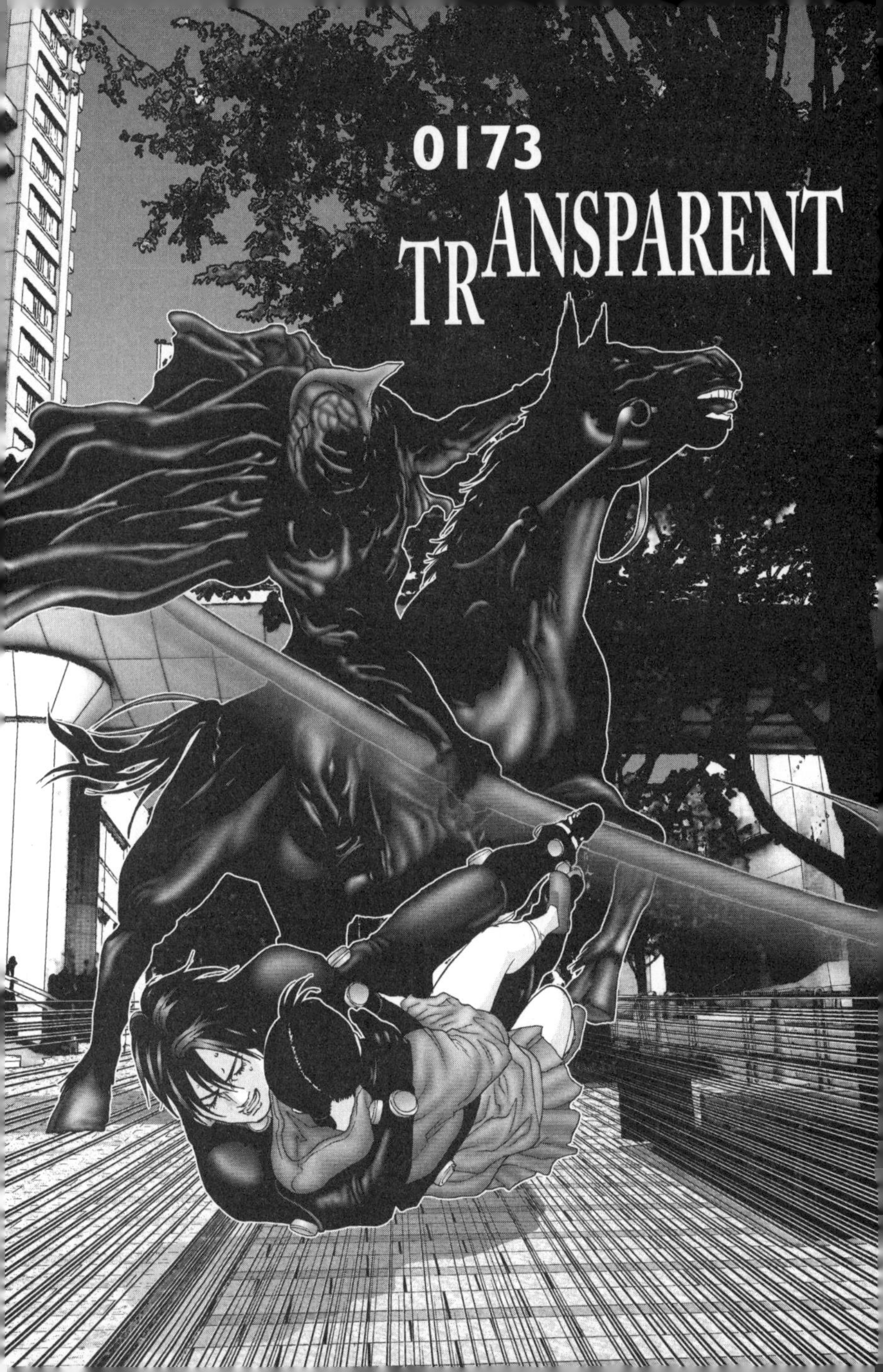
0173
TRANSPARENT

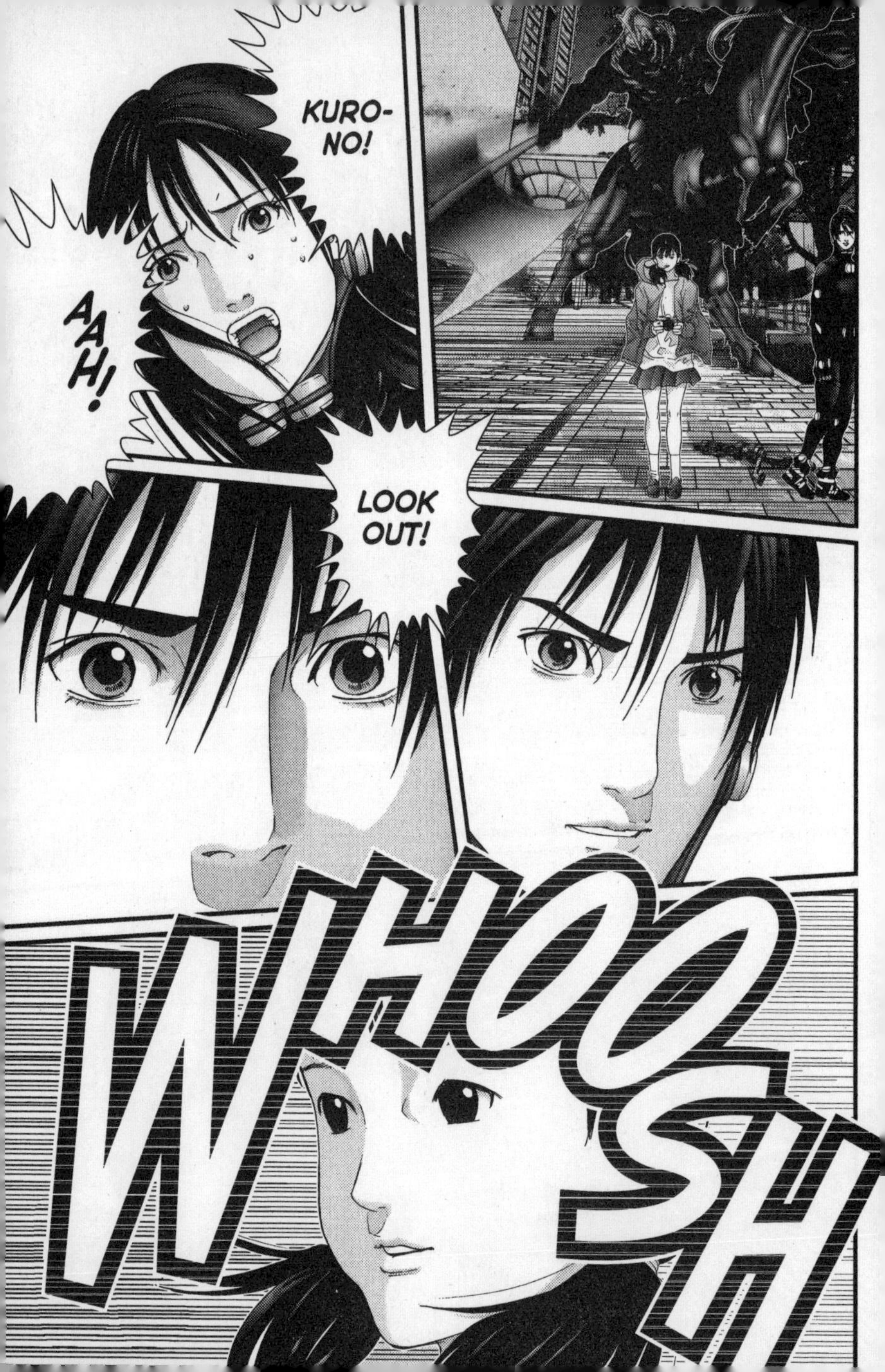
KURO-NO!
AAH!
LOOK OUT!
WHOOSH

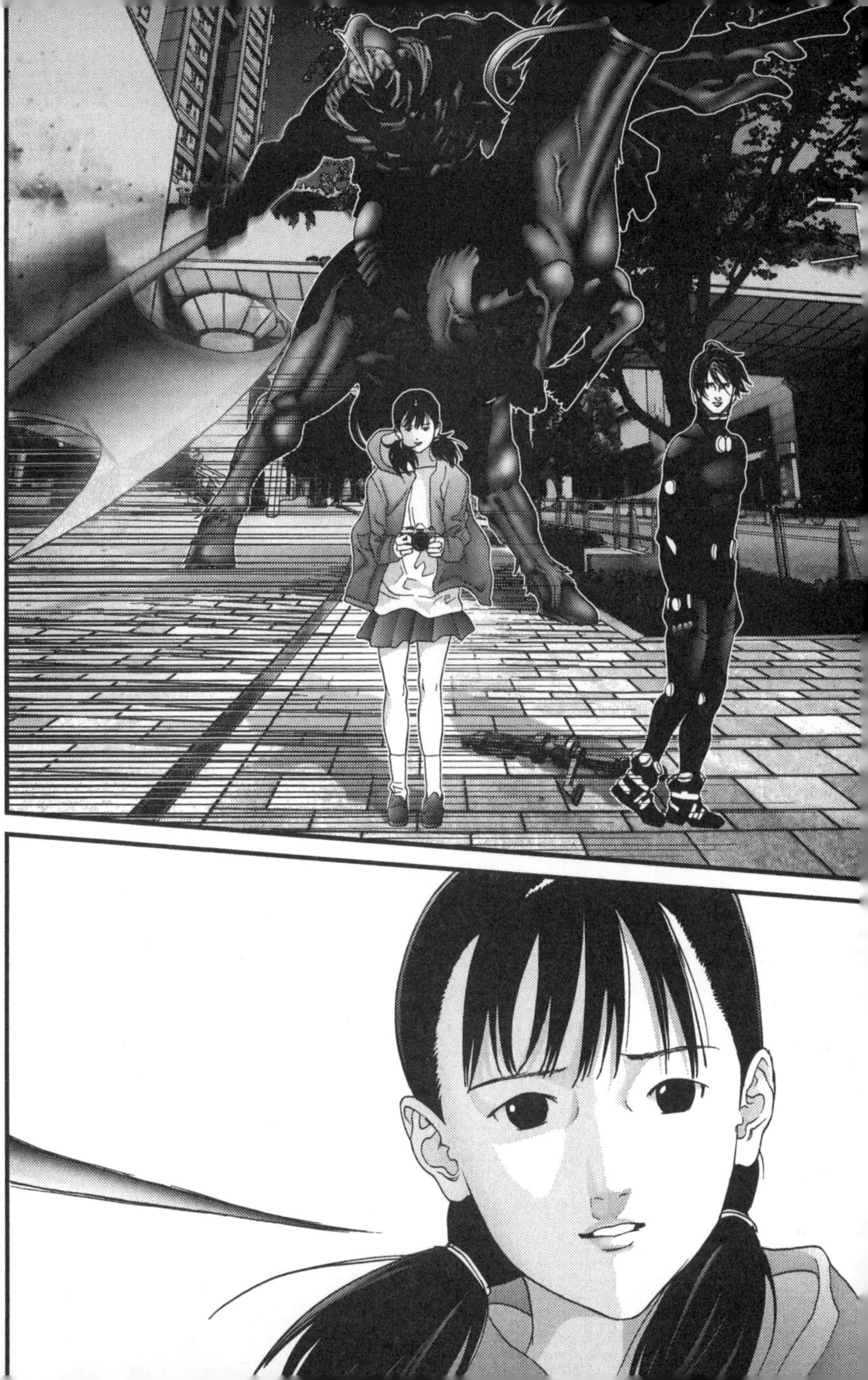

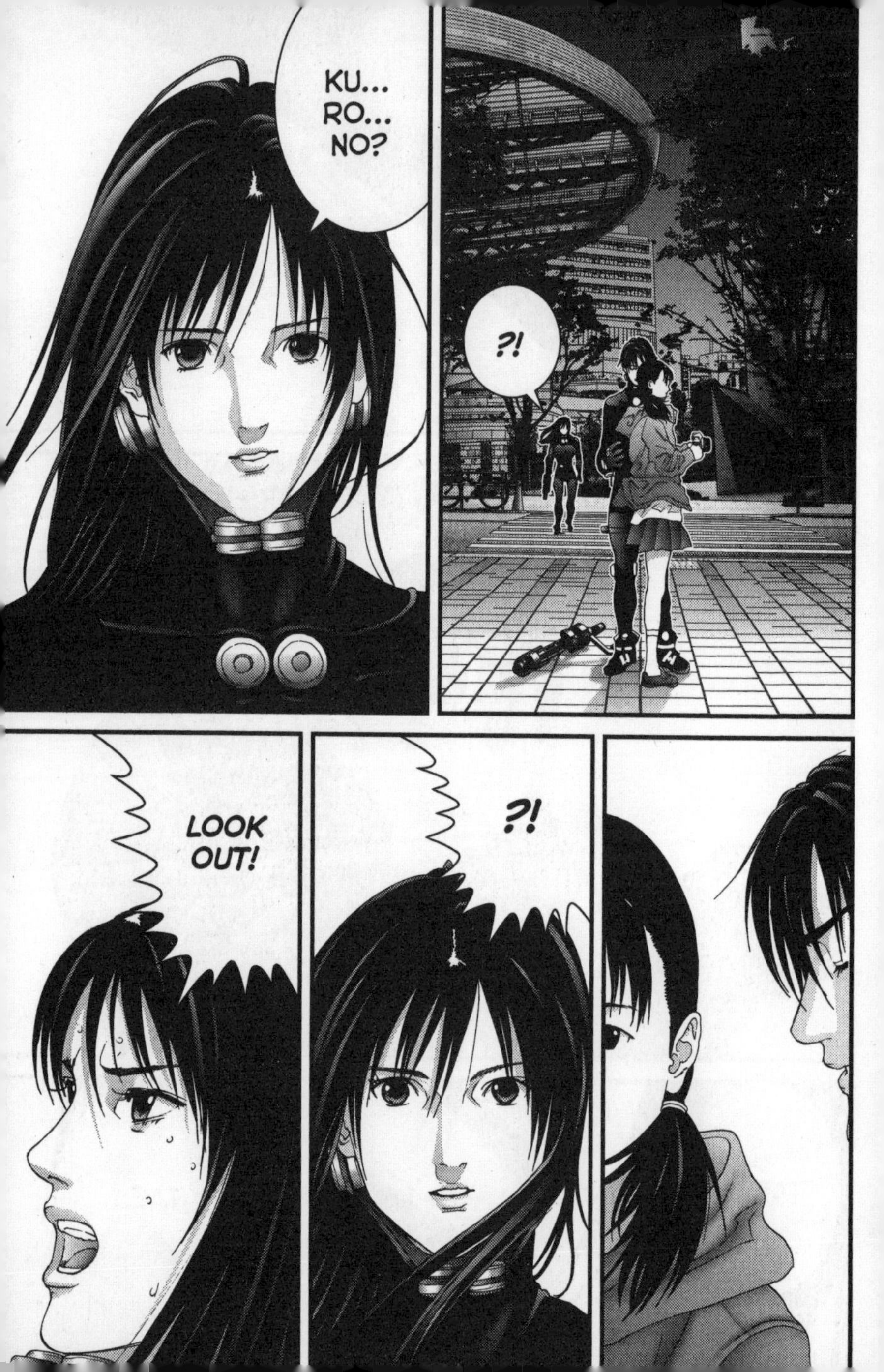
KU... RO... NO?
?!
LOOK OUT!
?!

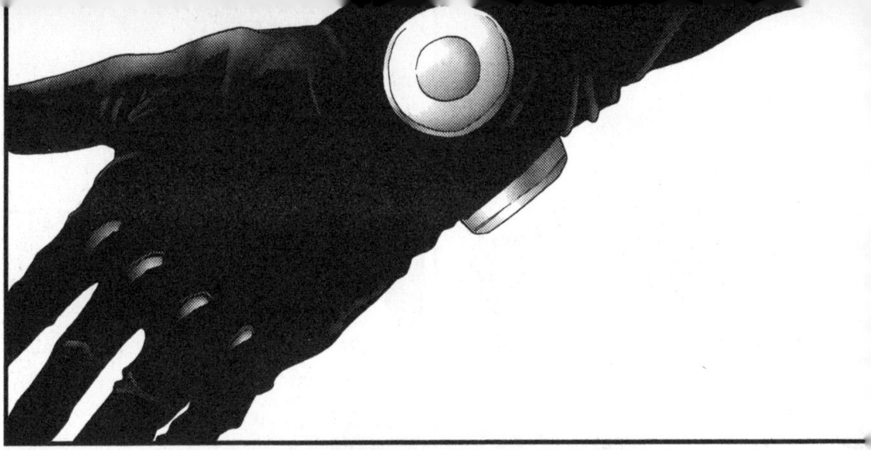

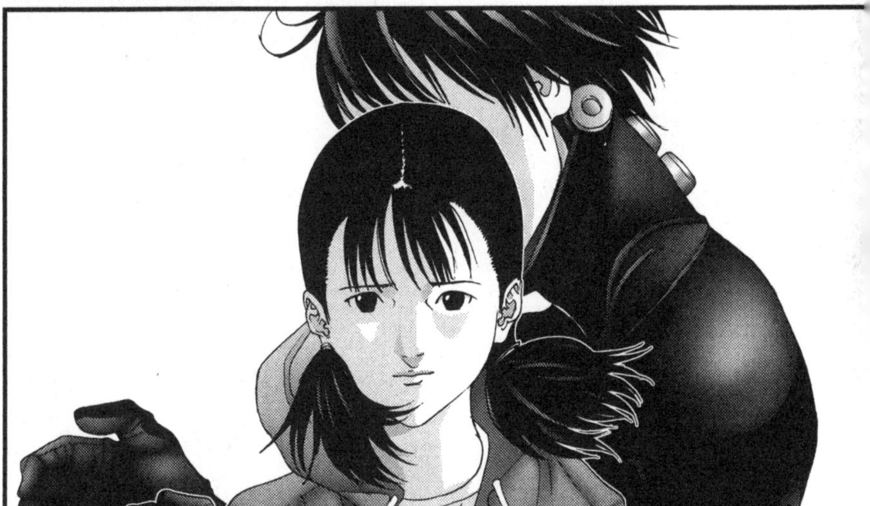

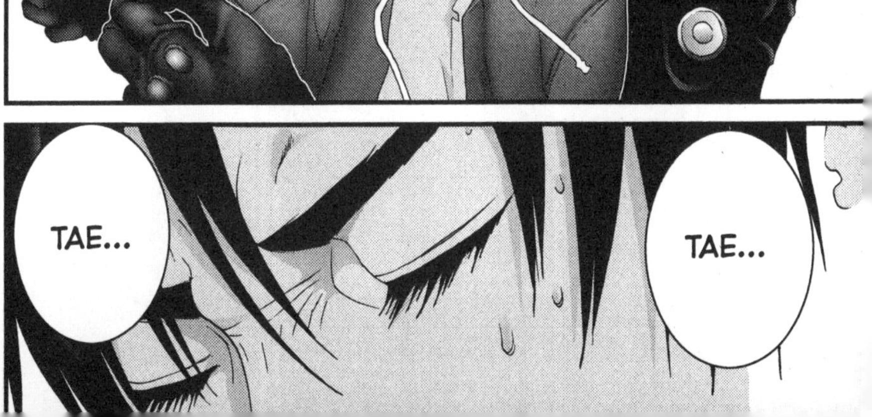
TAE...
TAE...

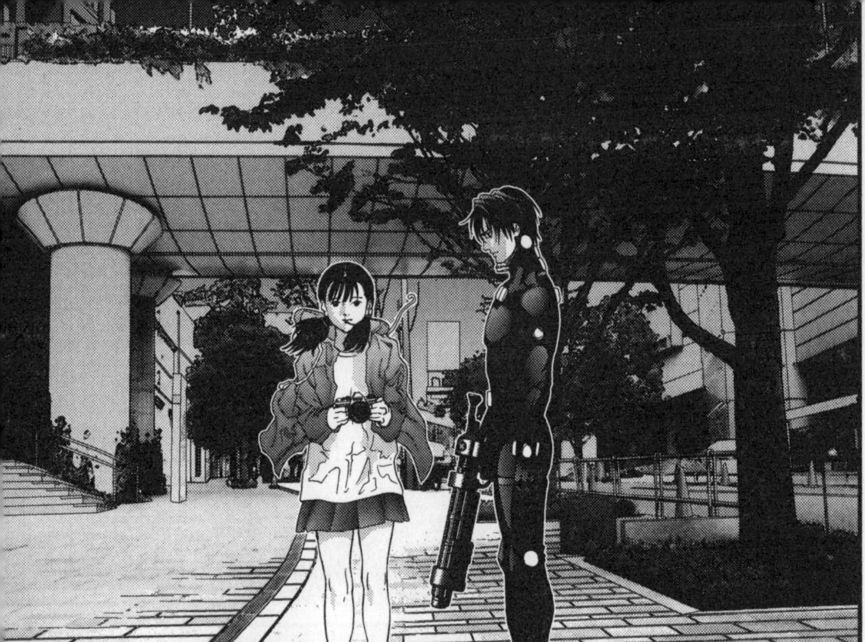
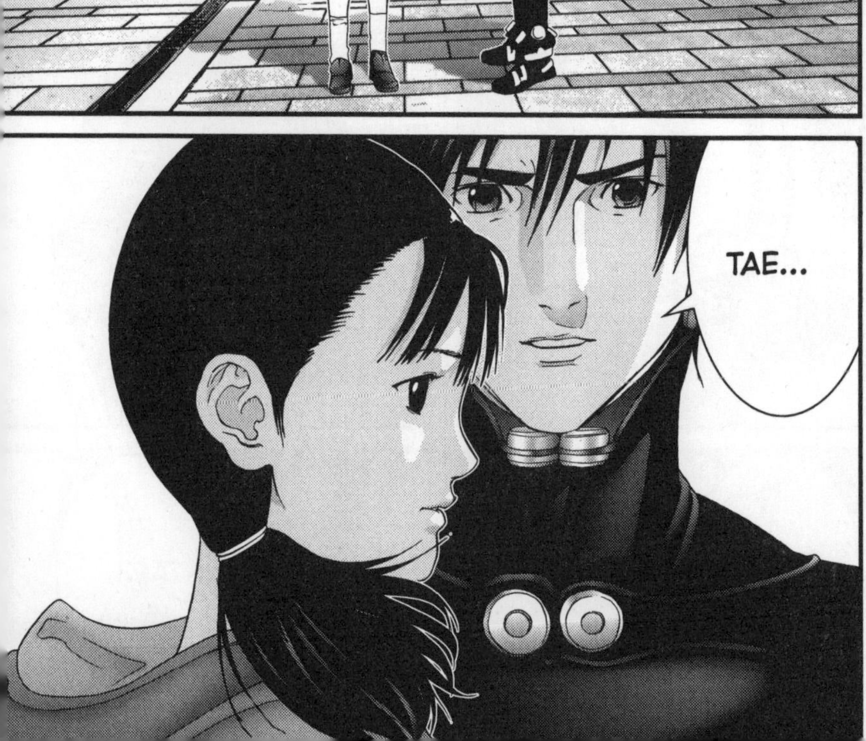
TAE...

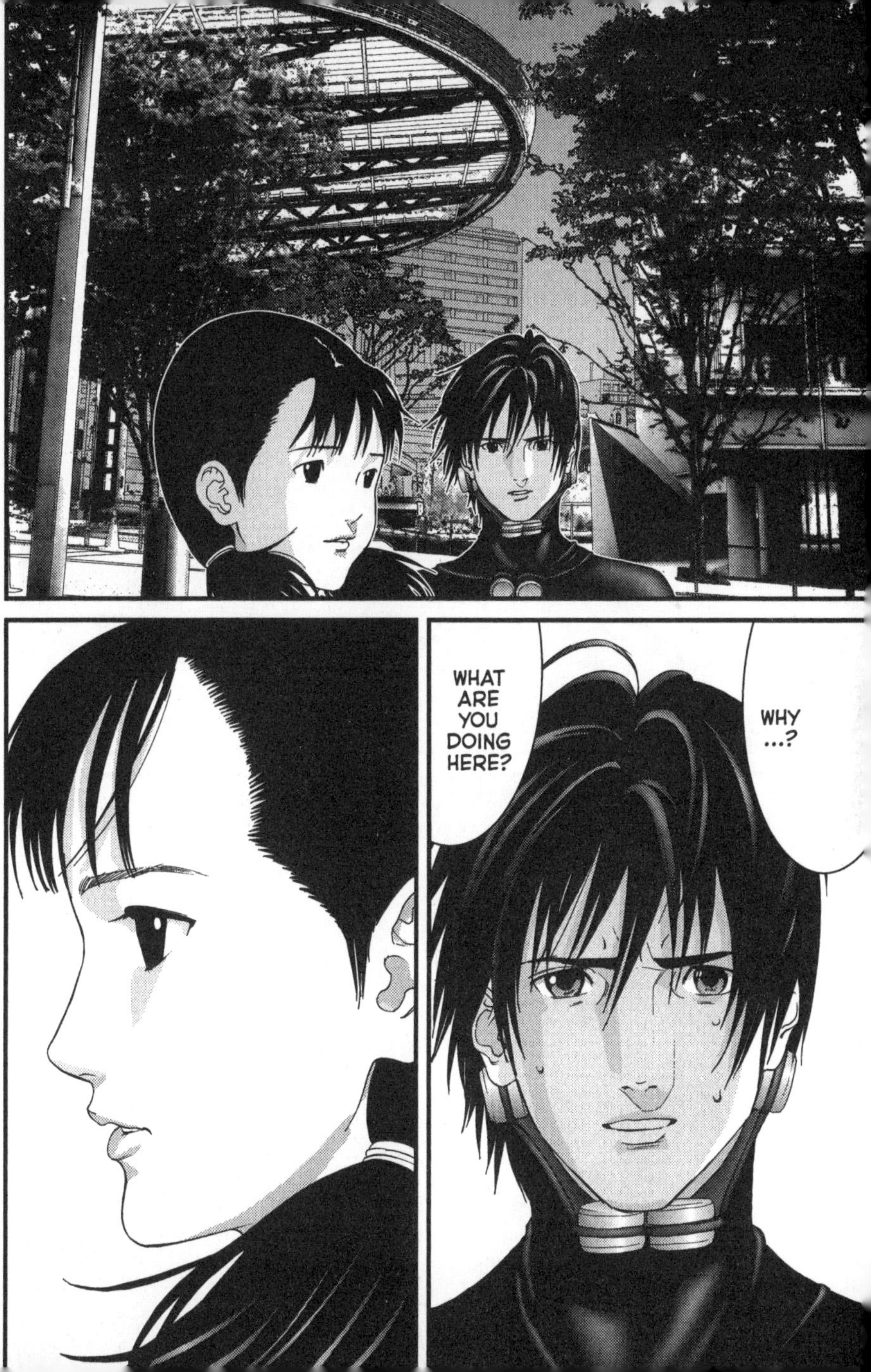
WHY ...?
WHAT ARE YOU DOING HERE?

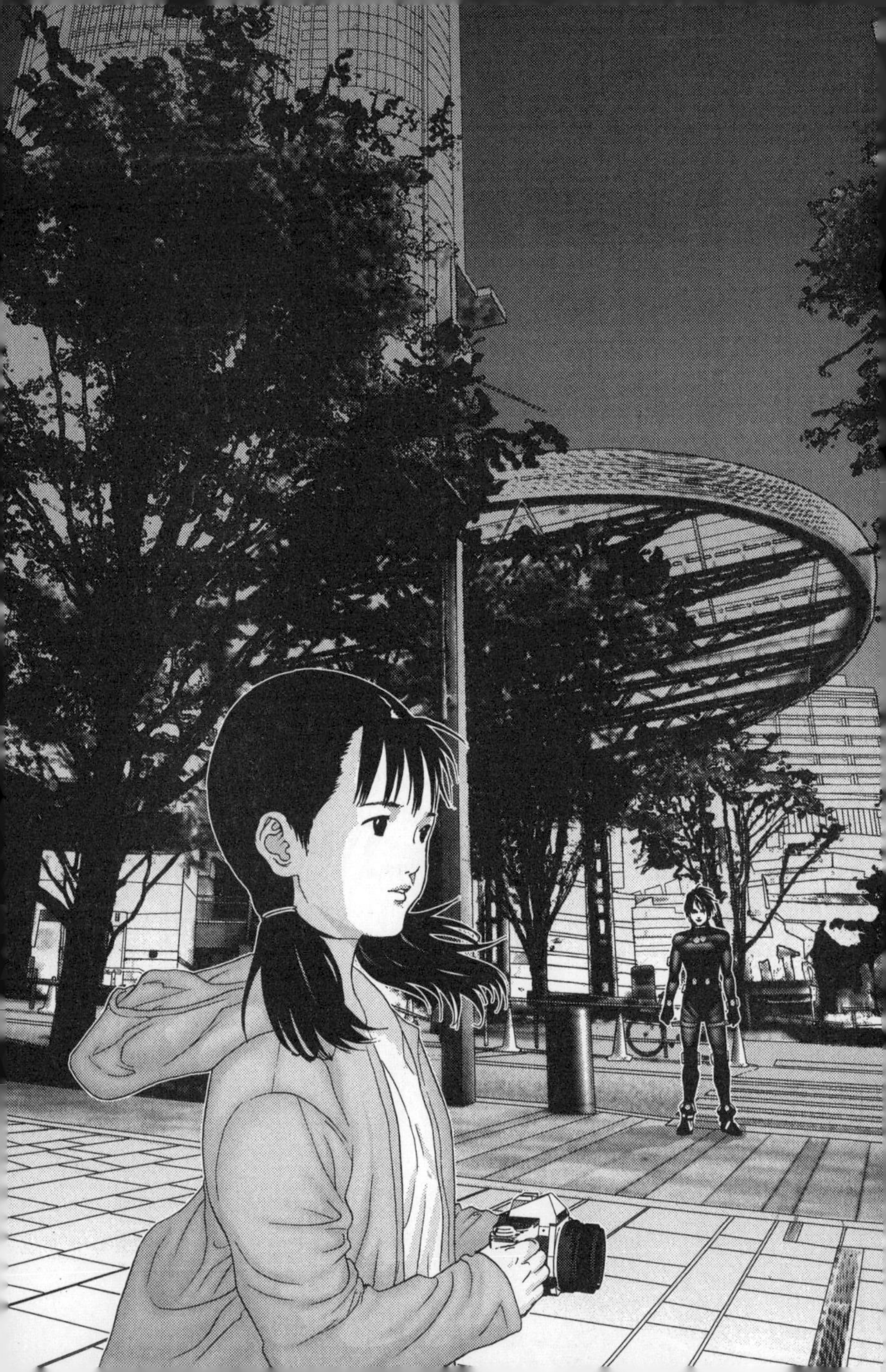

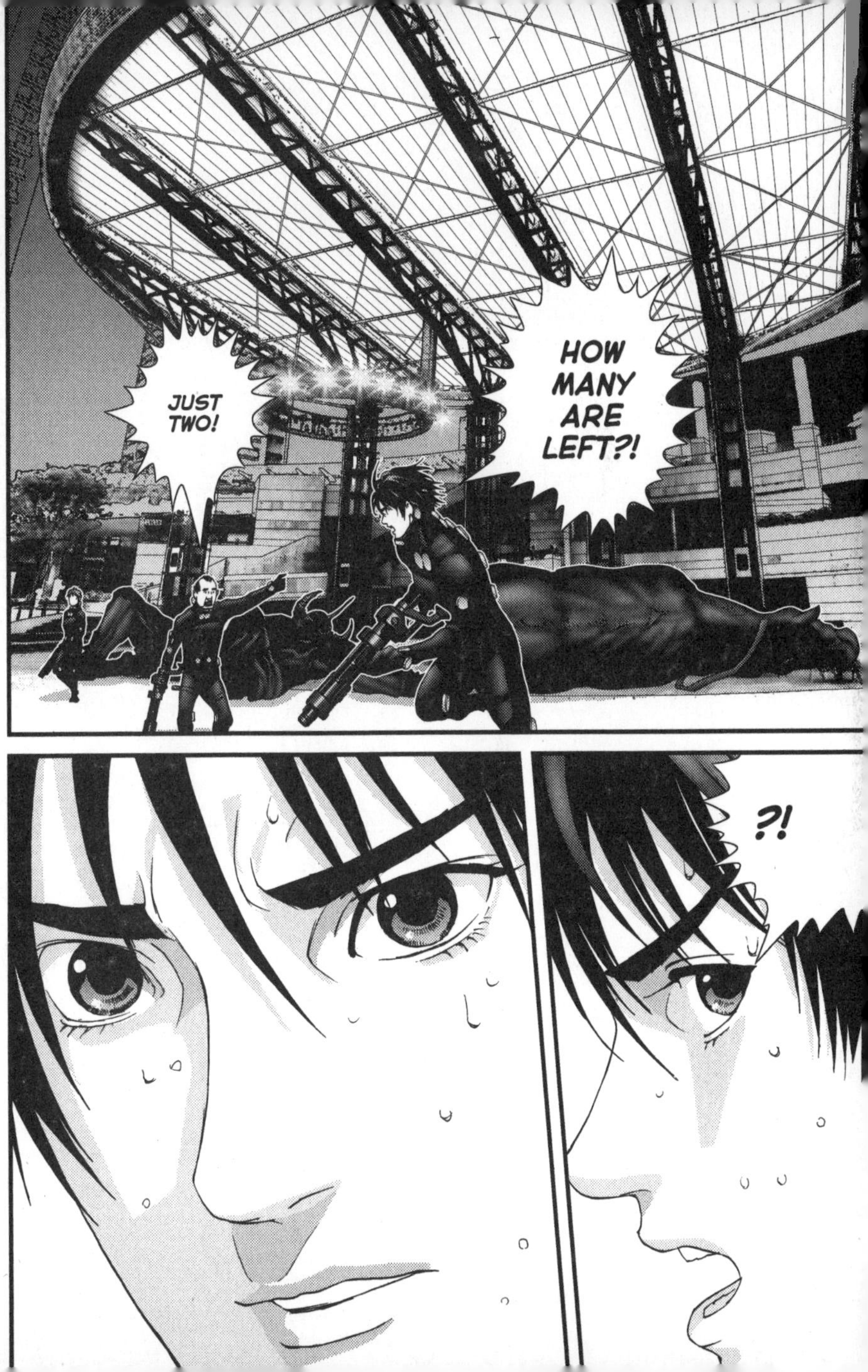
HOW MANY ARE LEFT?!
JUST TWO!
?!

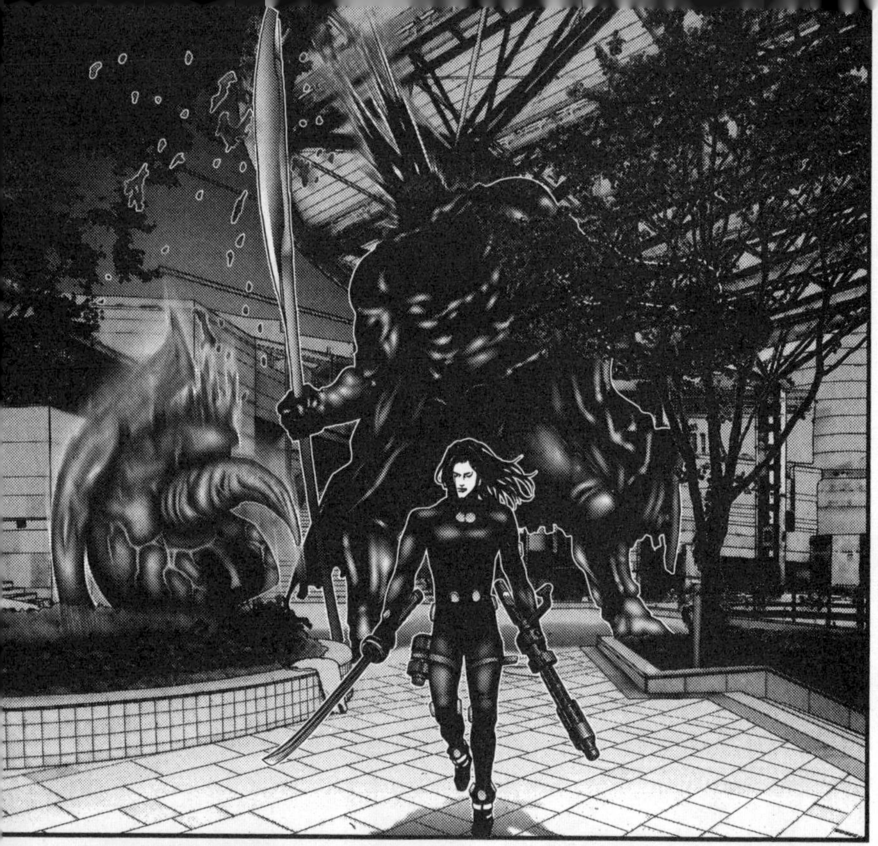
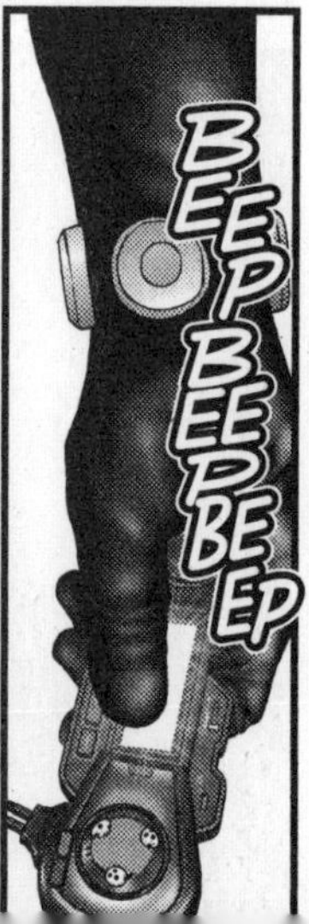
BEEP BEEP BEEBEEP
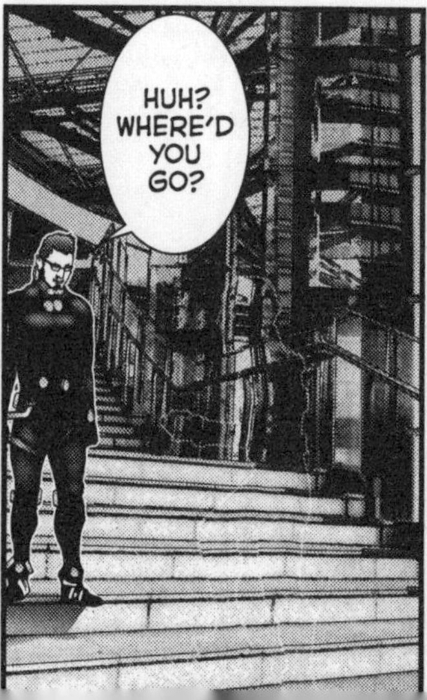
HUH? WHERE'D YOU GO?
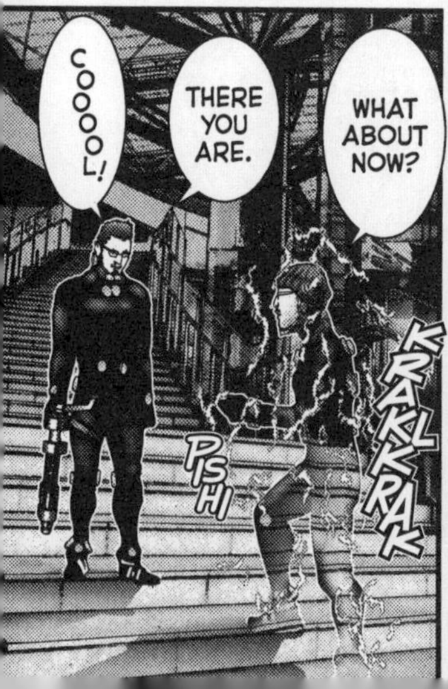
WHAT ABOUT NOW?
THERE YOU ARE.
COOOOL!
KRAKLKRAK
PISHI

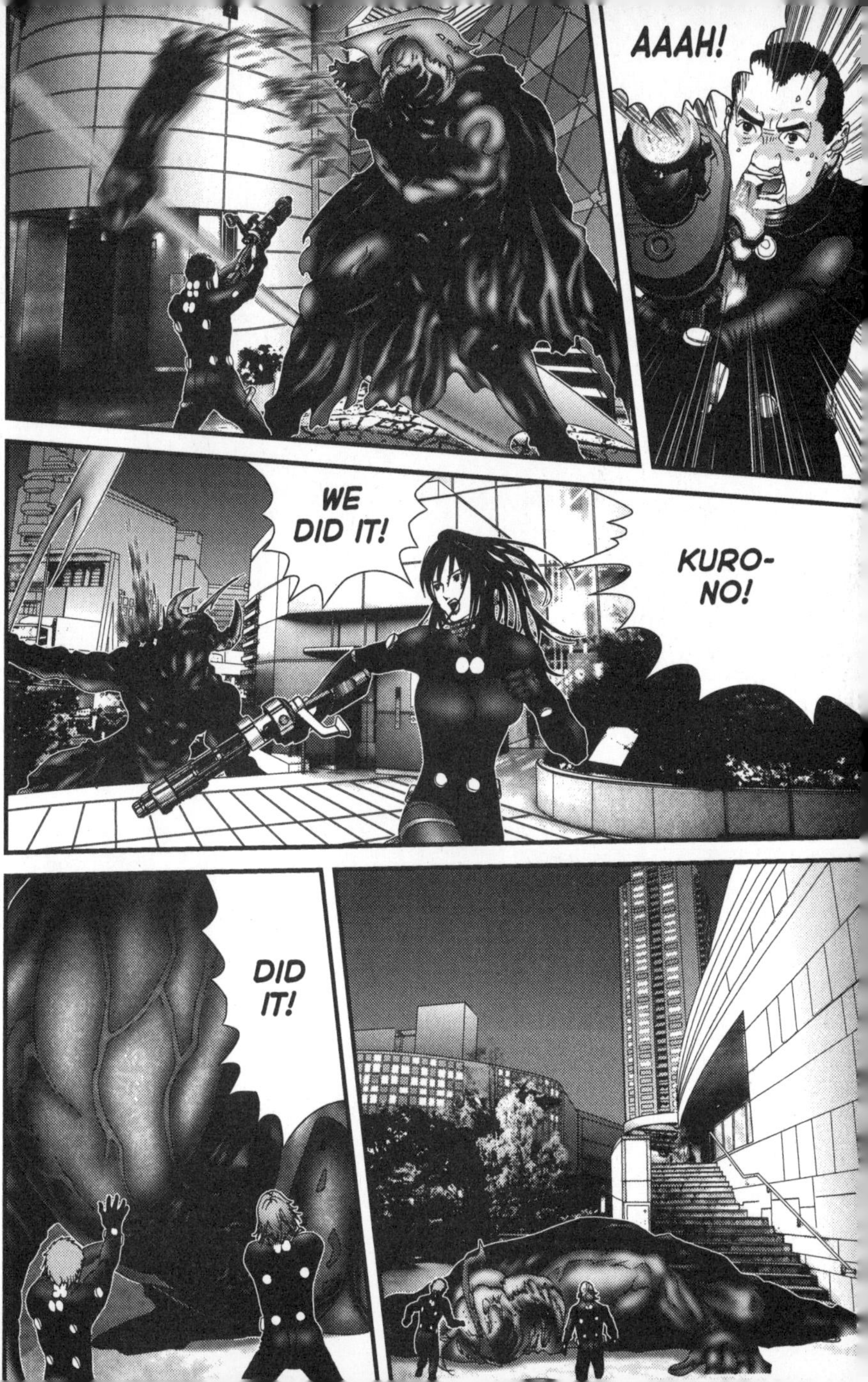
AAAH!
WE DID IT!
KURO-NO!
DID IT!

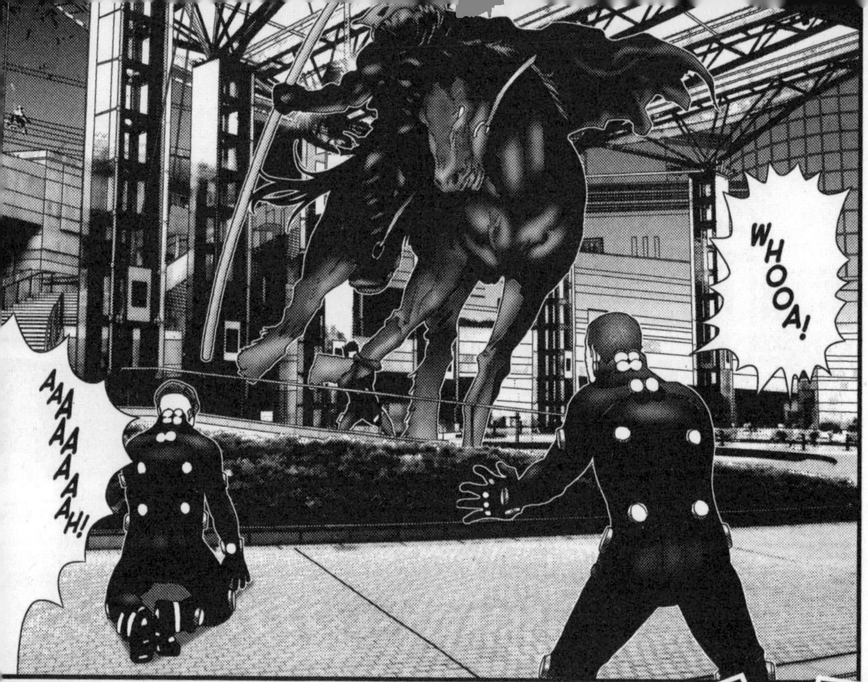
WHOOA!
AAAAAAAAAAH!
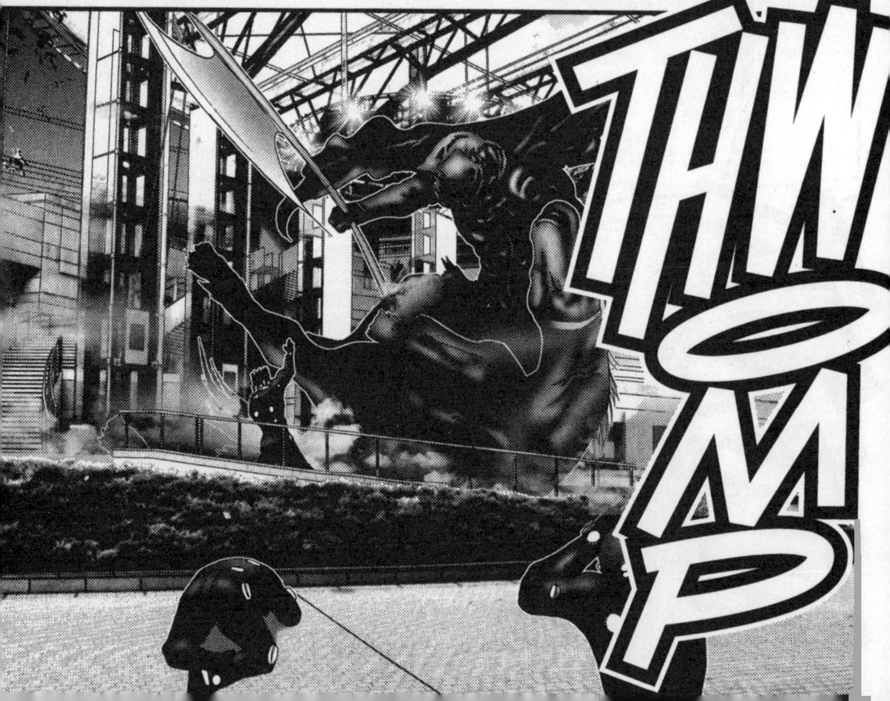
THWOMP

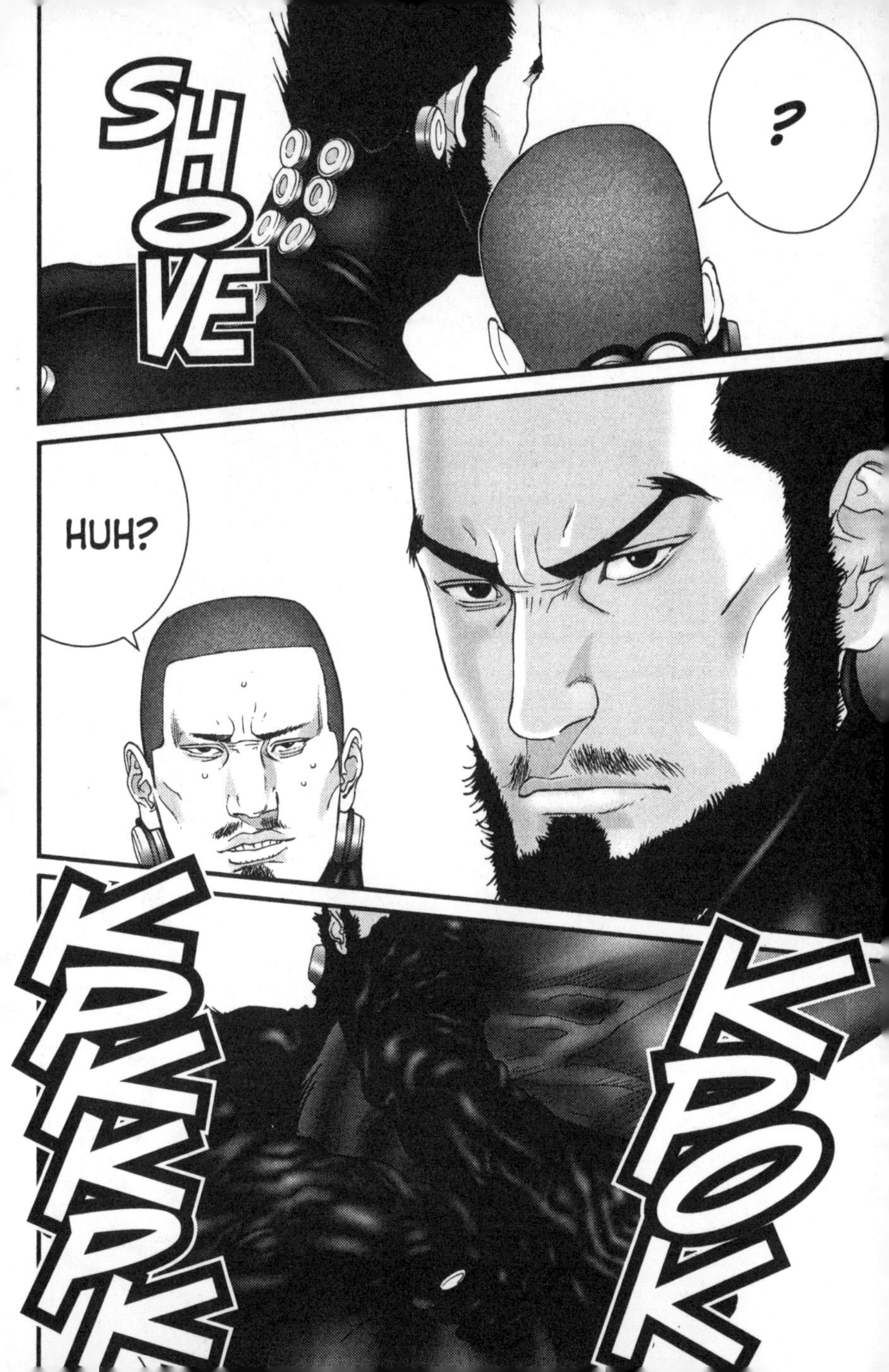
?
SHOVE
HUH?
KPOK
KPKPK

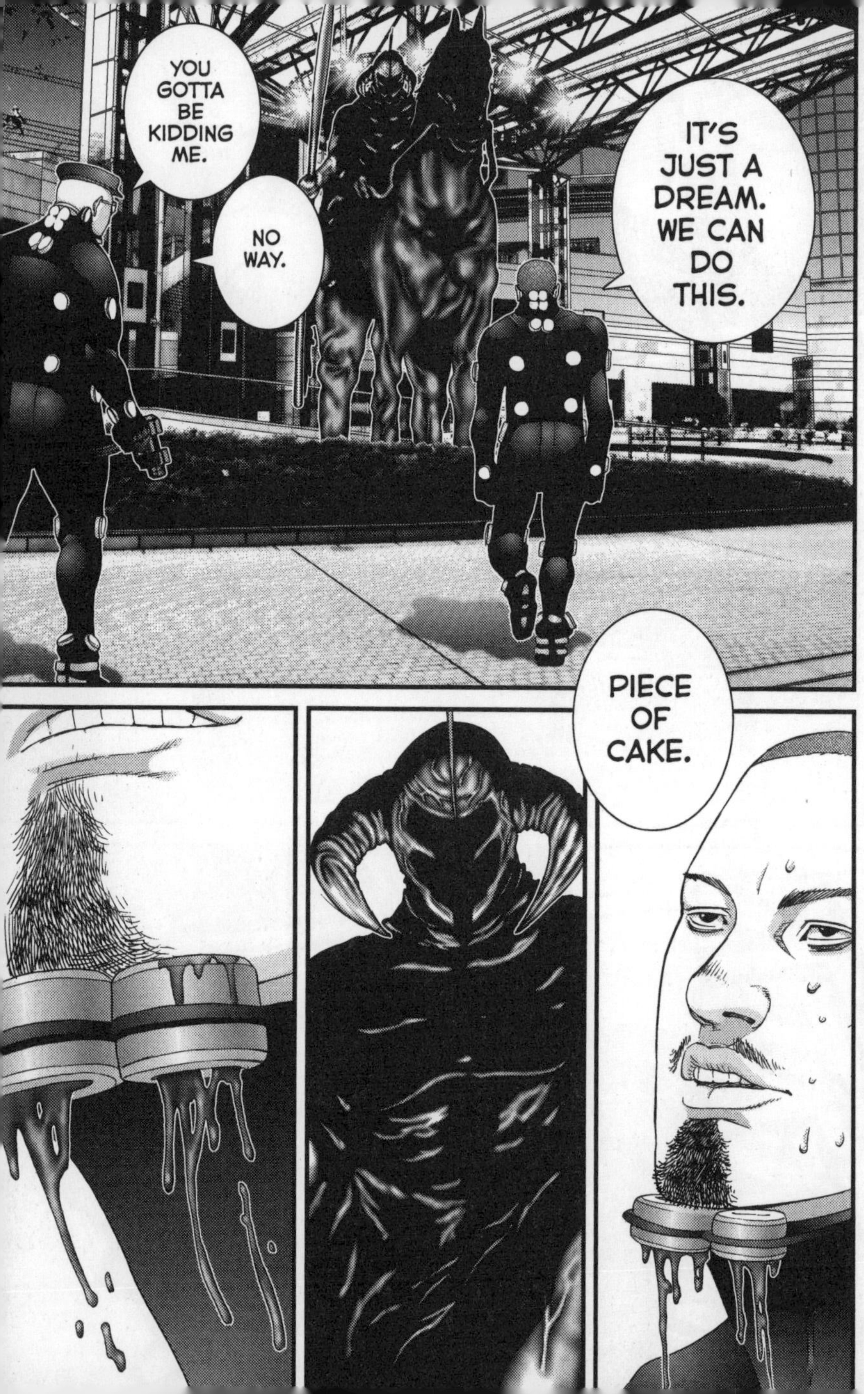
YOU GOTTA BE KIDDING ME.
NO WAY.
IT'S JUST A DREAM. WE CAN DO THIS.
PIECE OF CAKE.

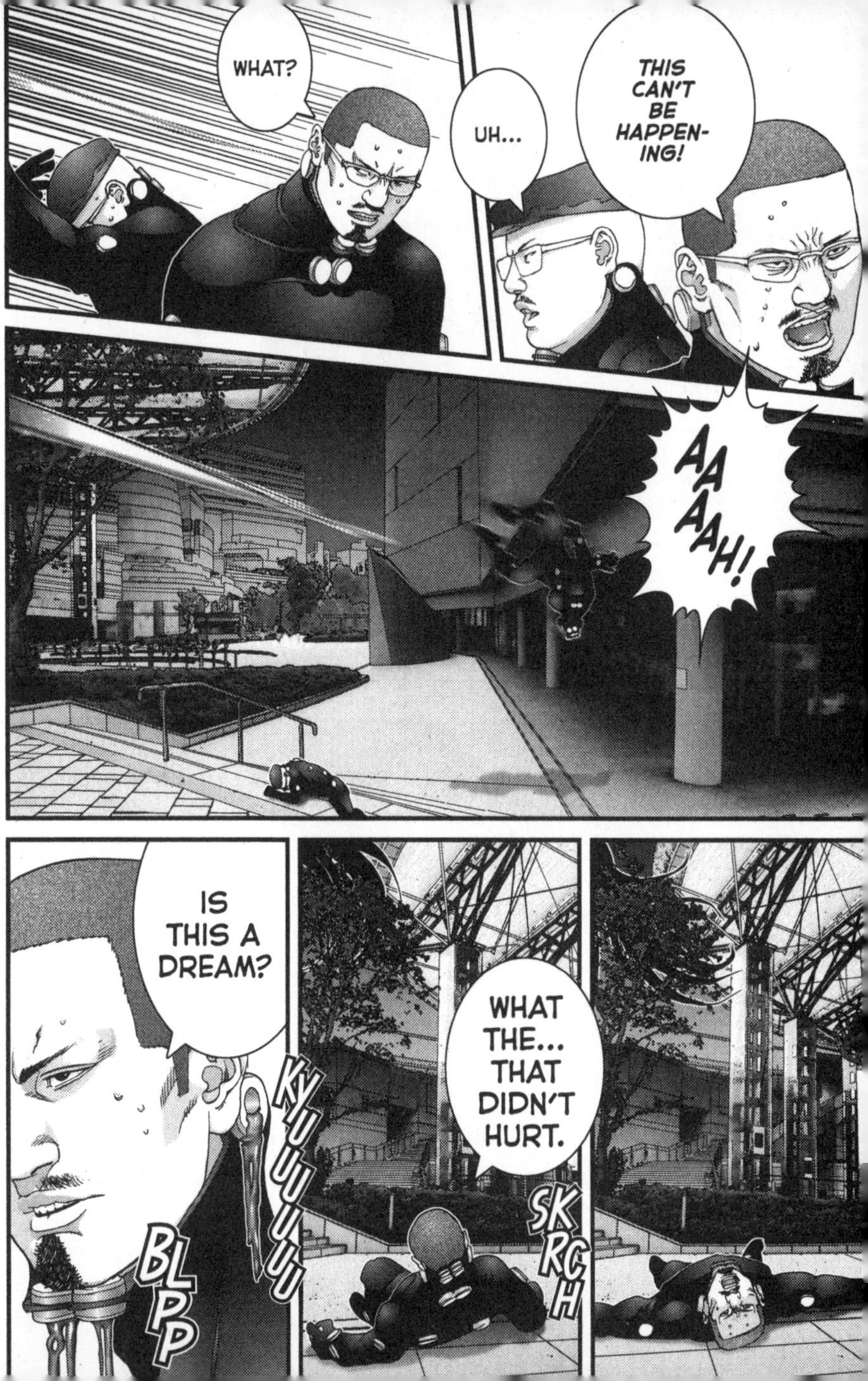
THIS CAN'T BE HAPPENING!
UH...
WHAT?
AAAAAH!
WHAT THE... THAT DIDN'T HURT.
SKRCH
IS THIS A DREAM?
KYUUUUUUU
BLPP

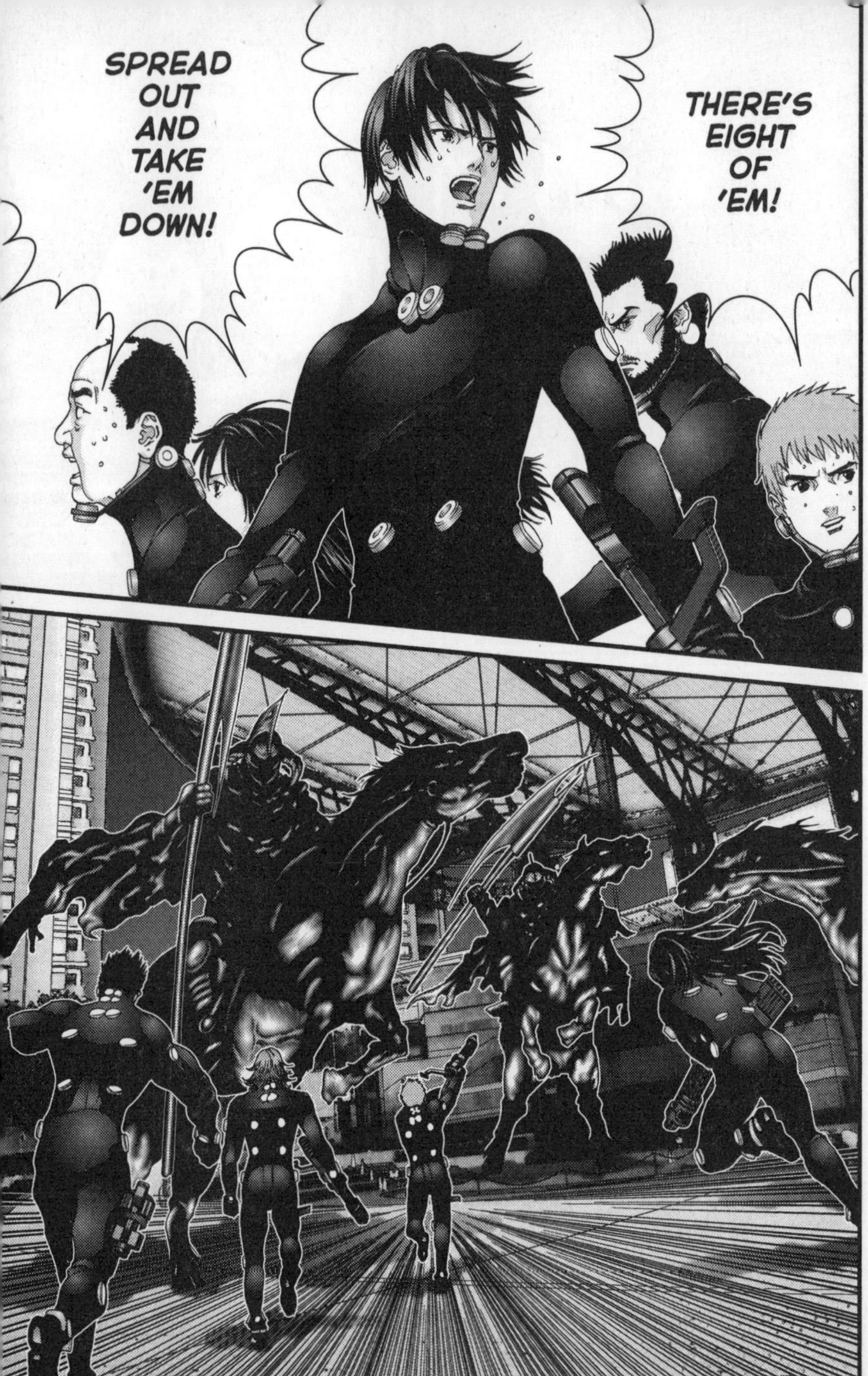
THERE'S EIGHT OF 'EM!
SPREAD OUT AND TAKE 'EM DOWN!

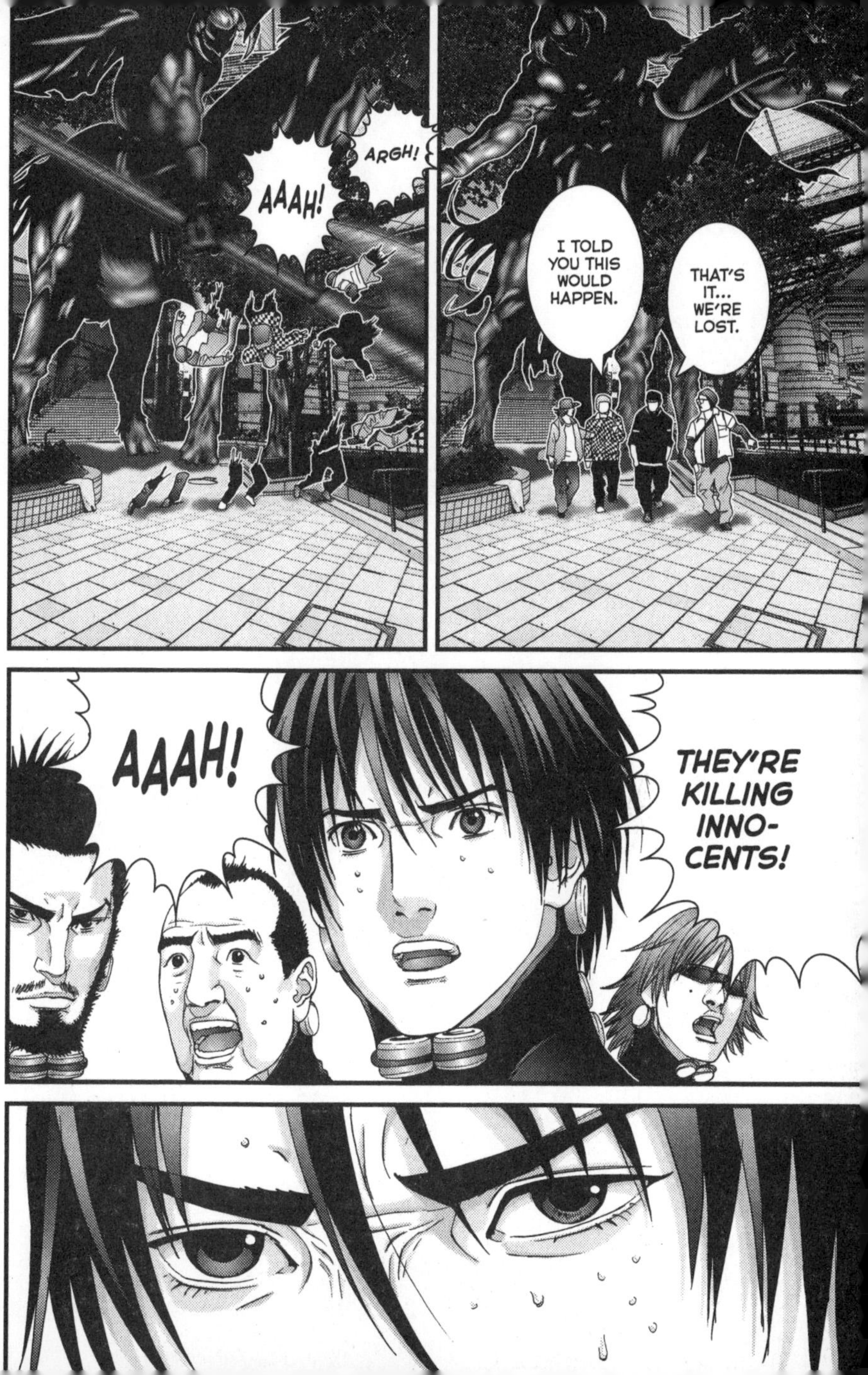
THAT'S IT... WE'RE LOST.
I TOLD YOU THIS WOULD HAPPEN.
ARGH!
AAAH!
THEY'RE KILLING INNO-CENTS!
AAAH!

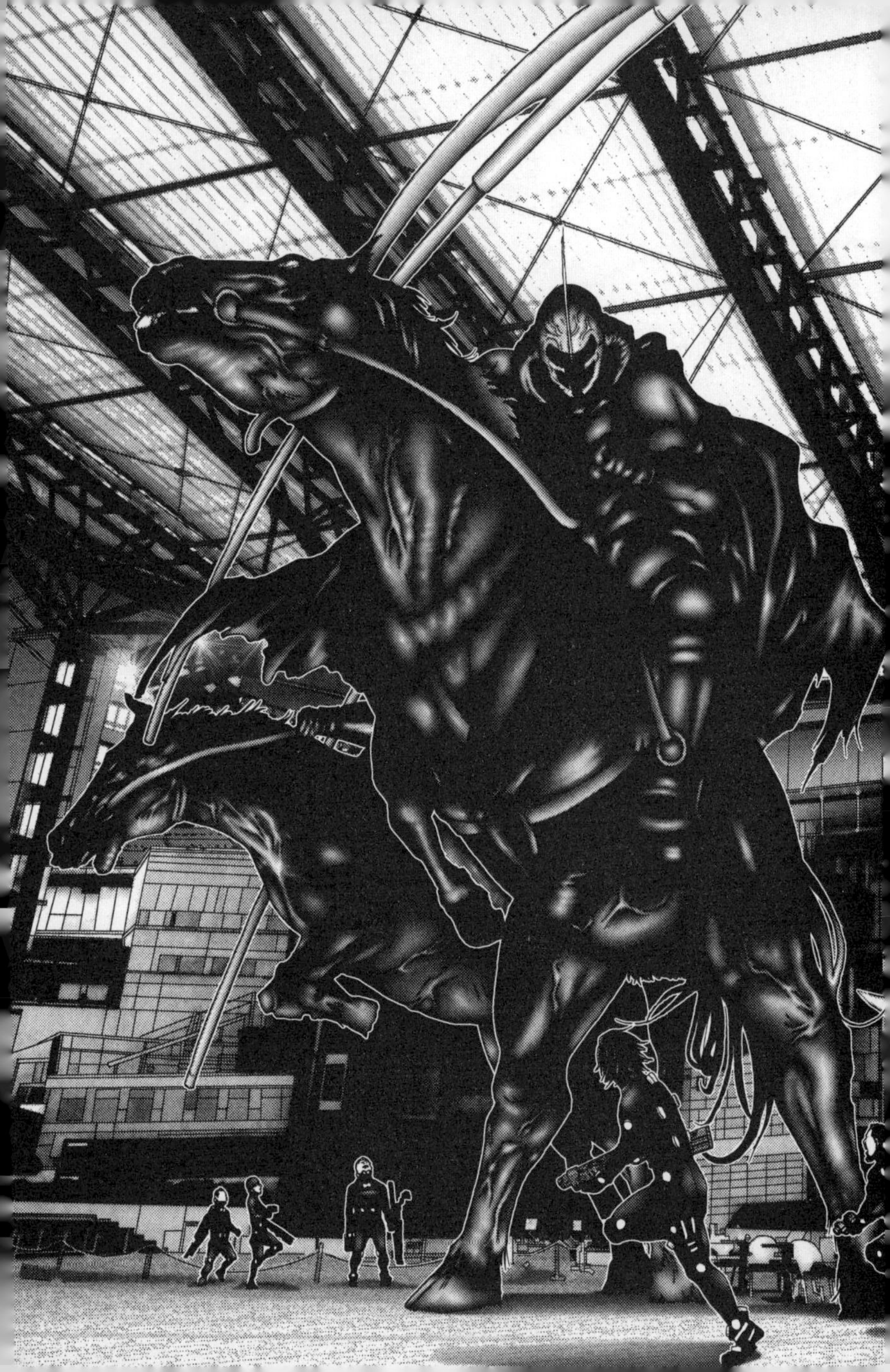

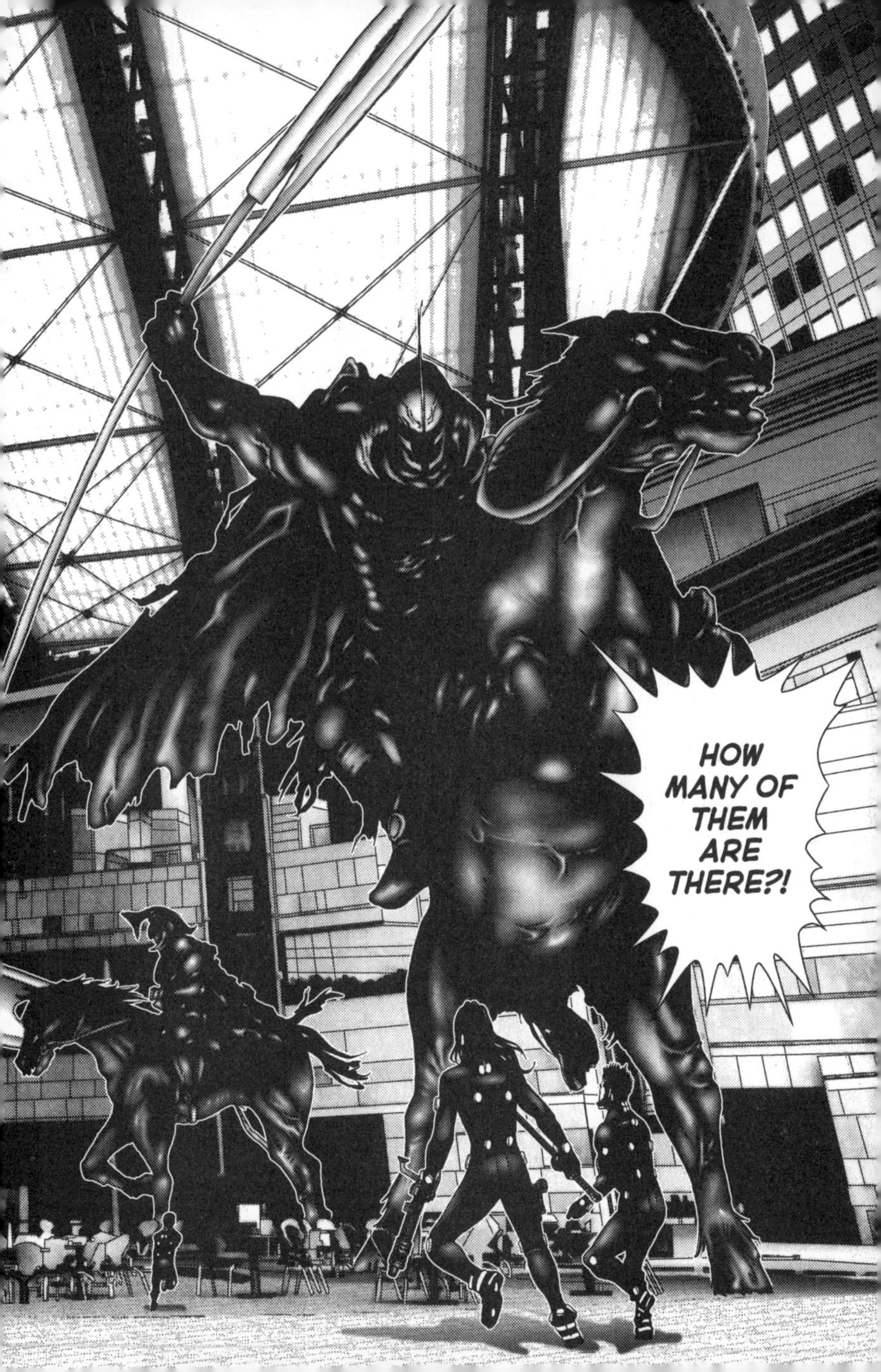
HOW MANY OF THEM ARE THERE?!

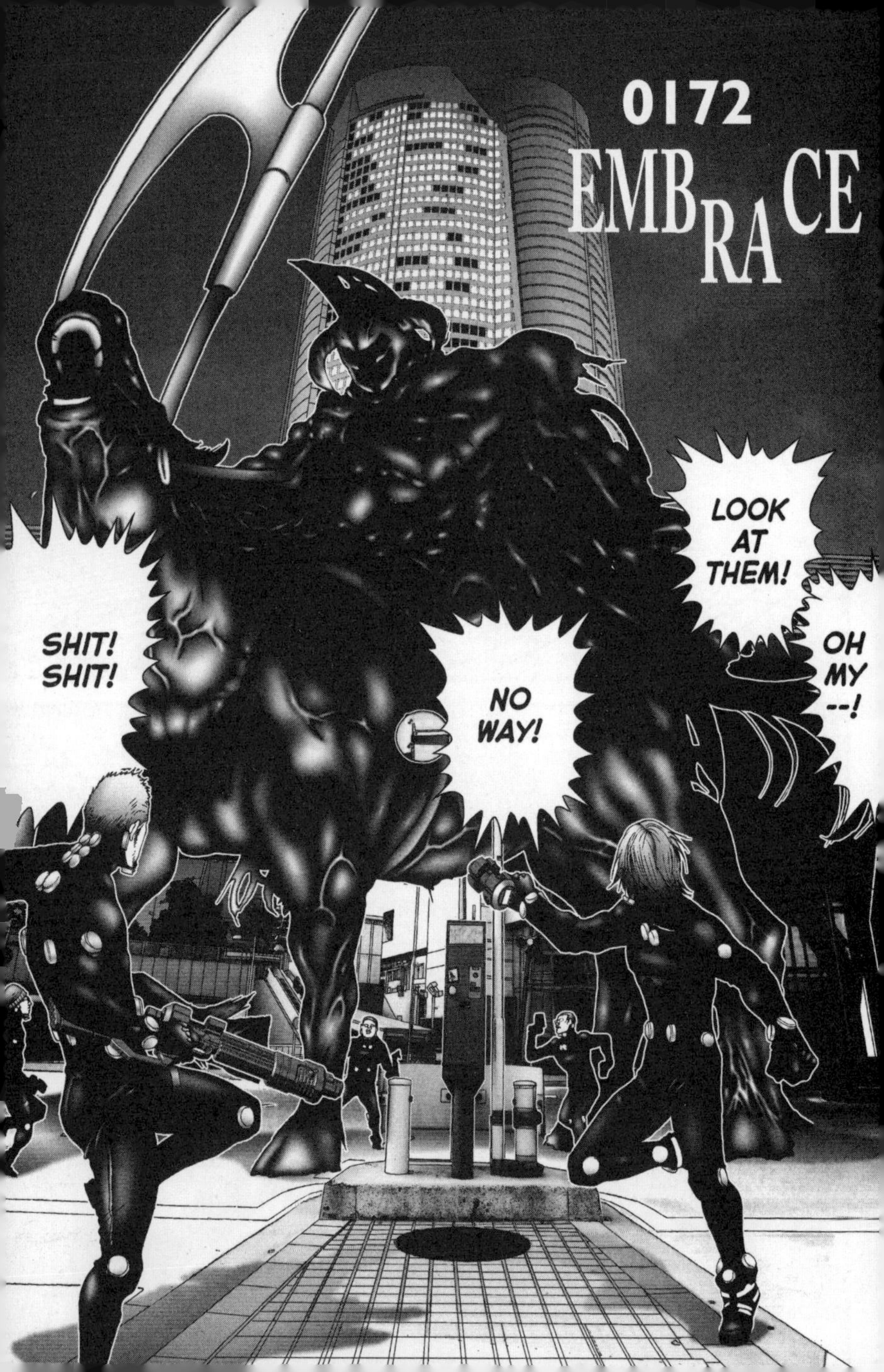
0172
EMBRACE
LOOK AT THEM!
OH MY --!
NO WAY!
SHIT! SHIT!

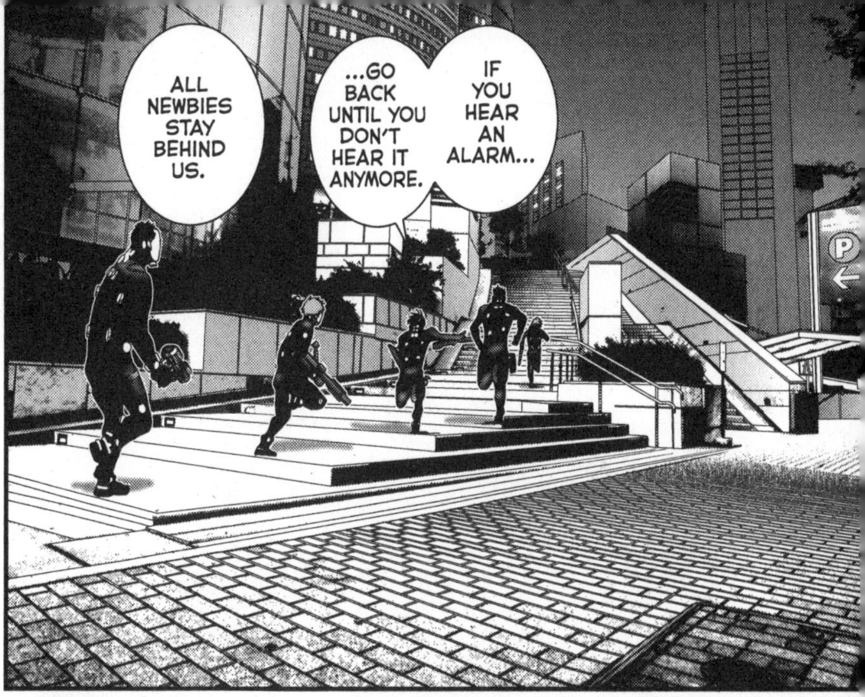
IF YOU HEAR AN ALARM...
...GO BACK UNTIL YOU DON'T HEAR IT ANYMORE.
ALL NEWBIES STAY BEHIND US.
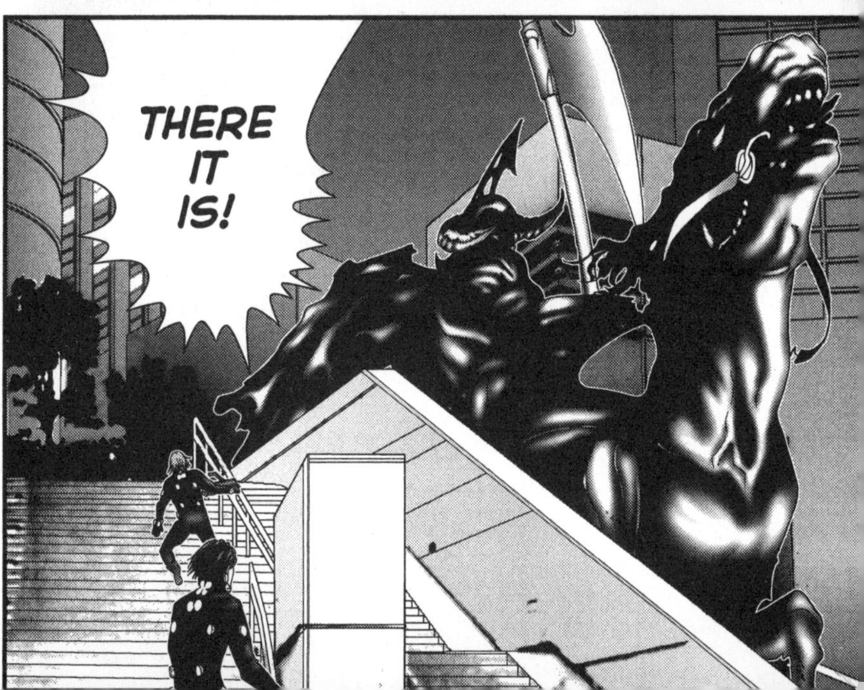
THERE IT IS!

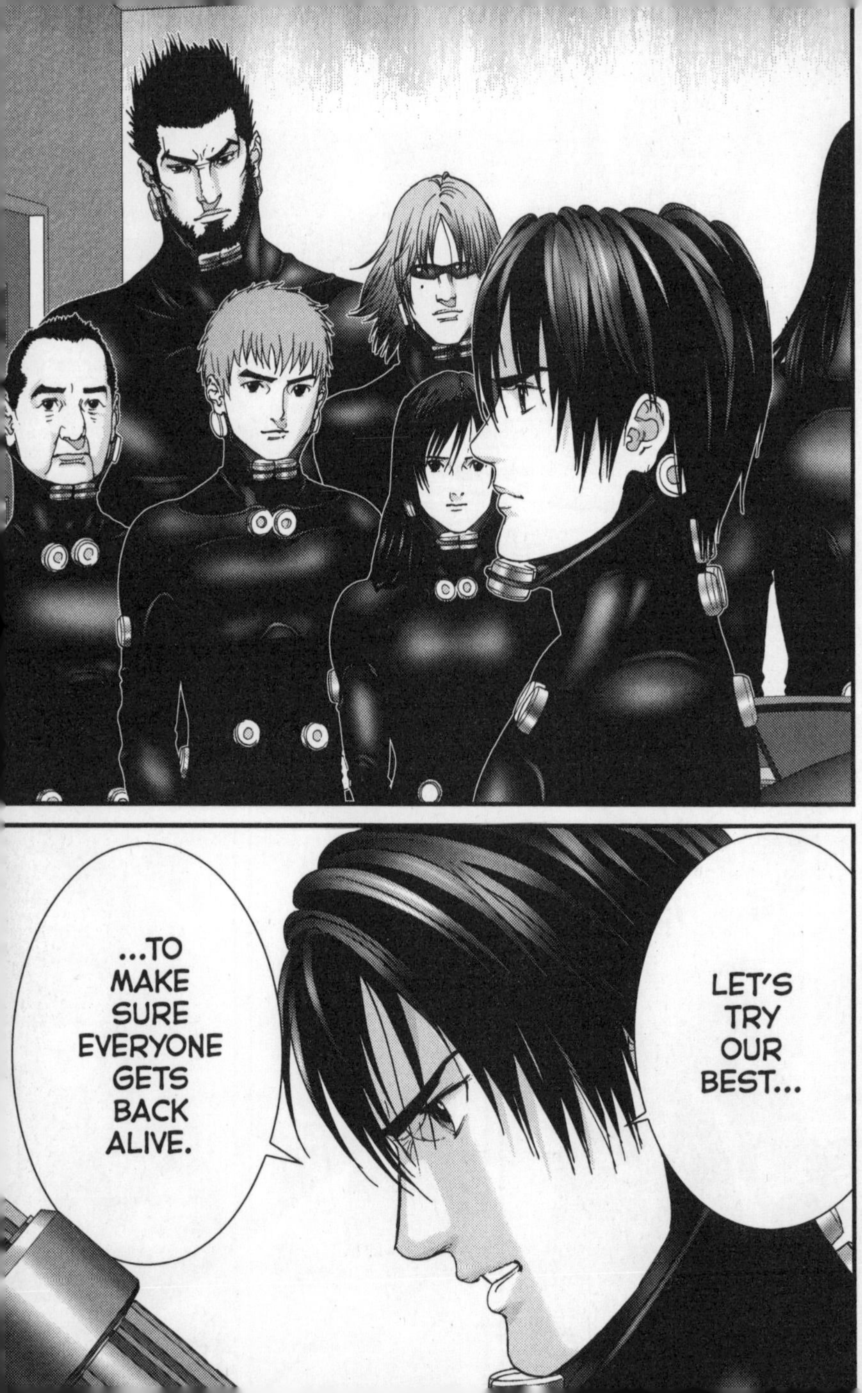
LET'S TRY OUR BEST...
...TO MAKE SURE EVERYONE GETS BACK ALIVE.

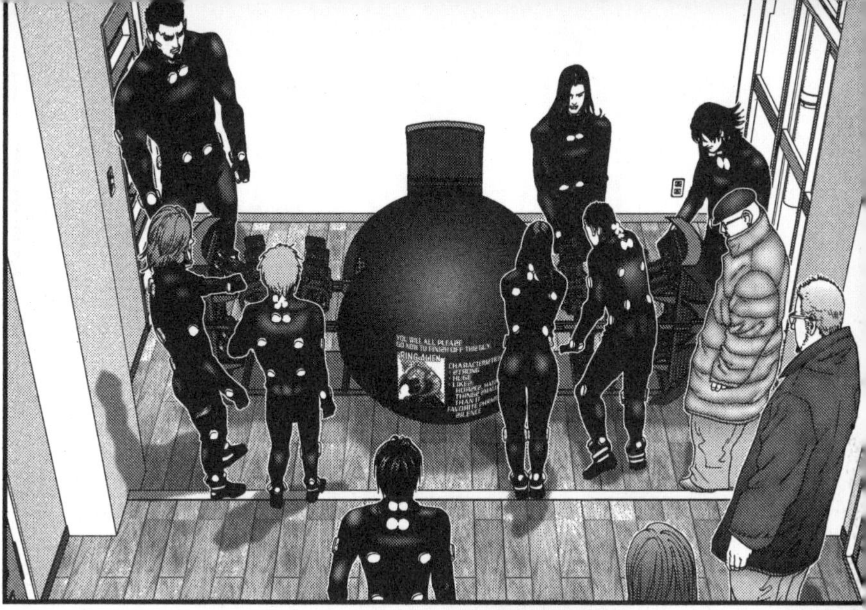
YOU WILL ALL PLEASE
GO NOW TO FINISH OFF THIS GUY.
RING ALIEN
• STRONG
• HUGE
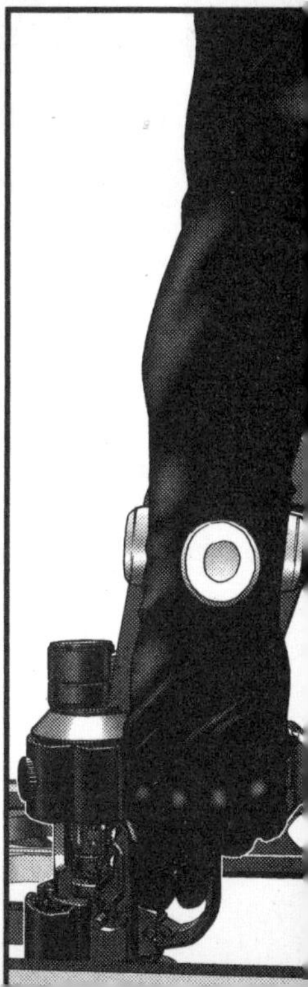
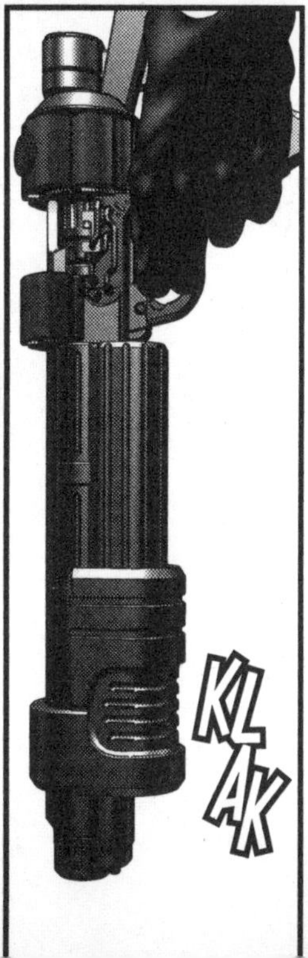
KLAK
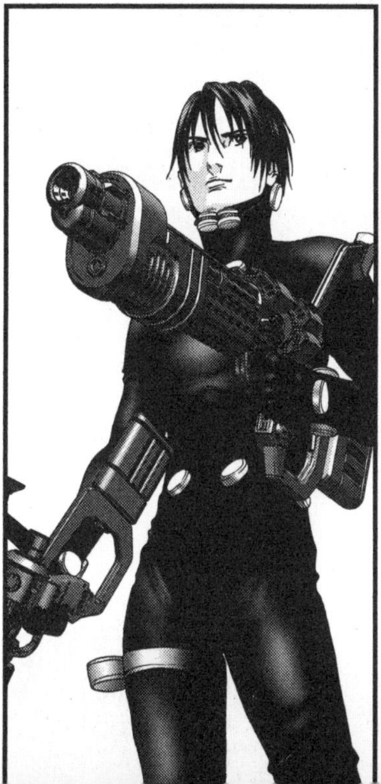

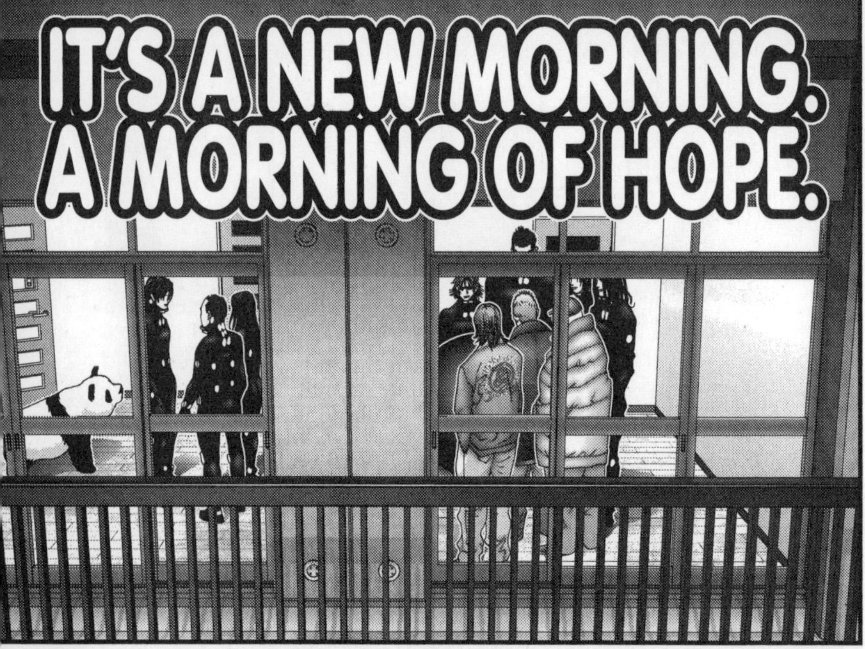
IT'S A NEW MORNING.
A MORNING OF HOPE.

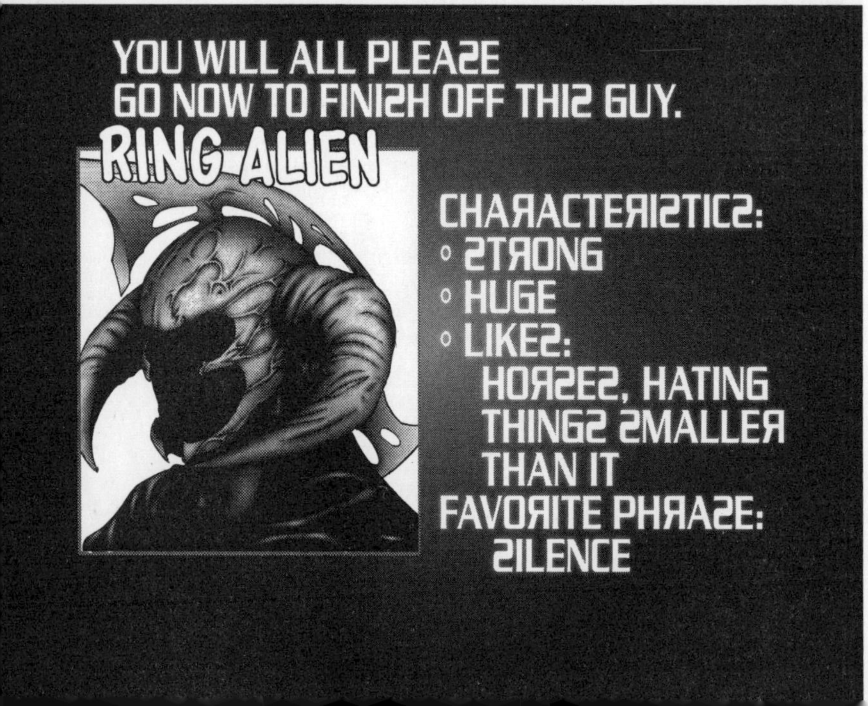
YOU WILL ALL PLEASE
GO NOW TO FINISH OFF THIS GUY.
RING ALIEN
CHARACTERISTICS:
◦ STRONG
◦ HUGE
◦ LIKES:
HORSES, HATING
THINGS SMALLER
THAN IT
FAVORITE PHRASE:
SILENCE

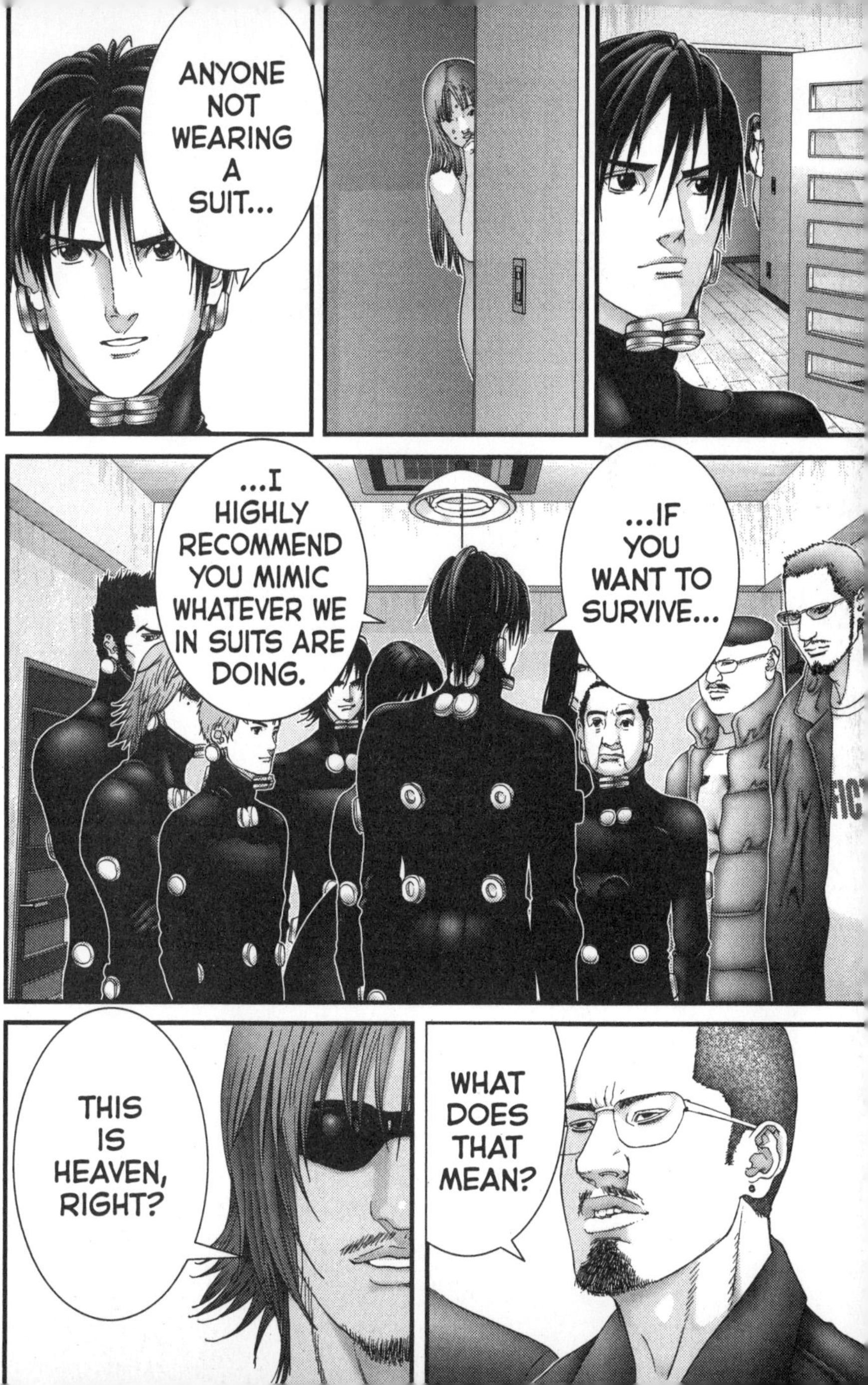
ANYONE NOT WEARING A SUIT...
...I HIGHLY RECOMMEND YOU MIMIC WHATEVER WE IN SUITS ARE DOING.
...IF YOU WANT TO SURVIVE...
THIS IS HEAVEN, RIGHT?
WHAT DOES THAT MEAN?

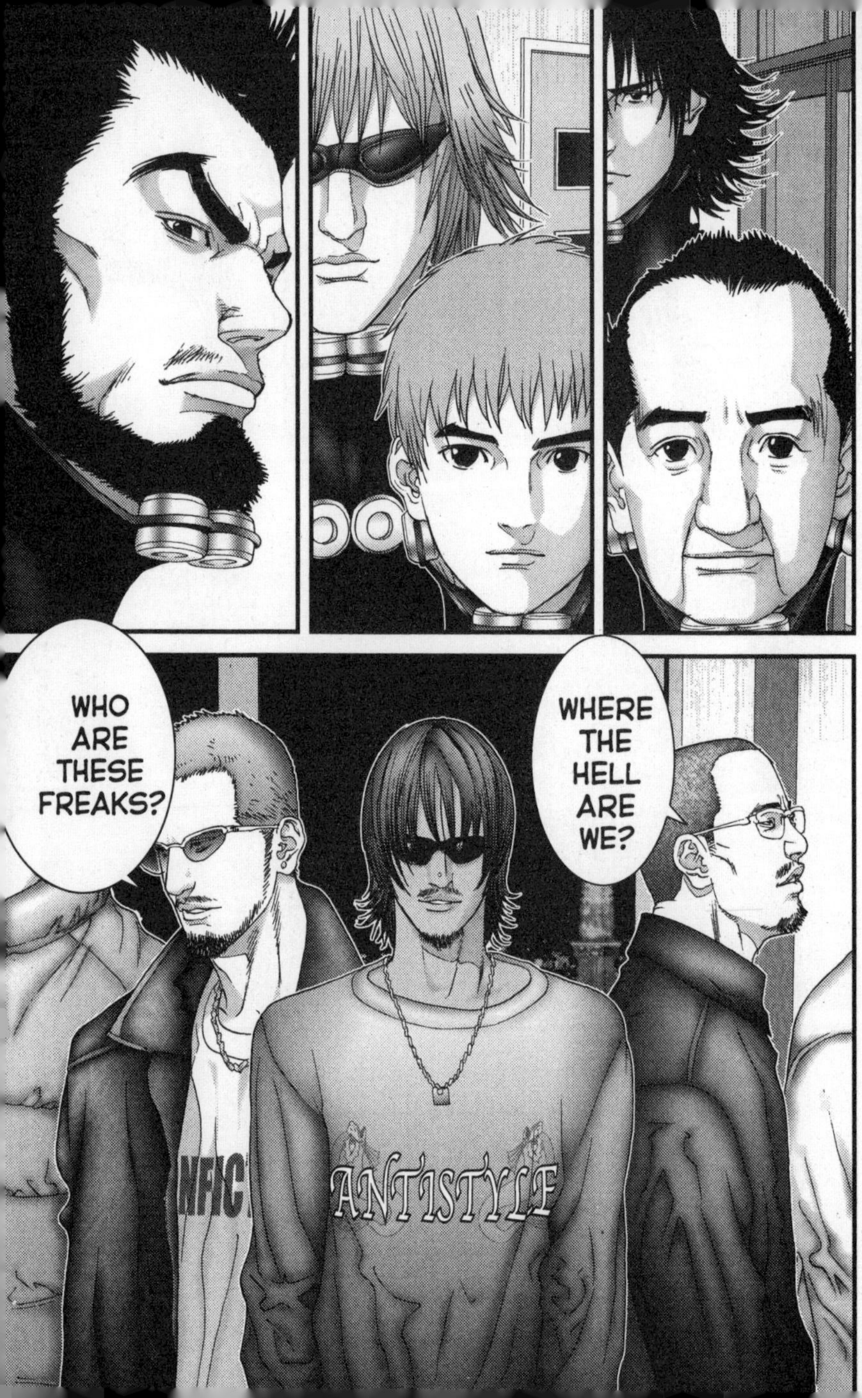
WHERE THE HELL ARE WE?
WHO ARE THESE FREAKS?
ANTISTYLE

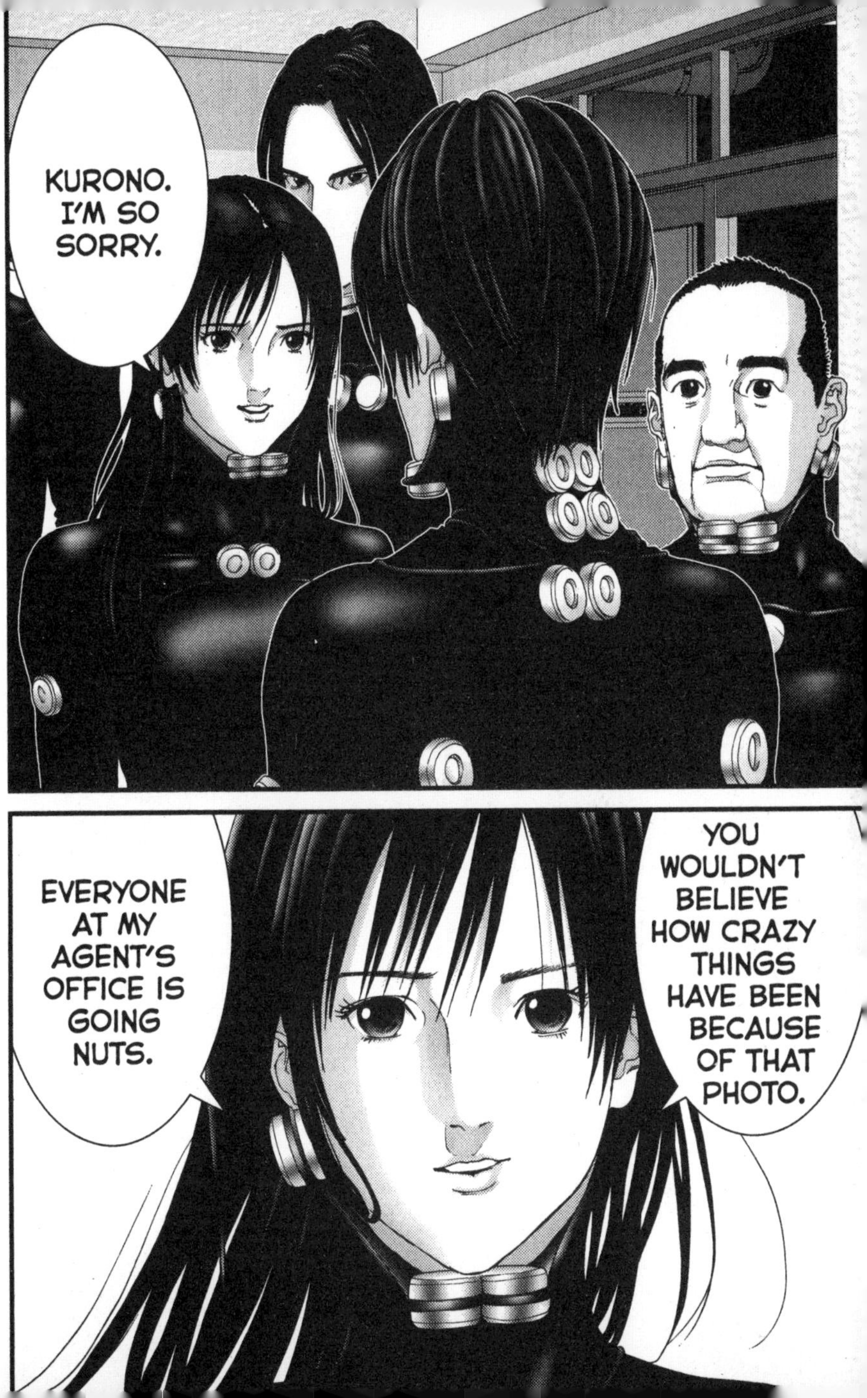
KURONO. I'M SO SORRY.
YOU WOULDN'T BELIEVE HOW CRAZY THINGS HAVE BEEN BECAUSE OF THAT PHOTO.
EVERYONE AT MY AGENT'S OFFICE IS GOING NUTS.

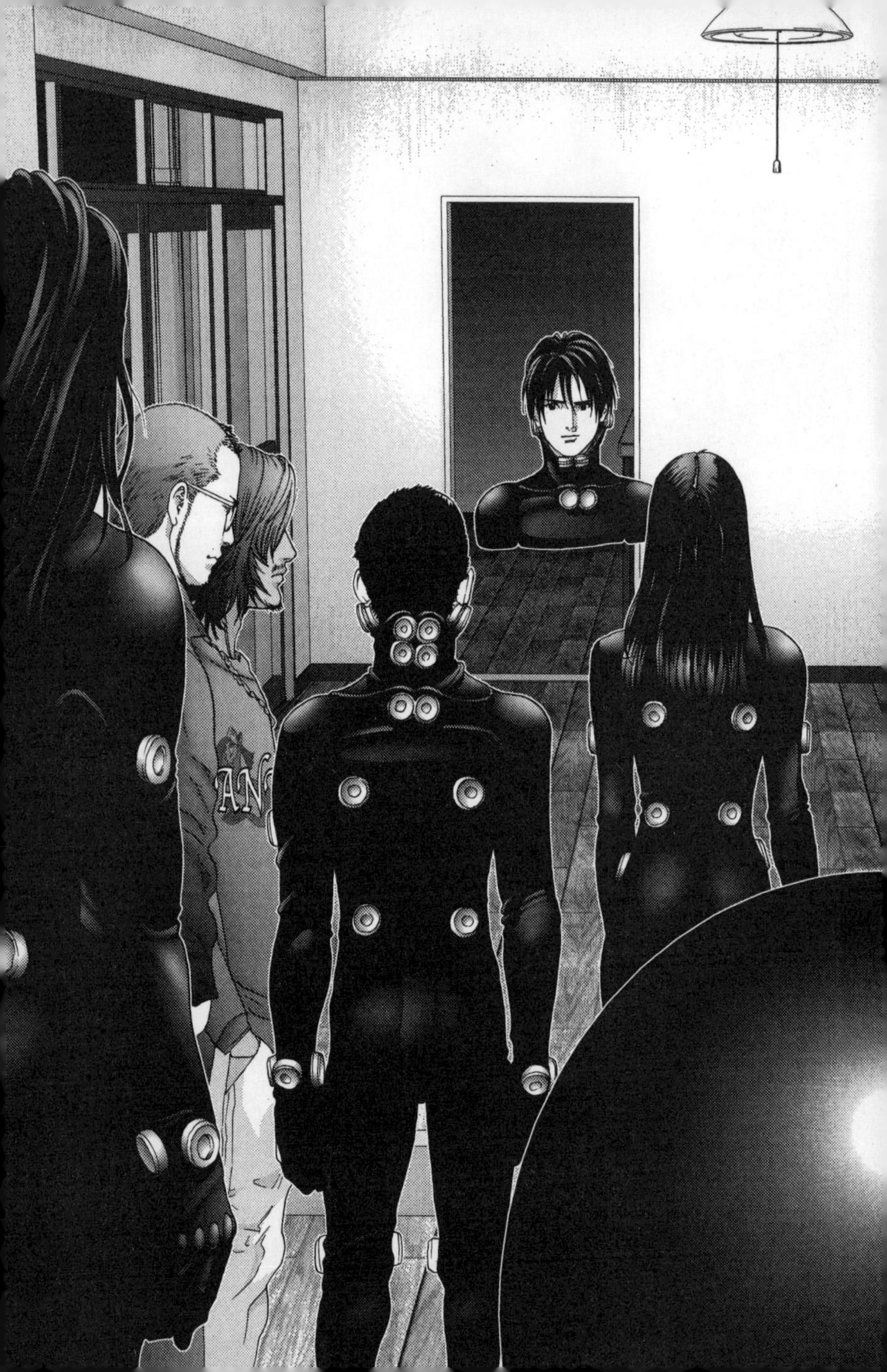

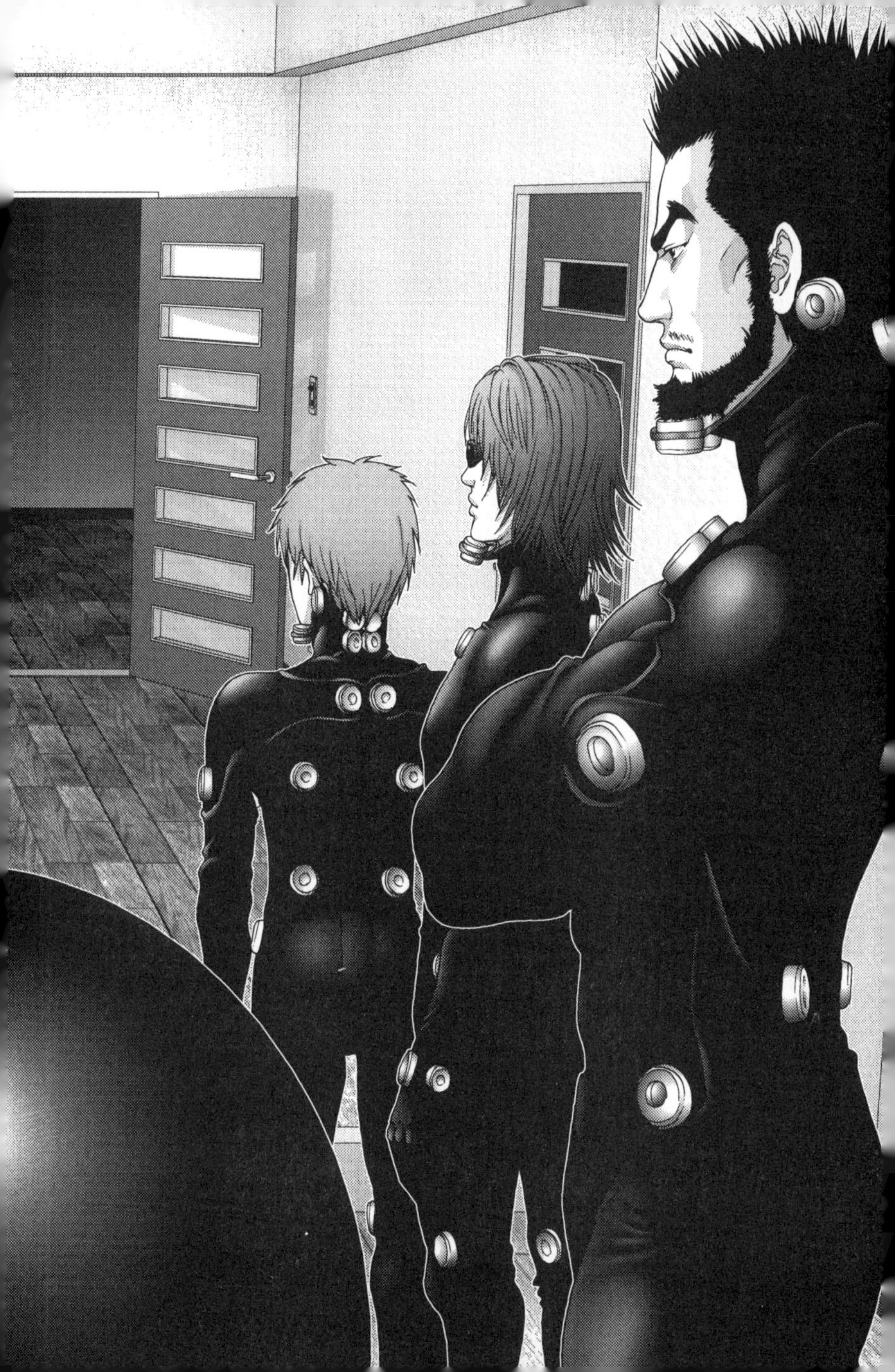

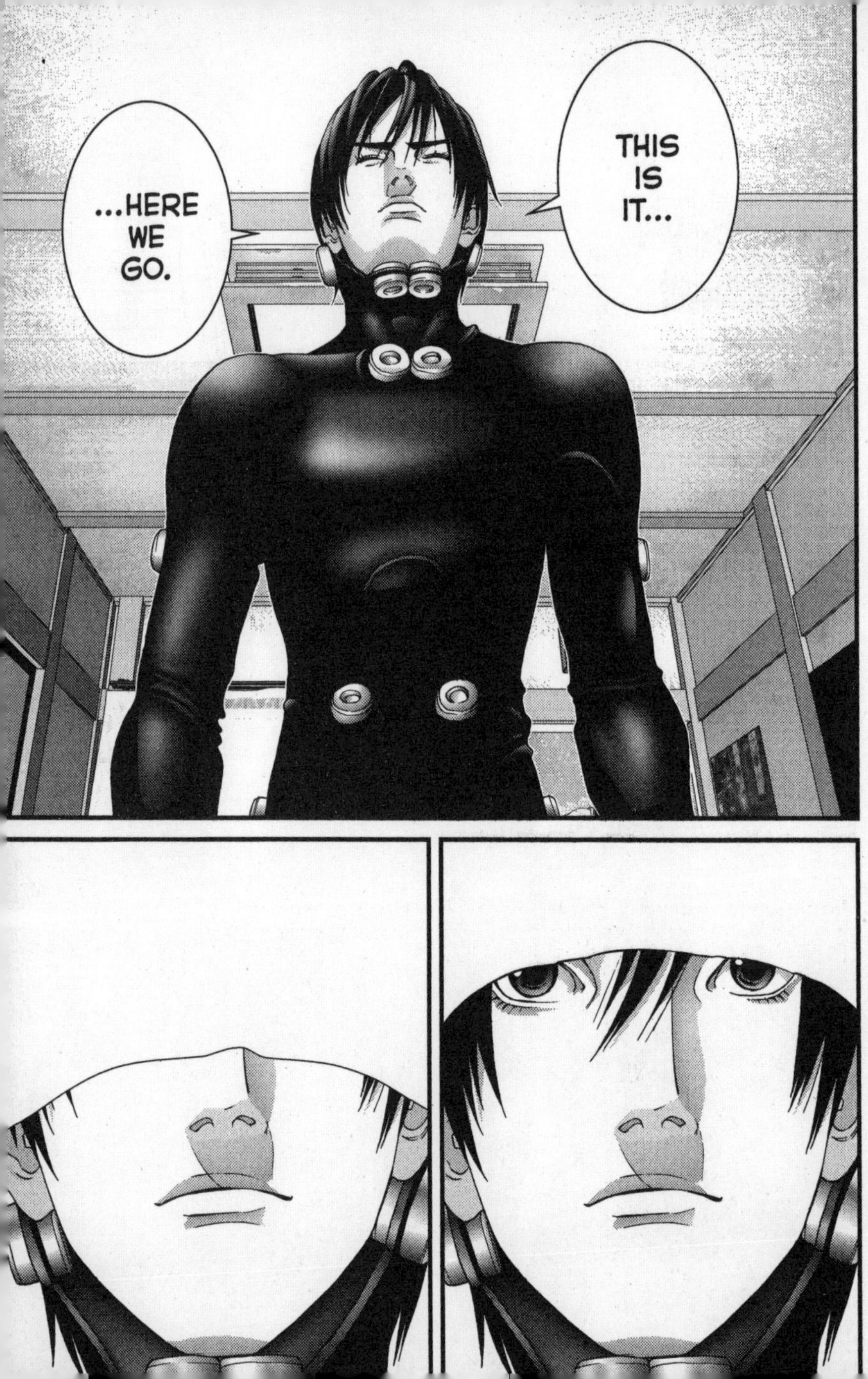
THIS IS IT...
...HERE WE GO.

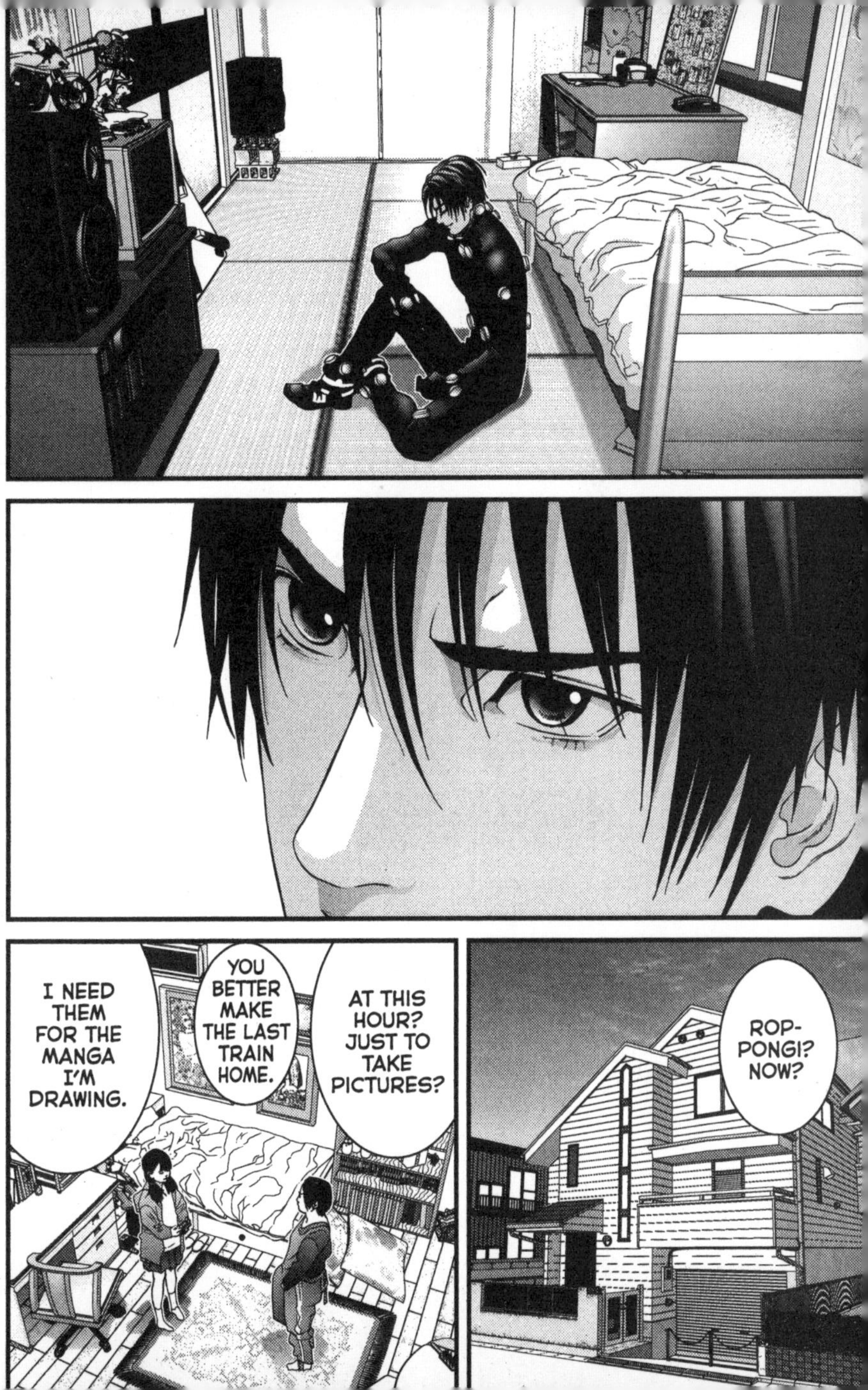
ROP-PONGI? NOW?
AT THIS HOUR? JUST TO TAKE PICTURES?
YOU BETTER MAKE THE LAST TRAIN HOME.
I NEED THEM FOR THE MANGA I'M DRAWING.

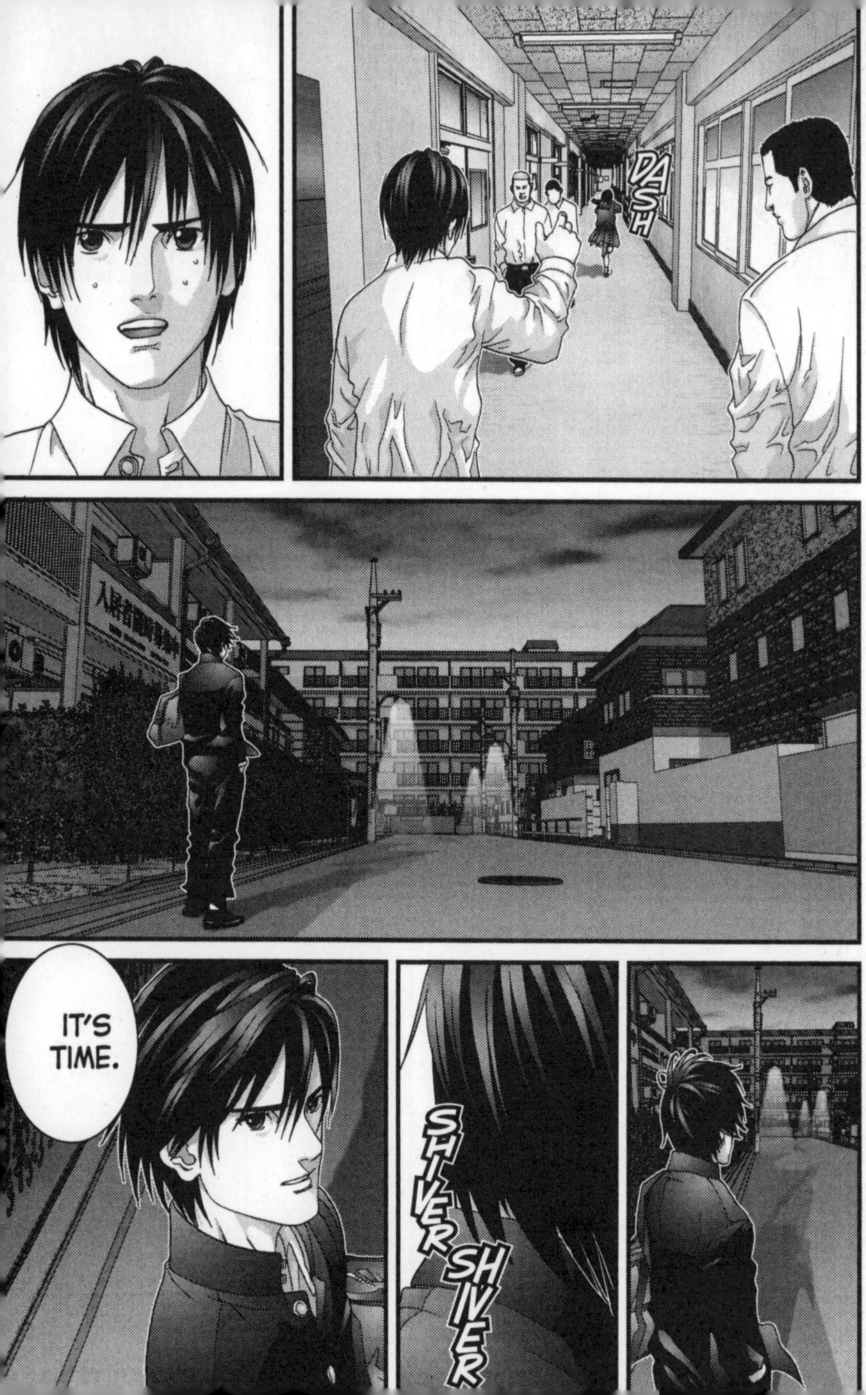
DASH
SHIVER SHIVER
IT'S TIME.

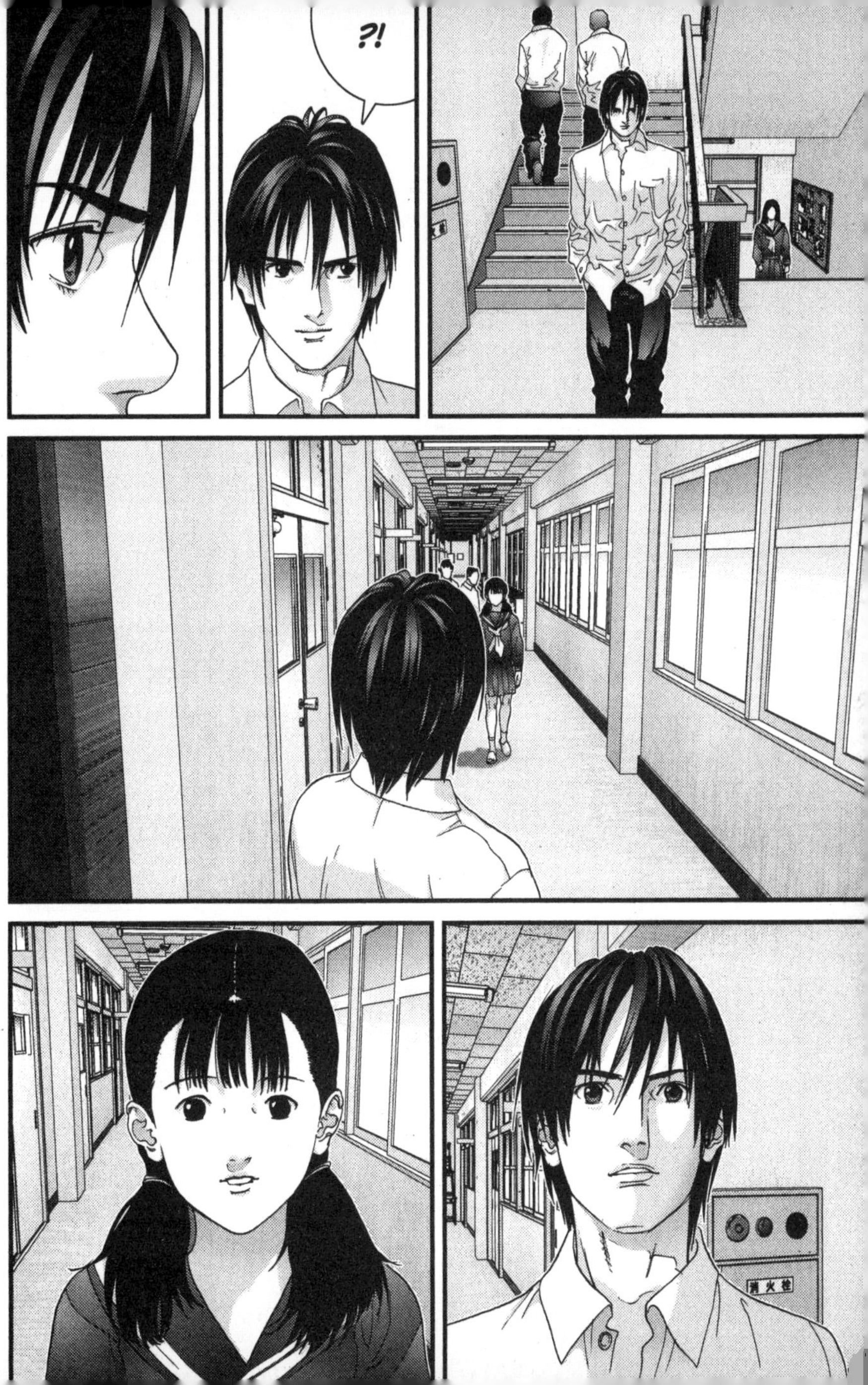
?!
消火栓

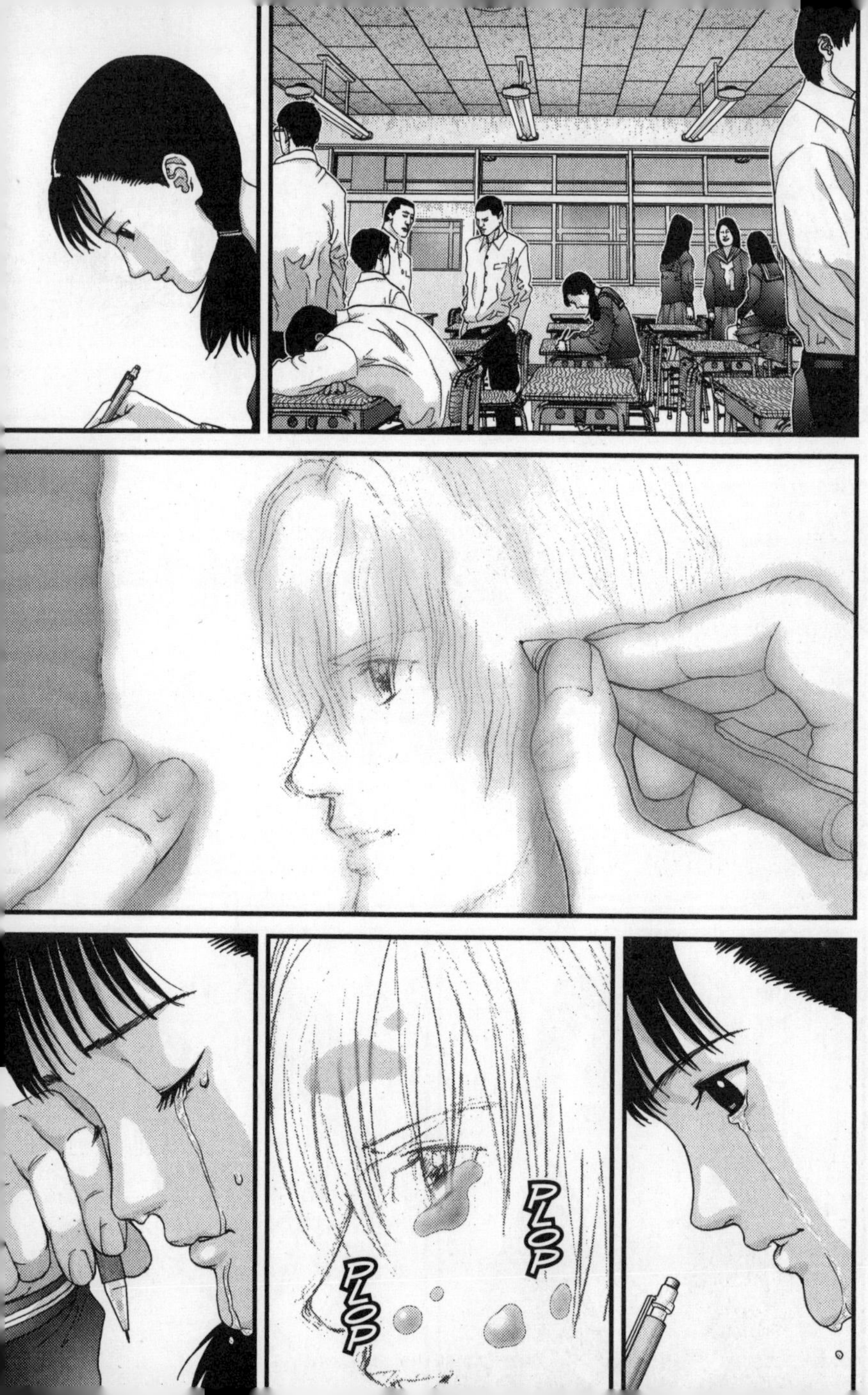
PLOP
PLOP

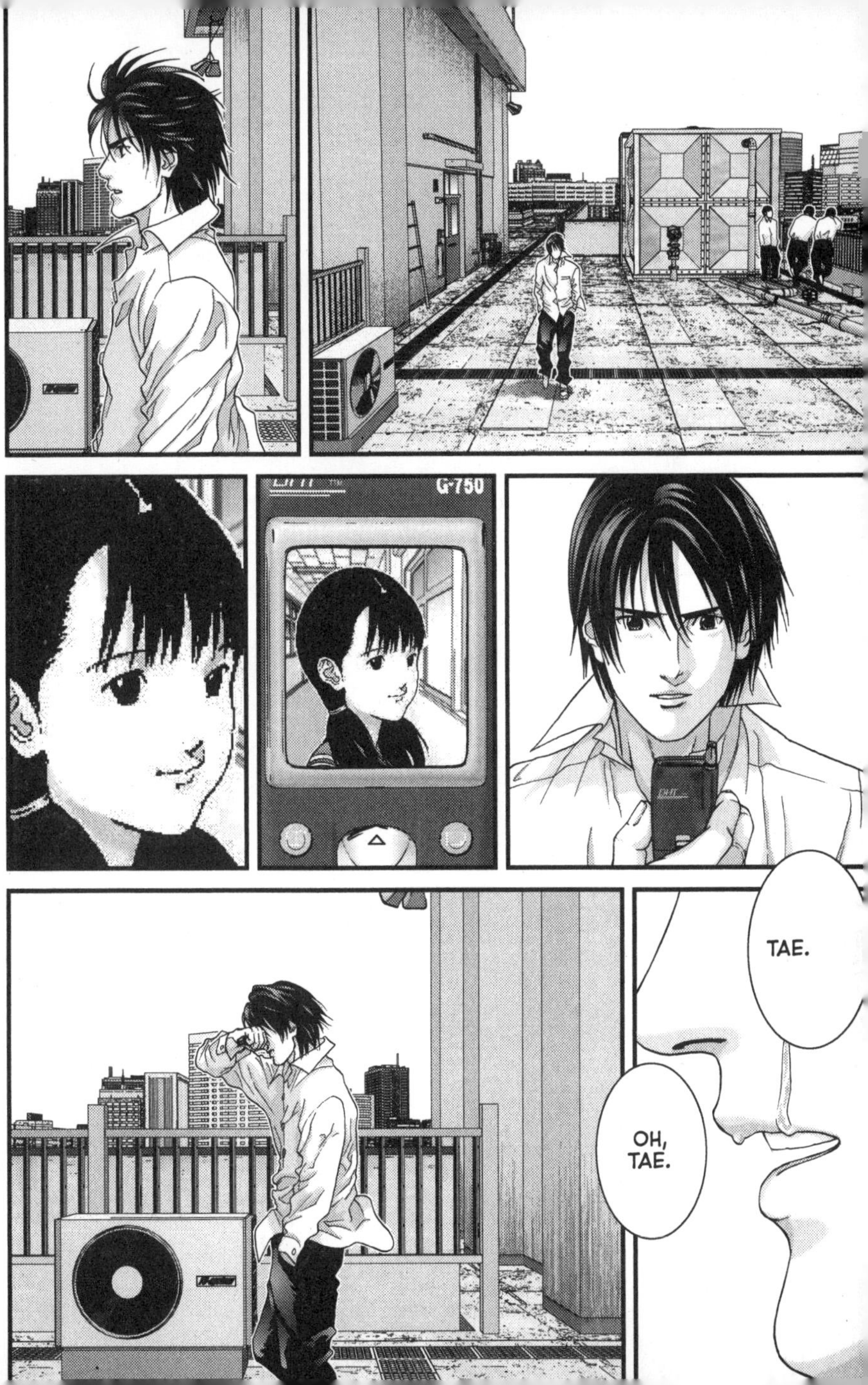
G-750
TAE.
OH, TAE.

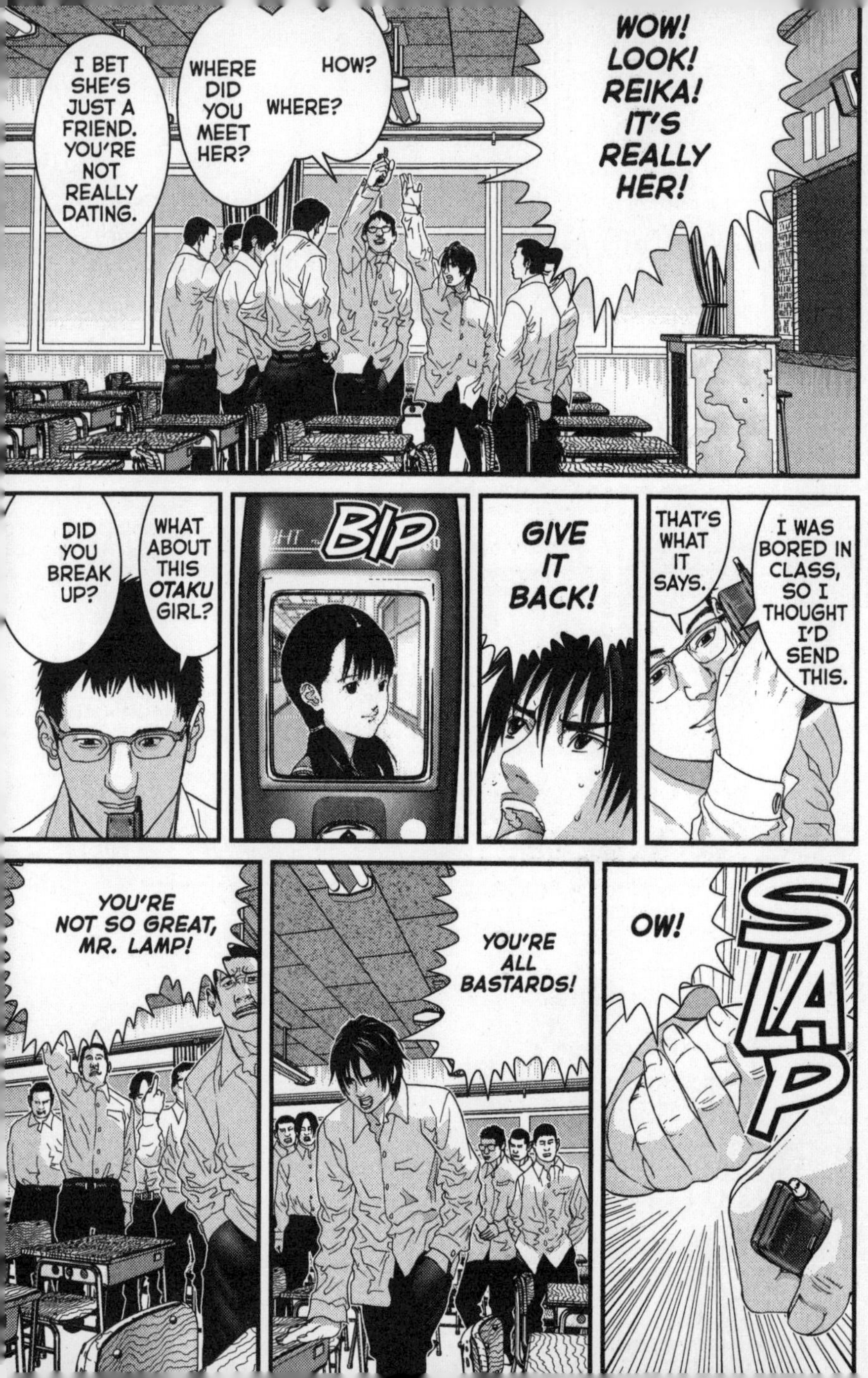
WOW! LOOK! REIKA! IT'S REALLY HER!
HOW?
WHERE?
WHERE DID YOU MEET HER?
I BET SHE'S JUST A FRIEND. YOU'RE NOT REALLY DATING.
I WAS BORED IN CLASS, SO I THOUGHT I'D SEND THIS.
THAT'S WHAT IT SAYS.
GIVE IT BACK!
BIP
WHAT ABOUT THIS OTAKU GIRL?
DID YOU BREAK UP?
SLAP
OW!
YOU'RE ALL BASTARDS!
YOU'RE NOT SO GREAT, MR. LAMP!

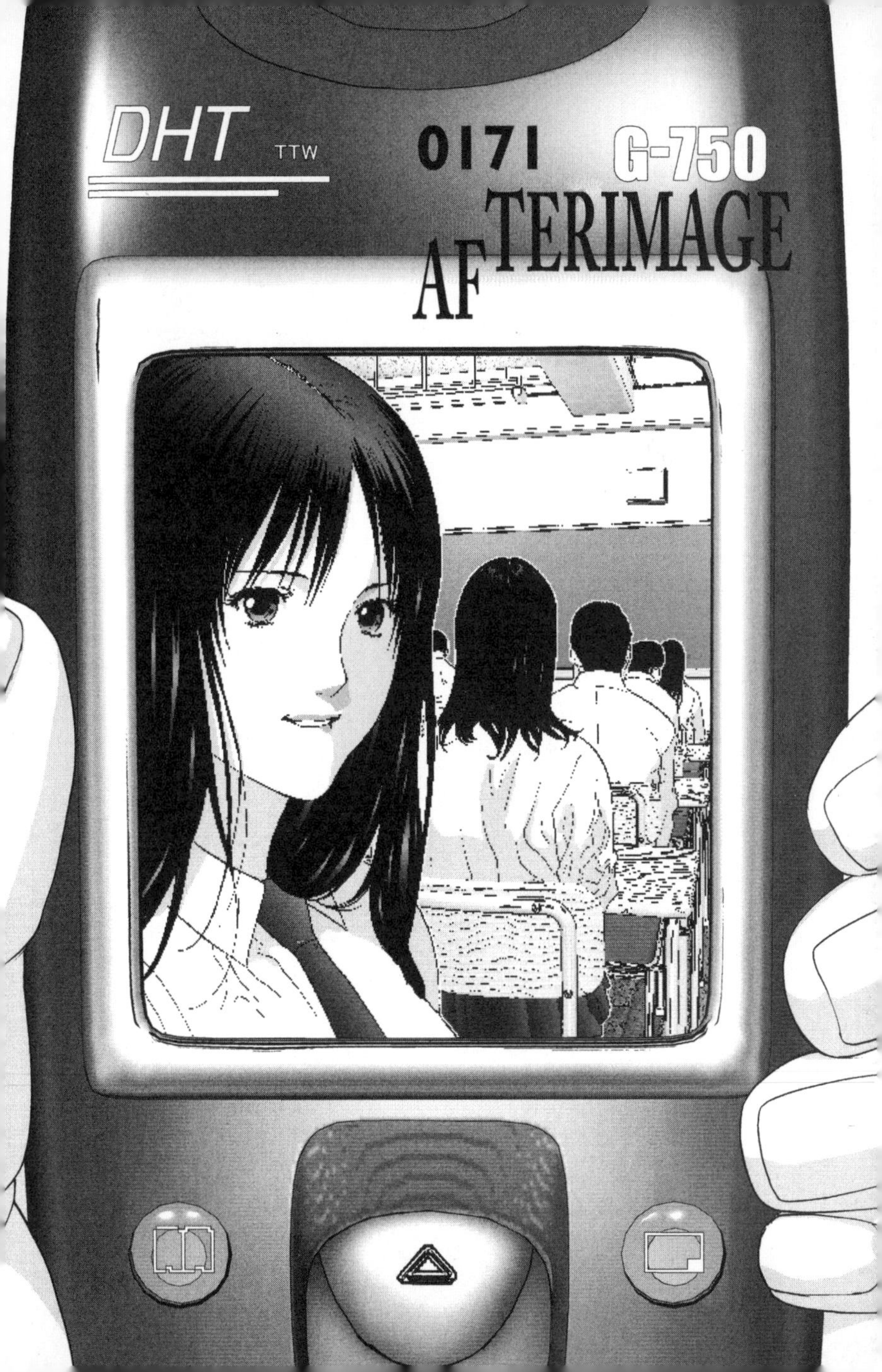
DHT
TTW
0171
G-750
AFTERIMAGE

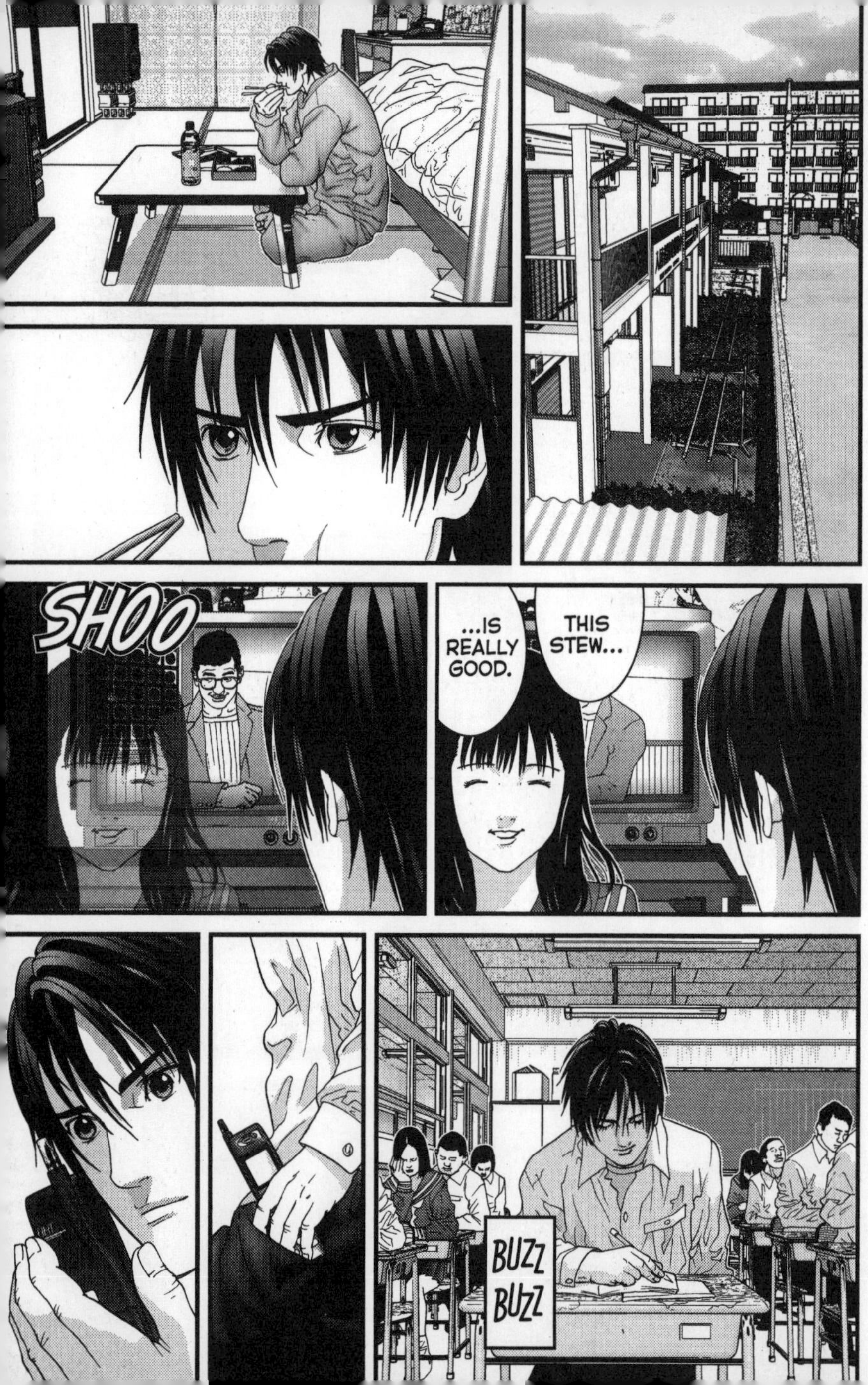
THIS STEW...
...IS REALLY GOOD.
SHOO
BUZZ BUZZ

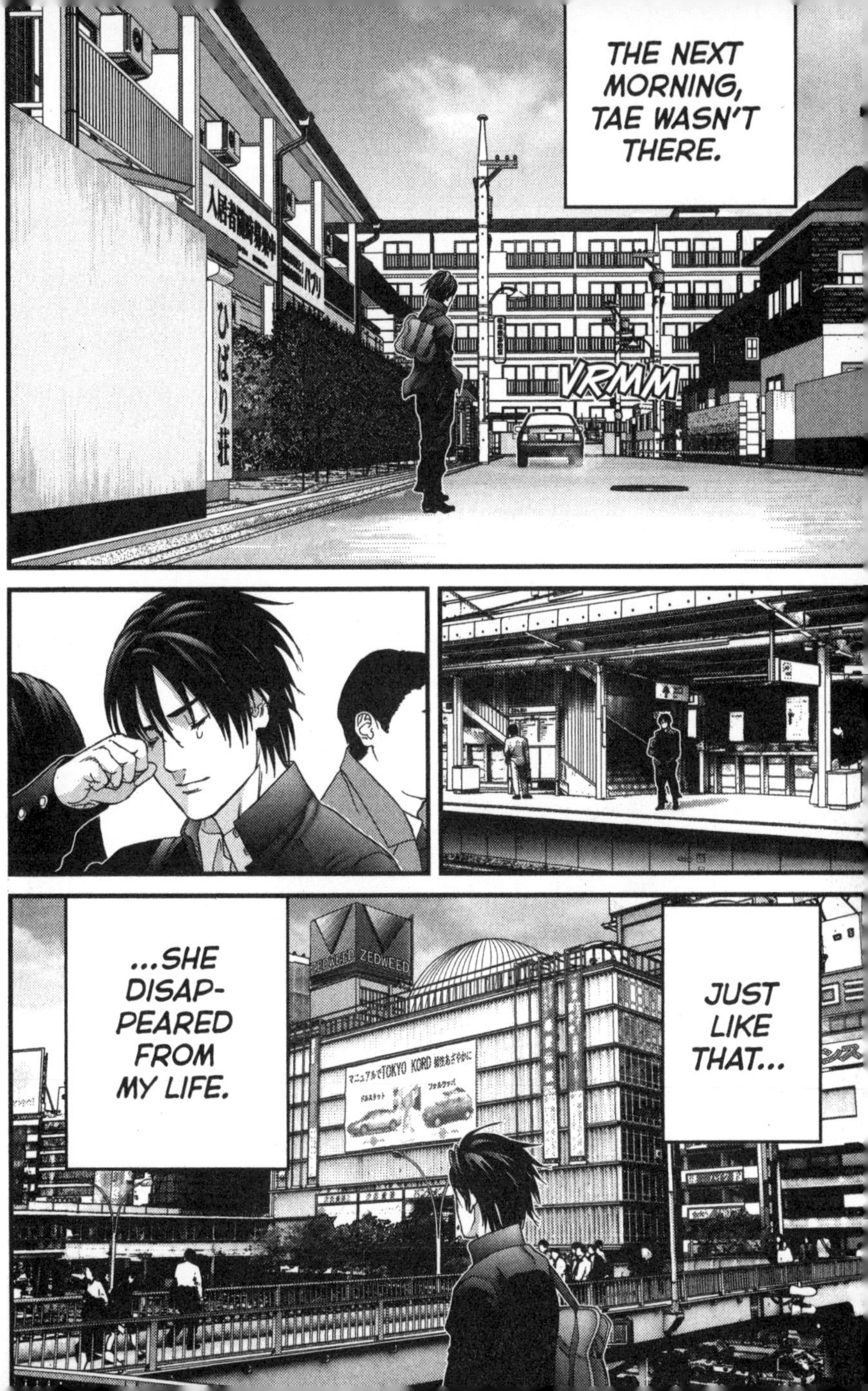
THE NEXT MORNING, TAE WASN'T THERE.
ひばり荘
VRMM
ZEDWEED
ZEDWEED
TOKYO KORD
JUST LIKE THAT...
...SHE DISAP-PEARED FROM MY LIFE.

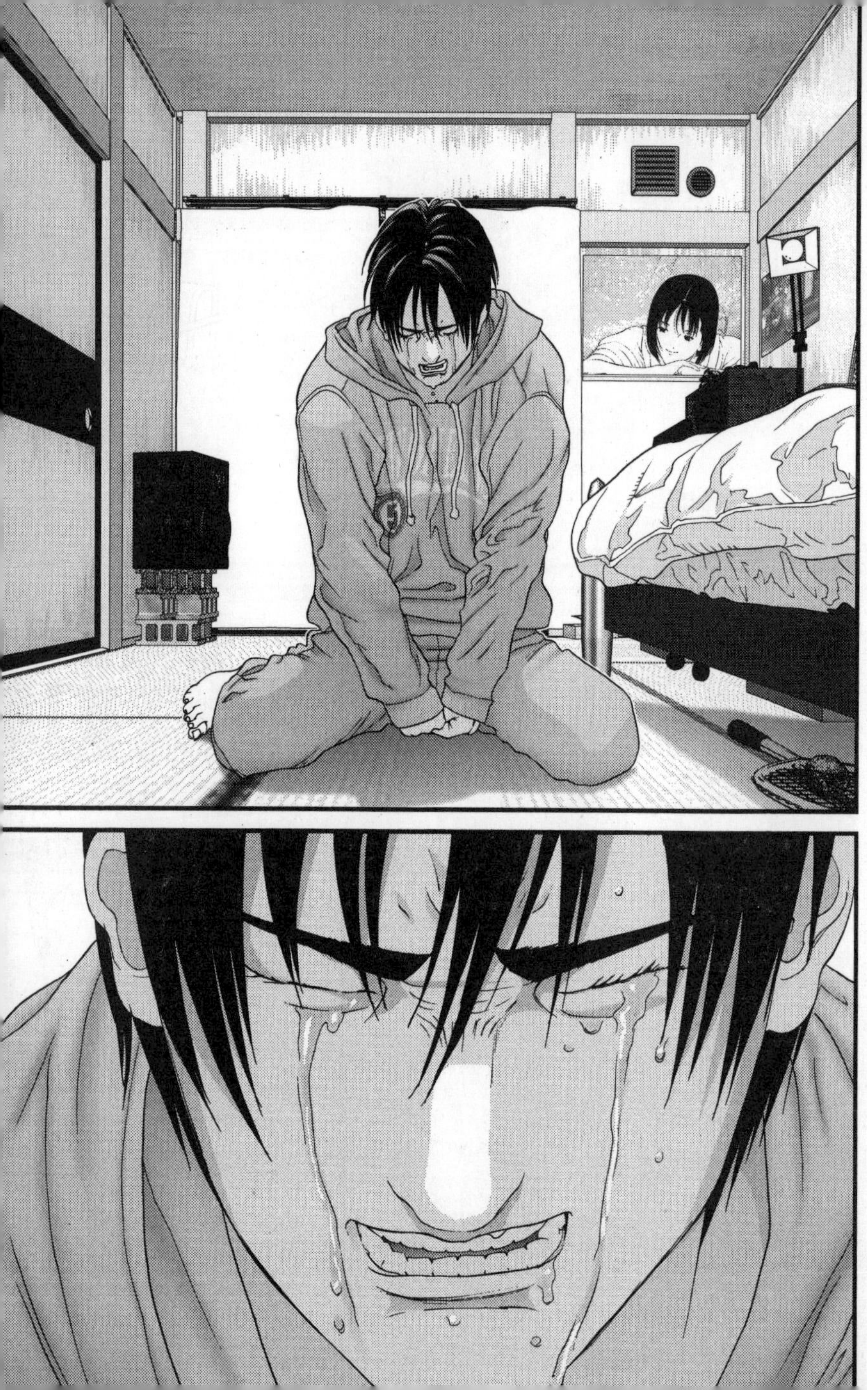

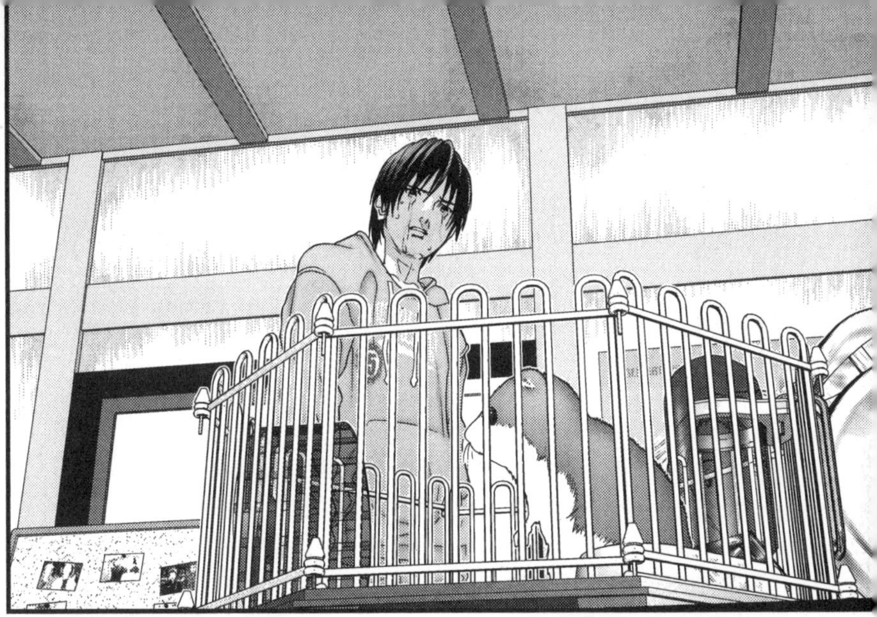
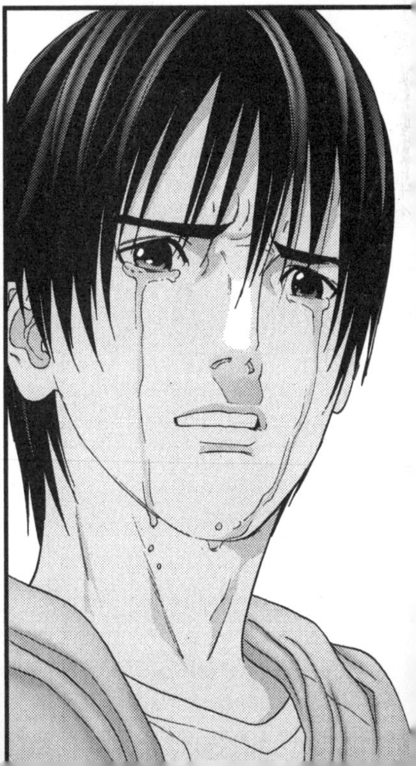
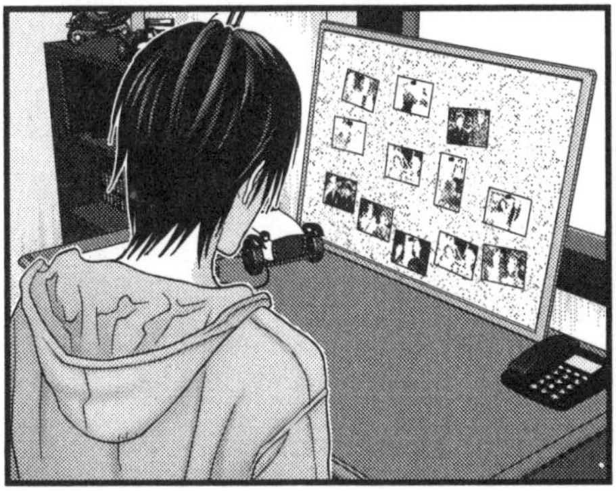
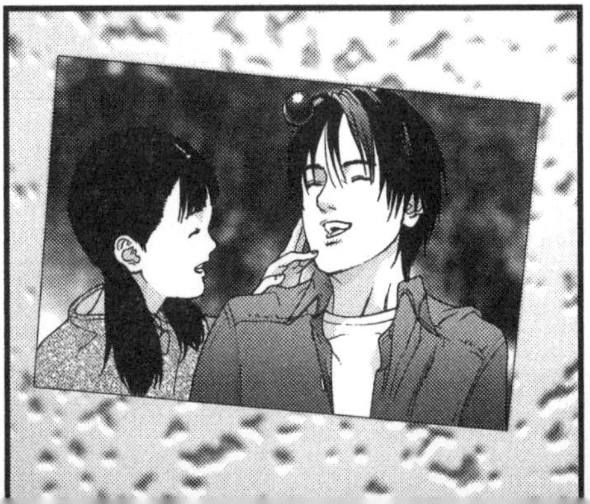

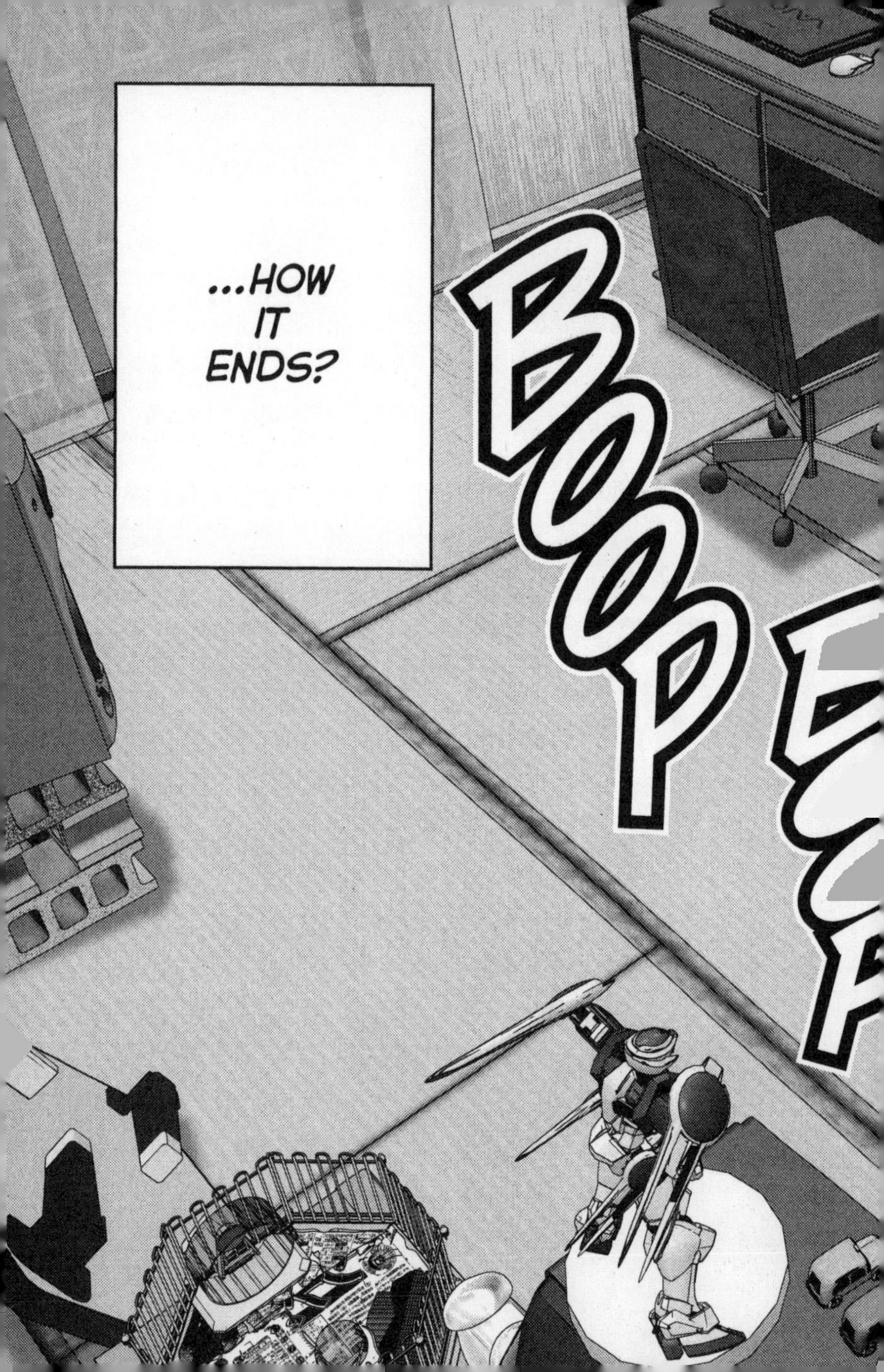
...HOW IT ENDS?
BOOP

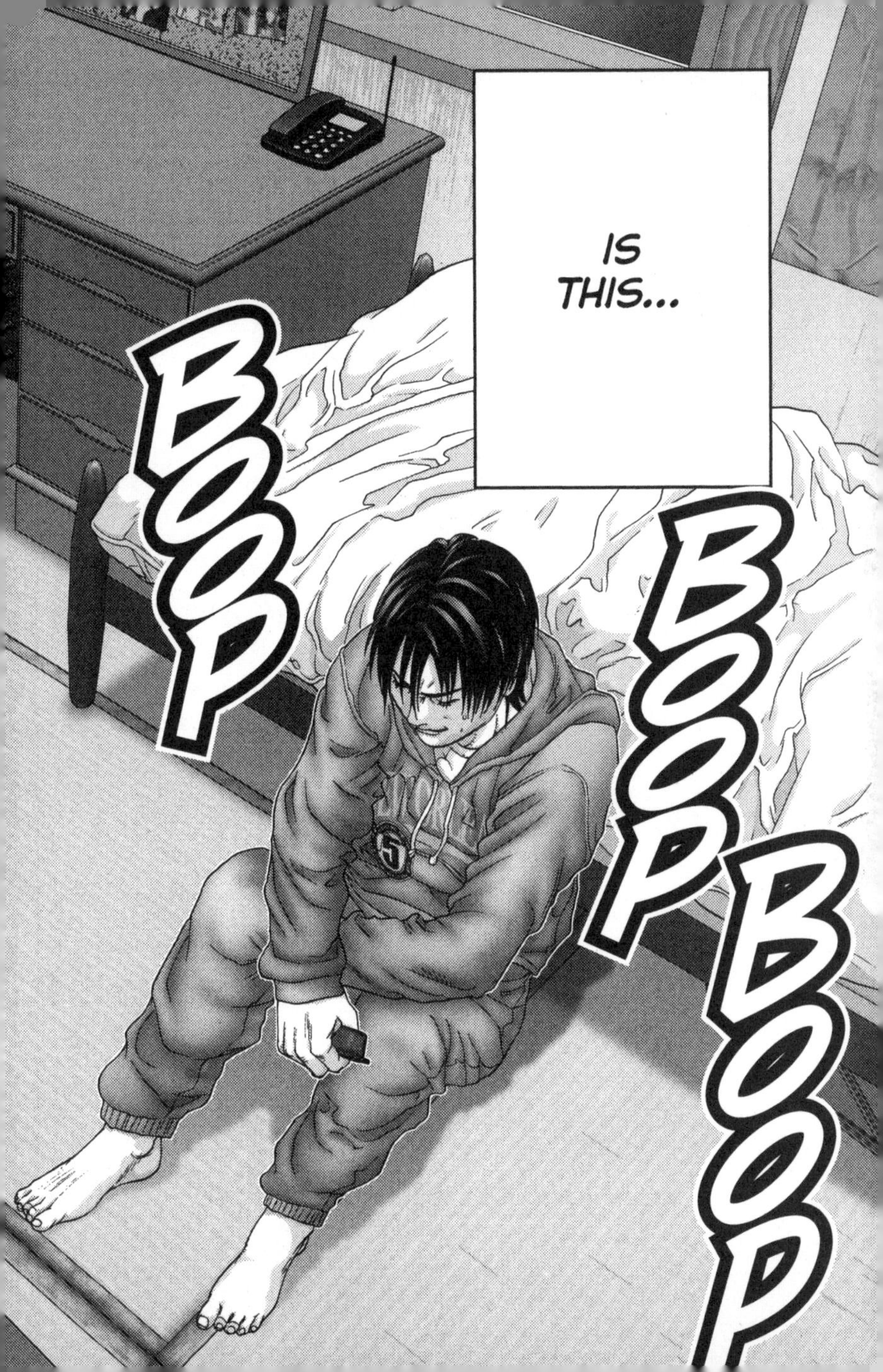
IS THIS...
BOOP
BOOP
BOOP

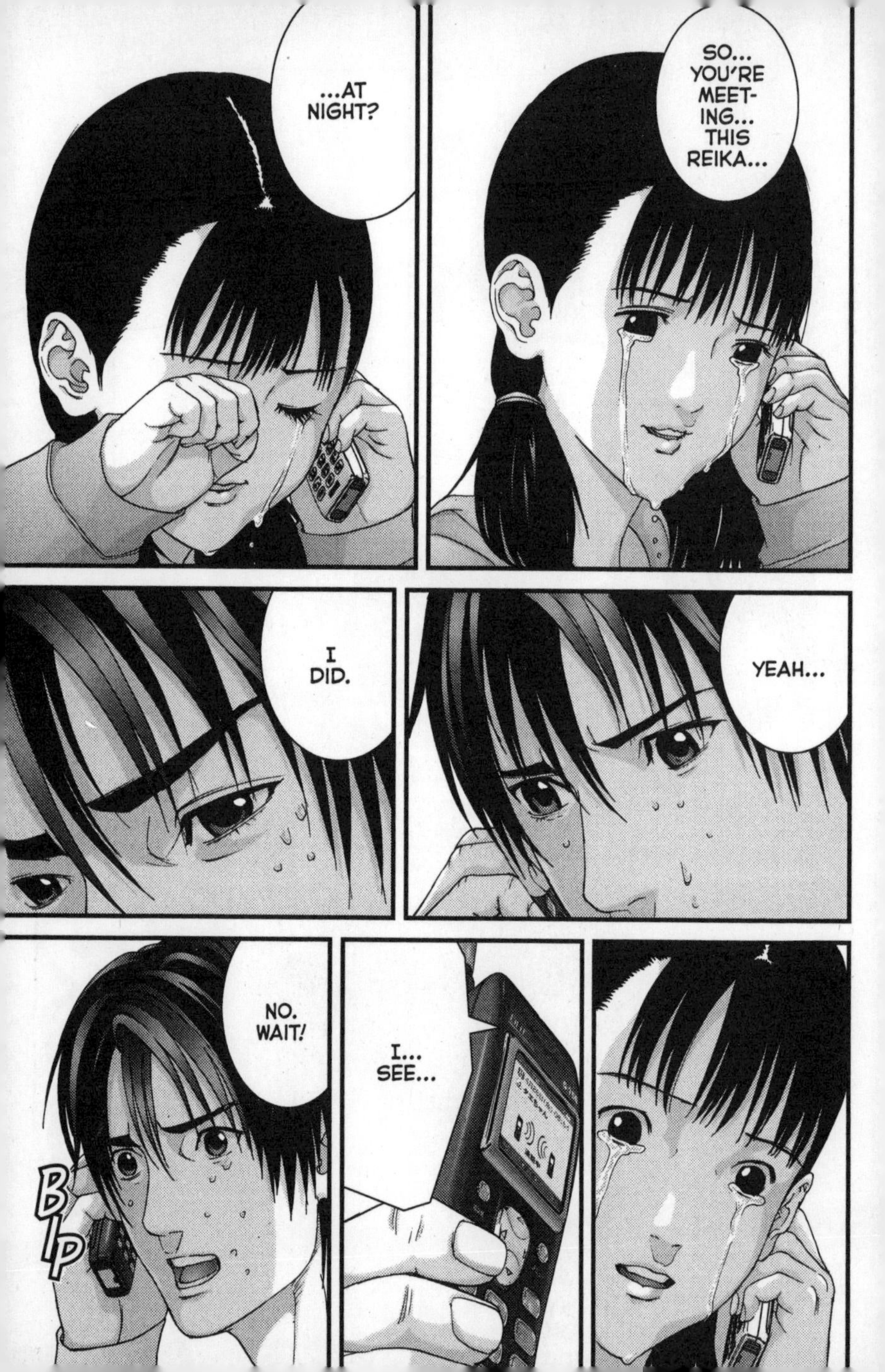
SO... YOU'RE MEETING... THIS REIKA...
...AT NIGHT?
YEAH...
I DID.
I... SEE...
NO. WAIT!
BIP

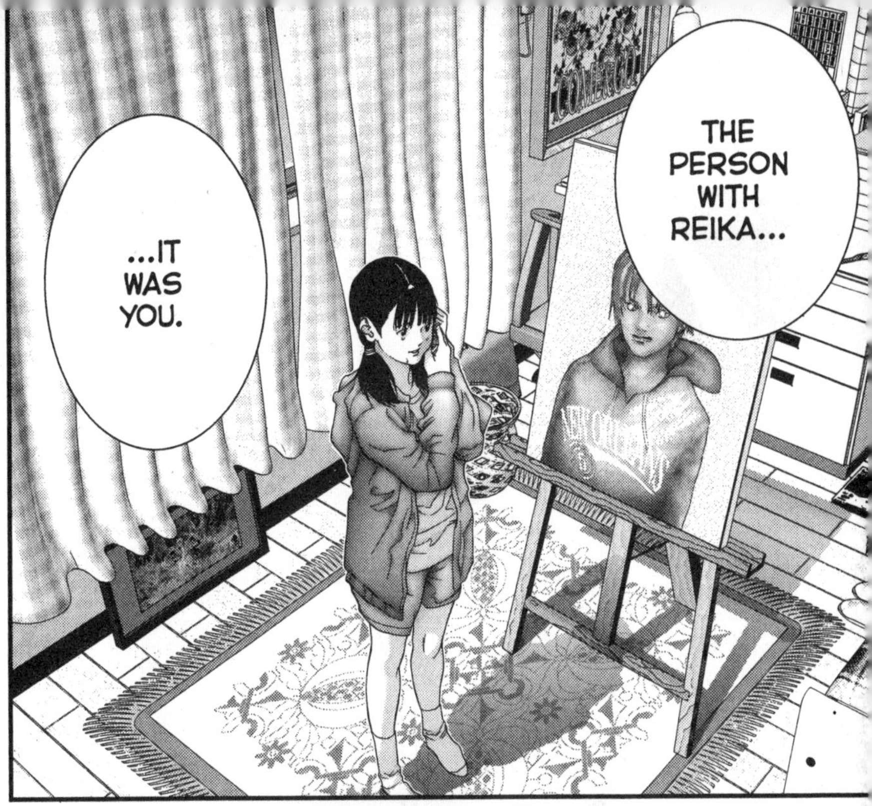
THE PERSON WITH REIKA...
...IT WAS YOU.
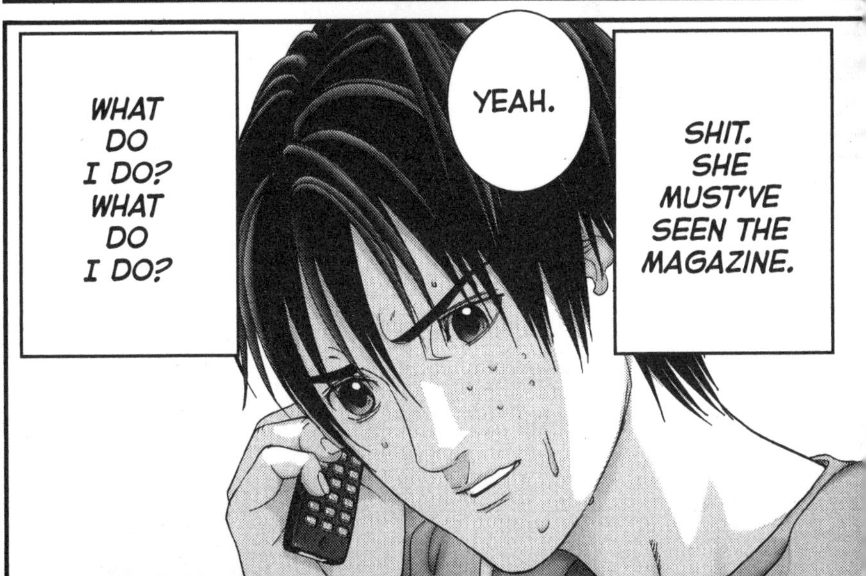
SHIT. SHE MUST'VE SEEN THE MAGAZINE.
YEAH.
WHAT DO I DO? WHAT DO I DO?

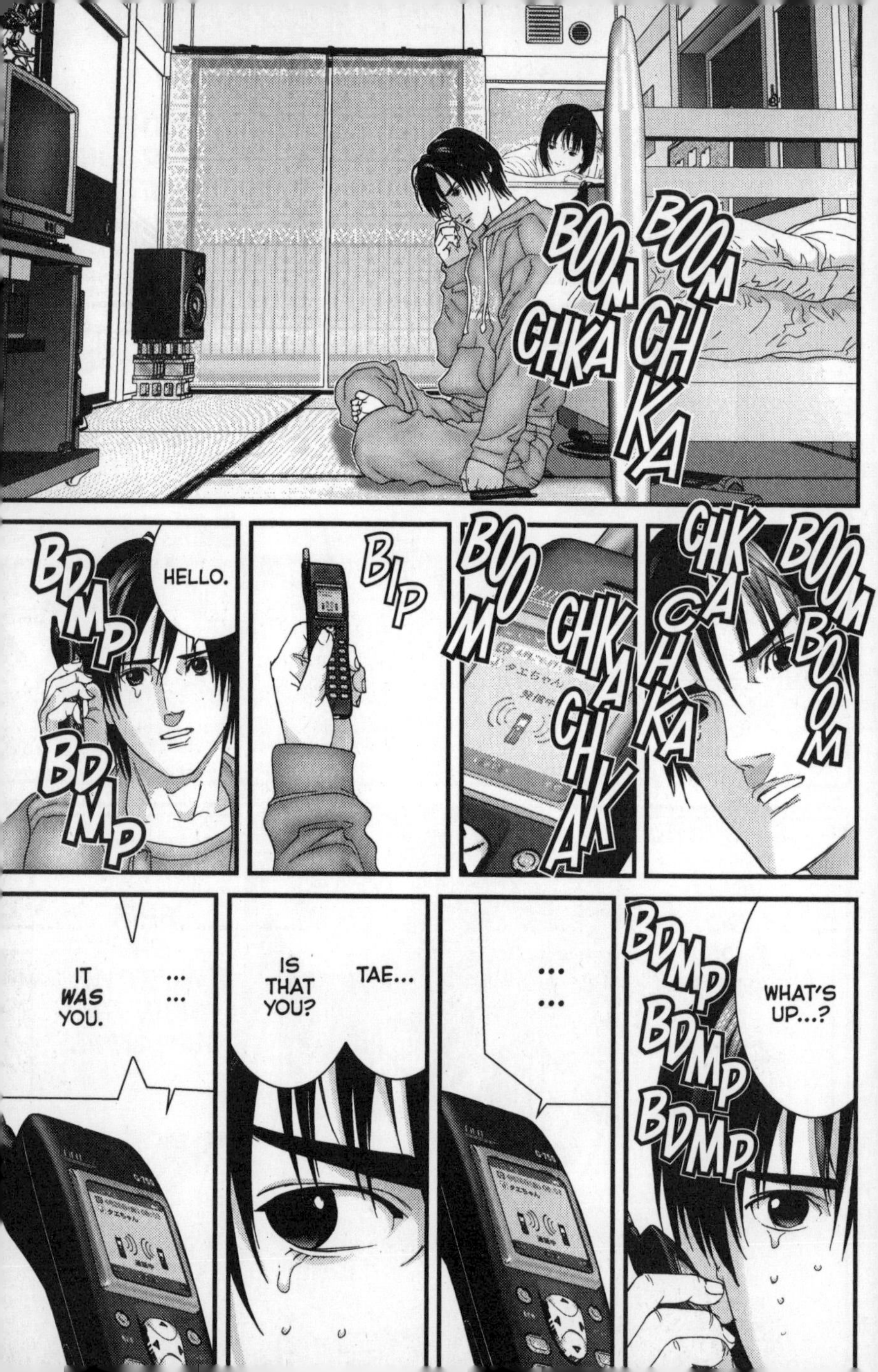
BOOM CHKA
BOOM CHKA
BOOM BOOOM
CHK CA CHKA
CHKA CHKAK
BOOOM
BIP
BDMP
HELLO.
BDMP
BDMP BDMP BDMP
WHAT'S UP...?
......
TAE...
IS THAT YOU?
......
IT WAS YOU.

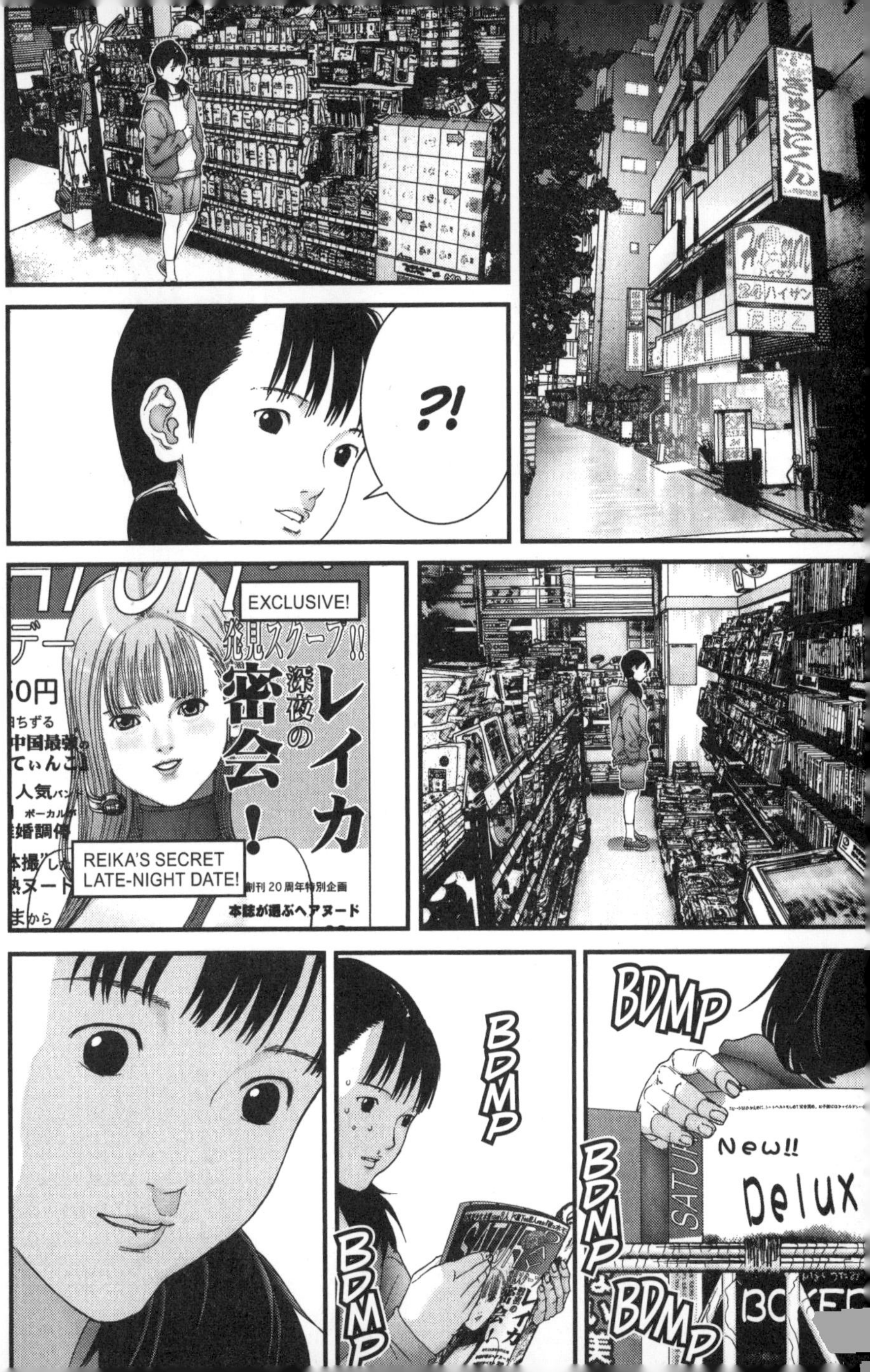
24ハイサン
?!
EXCLUSIVE!
発見スクープ!!
深夜の
レイカ
密会!
REIKA'S SECRET LATE-NIGHT DATE!
創刊20周年特別企画
本誌が選ぶヘアヌード
BDMP
New!!
Delux
BDMP
BDMP
BDMP
BDMP

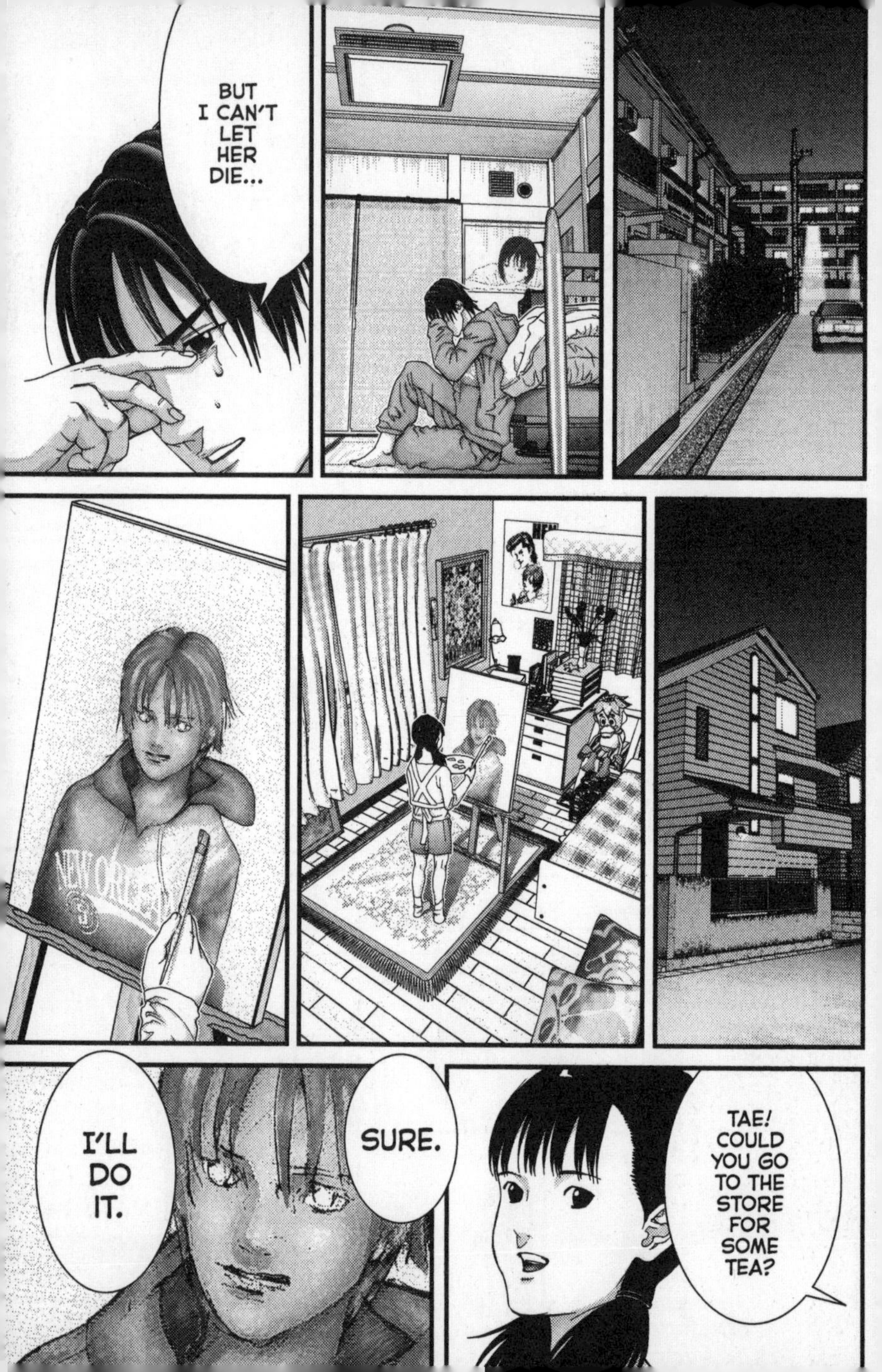
BUT I CAN'T LET HER DIE...
TAE! COULD YOU GO TO THE STORE FOR SOME TEA?
SURE.
I'LL DO IT.

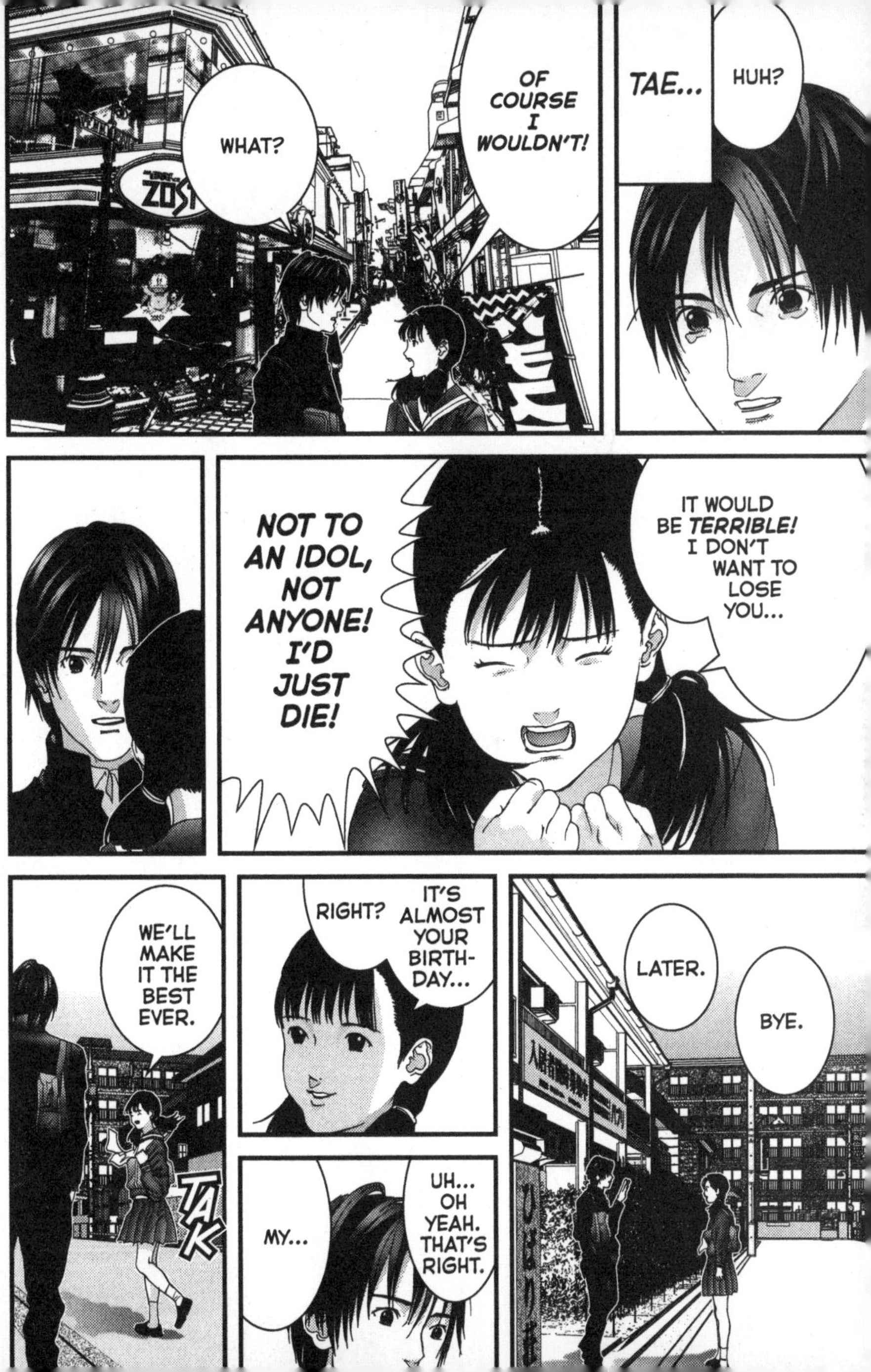
WHAT?
OF COURSE I WOULDN'T!
TAE...
HUH?
NOT TO AN IDOL, NOT ANYONE! I'D JUST DIE!
IT WOULD BE TERRIBLE! I DON'T WANT TO LOSE YOU...
WE'LL MAKE IT THE BEST EVER.
TAK
RIGHT?
IT'S ALMOST YOUR BIRTH-DAY...
MY...
UH... OH YEAH. THAT'S RIGHT.
LATER.
BYE.

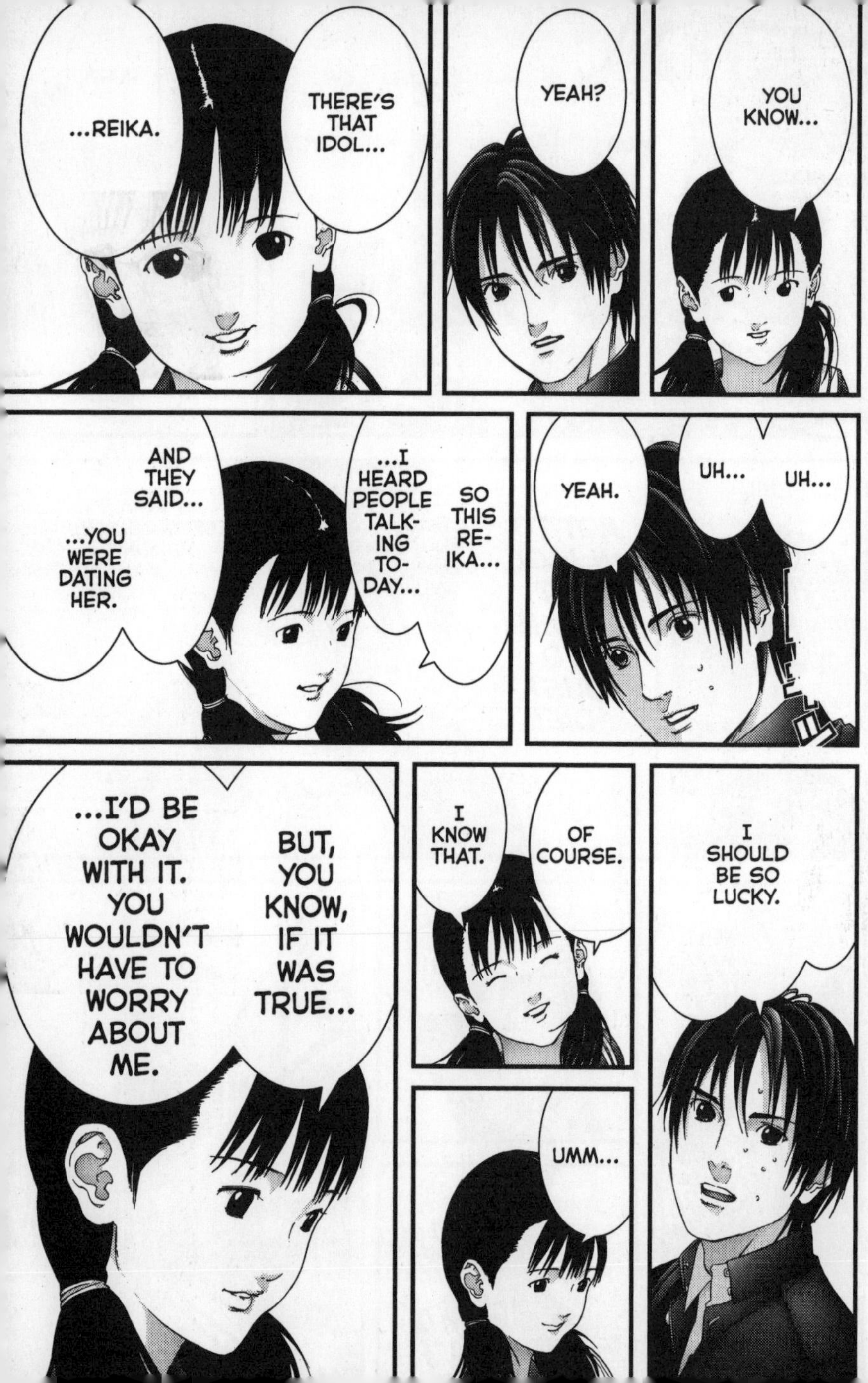
YOU KNOW...
YEAH?
THERE'S THAT IDOL...
...REIKA.
UH... UH...
YEAH.
SO THIS REIKA...
...I HEARD PEOPLE TALKING TODAY...
AND THEY SAID...
...YOU WERE DATING HER.
I SHOULD BE SO LUCKY.
OF COURSE.
I KNOW THAT.
UMM...
BUT, YOU KNOW, IF IT WAS TRUE...
...I'D BE OKAY WITH IT. YOU WOULDN'T HAVE TO WORRY ABOUT ME.

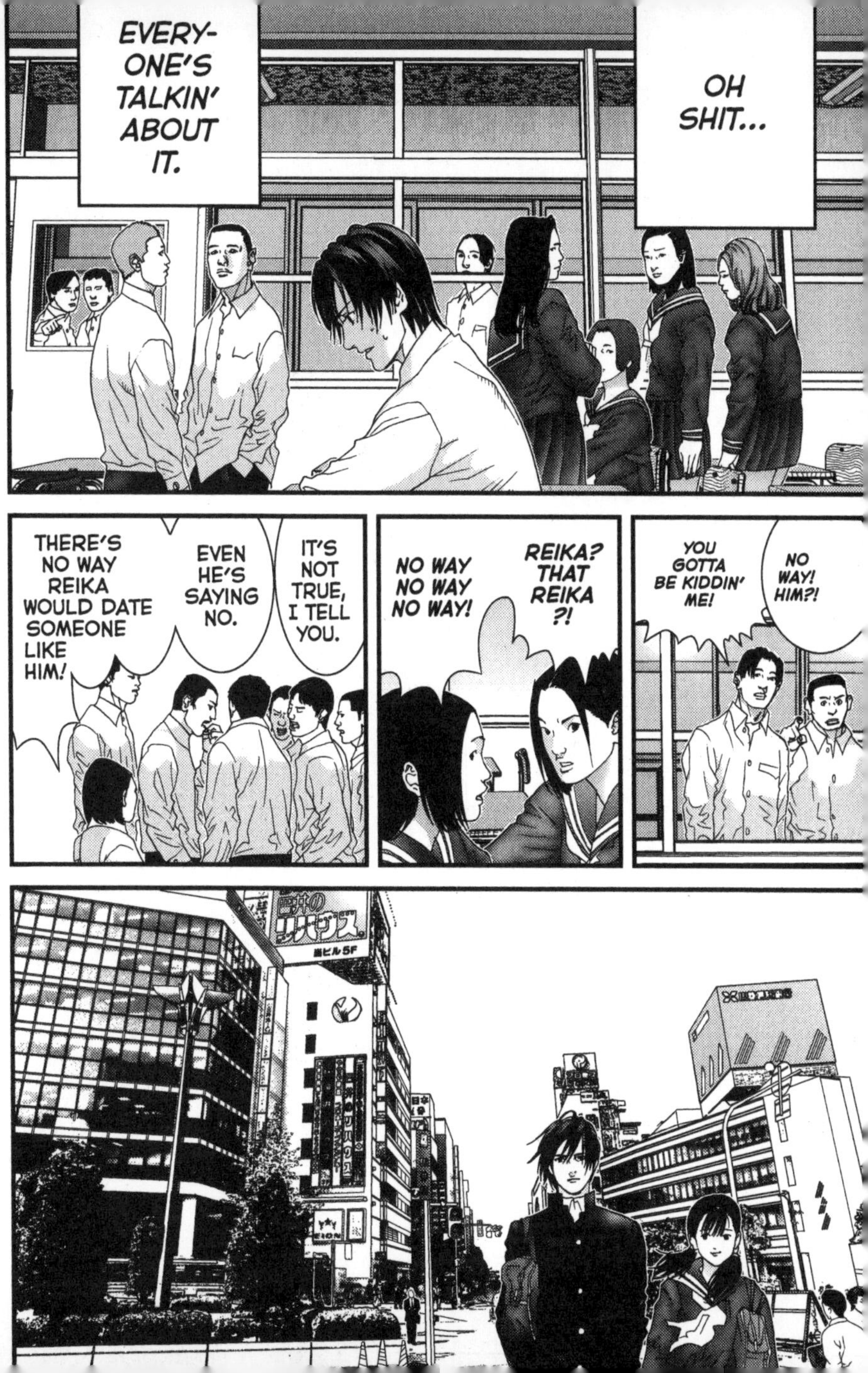
OH SHIT...
EVERY-ONE'S TALKIN' ABOUT IT.
NO WAY! HIM?!
YOU GOTTA BE KIDDIN' ME!
REIKA? THAT REIKA ?!
NO WAY NO WAY NO WAY!
IT'S NOT TRUE, I TELL YOU.
EVEN HE'S SAYING NO.
THERE'S NO WAY REIKA WOULD DATE SOMEONE LIKE HIM!

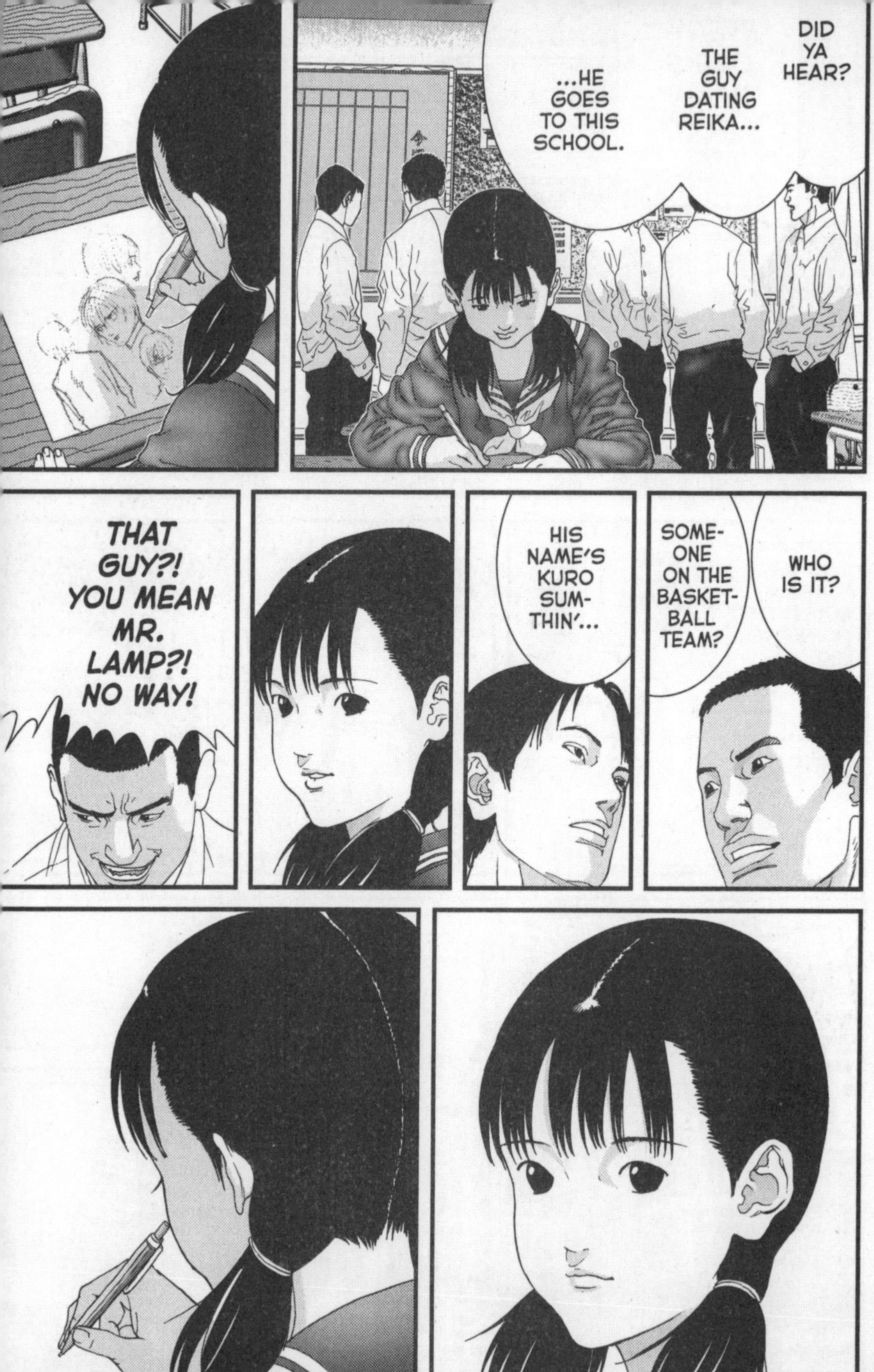
DID YA HEAR?
THE GUY DATING REIKA...
...HE GOES TO THIS SCHOOL.
WHO IS IT?
SOME-ONE ON THE BASKET-BALL TEAM?
HIS NAME'S KURO SUM-THIN'...
THAT GUY?! YOU MEAN MR. LAMP?! NO WAY!

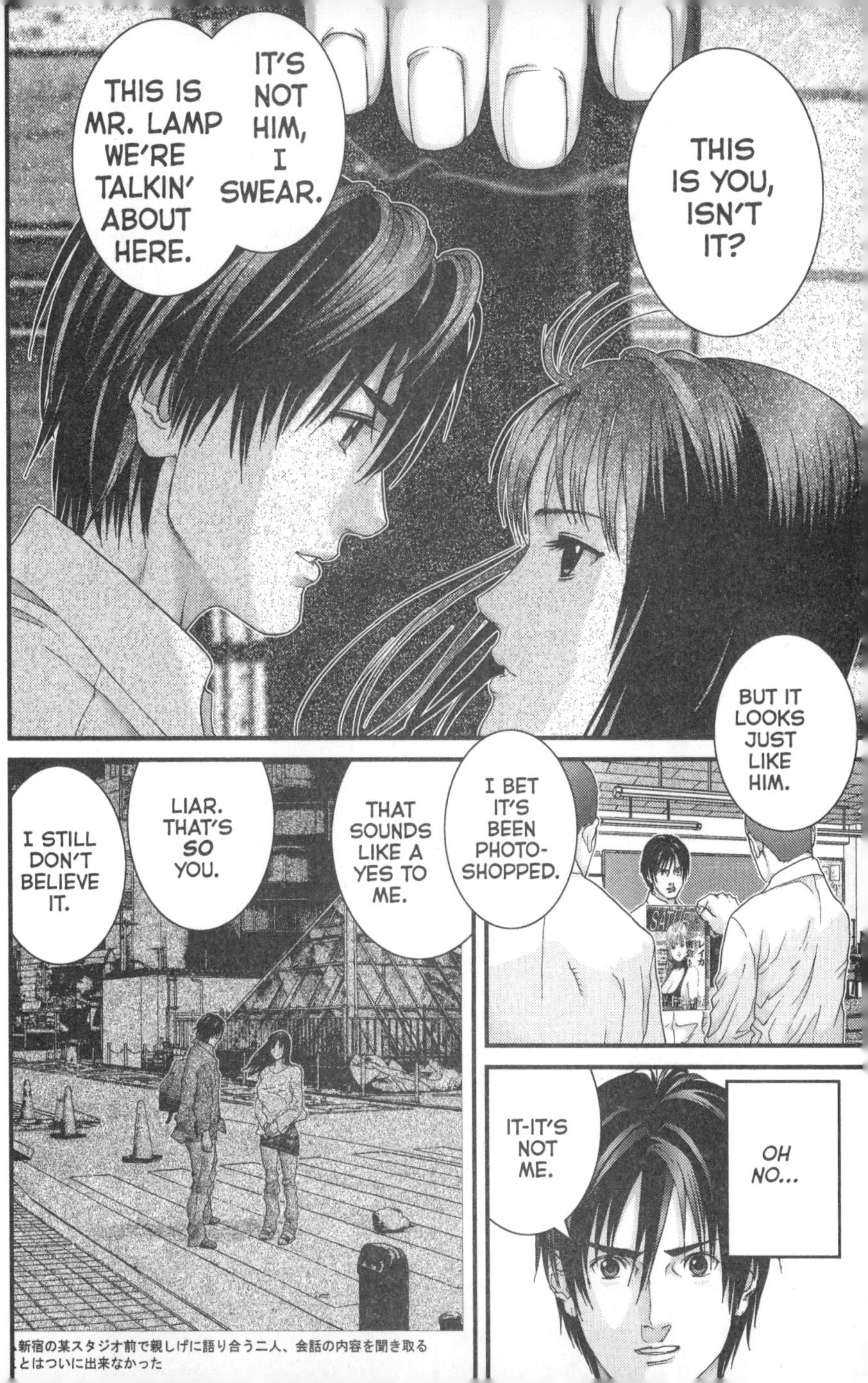
THIS IS YOU, ISN'T IT?
IT'S NOT HIM, I SWEAR.
THIS IS MR. LAMP WE'RE TALKIN' ABOUT HERE.
BUT IT LOOKS JUST LIKE HIM.
I BET IT'S BEEN PHOTO-SHOPPED.
OH NO...
IT-IT'S NOT ME.
THAT SOUNDS LIKE A YES TO ME.
LIAR. THAT'S SO YOU.
I STILL DON'T BELIEVE IT.
新宿の某スタジオ前で親しげに語り合う二人、会話の内容を聞き取る
とはついに出来なかった

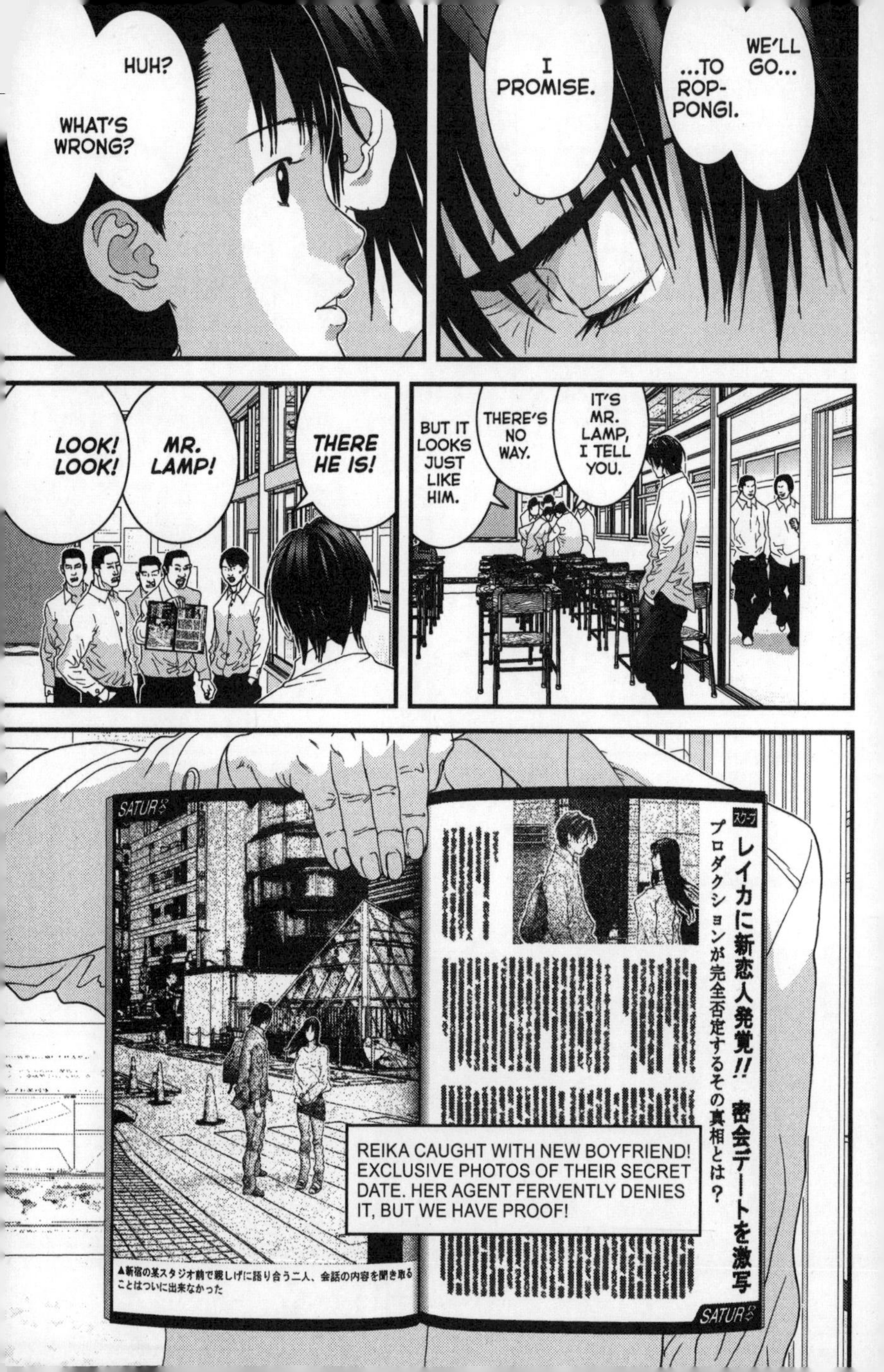
WE'LL GO...
...TO ROP-PONGI.
I PROMISE.
HUH?
WHAT'S WRONG?
IT'S MR. LAMP, I TELL YOU.
THERE'S NO WAY.
BUT IT LOOKS JUST LIKE HIM.
THERE HE IS!
MR. LAMP!
LOOK! LOOK!
スクープ
レイカに新恋人発覚!! 密会デートを激写
プロダクションが完全否定するその真相とは？
REIKA CAUGHT WITH NEW BOYFRIEND! EXCLUSIVE PHOTOS OF THEIR SECRET DATE. HER AGENT FERVENTLY DENIES IT, BUT WE HAVE PROOF!
▲新宿の某スタジオ前で親しげに語り合う二人、会話の内容を聞き取ることはついに出来なかった

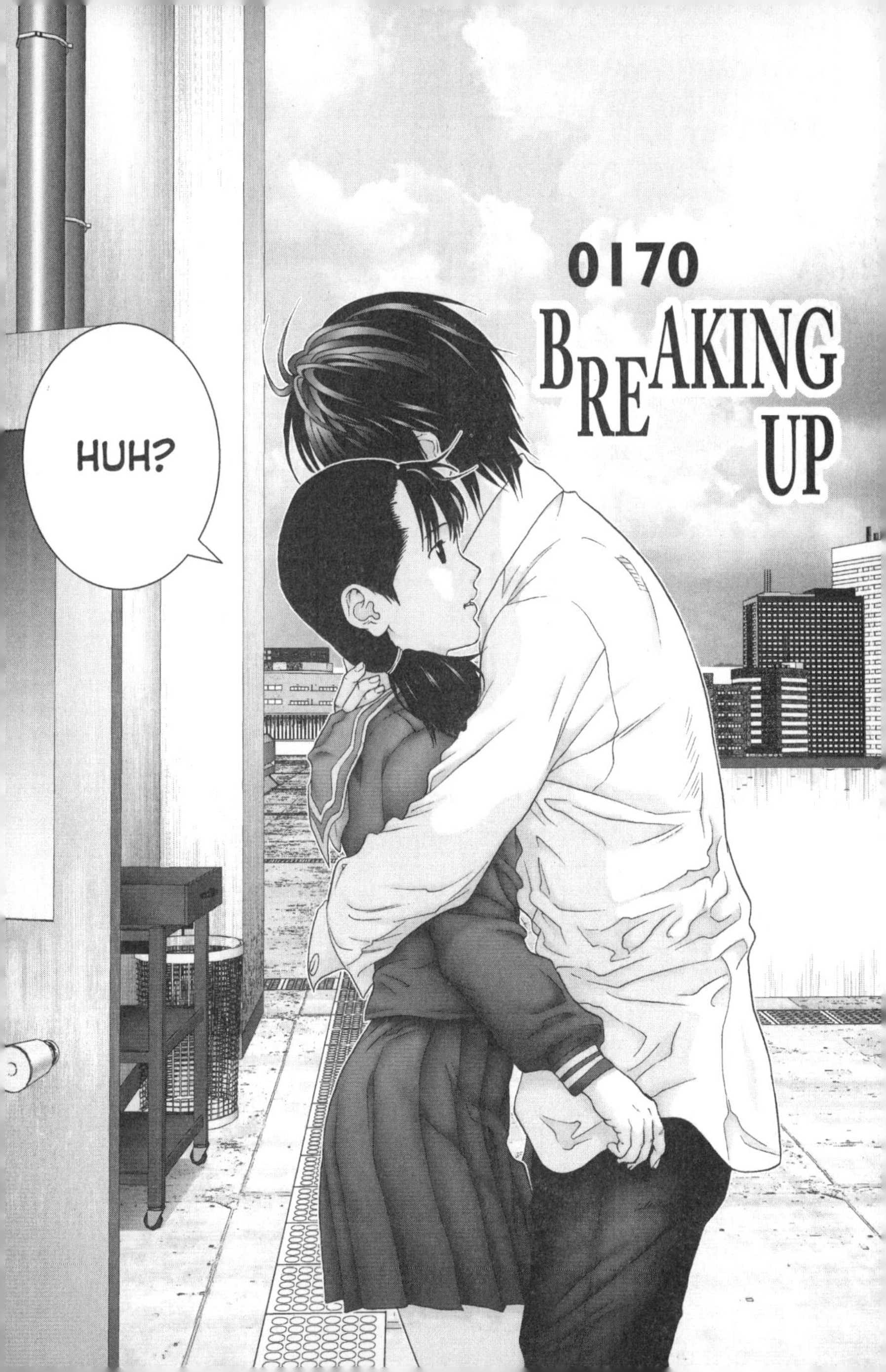
0170
BREAKING UP
HUH?

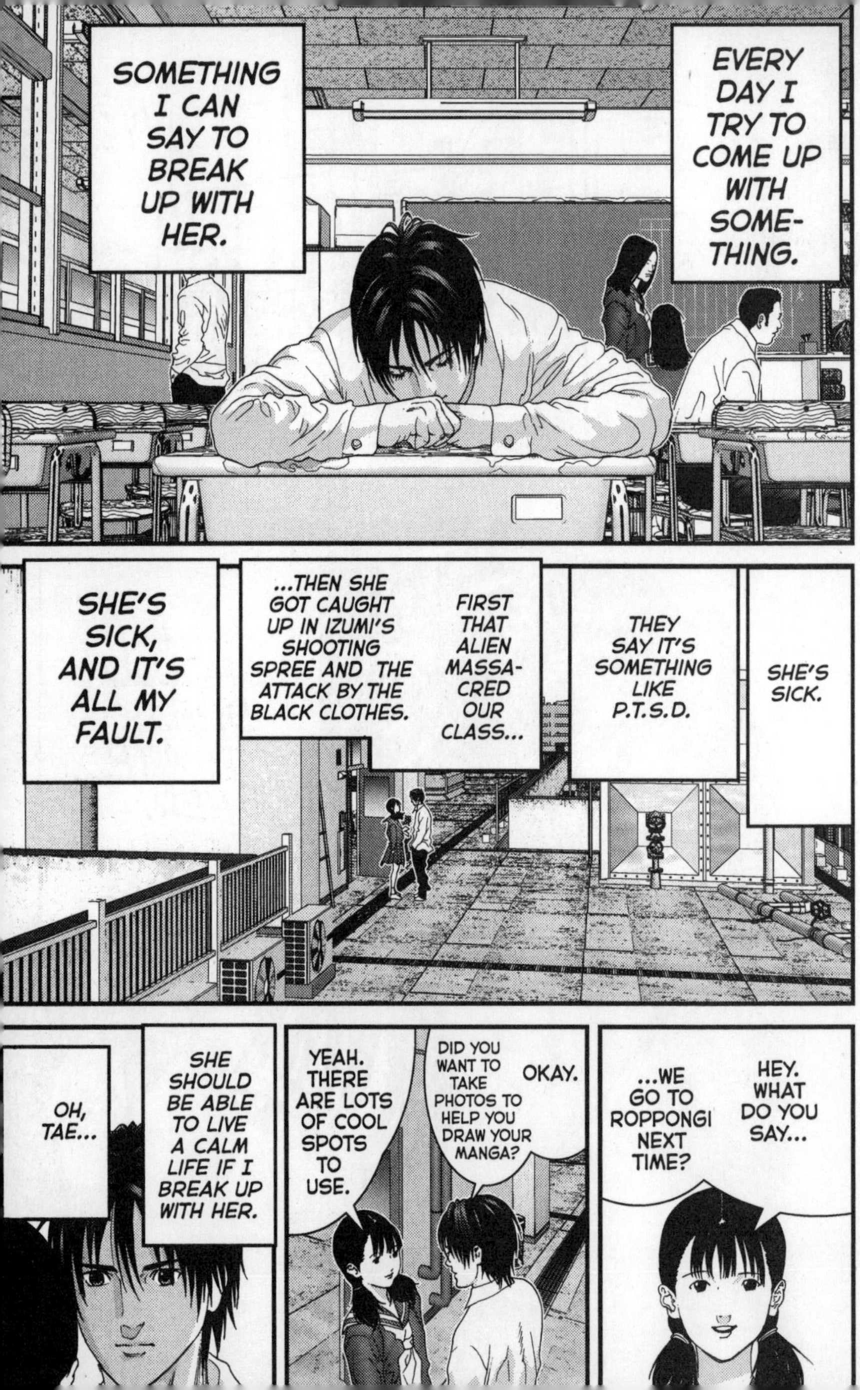
EVERY DAY I TRY TO COME UP WITH SOME-THING.
SOMETHING I CAN SAY TO BREAK UP WITH HER.
SHE'S SICK.
THEY SAY IT'S SOMETHING LIKE P.T.S.D.
FIRST THAT ALIEN MASSA-CRED OUR CLASS...
...THEN SHE GOT CAUGHT UP IN IZUMI'S SHOOTING SPREE AND THE ATTACK BY THE BLACK CLOTHES.
SHE'S SICK, AND IT'S ALL MY FAULT.
HEY. WHAT DO YOU SAY...
...WE GO TO ROPPONGI NEXT TIME?
OKAY.
DID YOU WANT TO TAKE PHOTOS TO HELP YOU DRAW YOUR MANGA?
YEAH. THERE ARE LOTS OF COOL SPOTS TO USE.
SHE SHOULD BE ABLE TO LIVE A CALM LIFE IF I BREAK UP WITH HER.
OH, TAE...

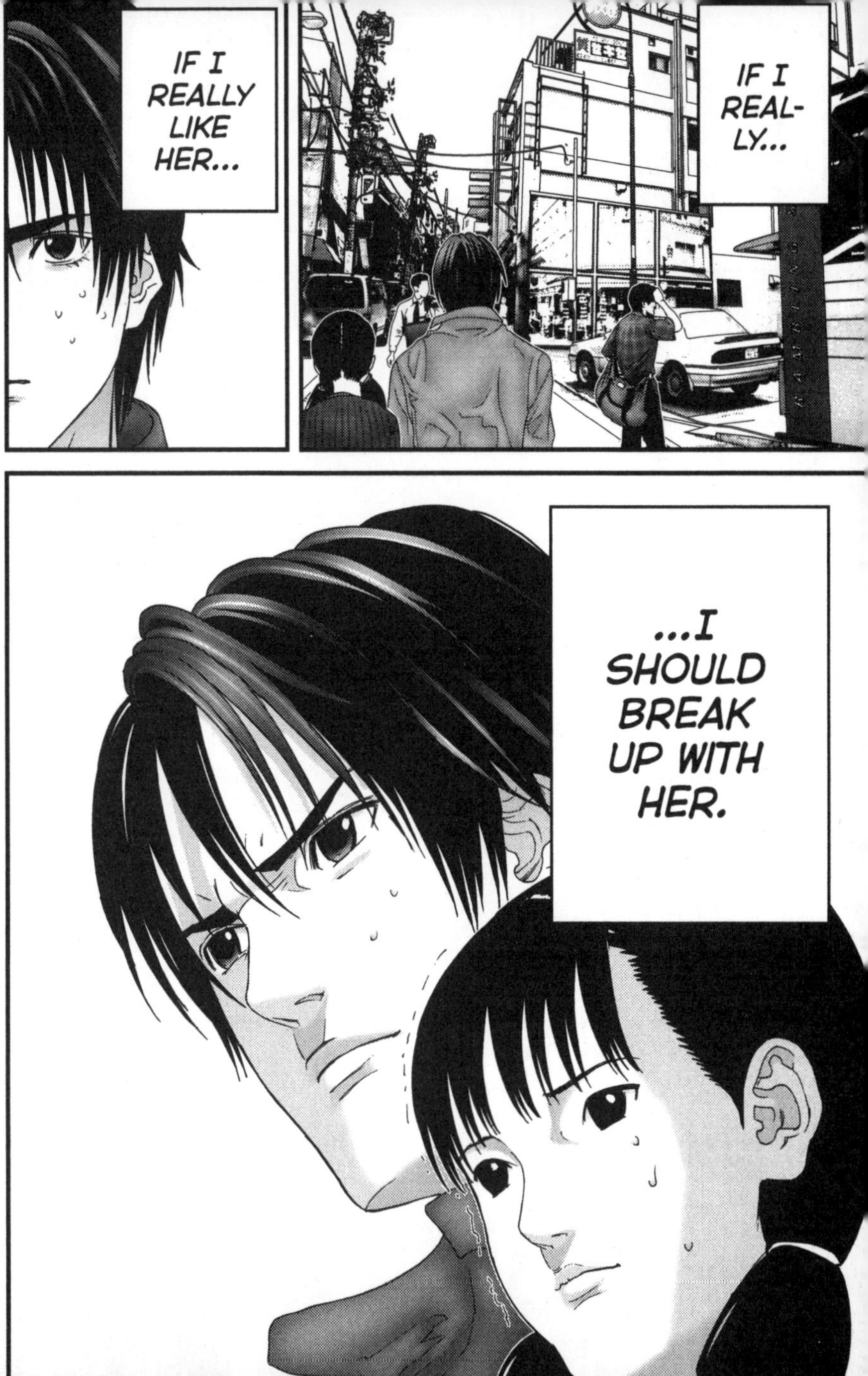
IF I REAL-LY...
IF I REALLY LIKE HER...
...I SHOULD BREAK UP WITH HER.

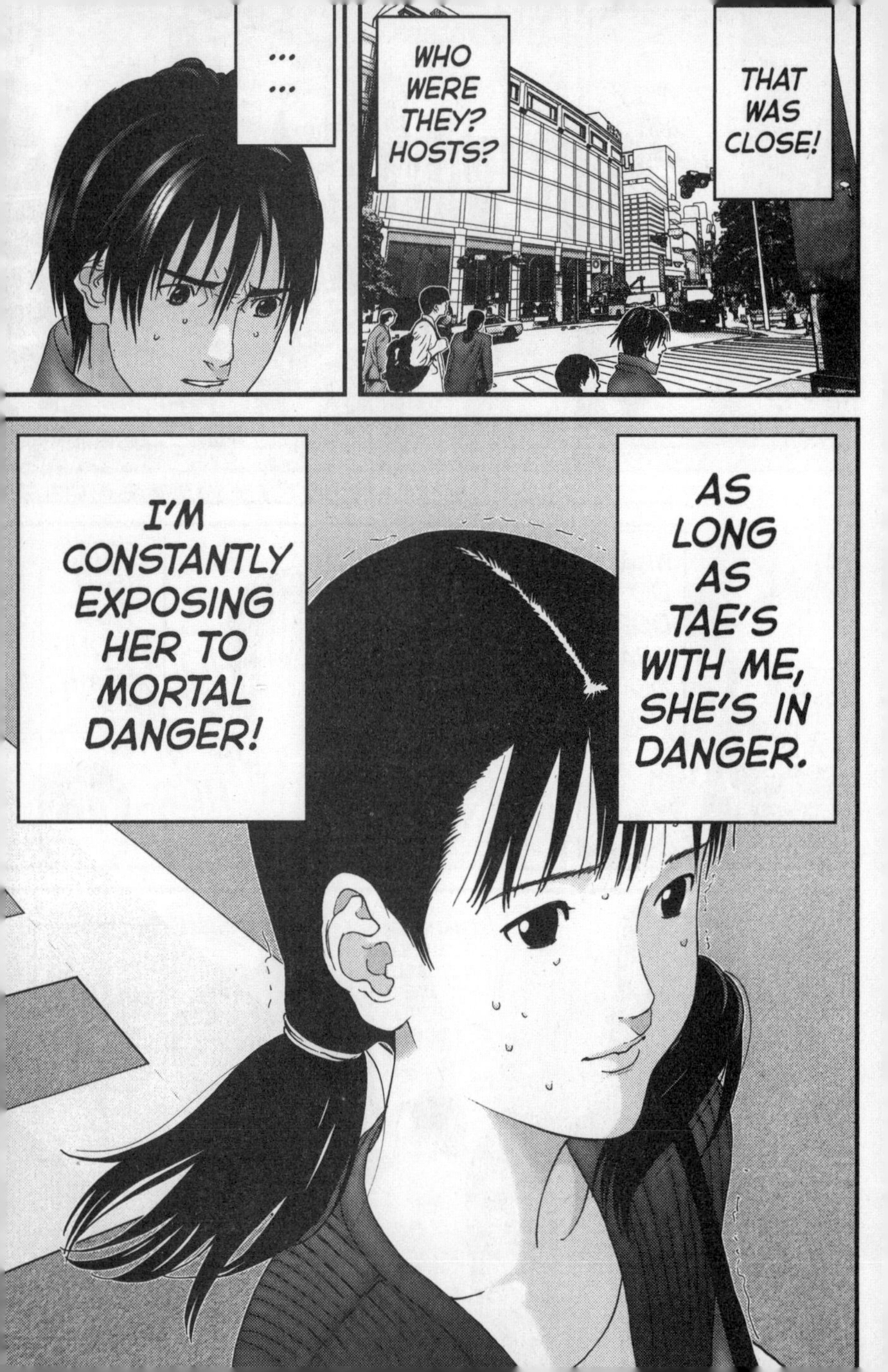
THAT WAS CLOSE!
WHO WERE THEY? HOSTS?
... ...
AS LONG AS TAE'S WITH ME, SHE'S IN DANGER.
I'M CONSTANTLY EXPOSING HER TO MORTAL DANGER!

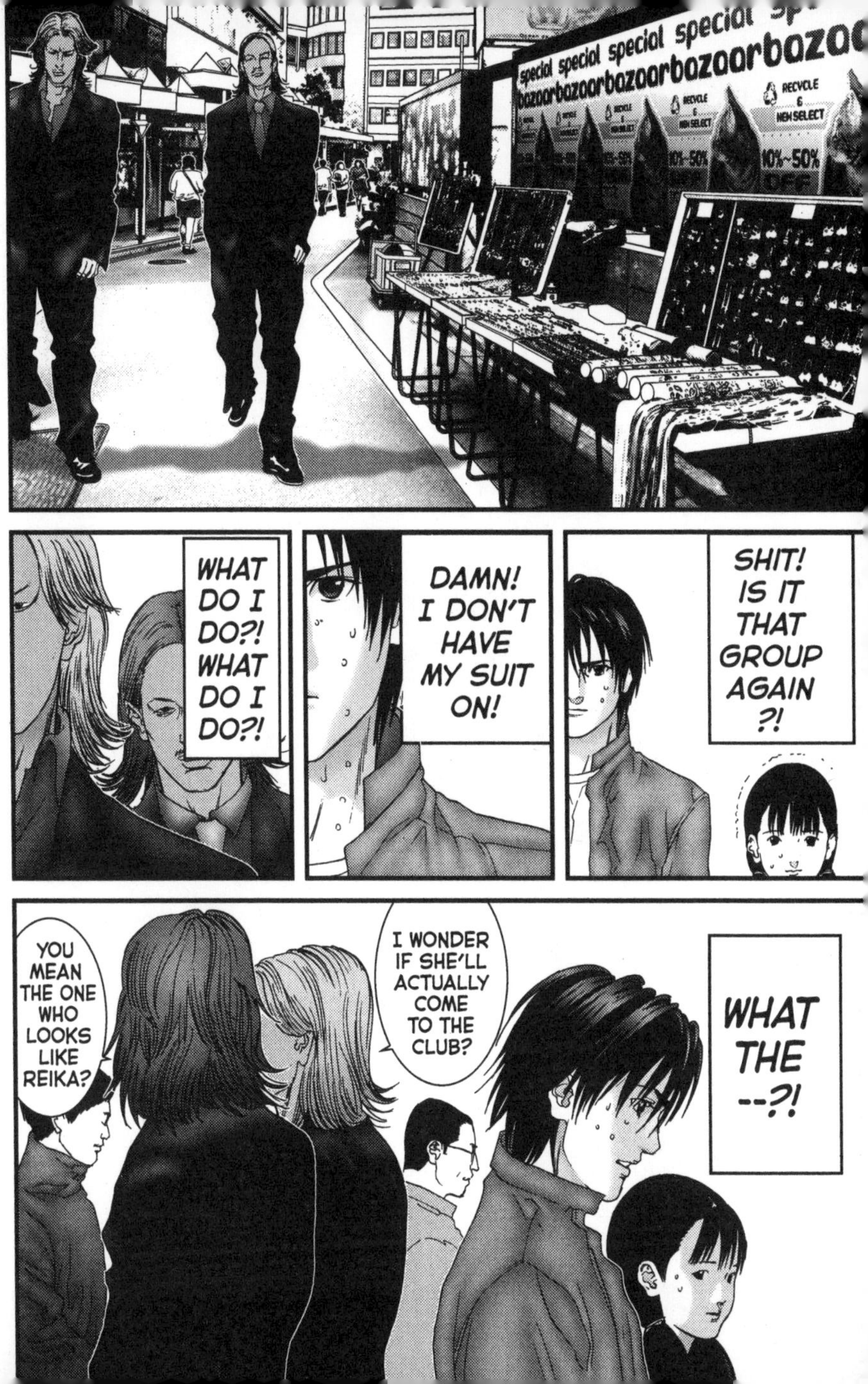
RECYCLE & NEW SELECT
10%~50% OFF
SHIT! IS IT THAT GROUP AGAIN?!
DAMN! I DON'T HAVE MY SUIT ON!
WHAT DO I DO?! WHAT DO I DO?!
WHAT THE --?!
I WONDER IF SHE'LL ACTUALLY COME TO THE CLUB?
YOU MEAN THE ONE WHO LOOKS LIKE REIKA?

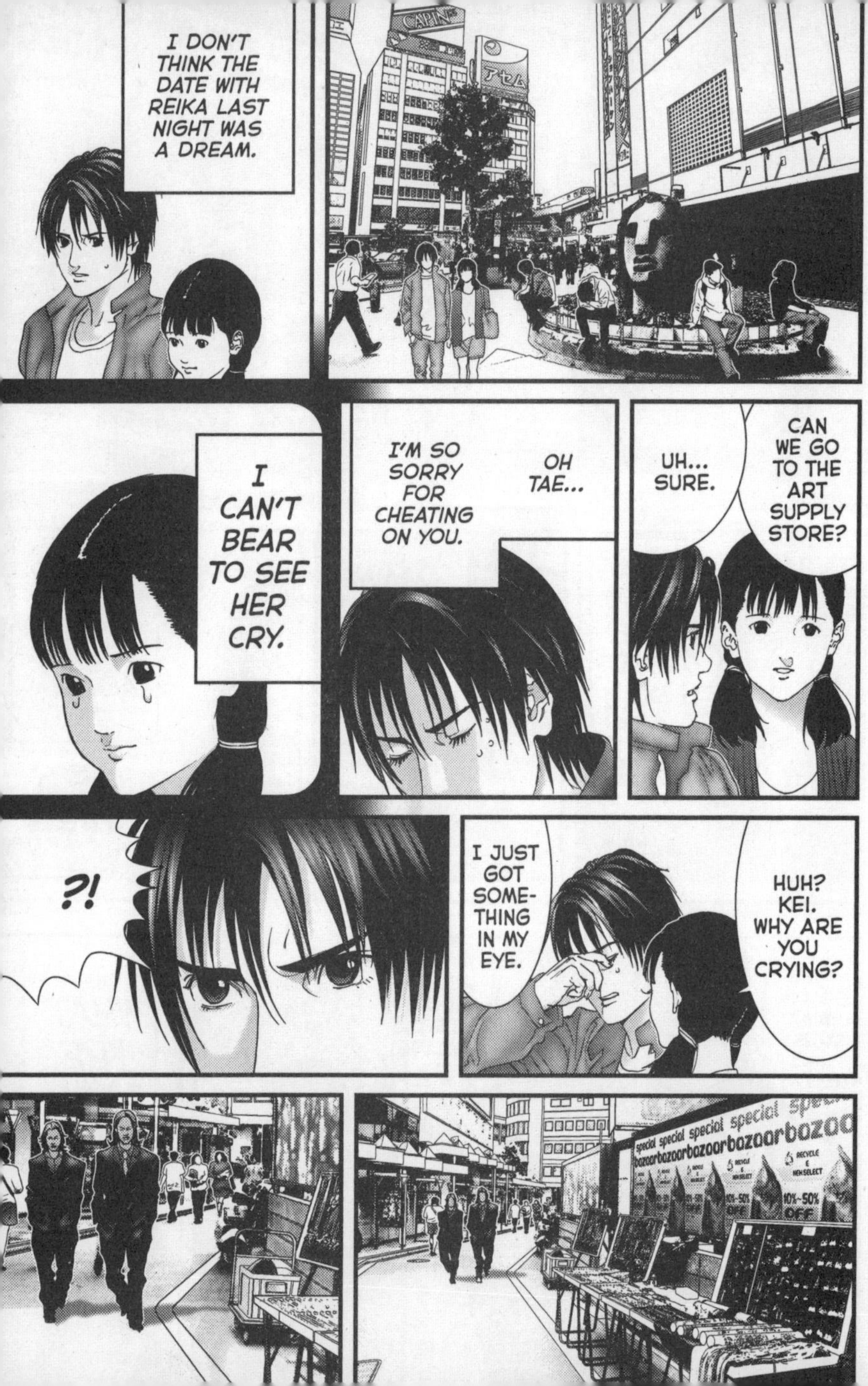
I DON'T THINK THE DATE WITH REIKA LAST NIGHT WAS A DREAM.
CAN WE GO TO THE ART SUPPLY STORE?
UH... SURE.
OH TAE...
I'M SO SORRY FOR CHEATING ON YOU.
I CAN'T BEAR TO SEE HER CRY.
HUH? KEI. WHY ARE YOU CRYING?
I JUST GOT SOME-THING IN MY EYE.
?!
special special special
RECYCLE & NEW SELECT
10%-50% OFF
10%-50% OFF

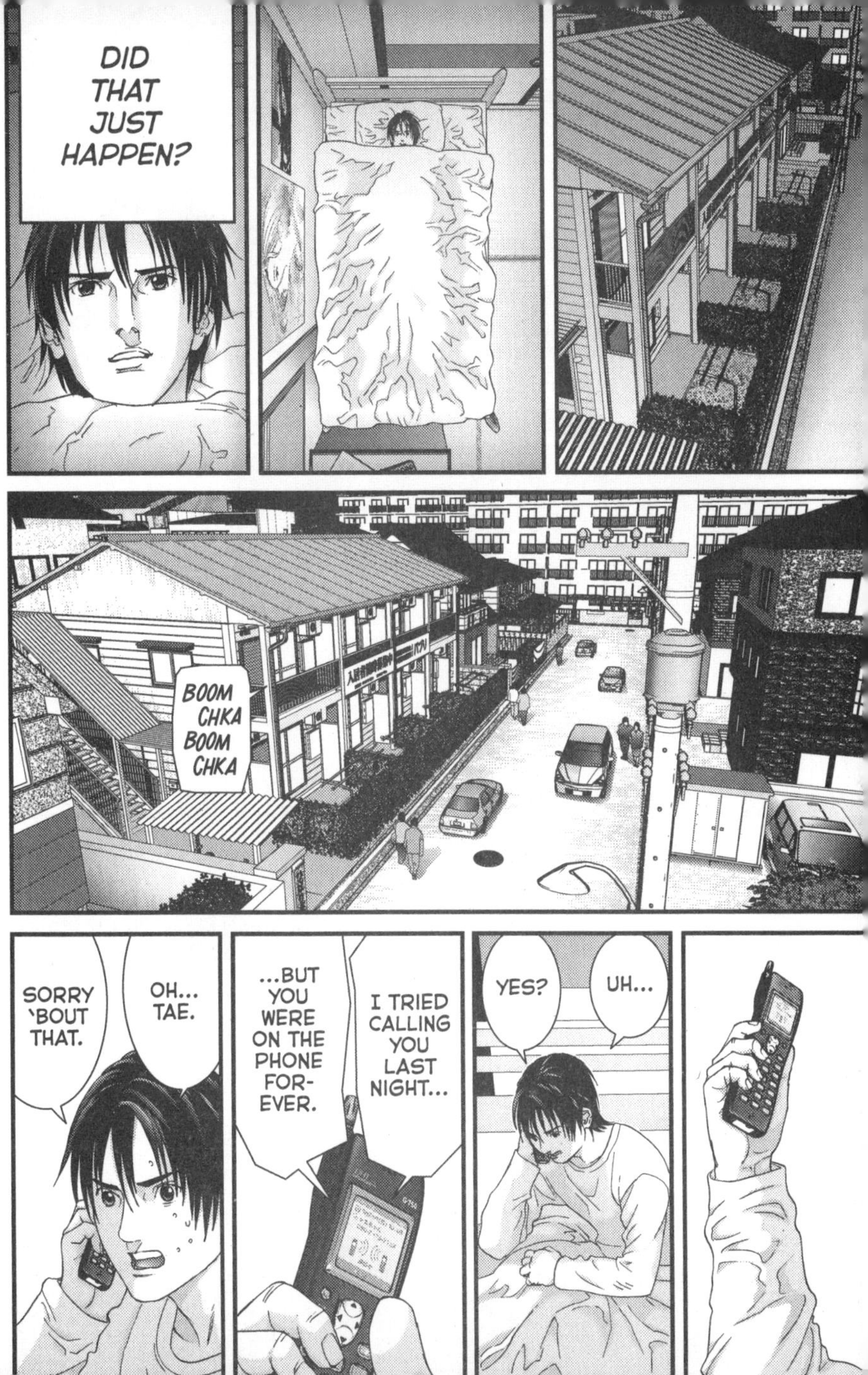
DID THAT JUST HAPPEN?
BOOM CHKA BOOM CHKA
UH...
YES?
I TRIED CALLING YOU LAST NIGHT...
...BUT YOU WERE ON THE PHONE FOR-EVER.
OH... TAE.
SORRY 'BOUT THAT.

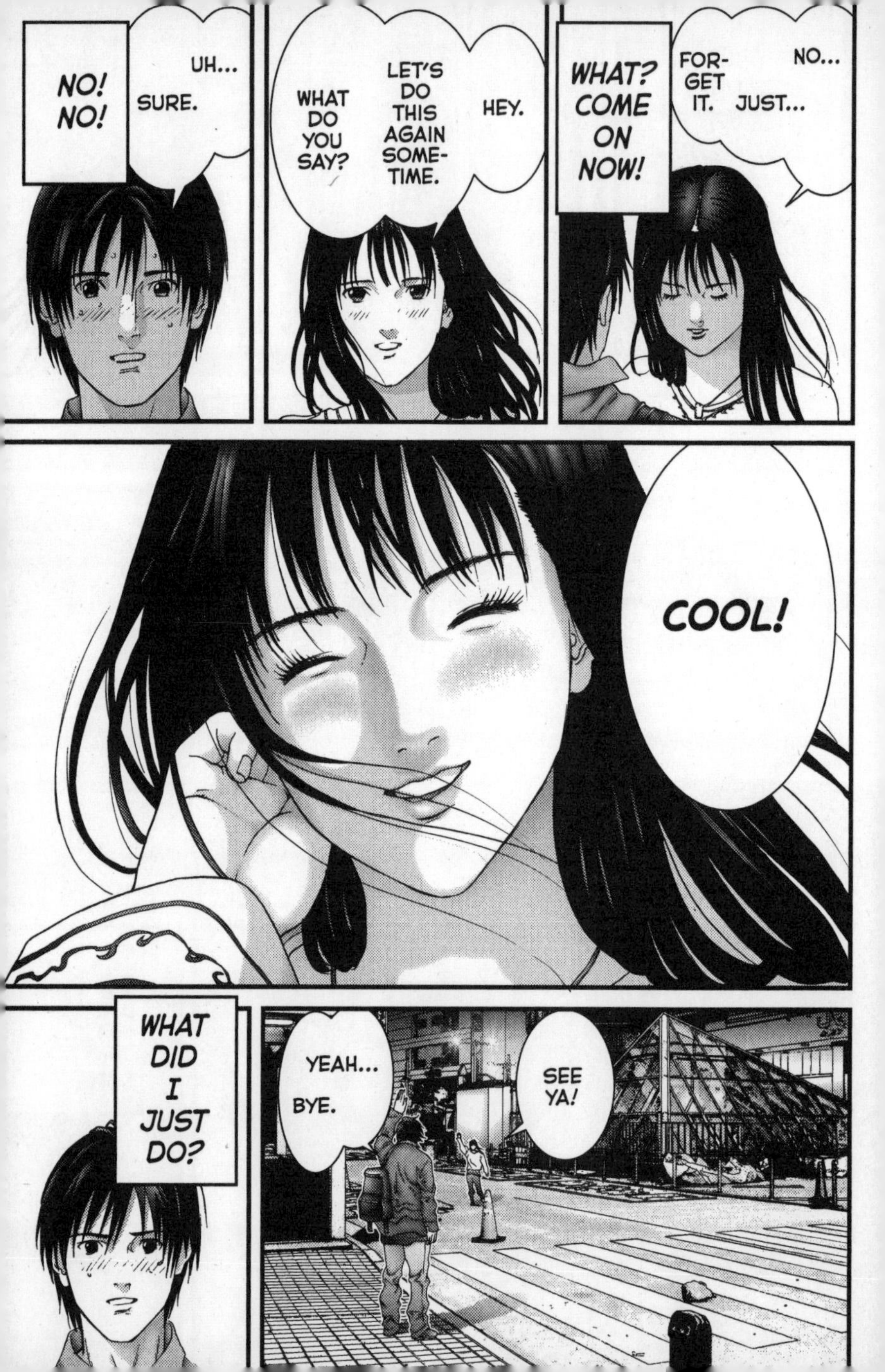
NO... JUST...
FOR-GET IT.
WHAT? COME ON NOW!
HEY.
LET'S DO THIS AGAIN SOME-TIME.
WHAT DO YOU SAY?
UH...
SURE.
NO! NO!
COOL!
SEE YA!
YEAH...
BYE.
WHAT DID I JUST DO?

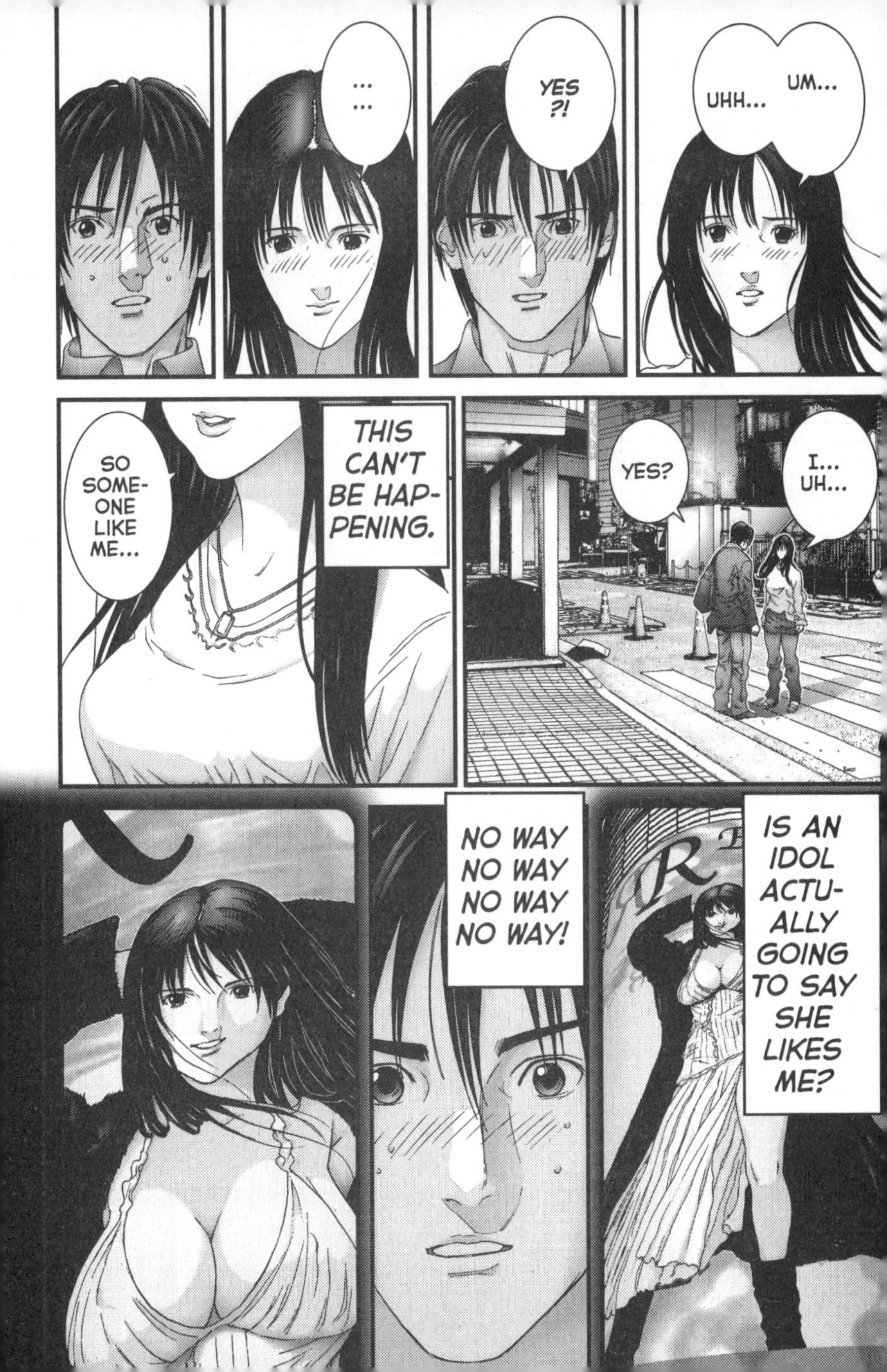
UHH... UM...
YES ?!
... ...
I... UH...
YES?
THIS CAN'T BE HAPPENING.
SO SOMEONE LIKE ME...
IS AN IDOL ACTUALLY GOING TO SAY SHE LIKES ME?
NO WAY NO WAY NO WAY NO WAY!

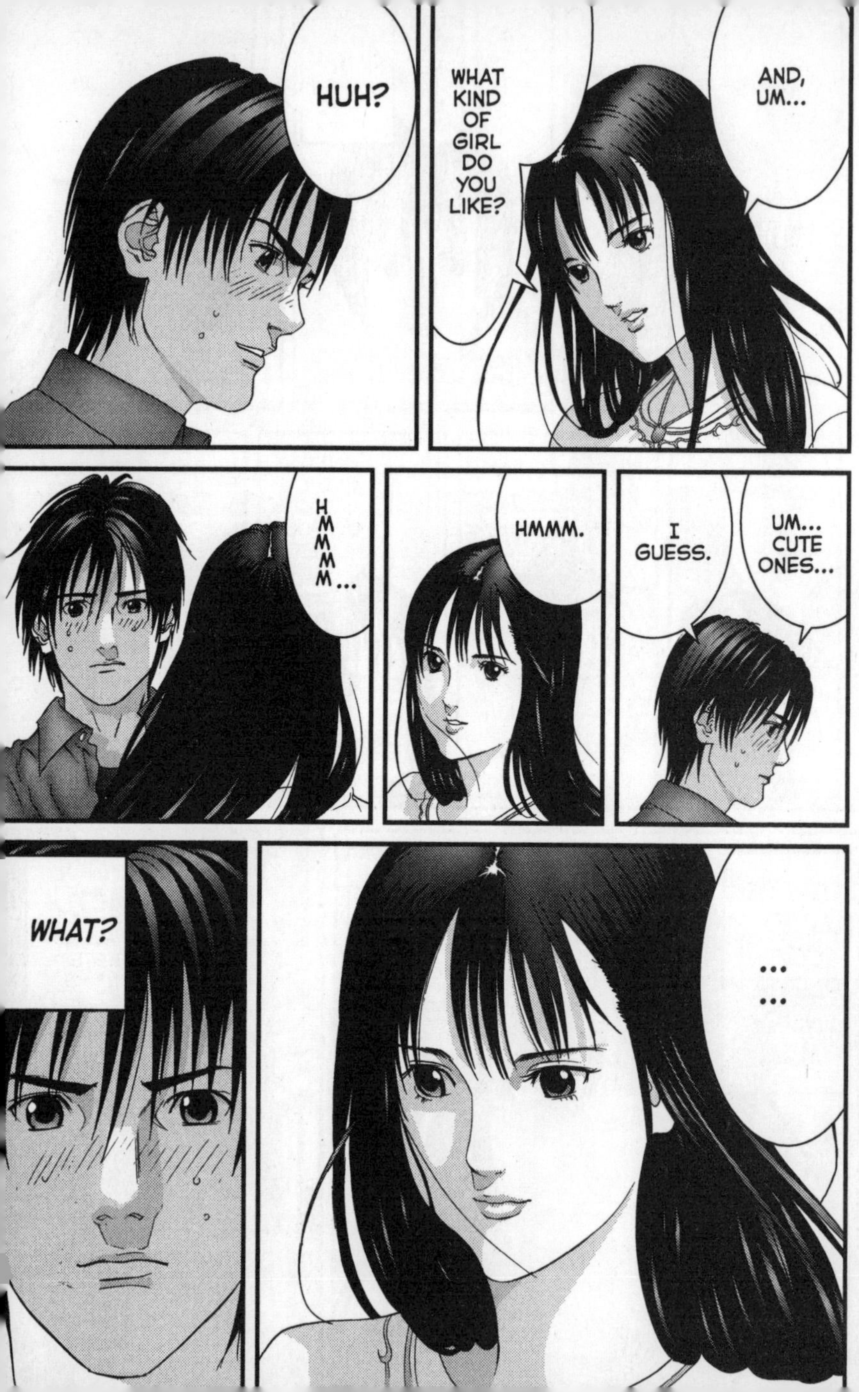
AND, UM...
WHAT KIND OF GIRL DO YOU LIKE?
HUH?
UM... CUTE ONES...
I GUESS.
HMMM.
HMMMM...
...
...
WHAT?

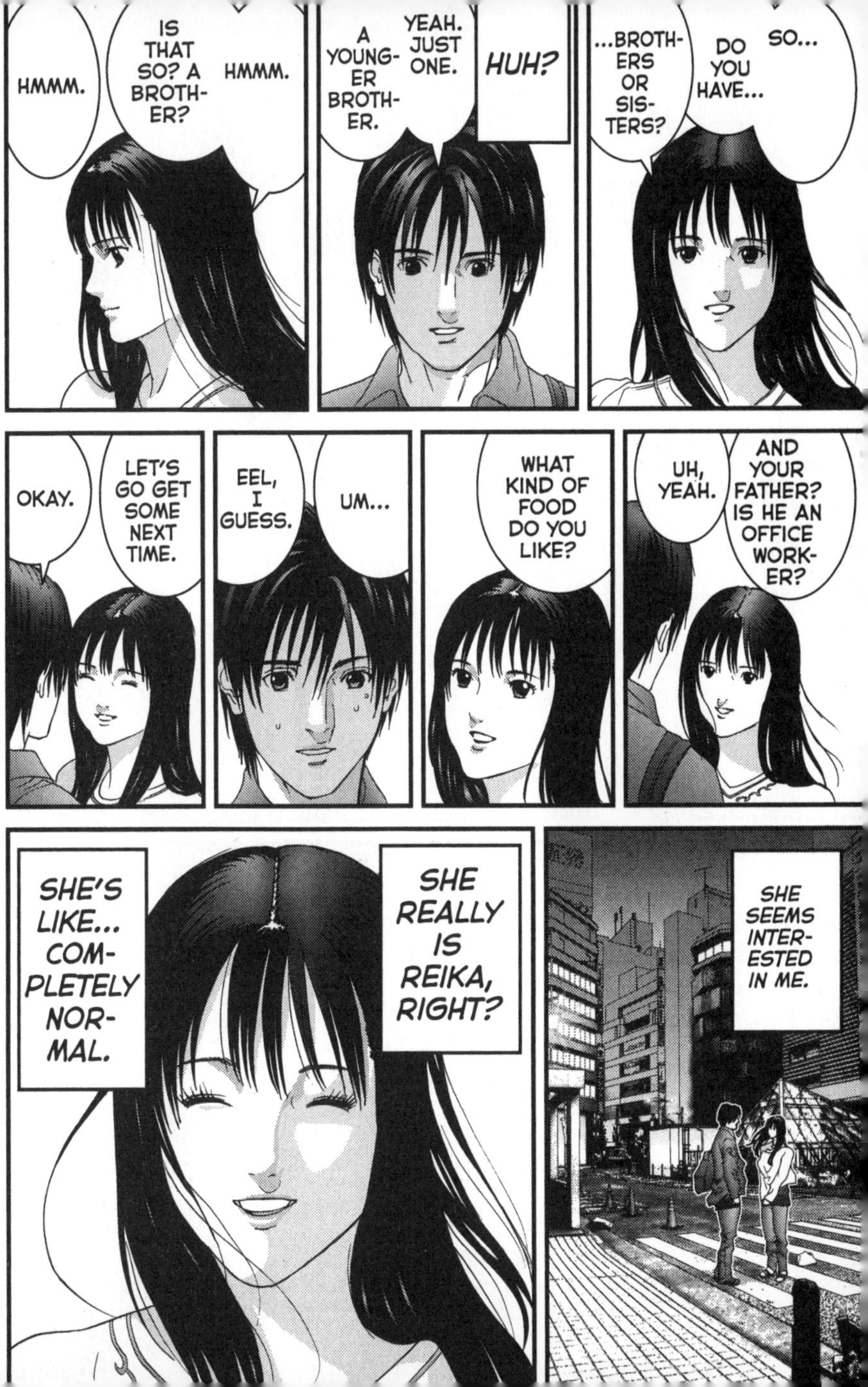
SO...
DO YOU HAVE...
...BROTH-ERS OR SIS-TERS?
HUH?
YEAH. JUST ONE.
A YOUNG-ER BROTH-ER.
HMMM.
IS THAT SO? A BROTH-ER?
HMMM.
AND YOUR FATHER? IS HE AN OFFICE WORK-ER?
UH, YEAH.
WHAT KIND OF FOOD DO YOU LIKE?
UM...
EEL, I GUESS.
LET'S GO GET SOME NEXT TIME.
OKAY.
SHE SEEMS INTER-ESTED IN ME.
SHE REALLY IS REIKA, RIGHT?
SHE'S LIKE... COM-PLETELY NOR-MAL.

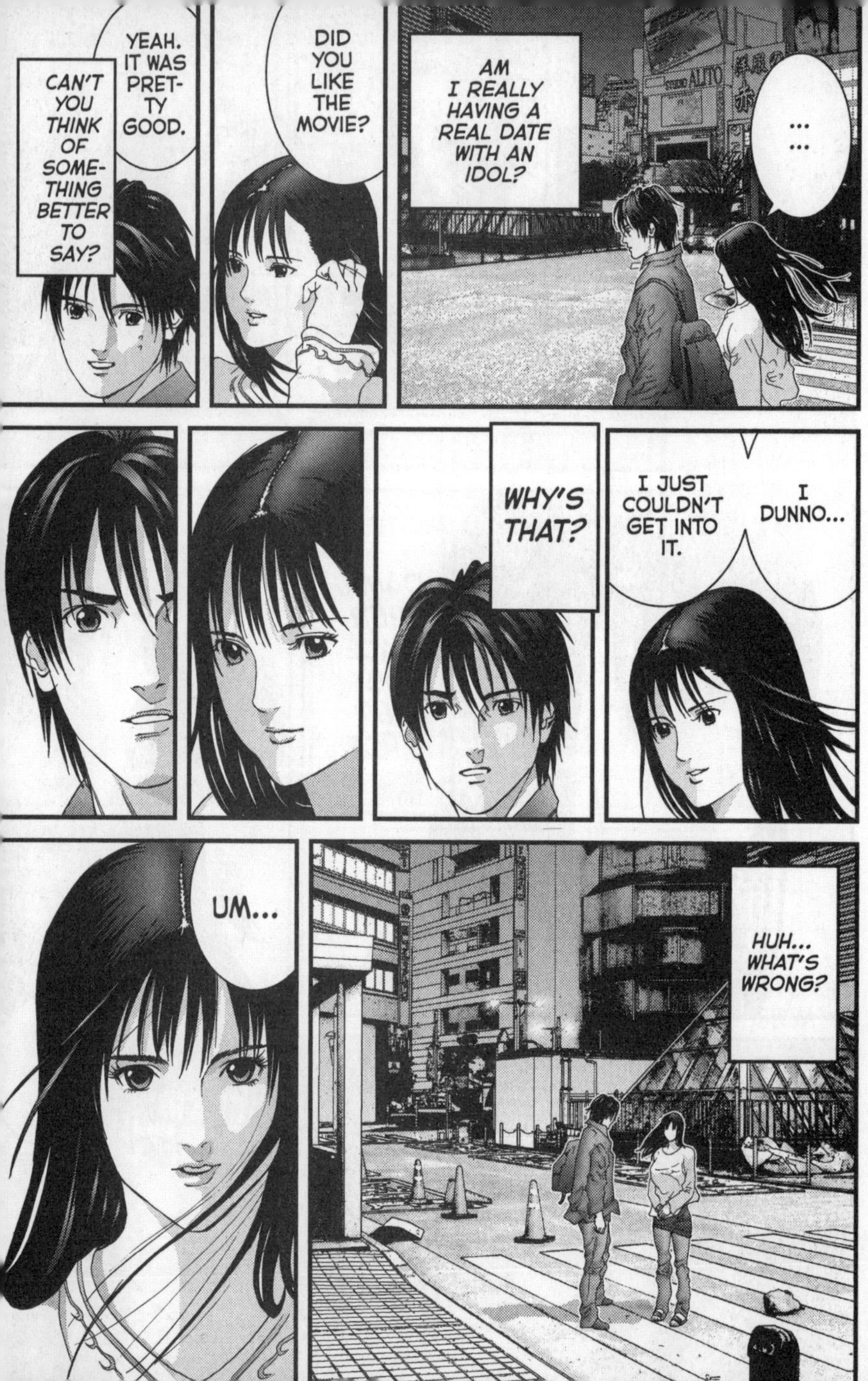
......
AM I REALLY HAVING A REAL DATE WITH AN IDOL?
DID YOU LIKE THE MOVIE?
YEAH. IT WAS PRET-TY GOOD.
CAN'T YOU THINK OF SOME-THING BETTER TO SAY?
I DUNNO...
I JUST COULDN'T GET INTO IT.
WHY'S THAT?
HUH... WHAT'S WRONG?
UM...

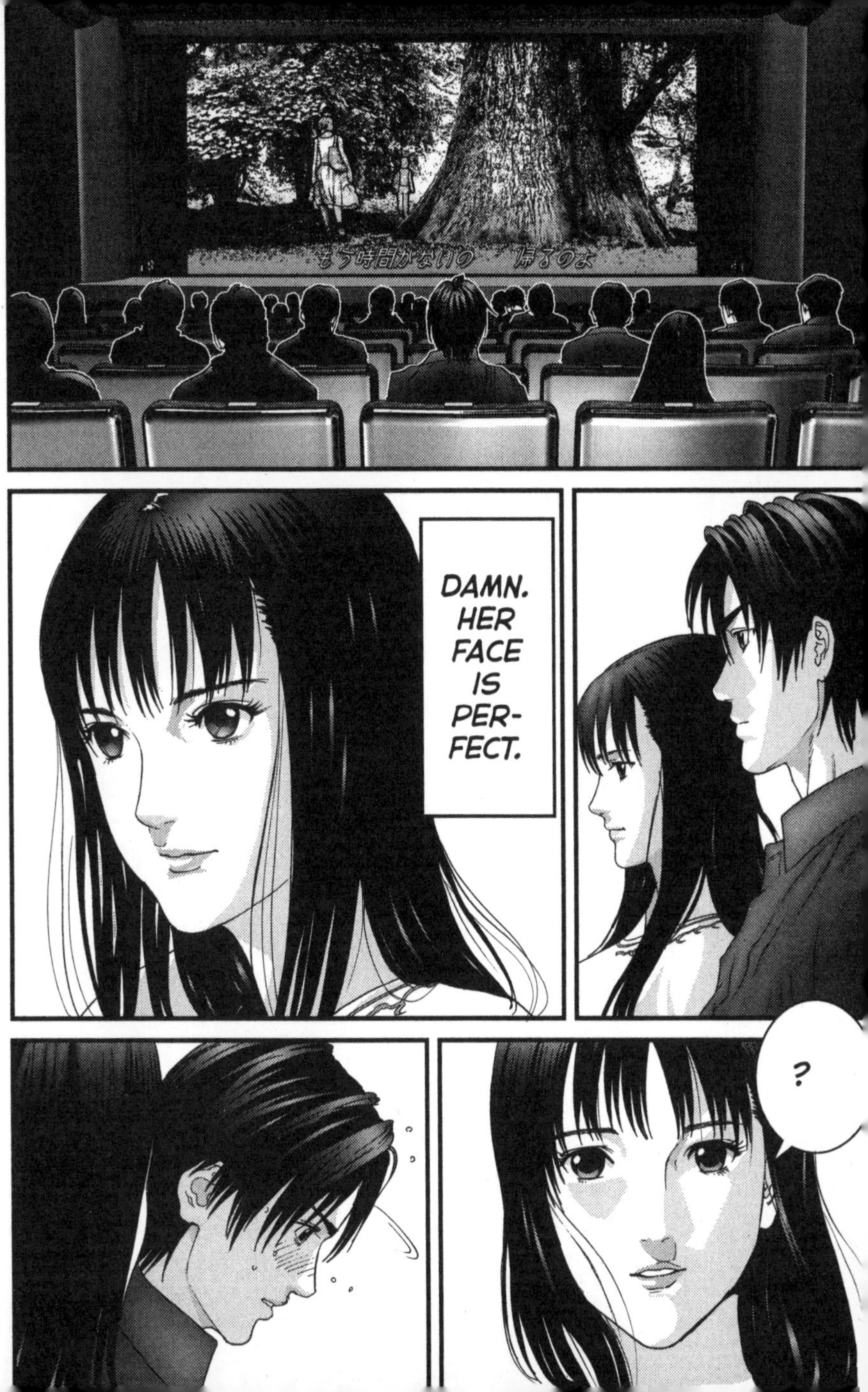
もう時間がないの　帰るのよ
DAMN. HER FACE IS PER- FECT.
?

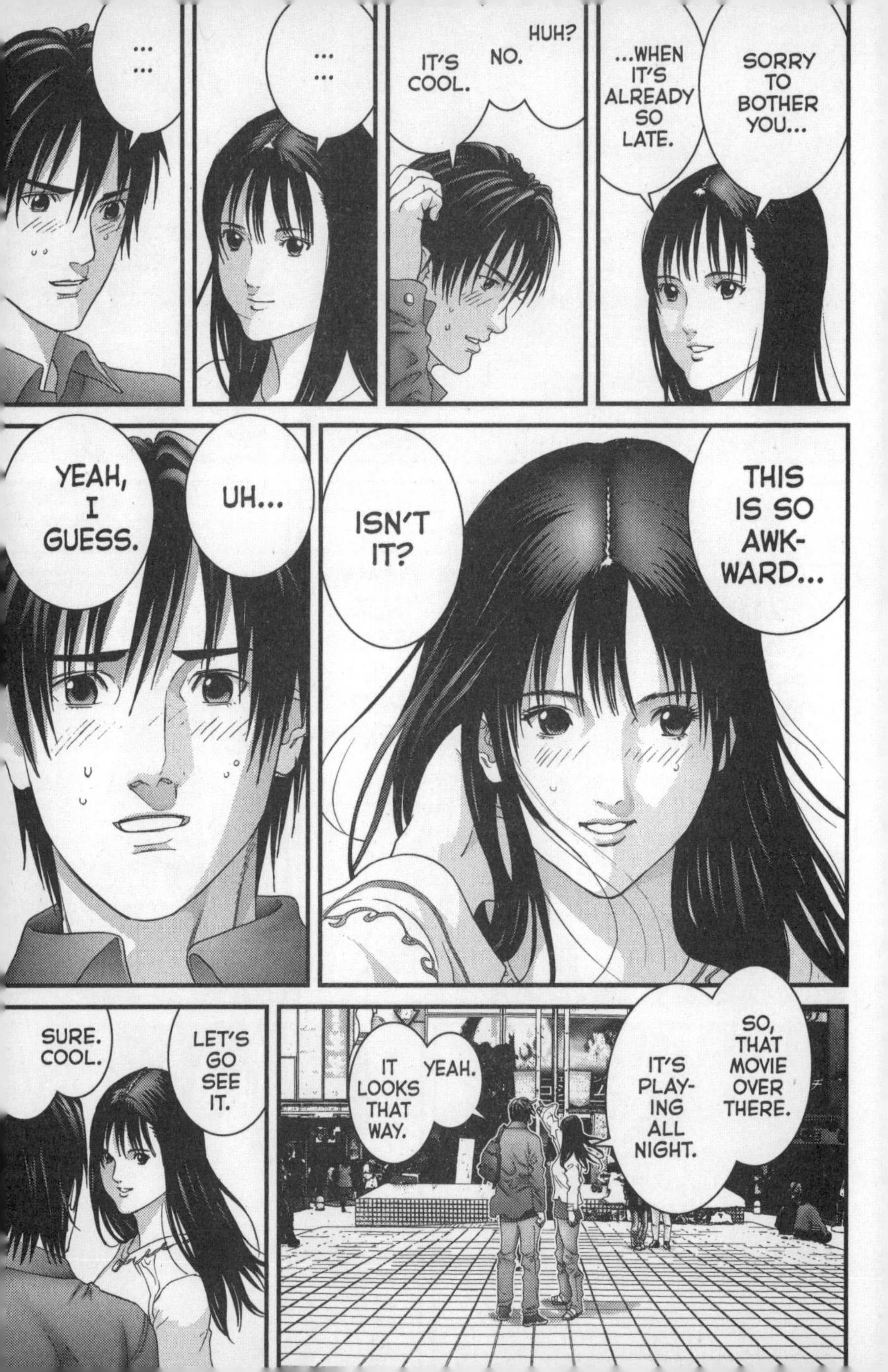
SORRY TO BOTHER YOU...
...WHEN IT'S ALREADY SO LATE.
HUH?
NO.
IT'S COOL.
...
...
THIS IS SO AWK-WARD...
ISN'T IT?
UH...
YEAH, I GUESS.
SO, THAT MOVIE OVER THERE.
IT'S PLAY-ING ALL NIGHT.
YEAH.
IT LOOKS THAT WAY.
LET'S GO SEE IT.
SURE. COOL.

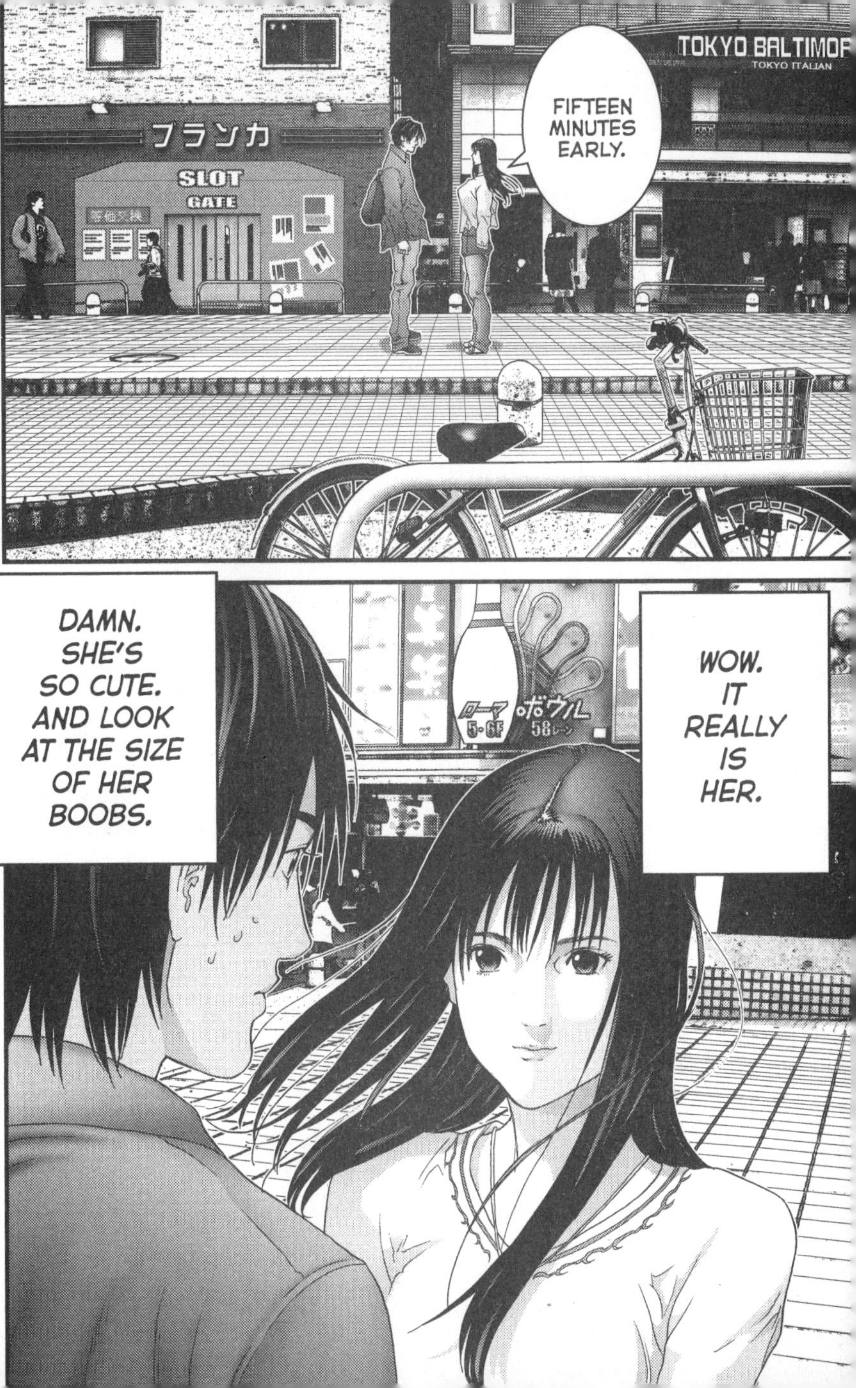
ブランカ
SLOT
GATE
TOKYO ITALIAN
FIFTEEN MINUTES EARLY.
WOW. IT REALLY IS HER.
DAMN. SHE'S SO CUTE. AND LOOK AT THE SIZE OF HER BOOBS.

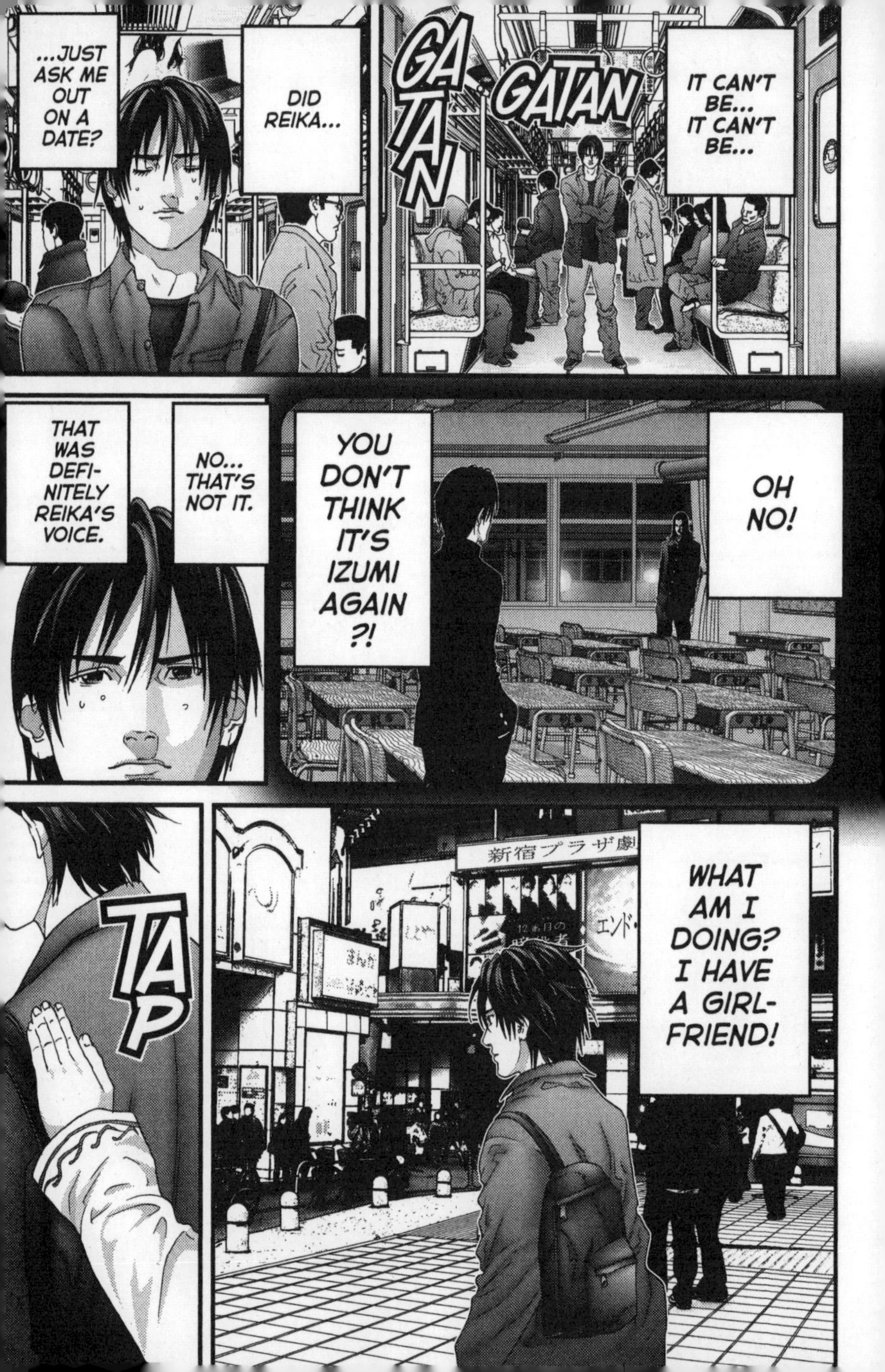
GA TAN
GATAN
IT CAN'T BE... IT CAN'T BE...
DID REIKA...
...JUST ASK ME OUT ON A DATE?
OH NO!
YOU DON'T THINK IT'S IZUMI AGAIN ?!
NO... THAT'S NOT IT.
THAT WAS DEFI- NITELY REIKA'S VOICE.
WHAT AM I DOING? I HAVE A GIRL- FRIEND!
新宿プラザ劇
TAP

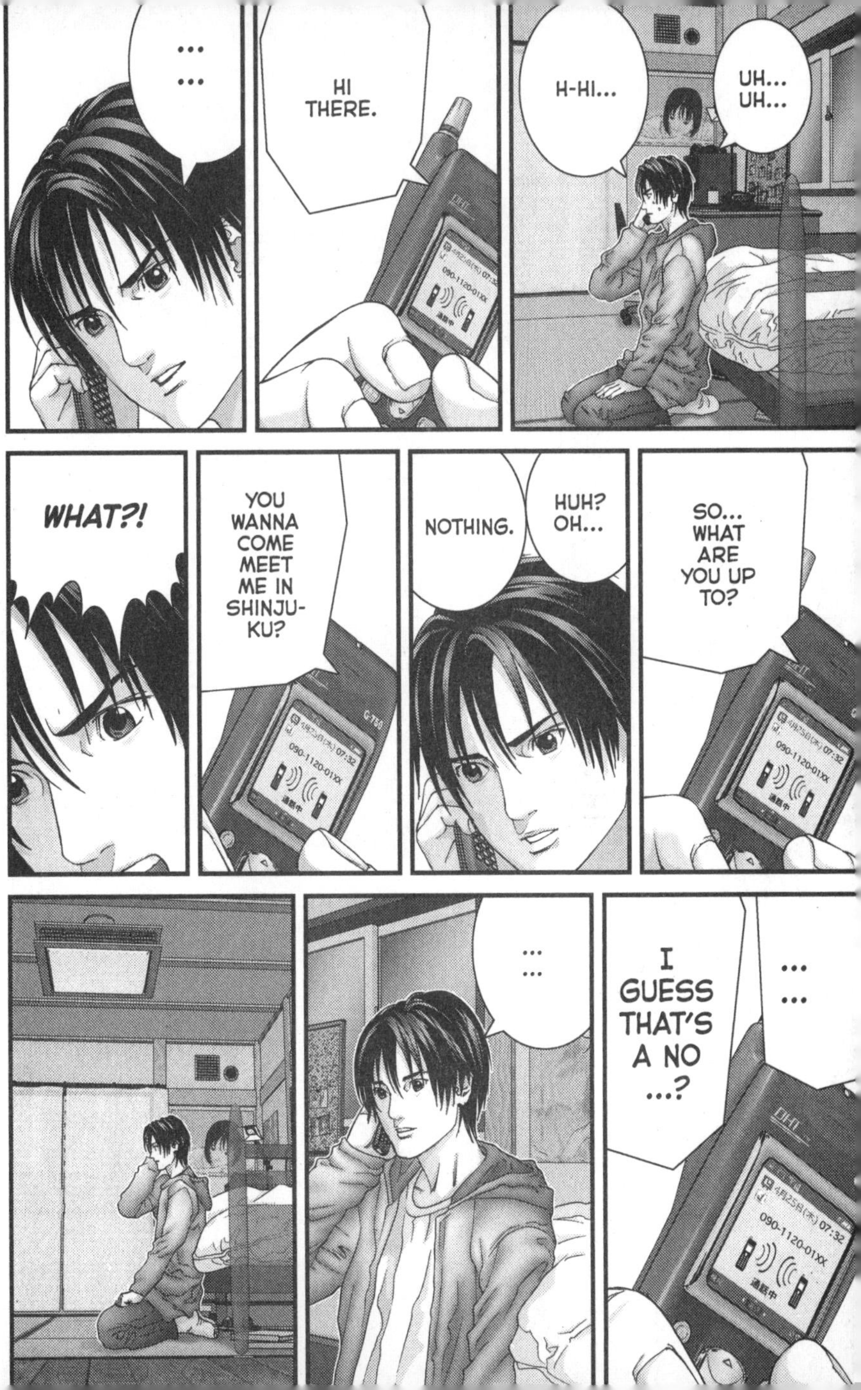
UH... UH...
H-HI...
HI THERE.
... ...
SO... WHAT ARE YOU UP TO?
HUH? OH...
NOTHING.
YOU WANNA COME MEET ME IN SHINJU-KU?
WHAT?!
... ...
I GUESS THAT'S A NO ...?
... ...

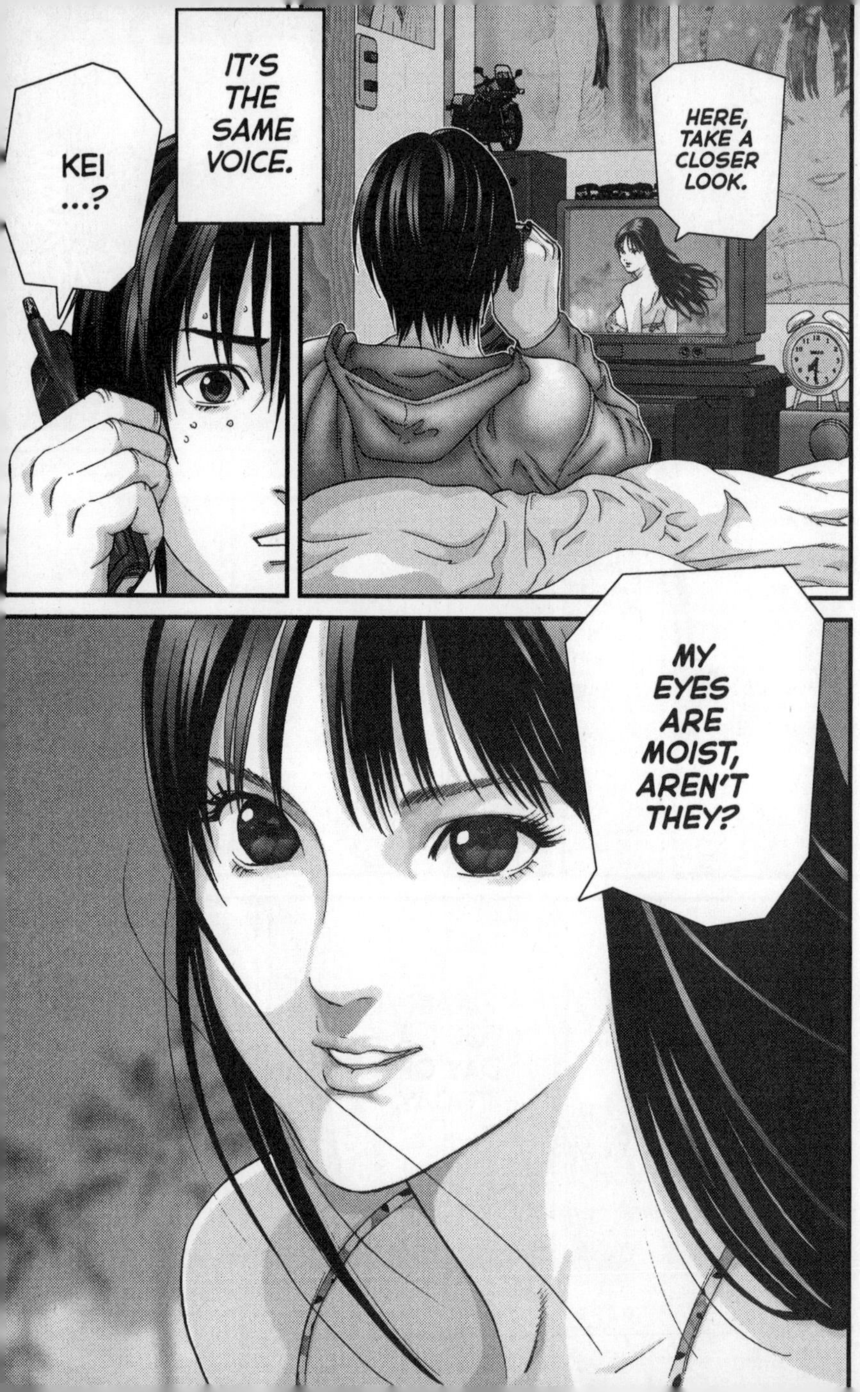
HERE, TAKE A CLOSER LOOK.
IT'S THE SAME VOICE.
KEI ...?
MY EYES ARE MOIST, AREN'T THEY?

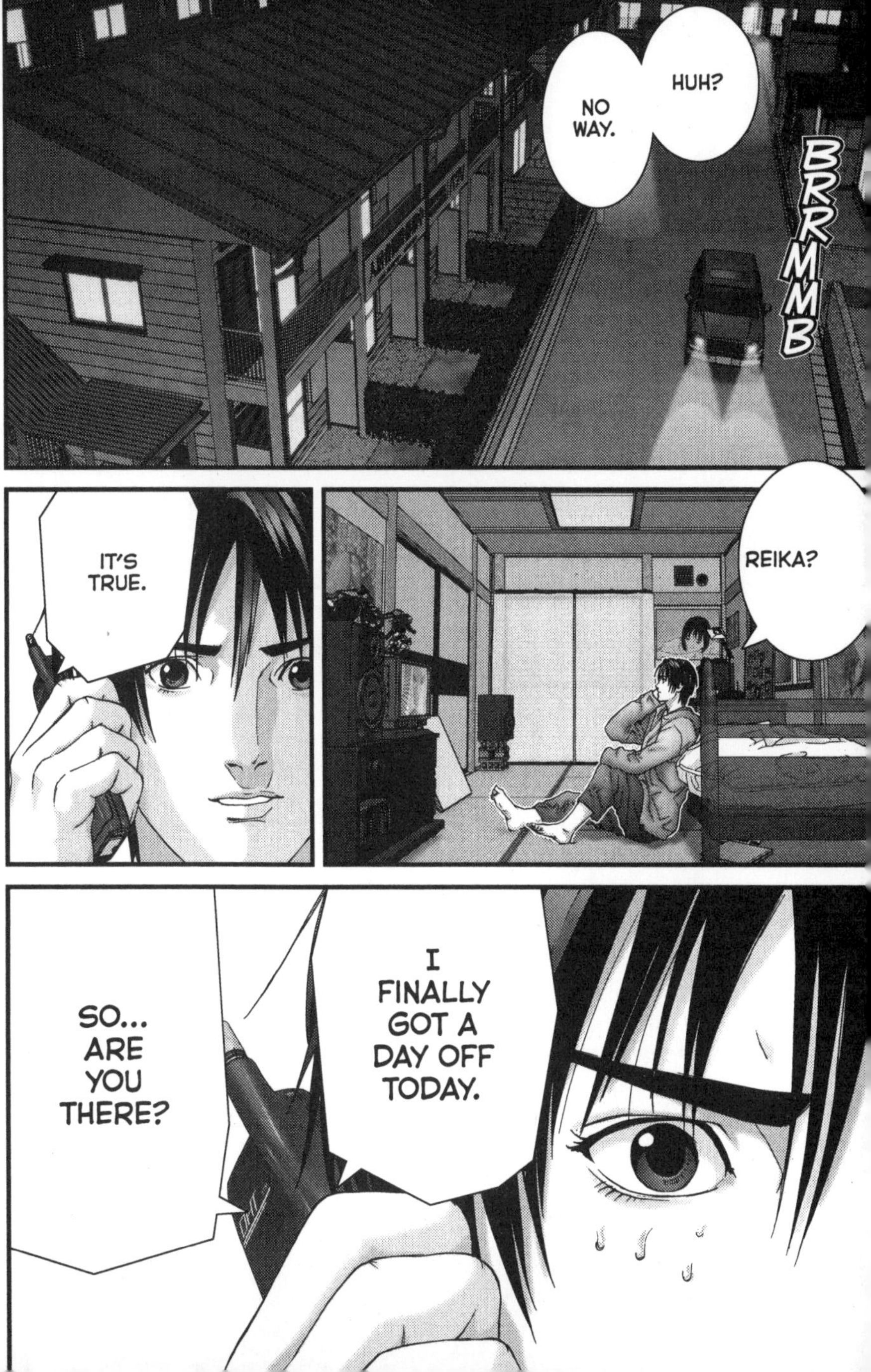
HUH?
NO WAY.
BRRMMB
REIKA?
IT'S TRUE.
I FINALLY GOT A DAY OFF TODAY.
SO... ARE YOU THERE?

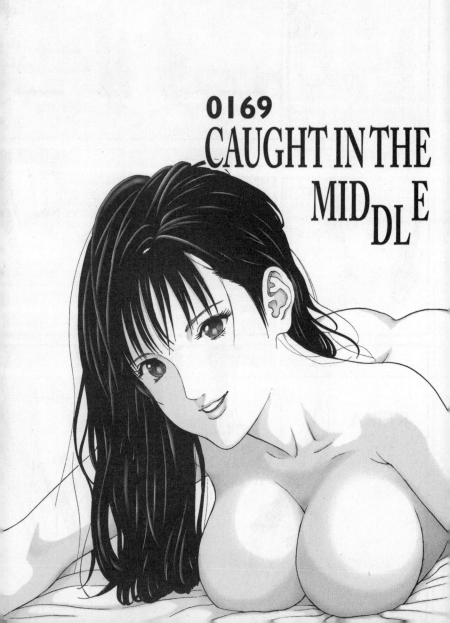

0169 CAUGHT IN THE MIDDLE

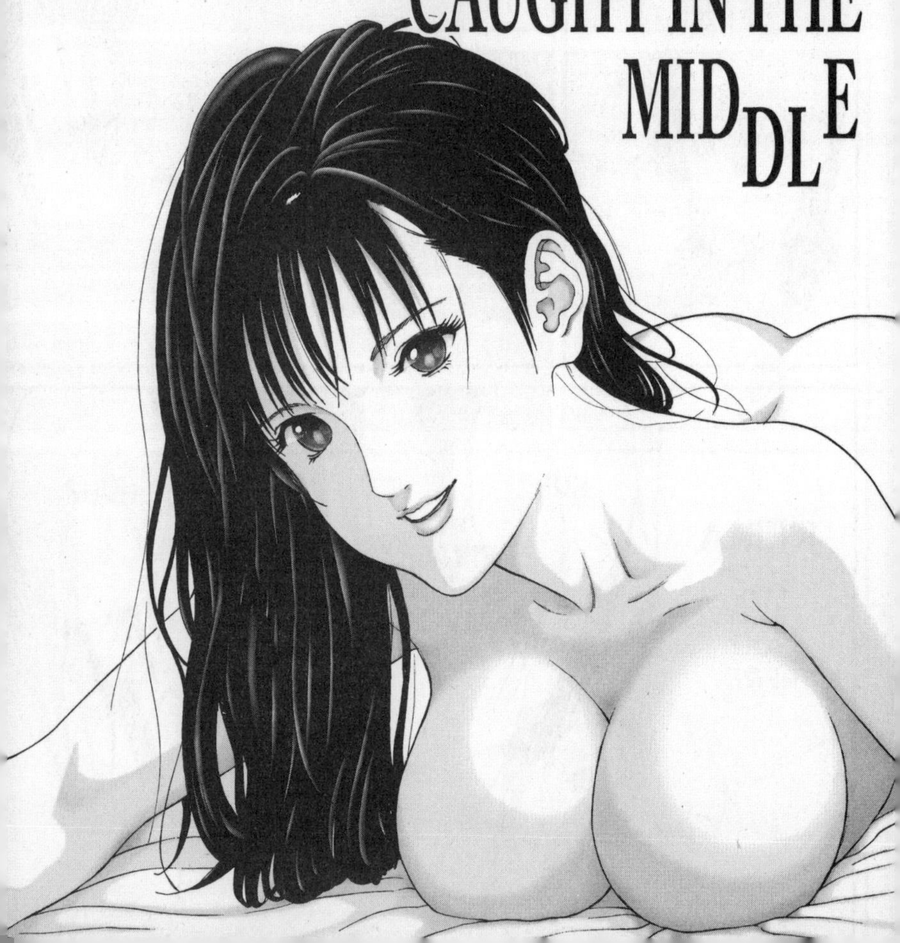

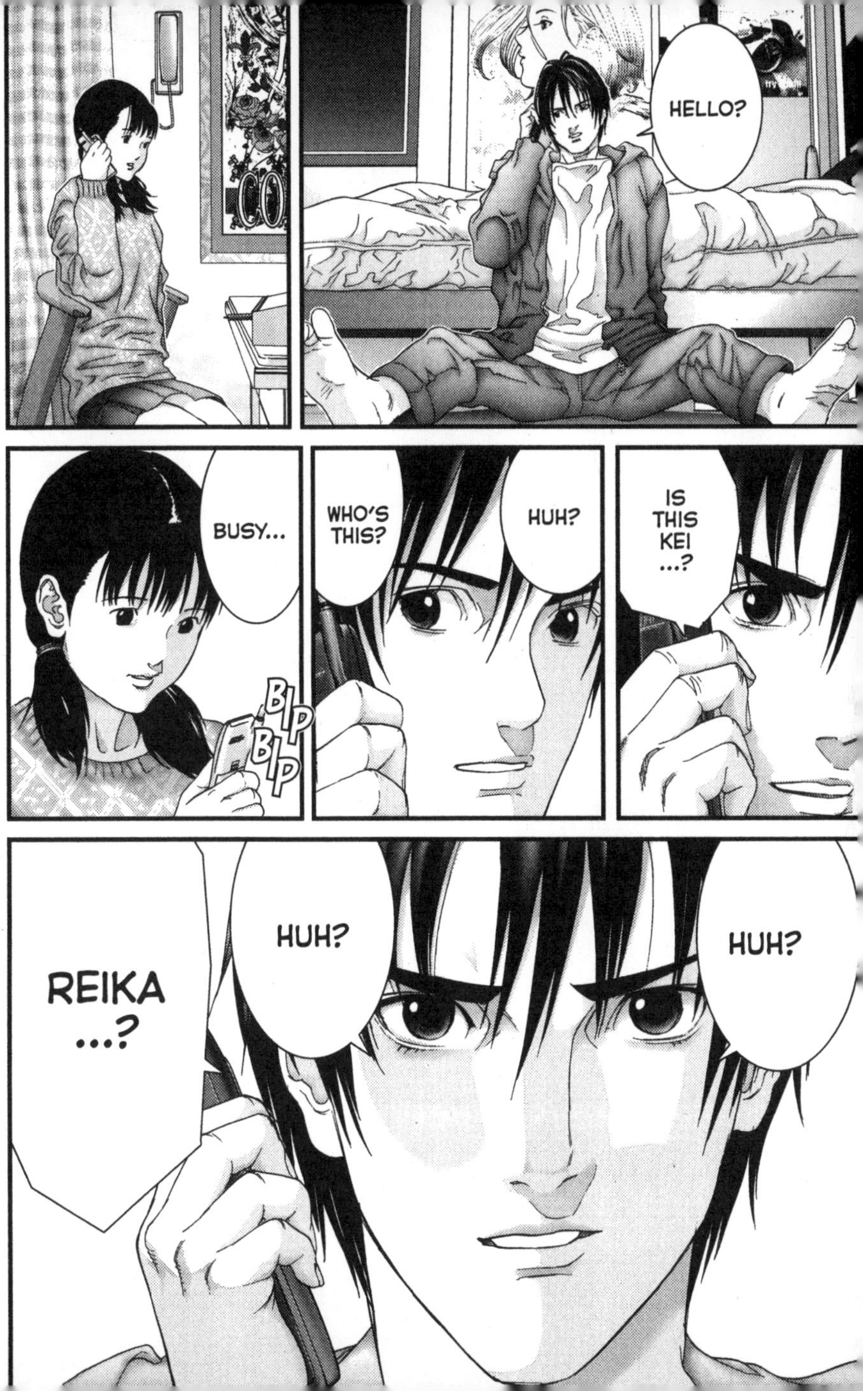
HELLO?
IS THIS KEI ...?
HUH?
WHO'S THIS?
BUSY...
BIP BIP
HUH?
HUH?
REIKA ...?

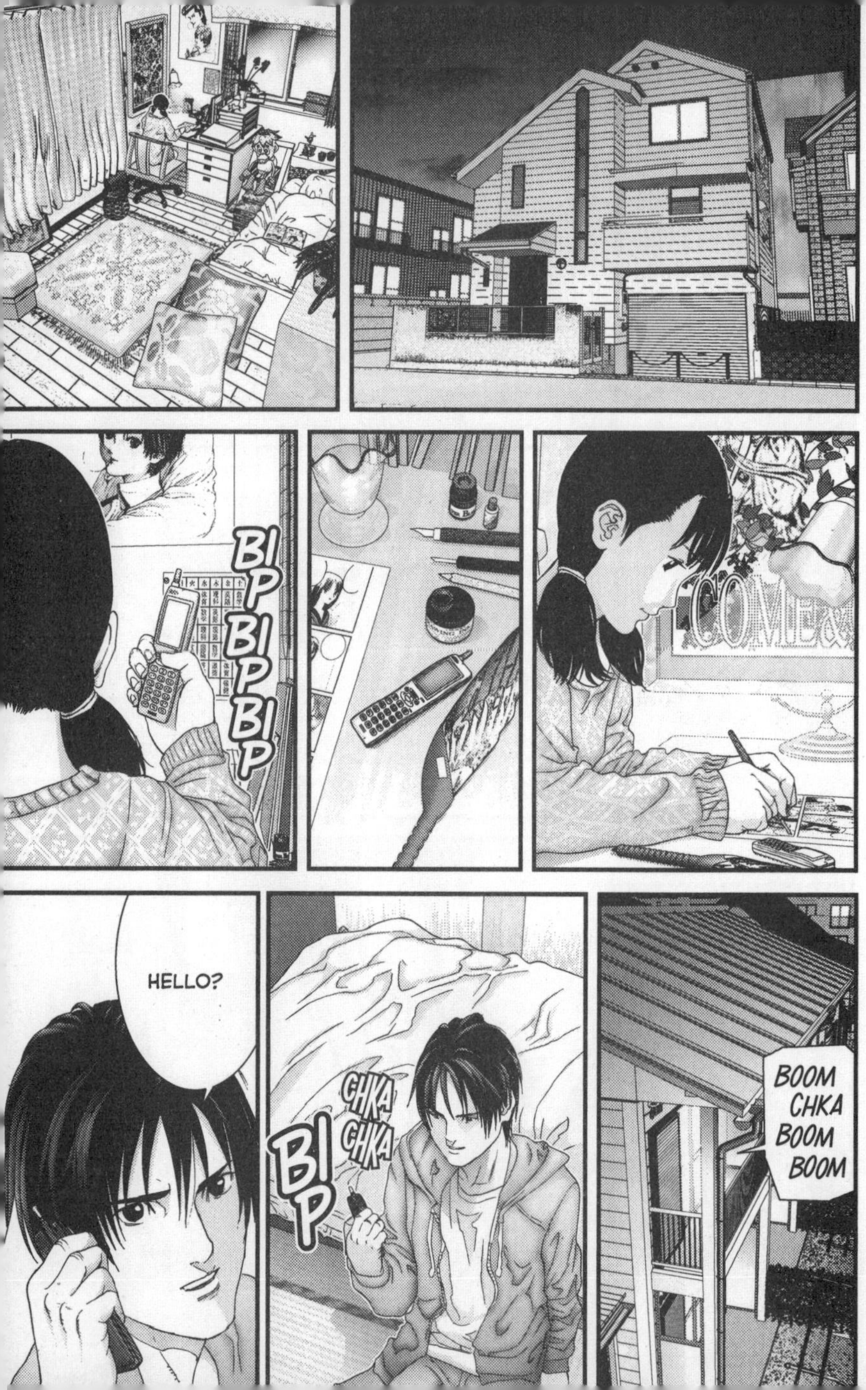
BIP BIP BIP BIP
BOOM CHKA BOOM BOOM
CHKA CHKA
BIP
HELLO?

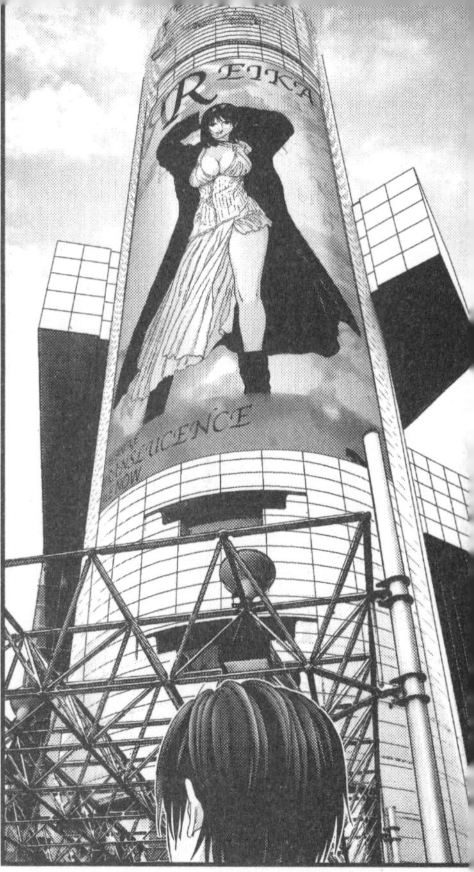
REIKA
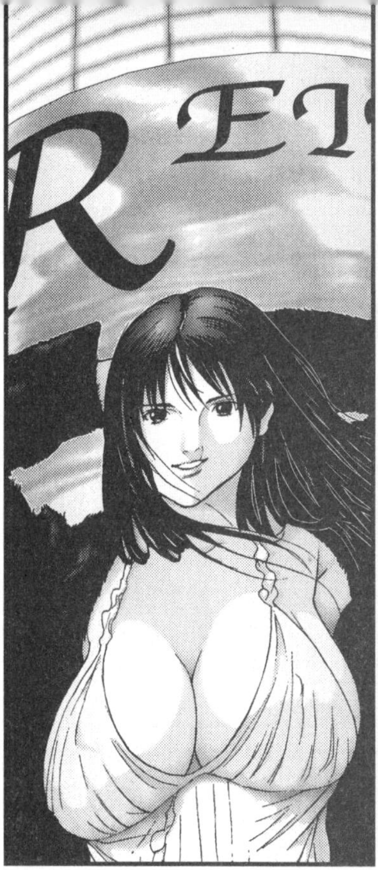
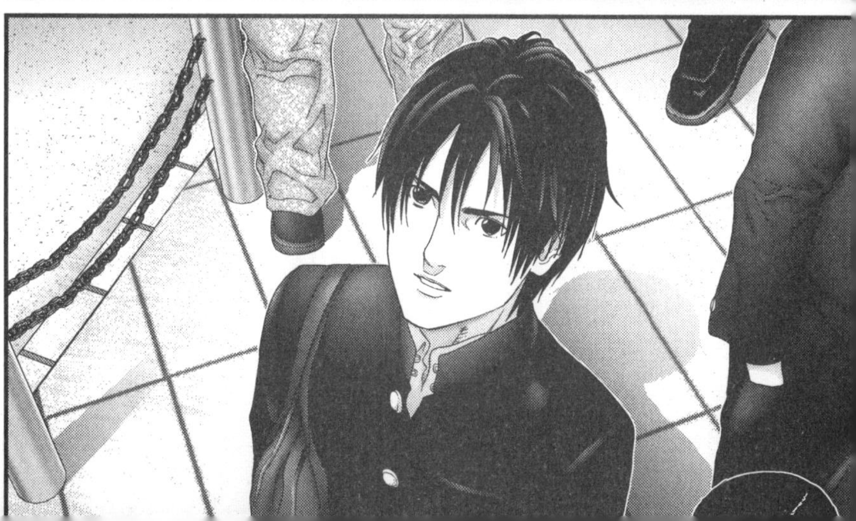

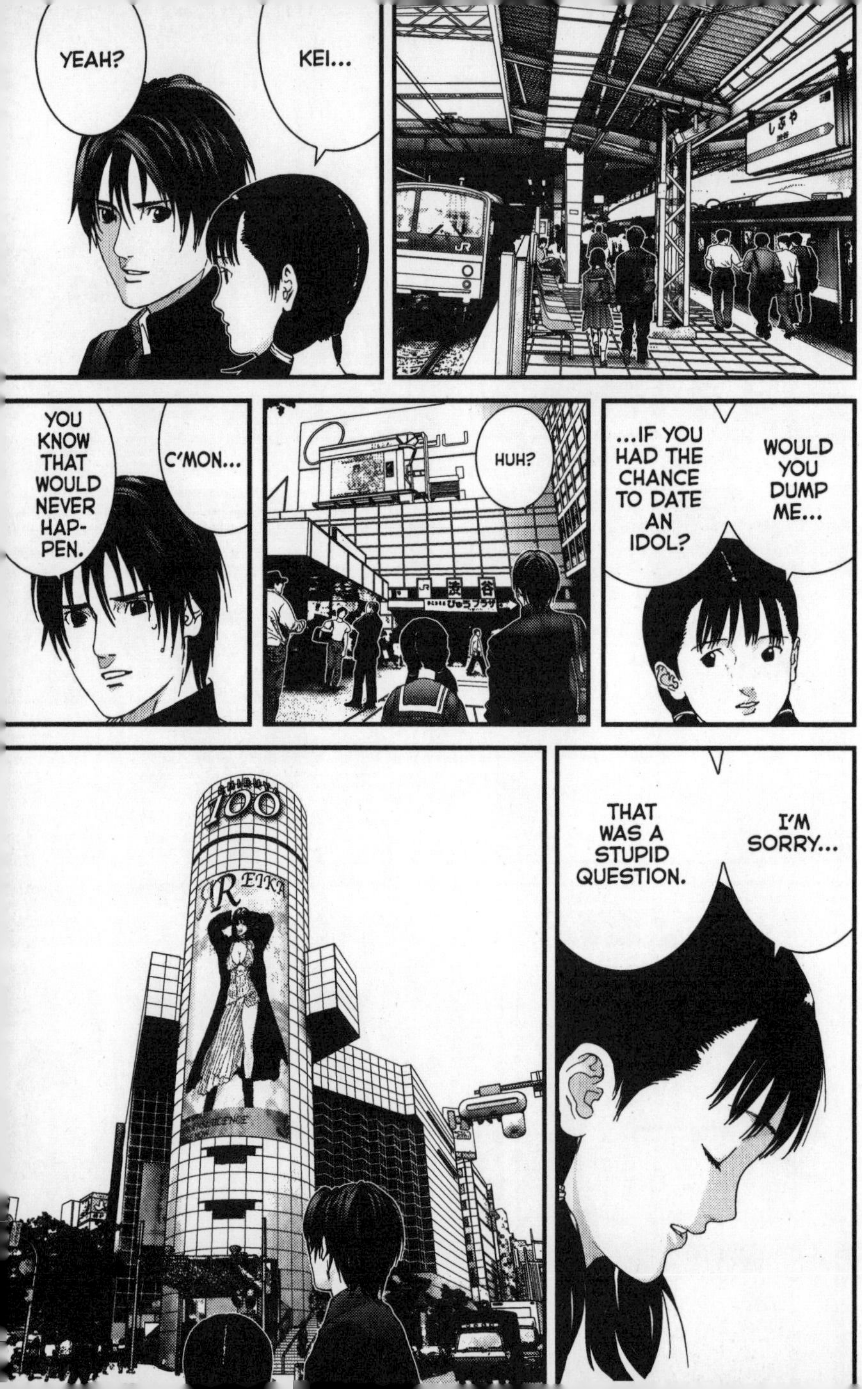
KEI...
YEAH?
WOULD YOU DUMP ME...
...IF YOU HAD THE CHANCE TO DATE AN IDOL?
HUH?
C'MON...
YOU KNOW THAT WOULD NEVER HAP-PEN.
I'M SORRY...
THAT WAS A STUPID QUESTION.

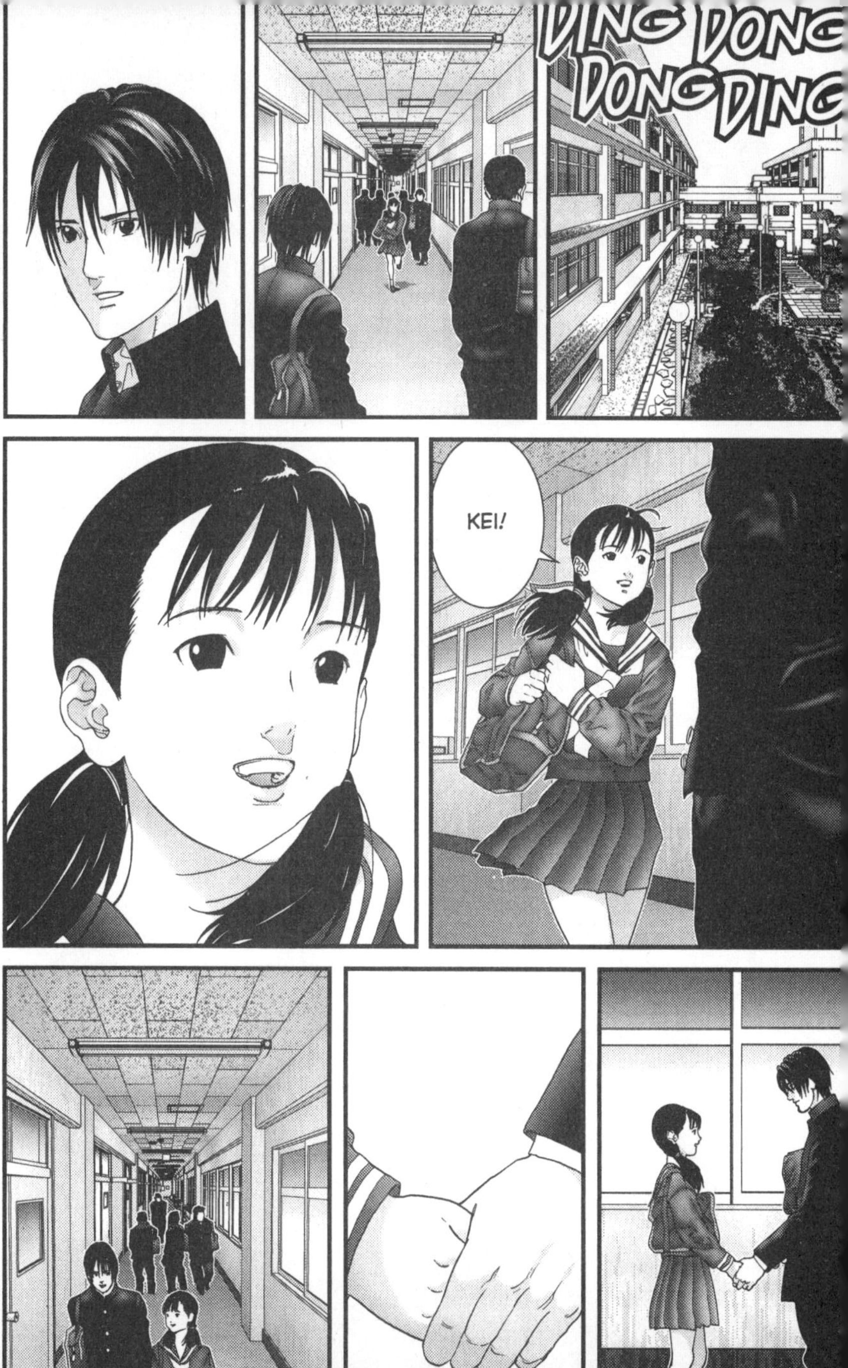
DING DONG
DONG DING
KEI!

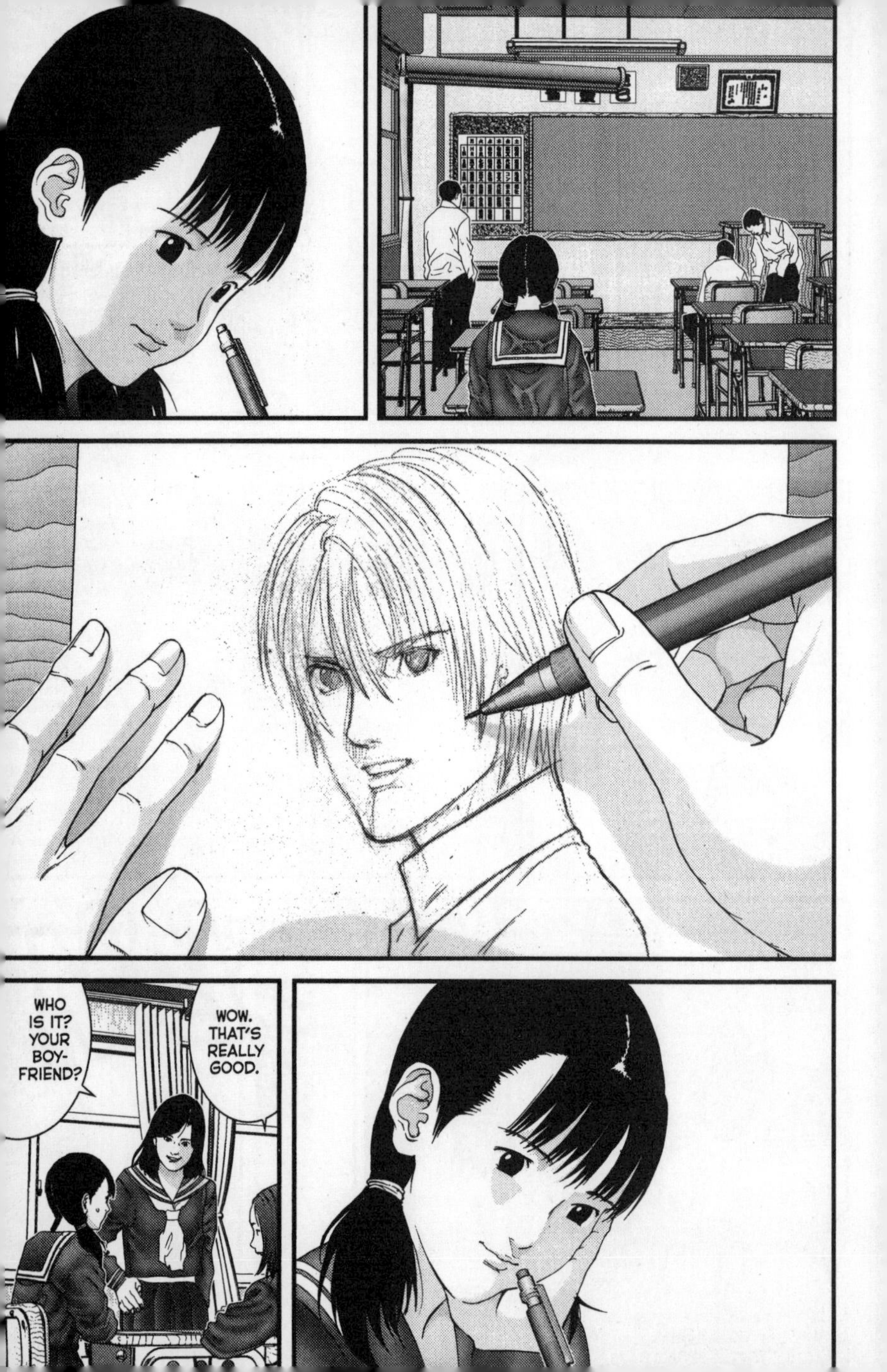
WOW. THAT'S REALLY GOOD.
WHO IS IT? YOUR BOY-FRIEND?

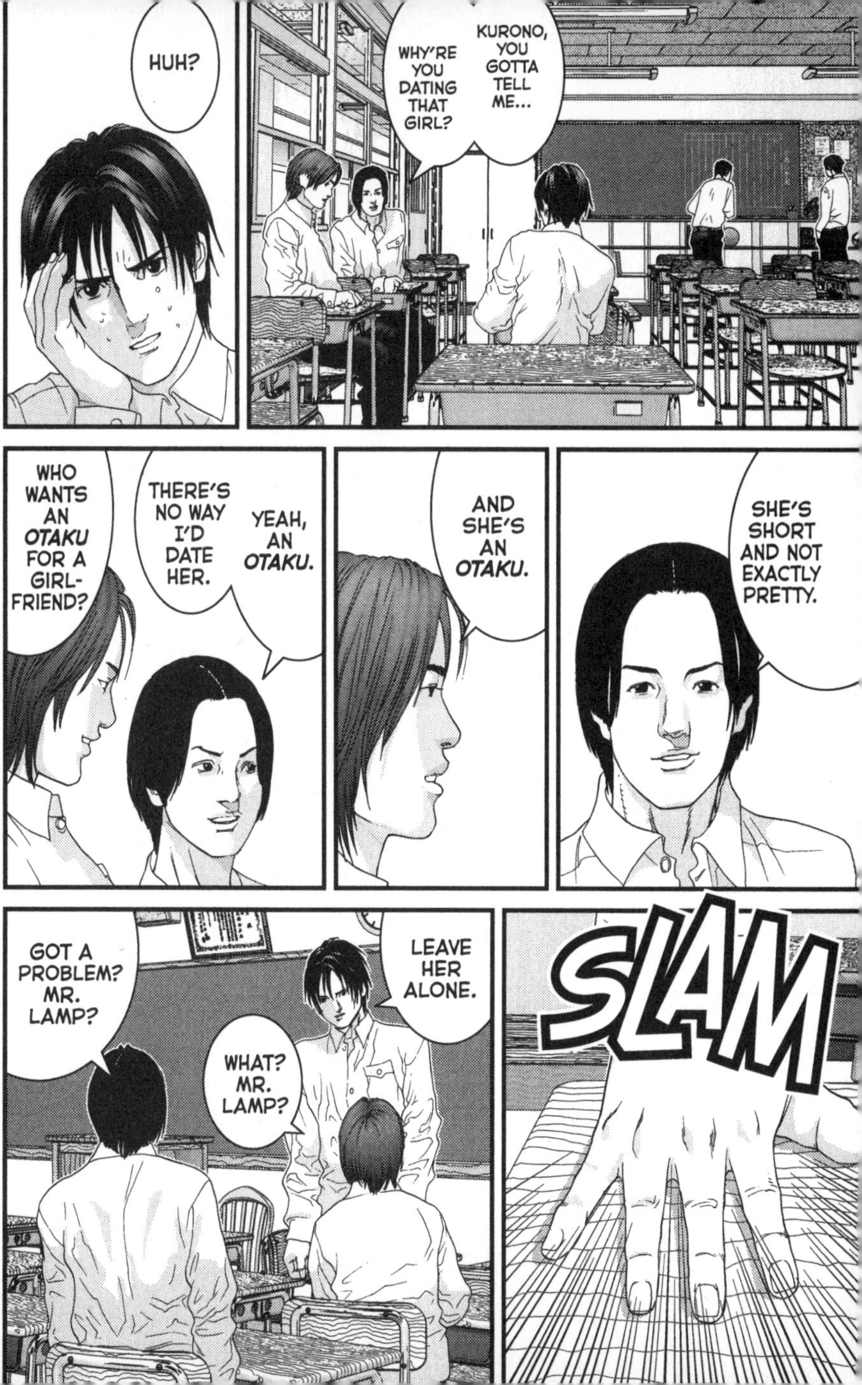
KURONO, YOU GOTTA TELL ME...
WHY'RE YOU DATING THAT GIRL?
HUH?
SHE'S SHORT AND NOT EXACTLY PRETTY.
AND SHE'S AN *OTAKU*.
YEAH, AN *OTAKU*.
THERE'S NO WAY I'D DATE HER.
WHO WANTS AN *OTAKU* FOR A GIRL-FRIEND?
SLAM
LEAVE HER ALONE.
WHAT? MR. LAMP?
GOT A PROBLEM? MR. LAMP?

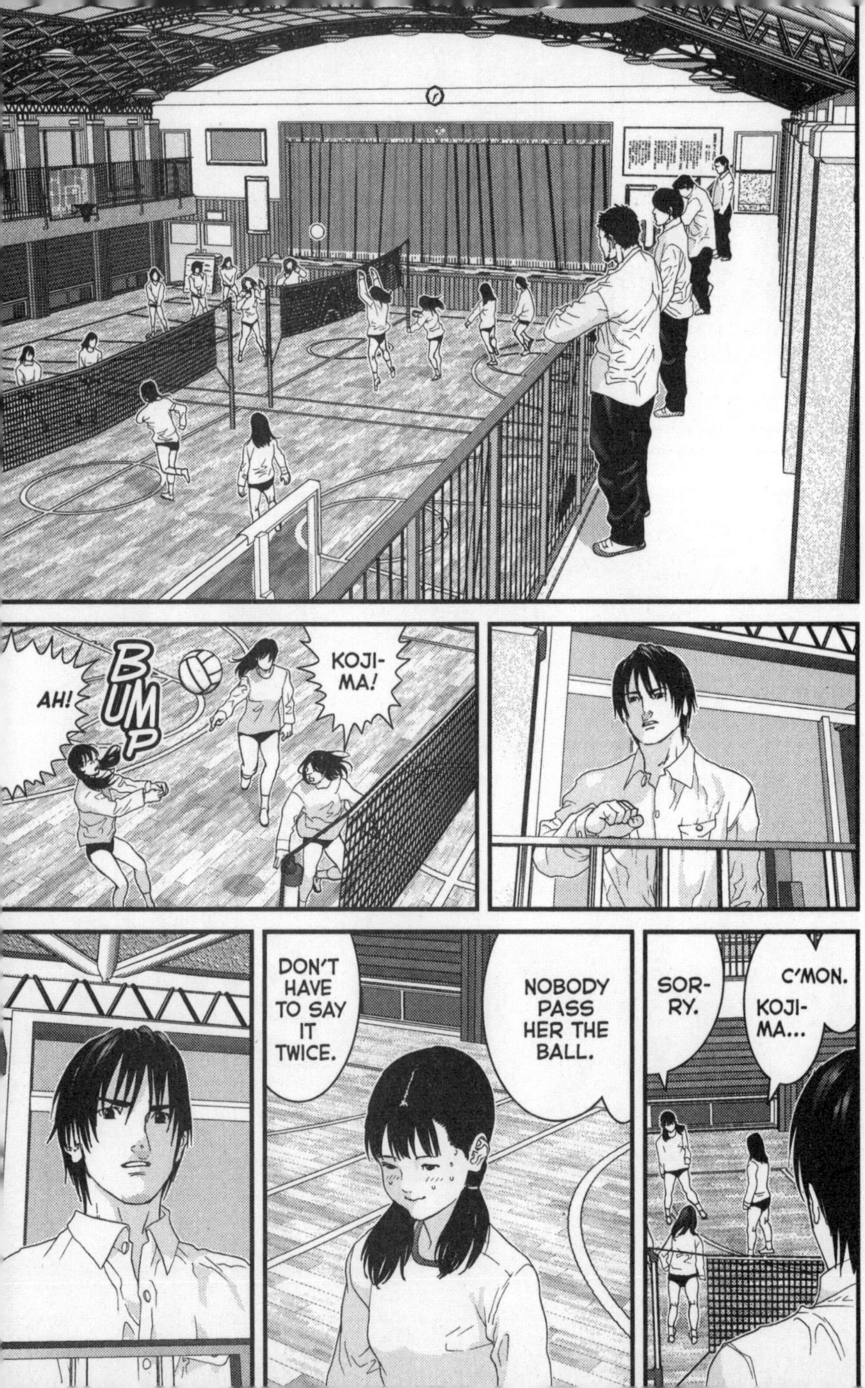
KOJI-MA!
BUMP
AH!
C'MON. KOJI-MA...
SOR-RY.
NOBODY PASS HER THE BALL.
DON'T HAVE TO SAY IT TWICE.

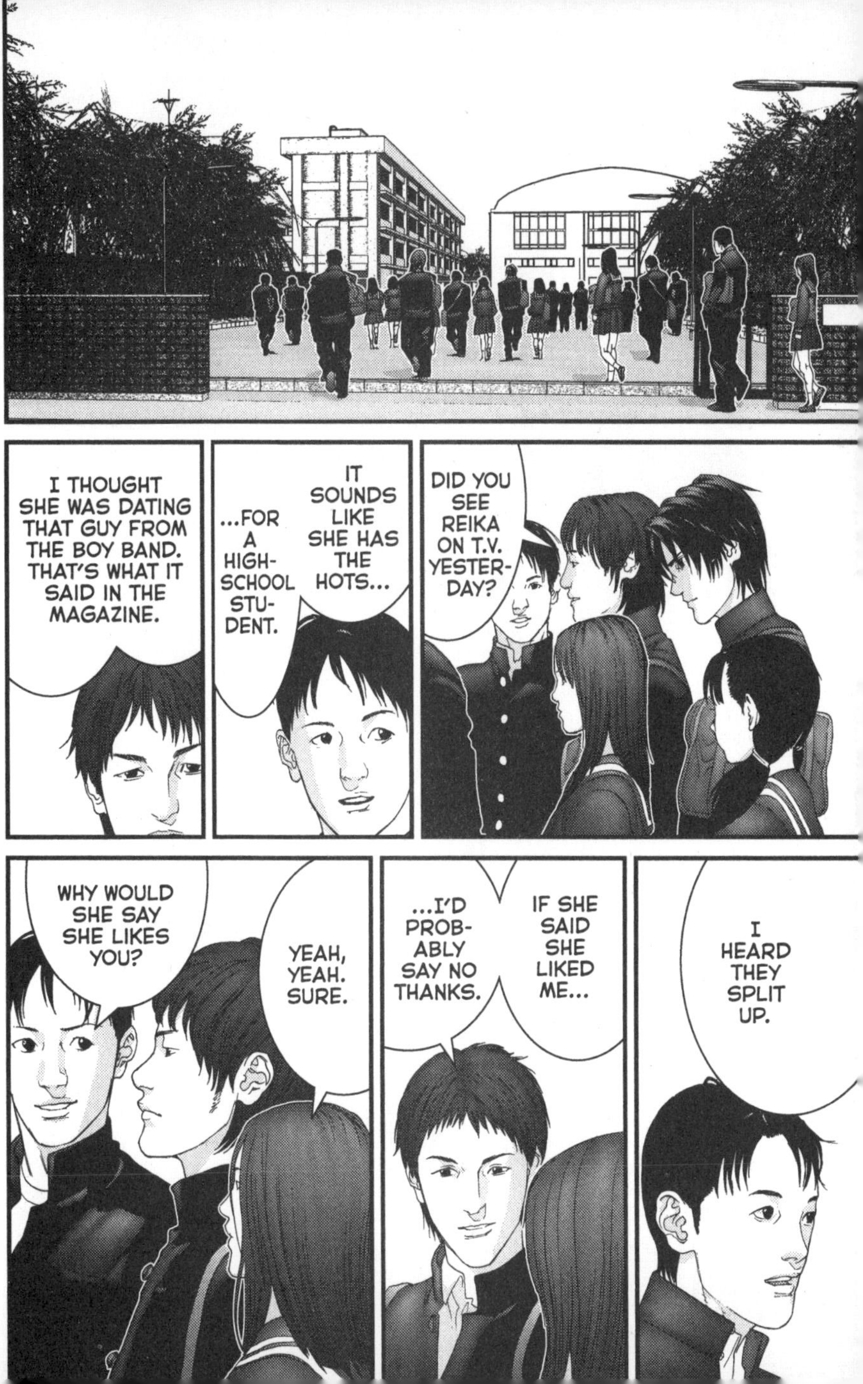
DID YOU SEE REIKA ON T.V. YESTERDAY?
IT SOUNDS LIKE SHE HAS THE HOTS...
...FOR A HIGH-SCHOOL STUDENT.
I THOUGHT SHE WAS DATING THAT GUY FROM THE BOY BAND. THAT'S WHAT IT SAID IN THE MAGAZINE.
I HEARD THEY SPLIT UP.
IF SHE SAID SHE LIKED ME...
...I'D PROBABLY SAY NO THANKS.
YEAH, YEAH. SURE.
WHY WOULD SHE SAY SHE LIKES YOU?

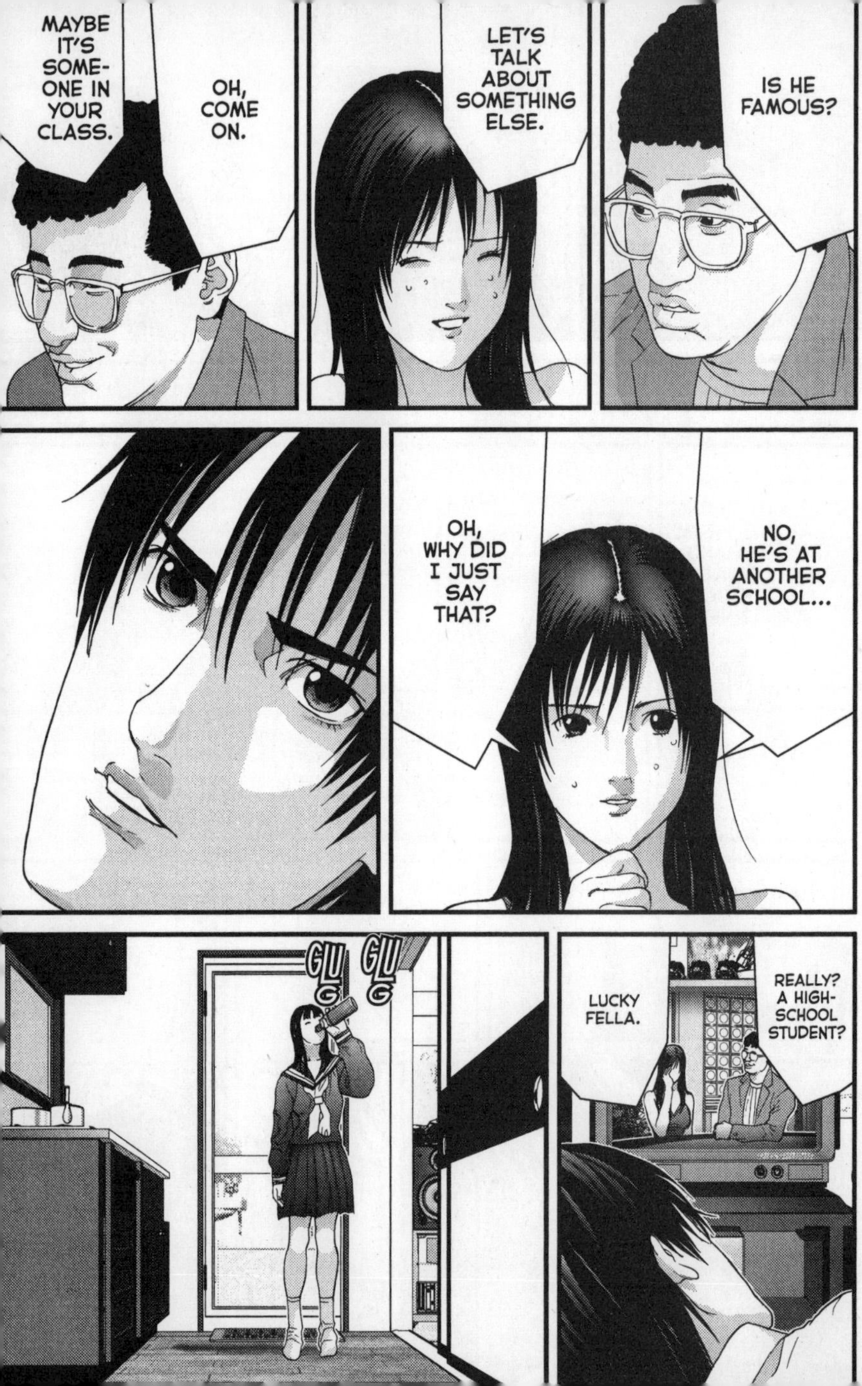
IS HE FAMOUS?
LET'S TALK ABOUT SOMETHING ELSE.
OH, COME ON.
MAYBE IT'S SOME-ONE IN YOUR CLASS.
NO, HE'S AT ANOTHER SCHOOL...
OH, WHY DID I JUST SAY THAT?
REALLY? A HIGH-SCHOOL STUDENT?
LUCKY FELLA.
GLUG GLUG

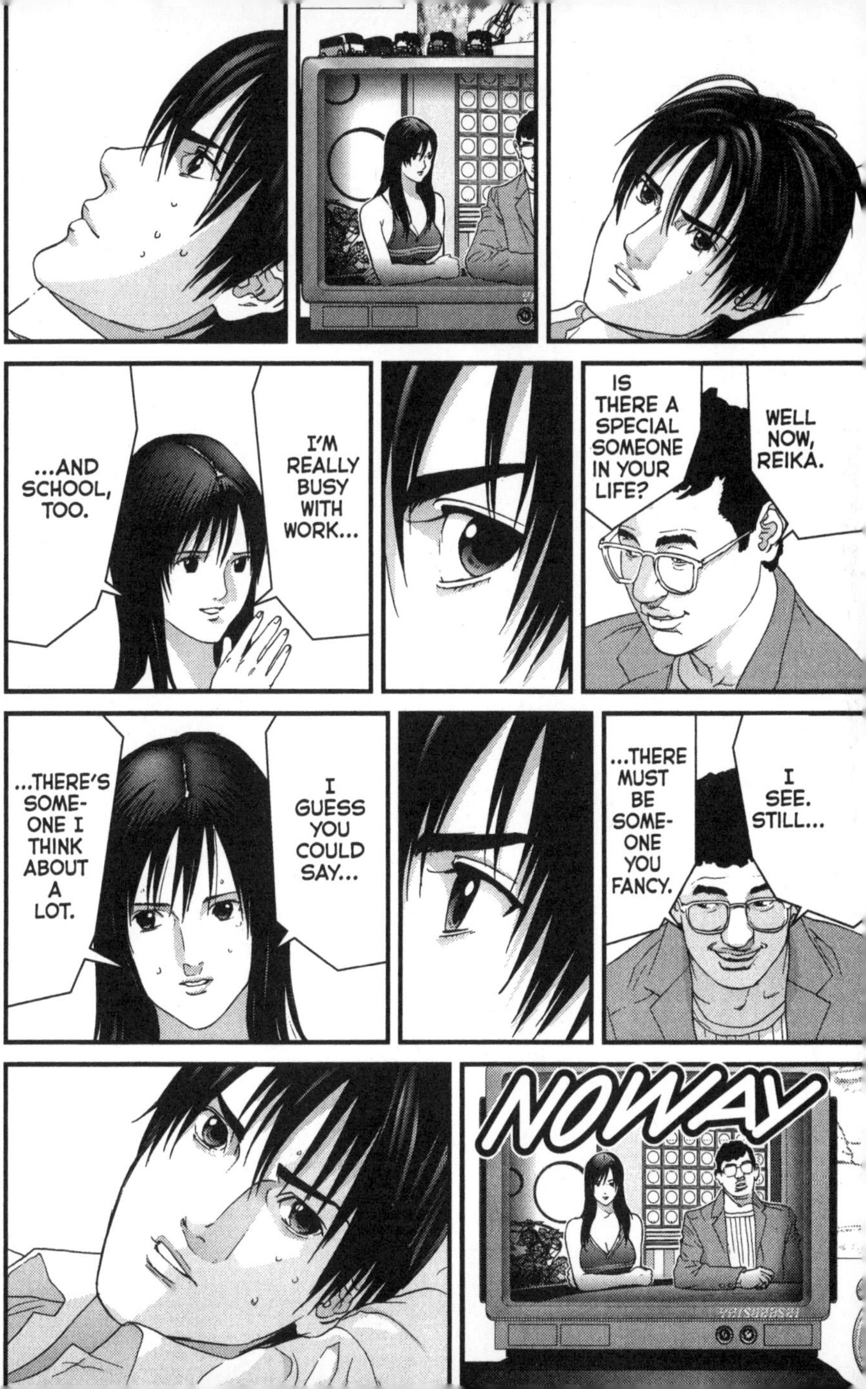
WELL NOW, REIKA.
IS THERE A SPECIAL SOMEONE IN YOUR LIFE?
I'M REALLY BUSY WITH WORK...
...AND SCHOOL, TOO.
I SEE. STILL...
...THERE MUST BE SOME-ONE YOU FANCY.
I GUESS YOU COULD SAY...
...THERE'S SOME-ONE I THINK ABOUT A LOT.
NOWAY

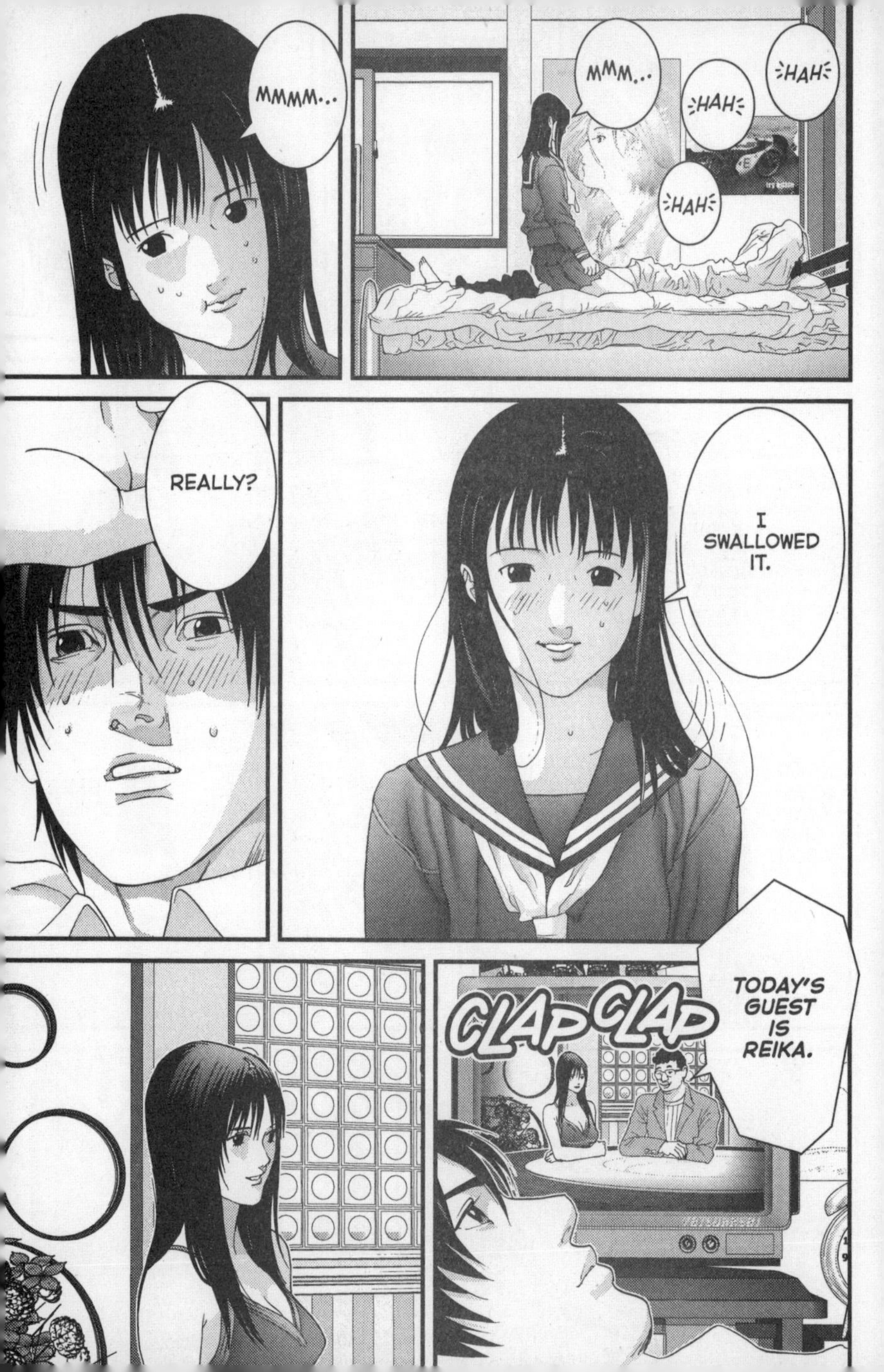
MMM...
HAH
HAH
HAH
MMMM...
I SWALLOWED IT.
REALLY?
CLAP CLAP
TODAY'S GUEST IS REIKA.

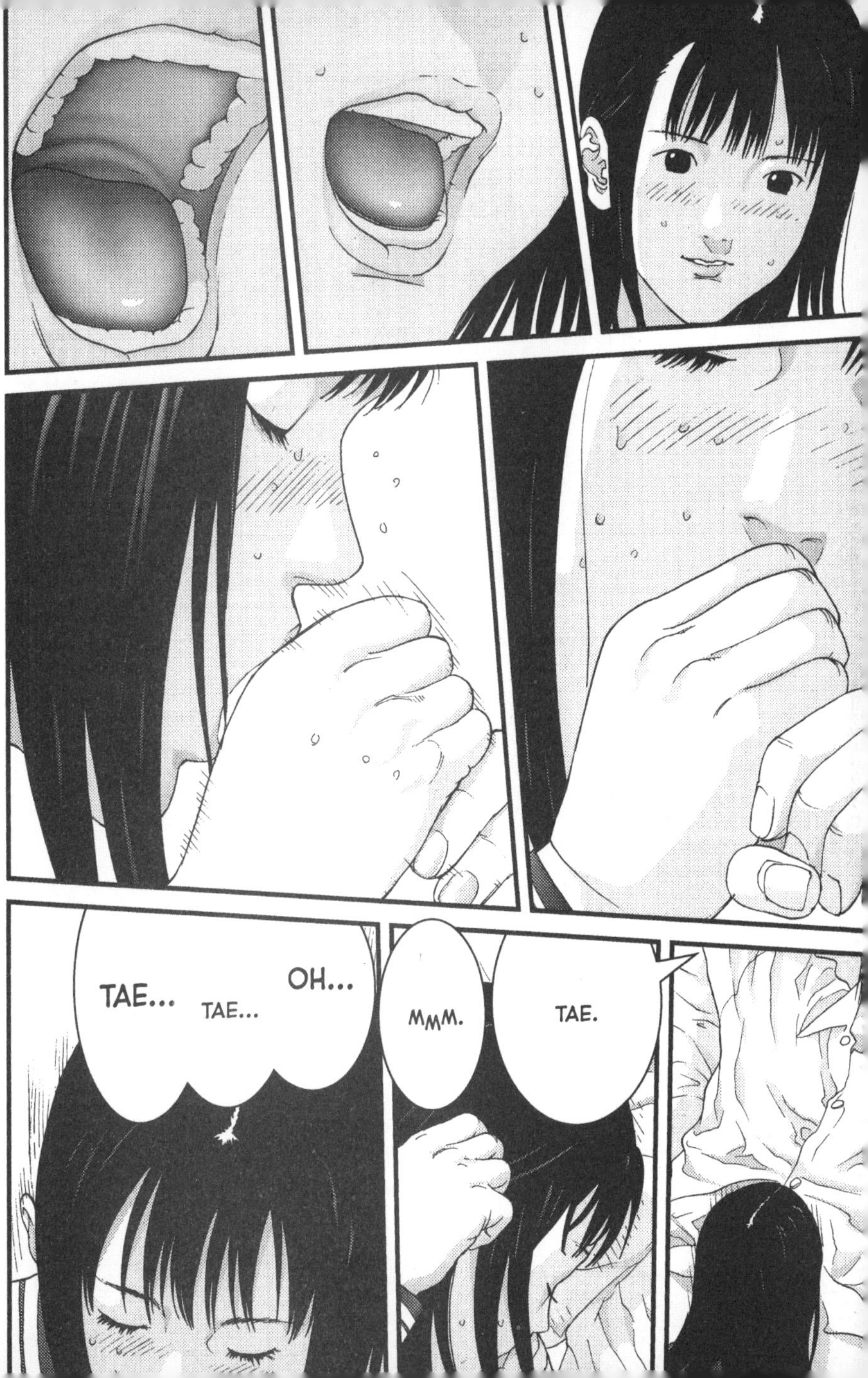
TAE.
MMM.
TAE... TAE... OH...

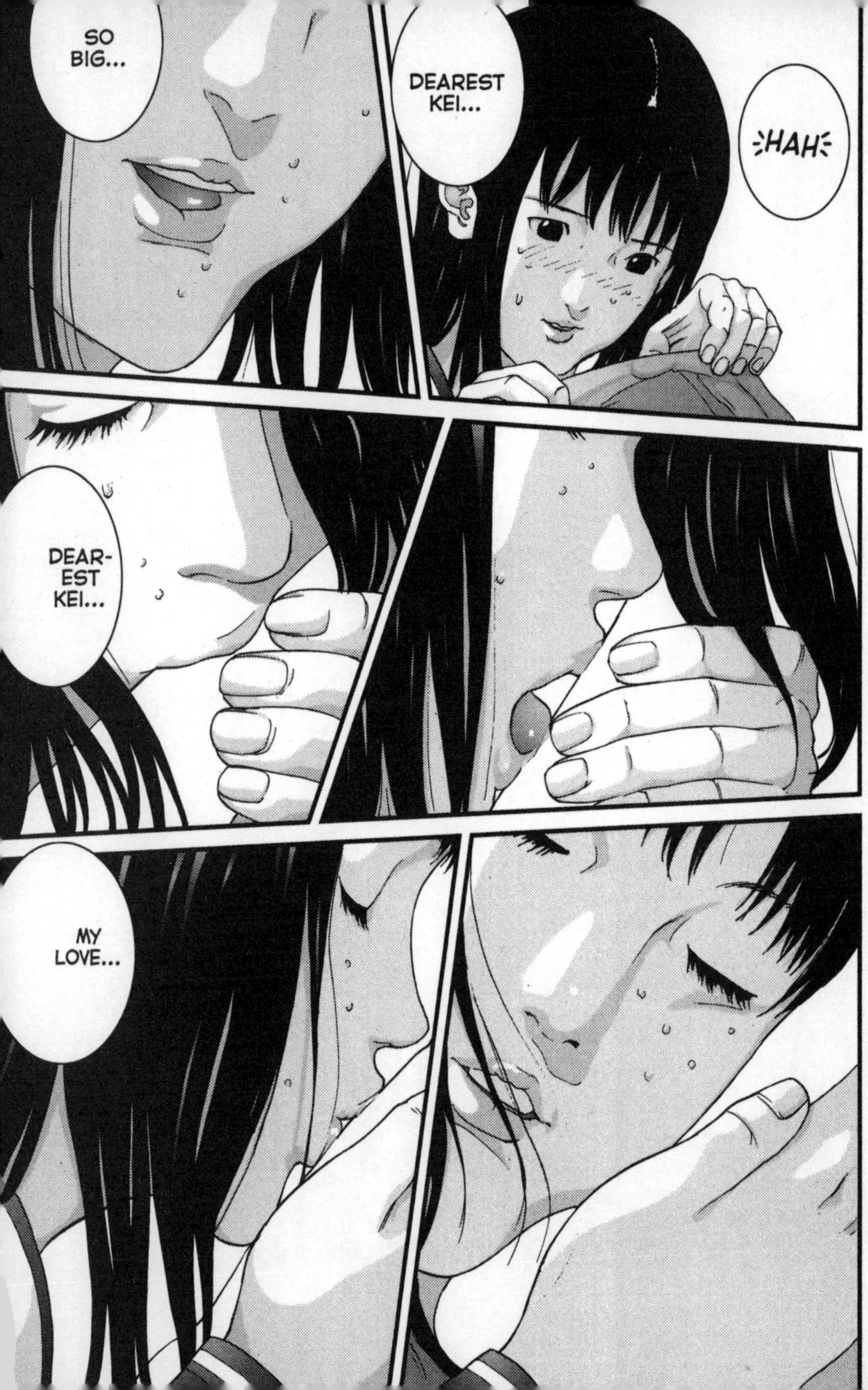
HAH
DEAREST KEI...
SO BIG...
DEAR-EST KEI...
MY LOVE...

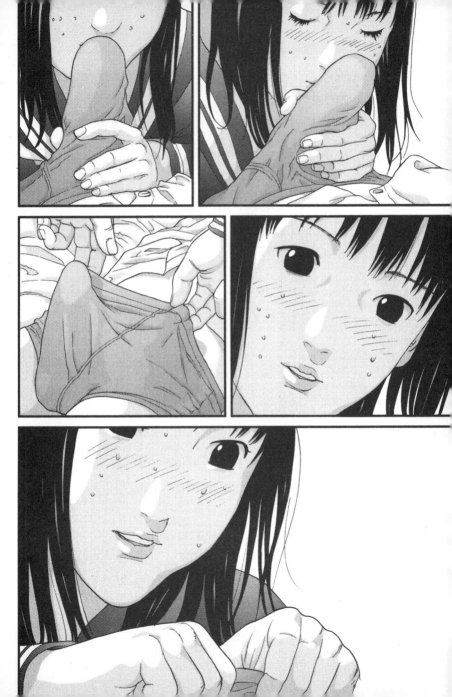

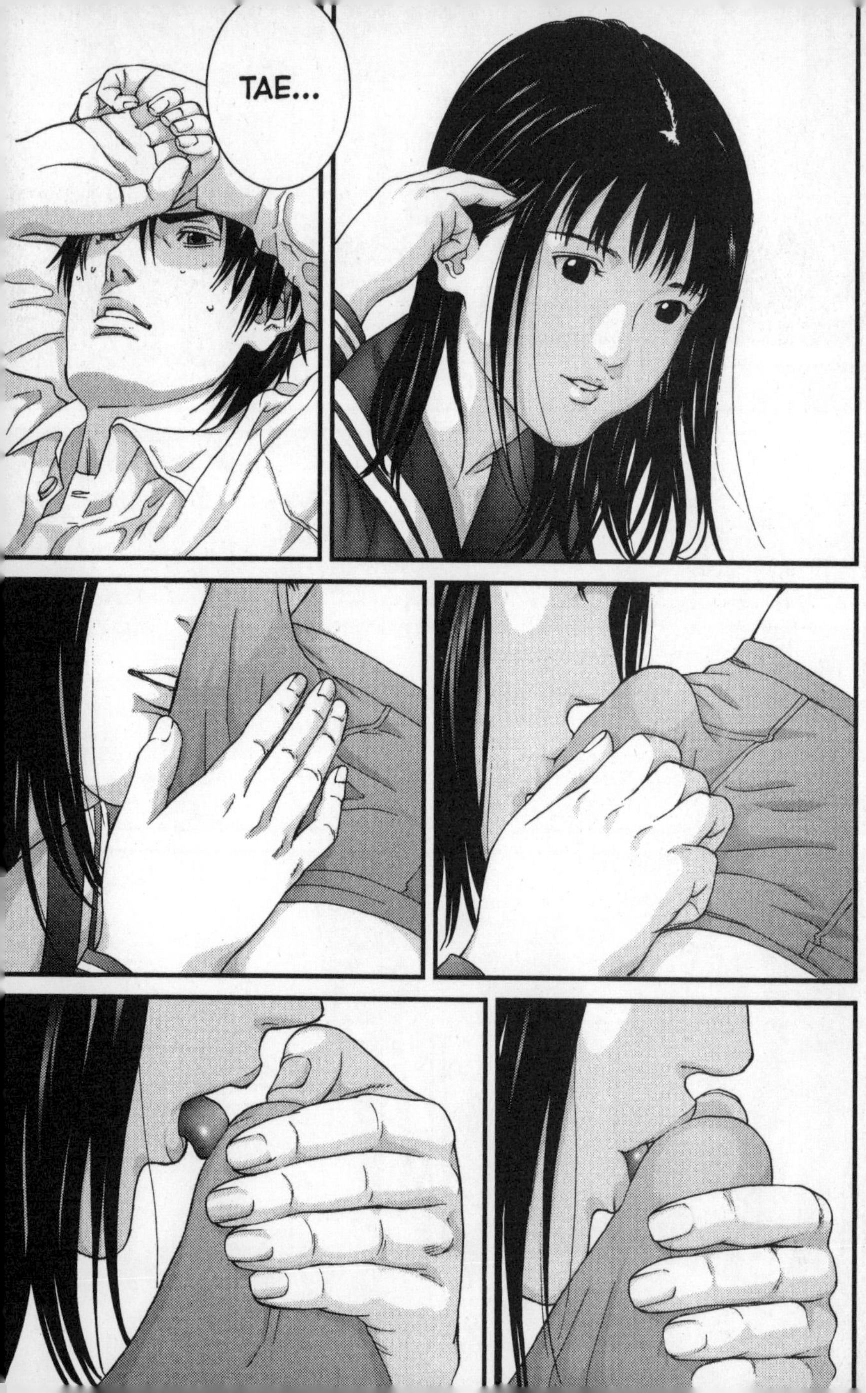
TAE...

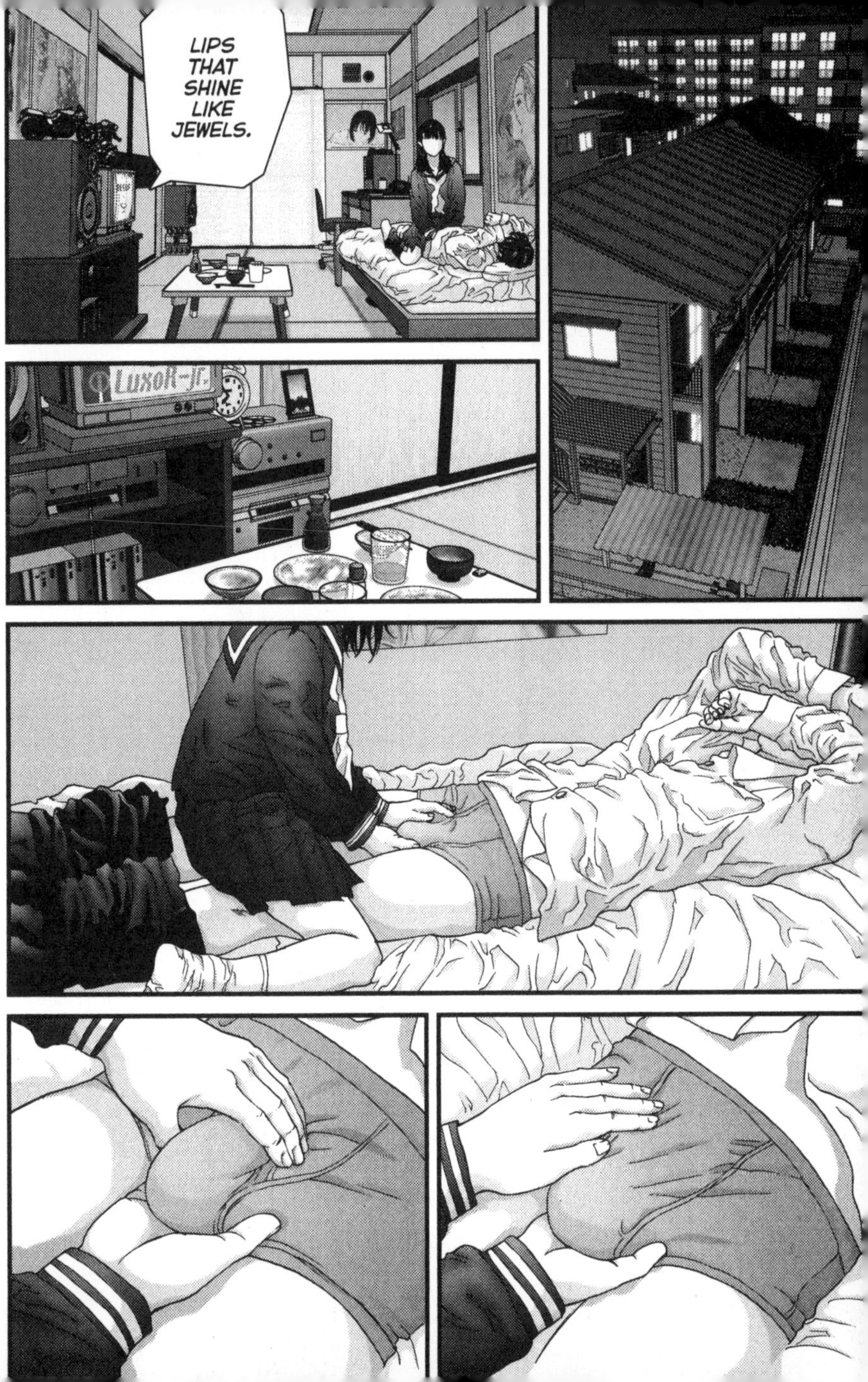
LIPS THAT SHINE LIKE JEWELS.
LuxoR-jr.

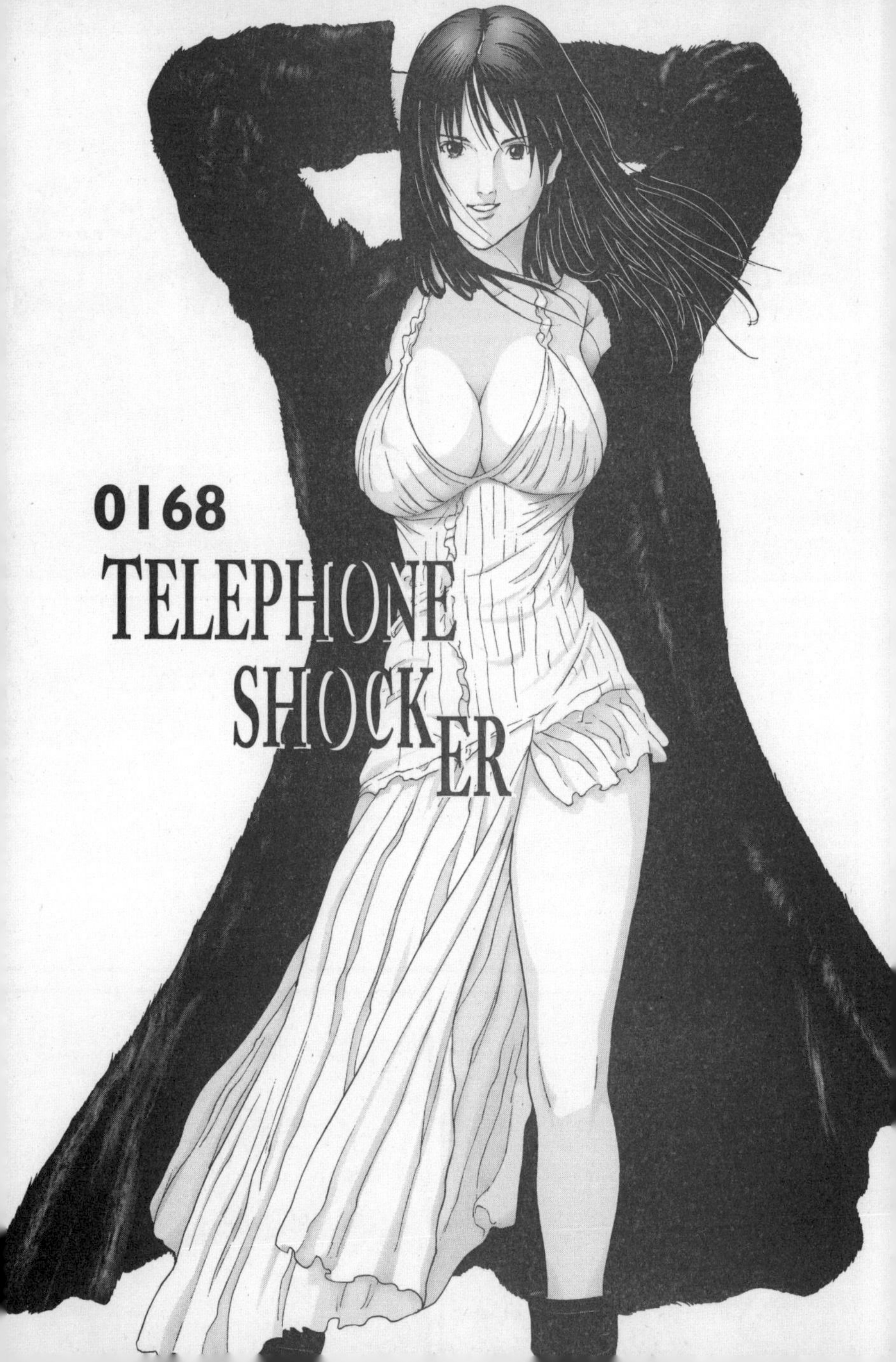
0168
TELEPHONE
SHOCKER

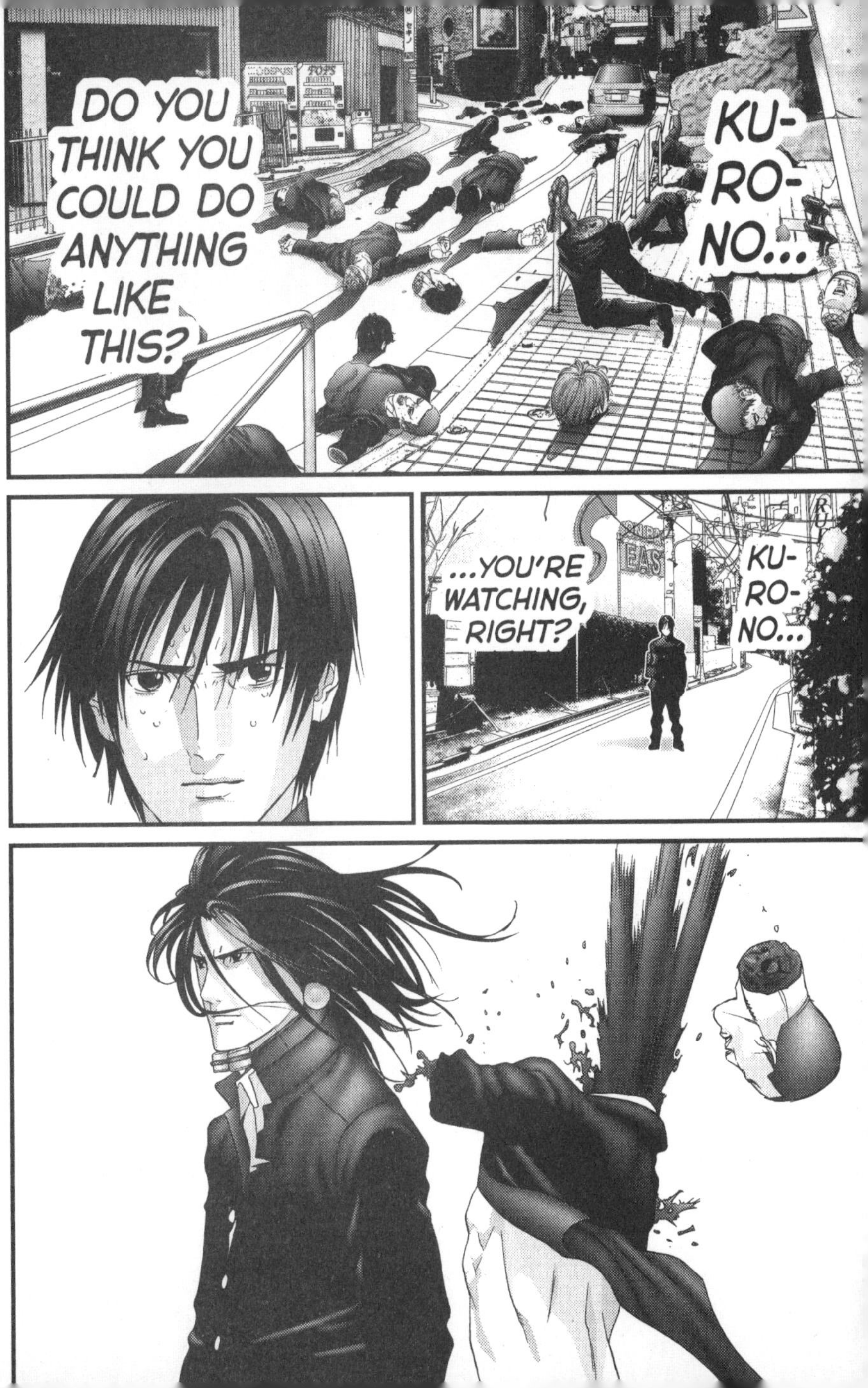
KU-RO-NO...
DO YOU THINK YOU COULD DO ANYTHING LIKE THIS?
KU-RO-NO...
...YOU'RE WATCHING, RIGHT?

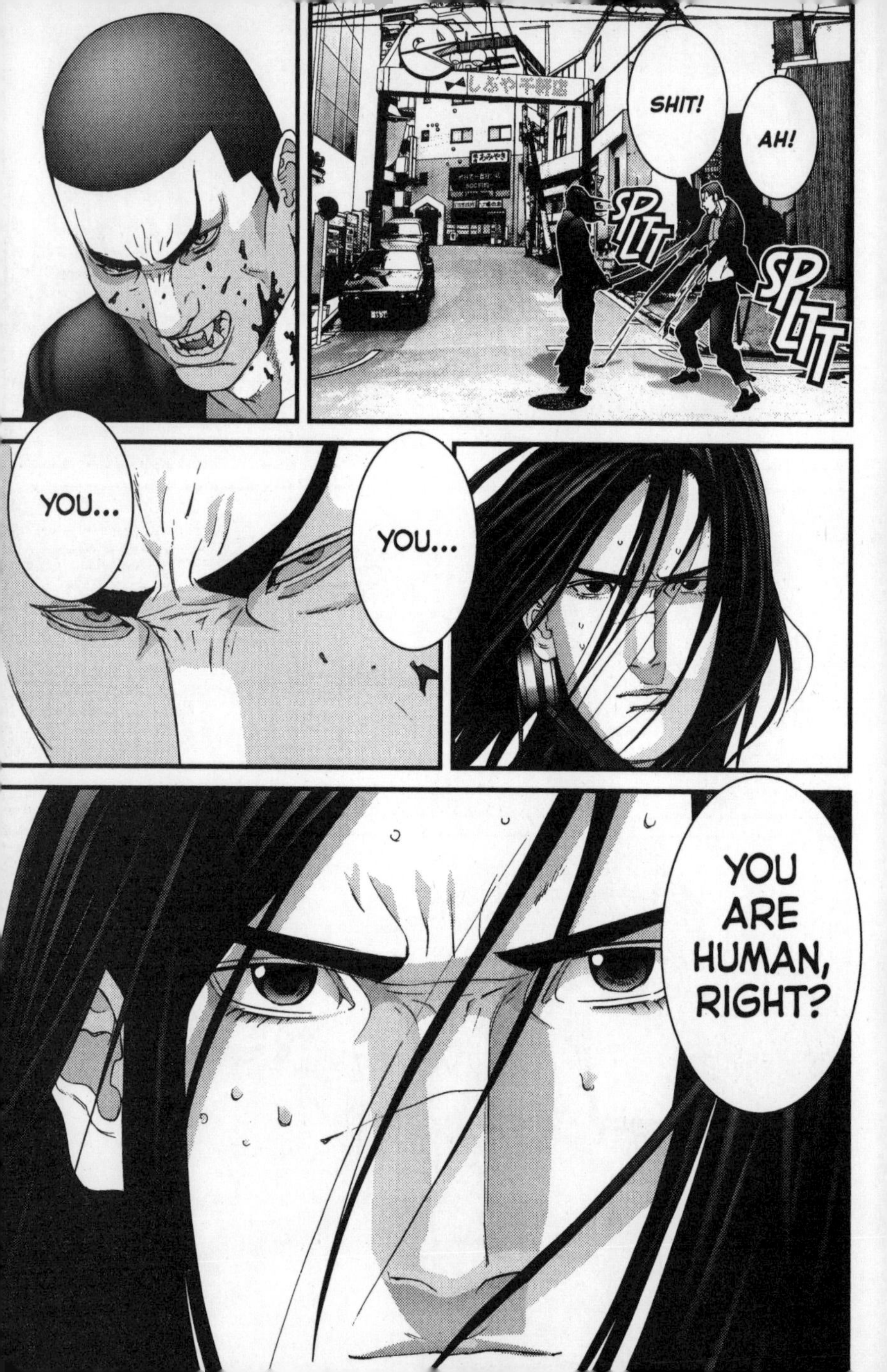
AH!
SHIT!
SPLTT
SPLTT
YOU...
YOU...
YOU ARE HUMAN, RIGHT?

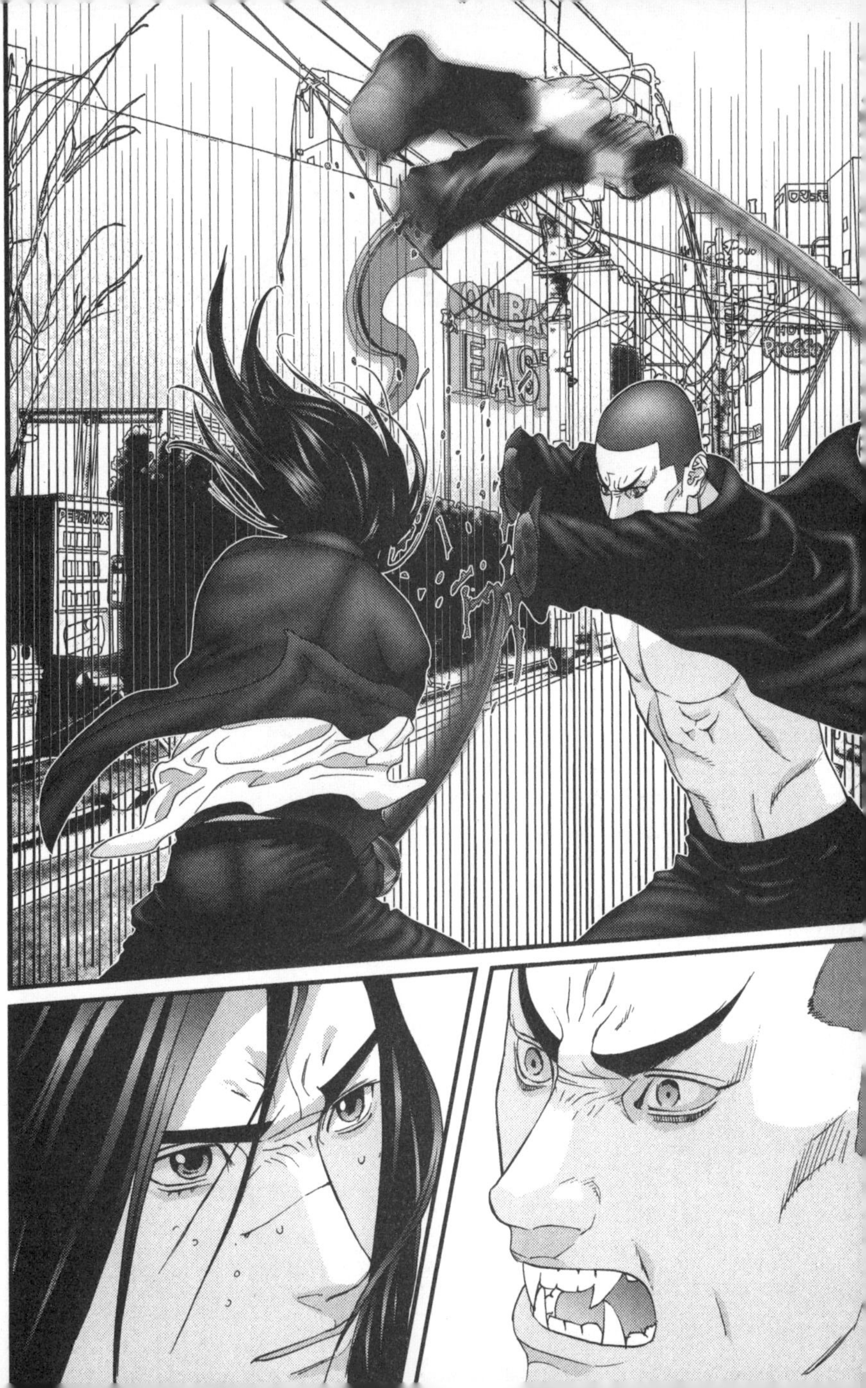

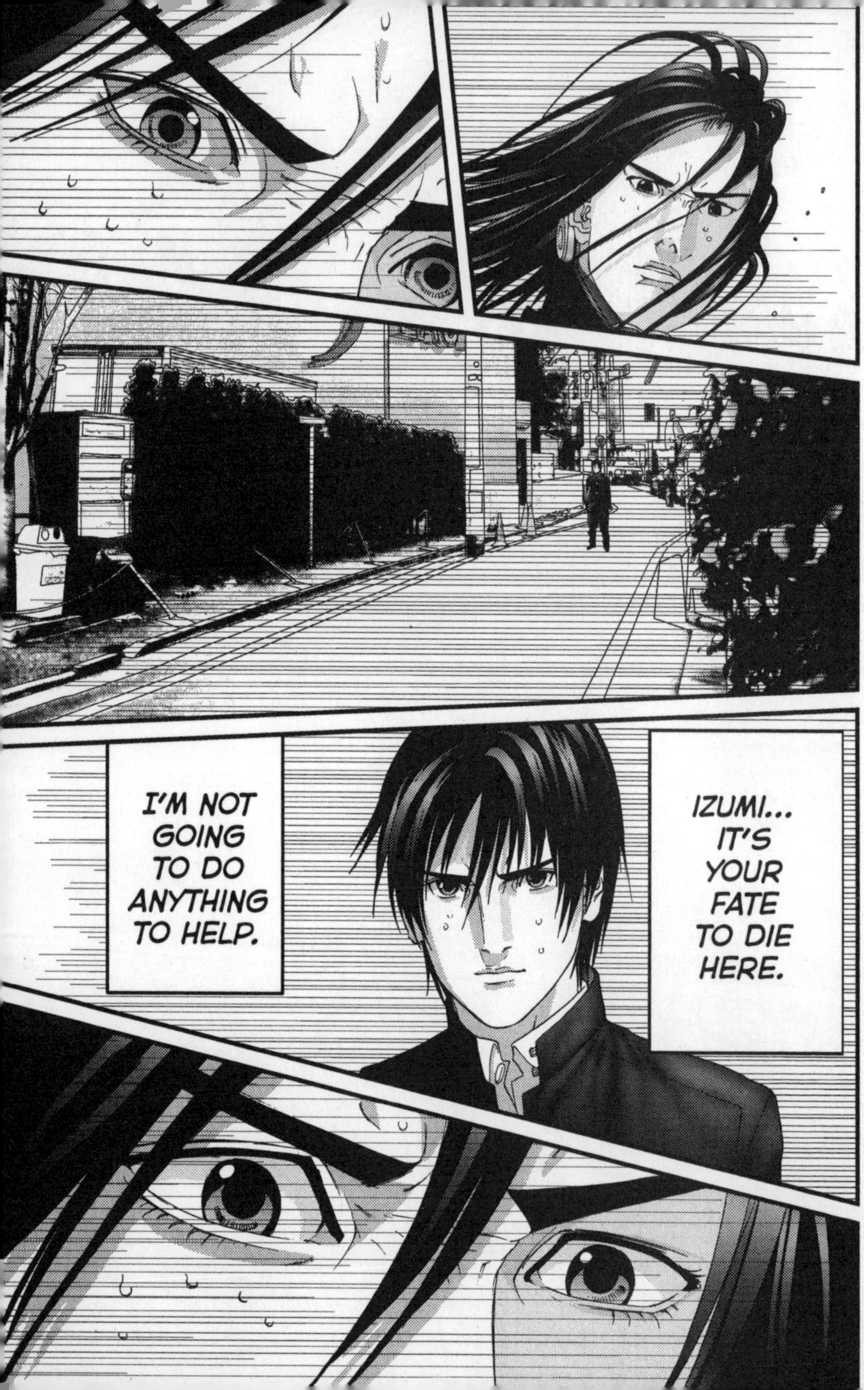
IZUMI... IT'S YOUR FATE TO DIE HERE.
I'M NOT GOING TO DO ANYTHING TO HELP.

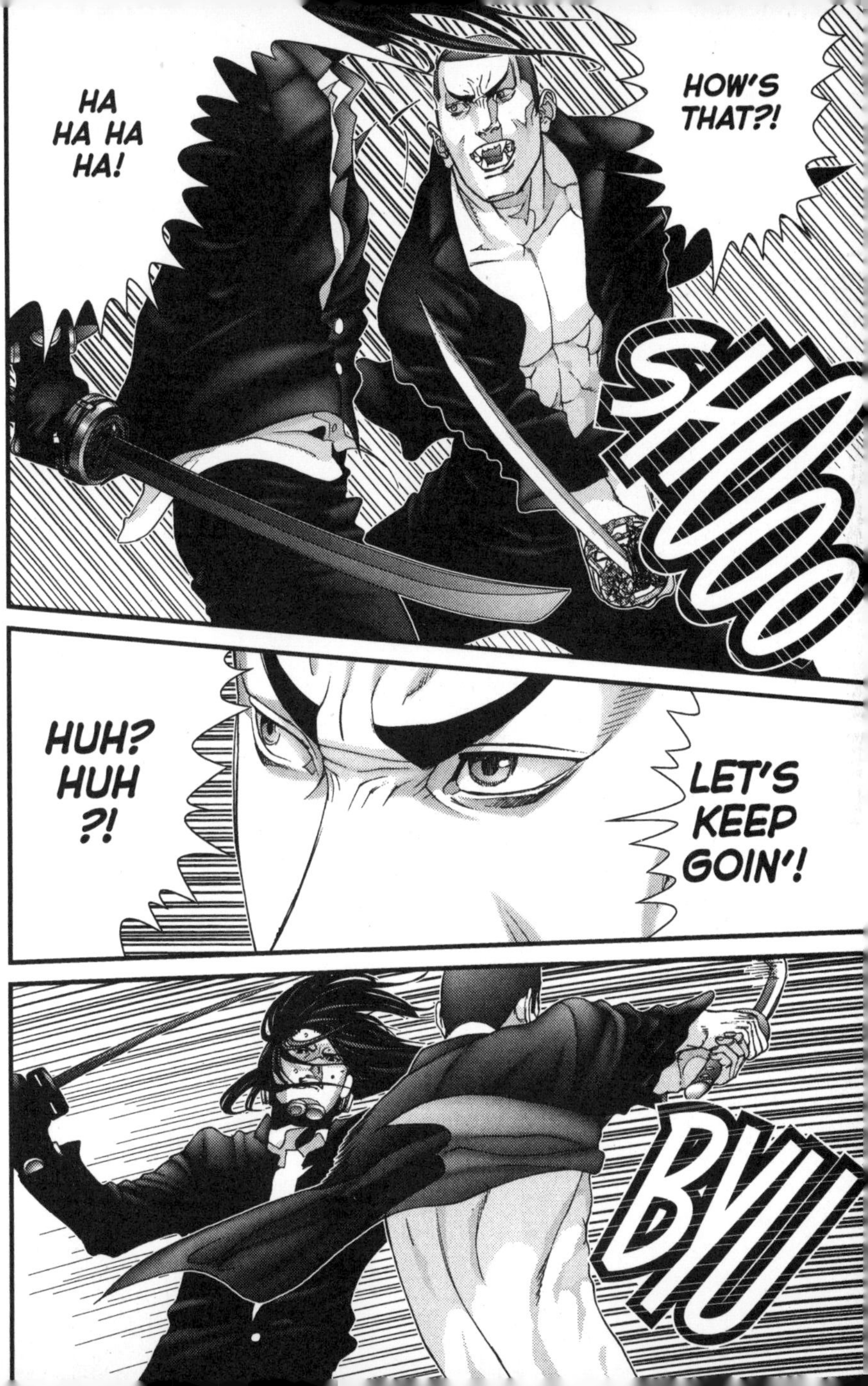
HOW'S THAT?!
SHOOO
HA HA HA HA!
LET'S KEEP GOIN'!
HUH? HUH ?!
BYU

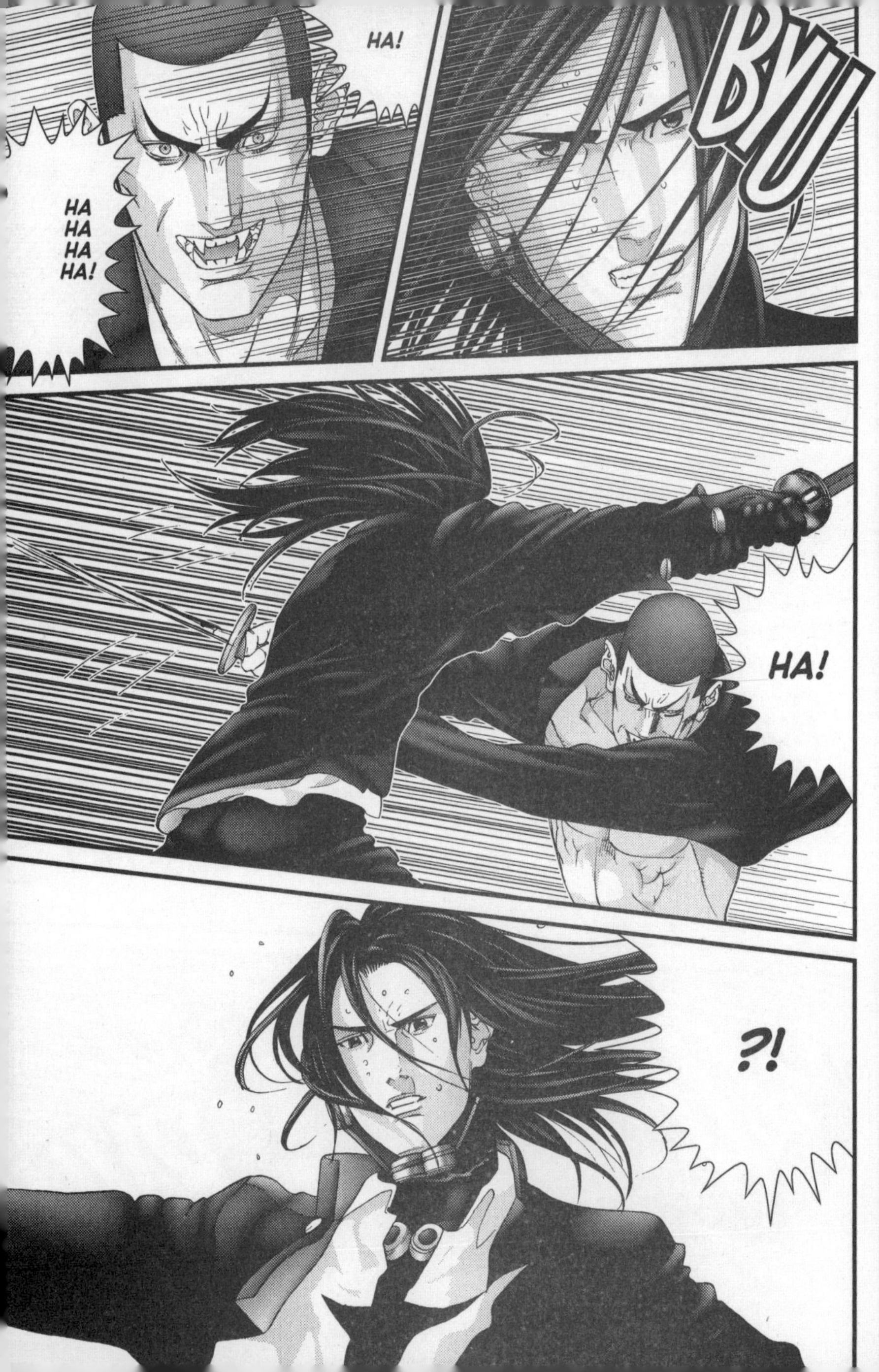
BYU
HA!
HA HA HA HA!
HA!
?!

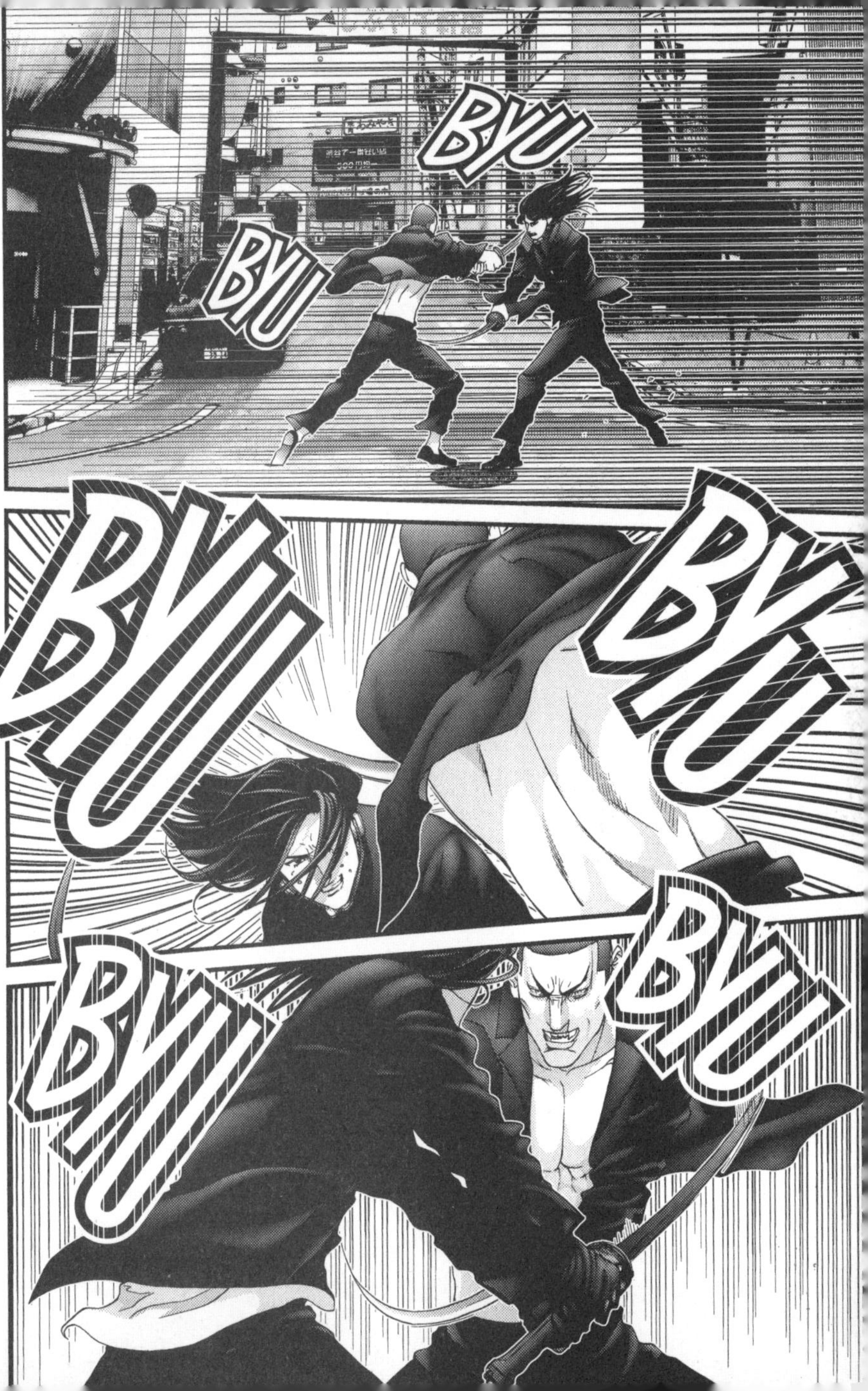
BYU
BYU
BYU
BYU
BYU
BYU

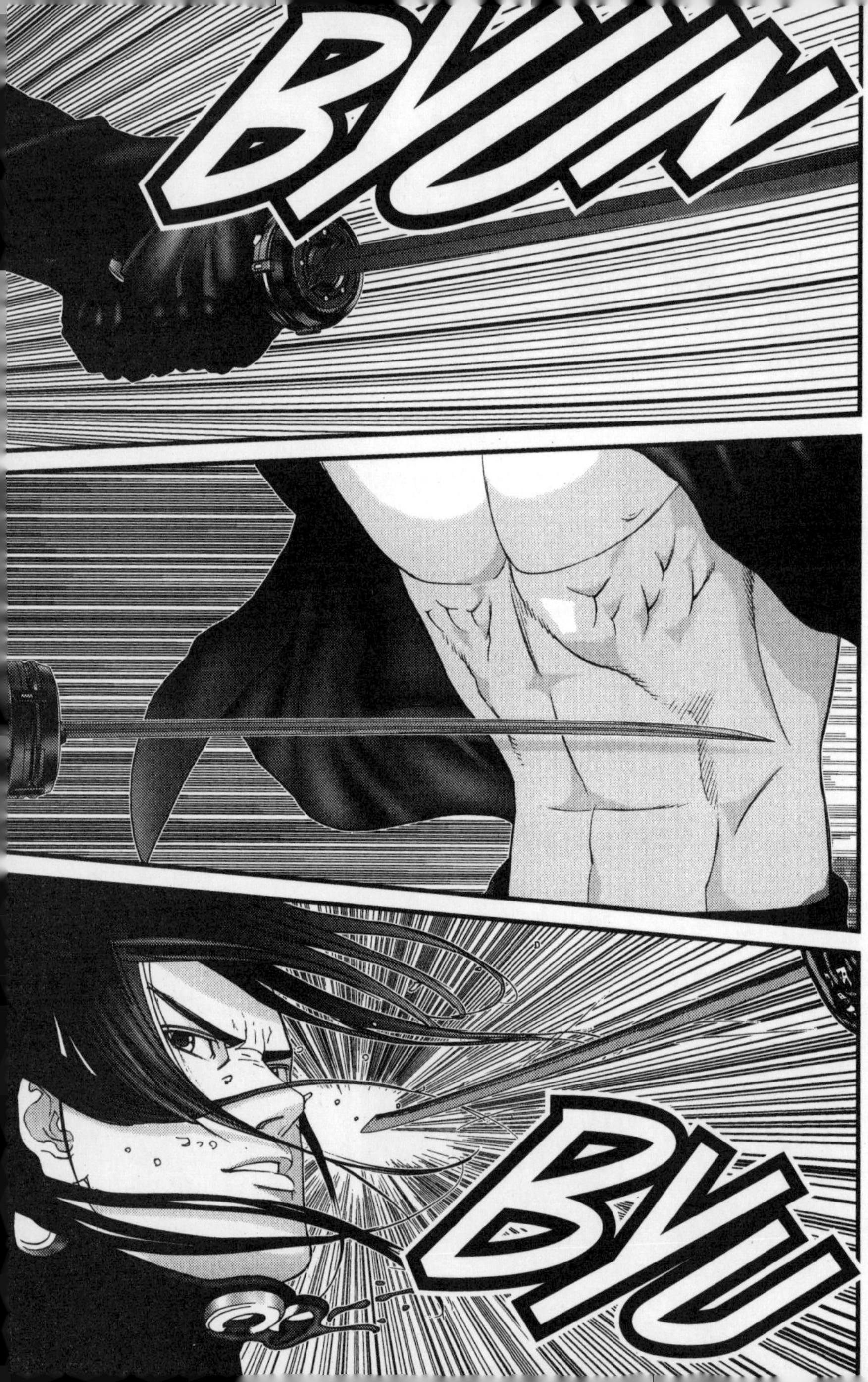
BYUN
BYU

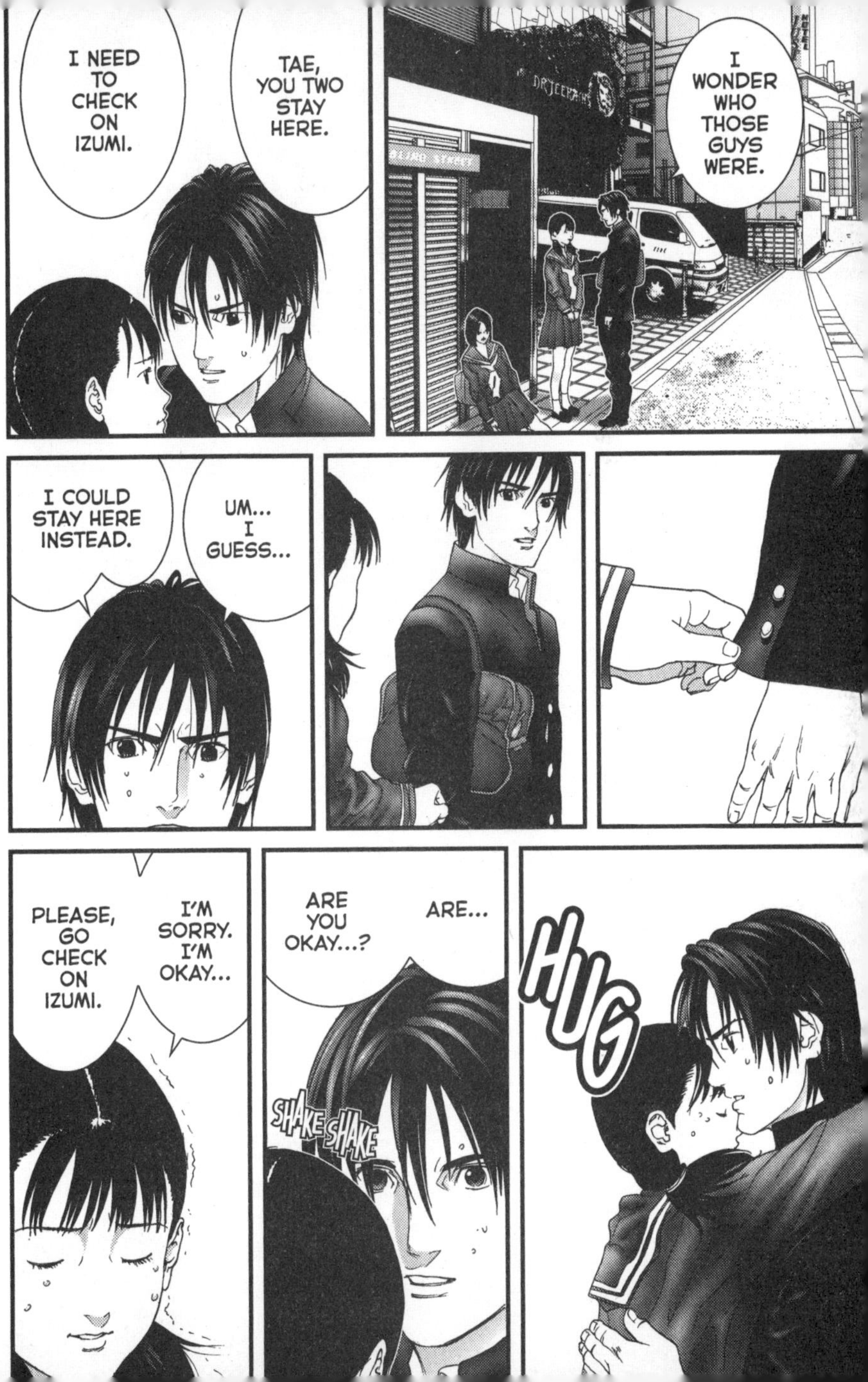
I WONDER WHO THOSE GUYS WERE.
TAE, YOU TWO STAY HERE.
I NEED TO CHECK ON IZUMI.
UM... I GUESS...
I COULD STAY HERE INSTEAD.
HUG
ARE...
ARE YOU OKAY...?
SHAKE SHAKE
I'M SORRY. I'M OKAY...
PLEASE, GO CHECK ON IZUMI.

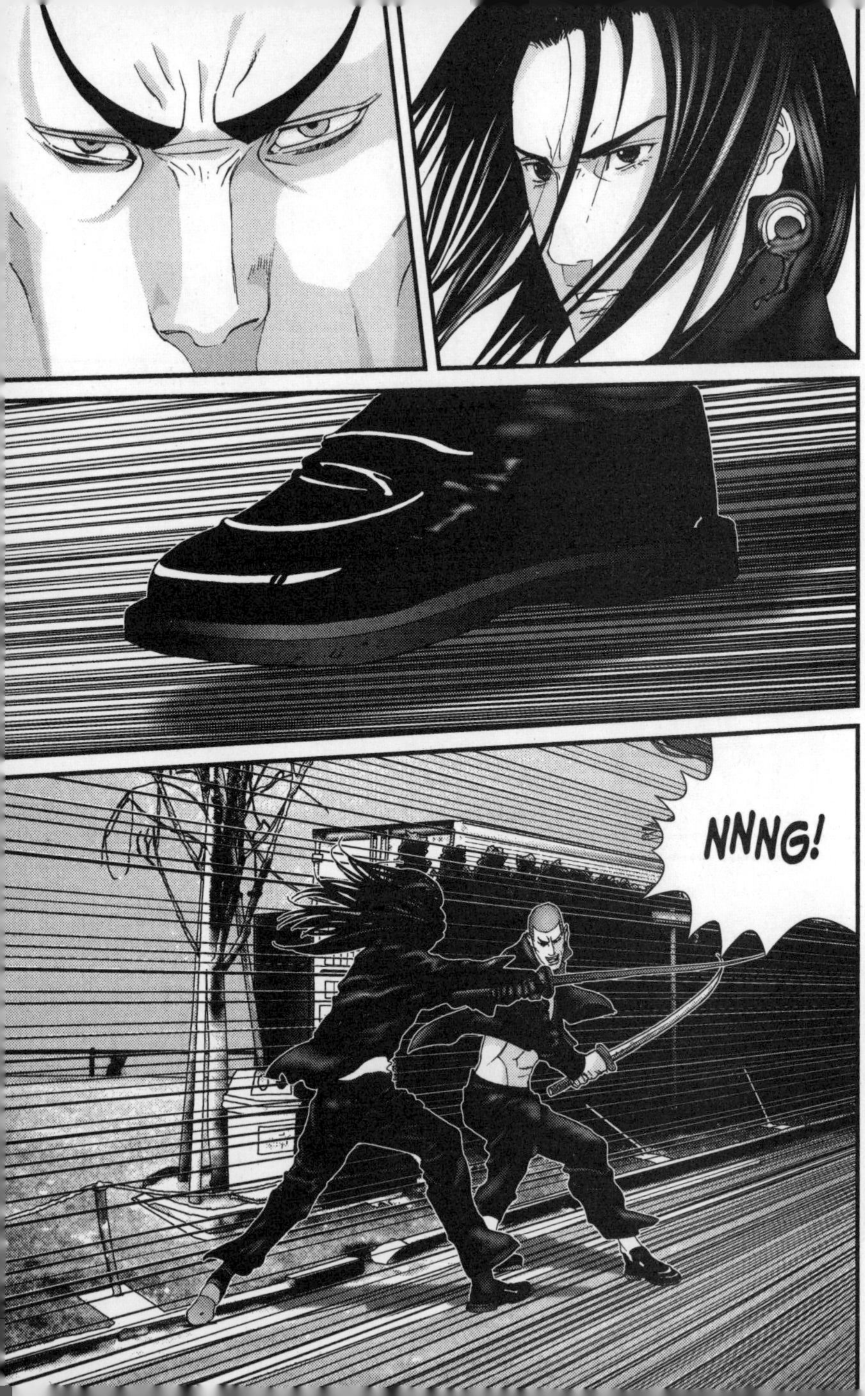
NNNG!

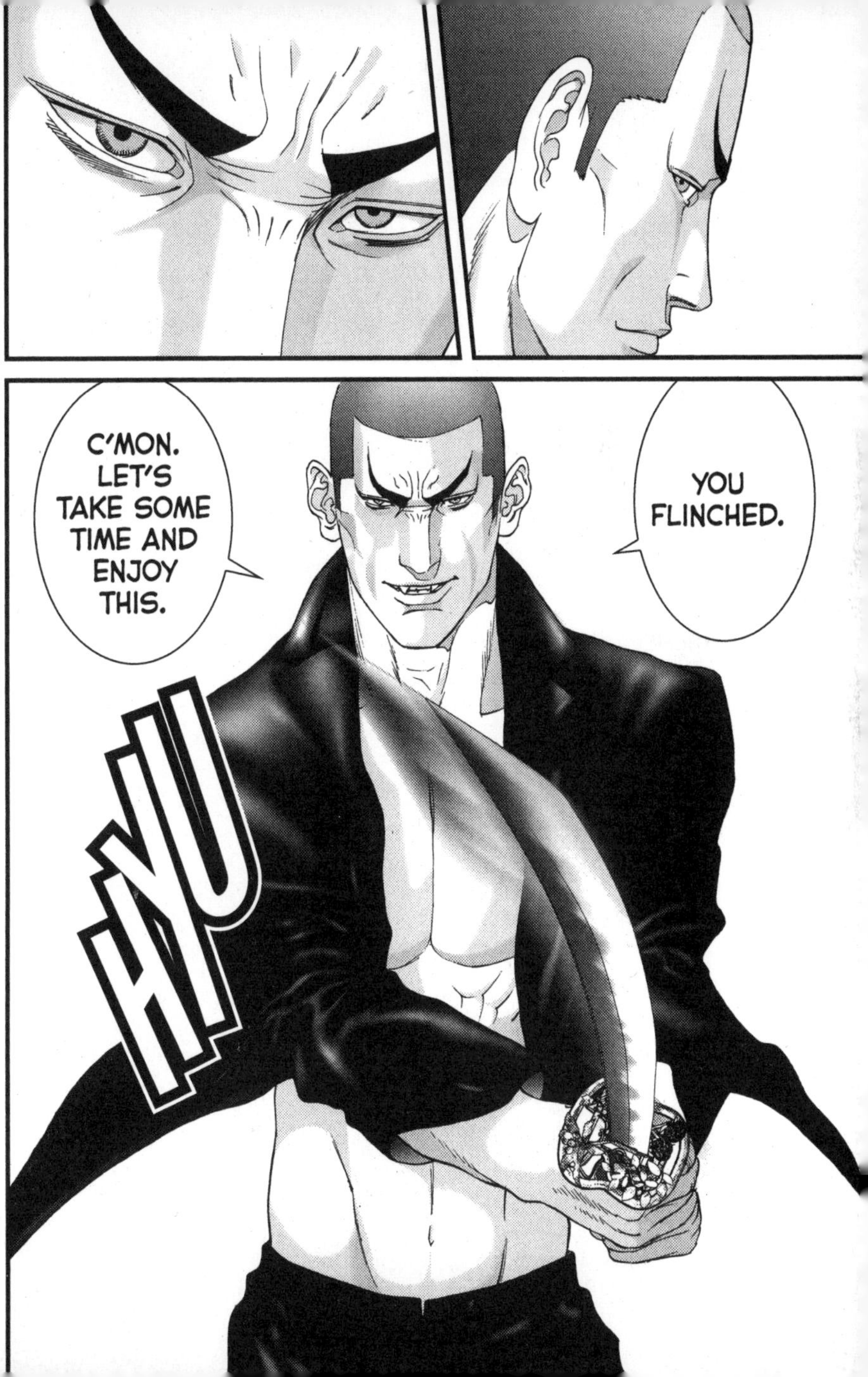
YOU FLINCHED.
C'MON. LET'S TAKE SOME TIME AND ENJOY THIS.
HYU

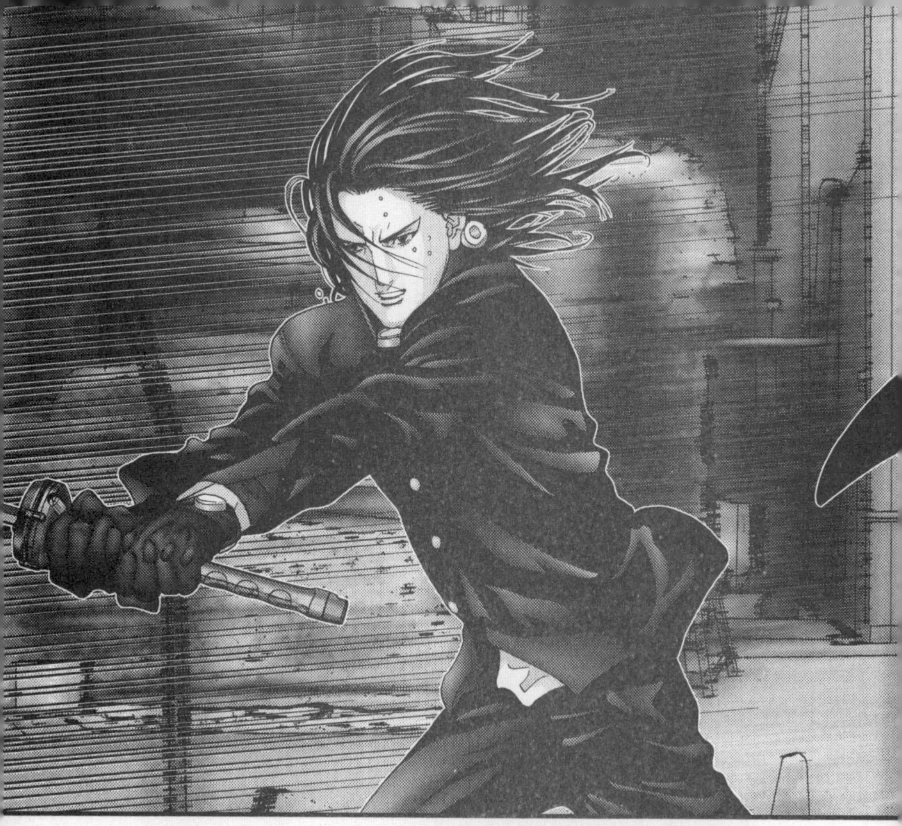
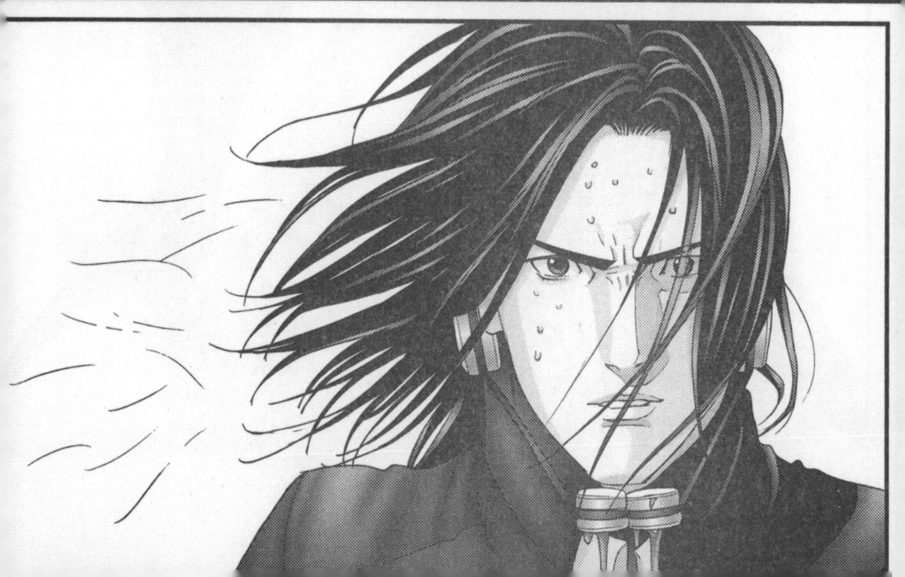

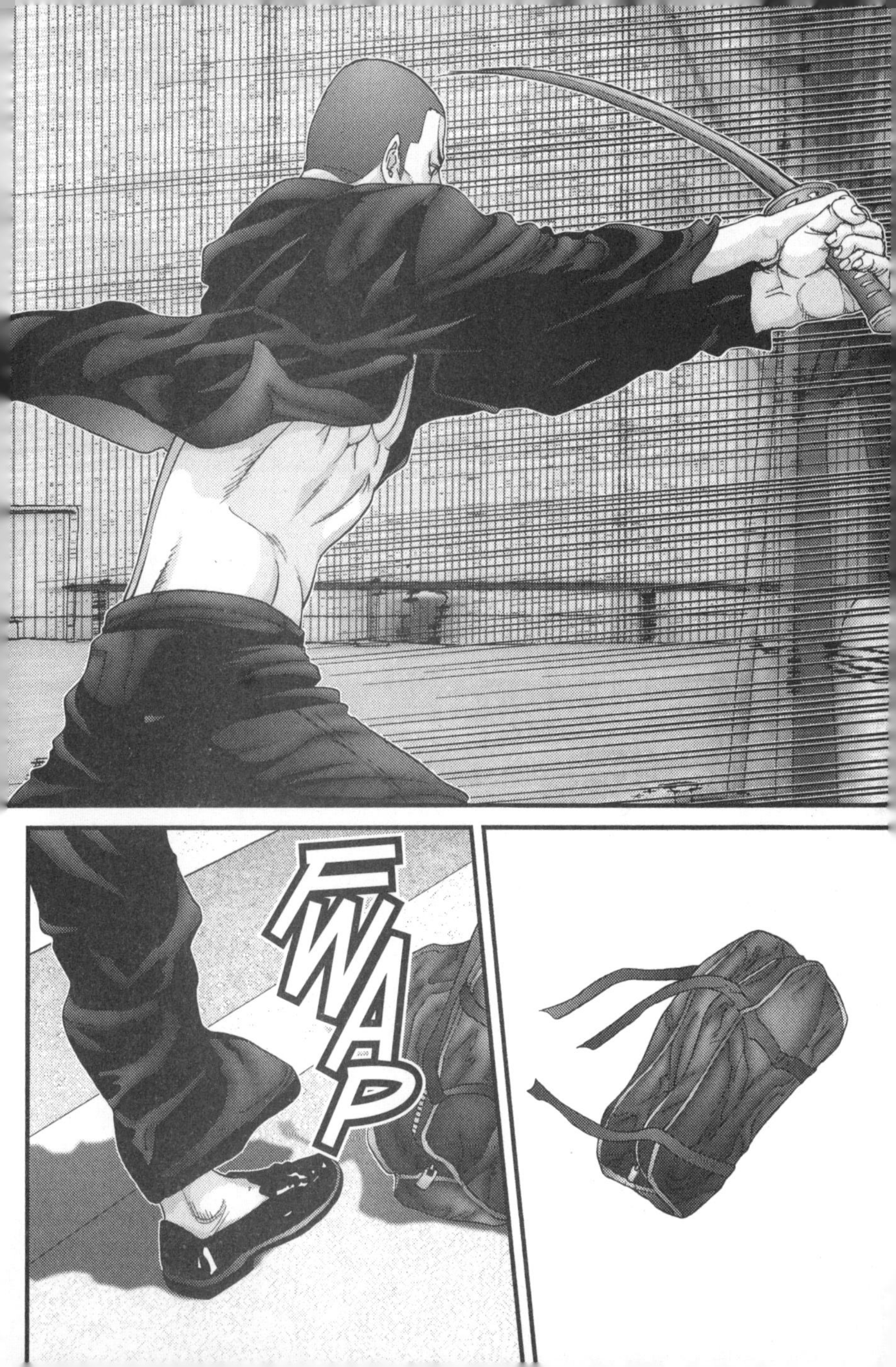
FWAP

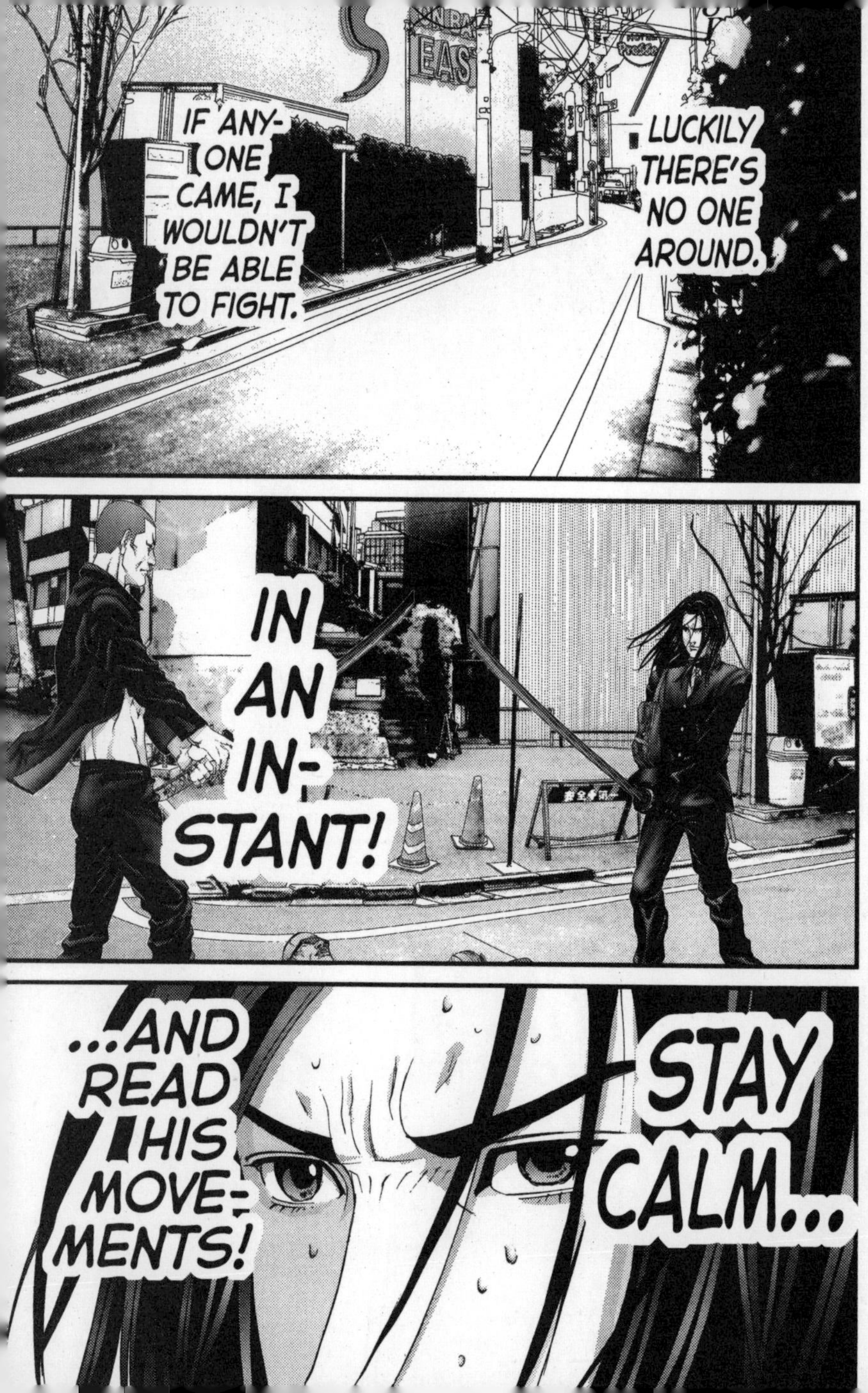
LUCKILY THERE'S NO ONE AROUND.
IF ANYONE CAME, I WOULDN'T BE ABLE TO FIGHT.
IN AN INSTANT!
STAY CALM...
...AND READ HIS MOVEMENTS!

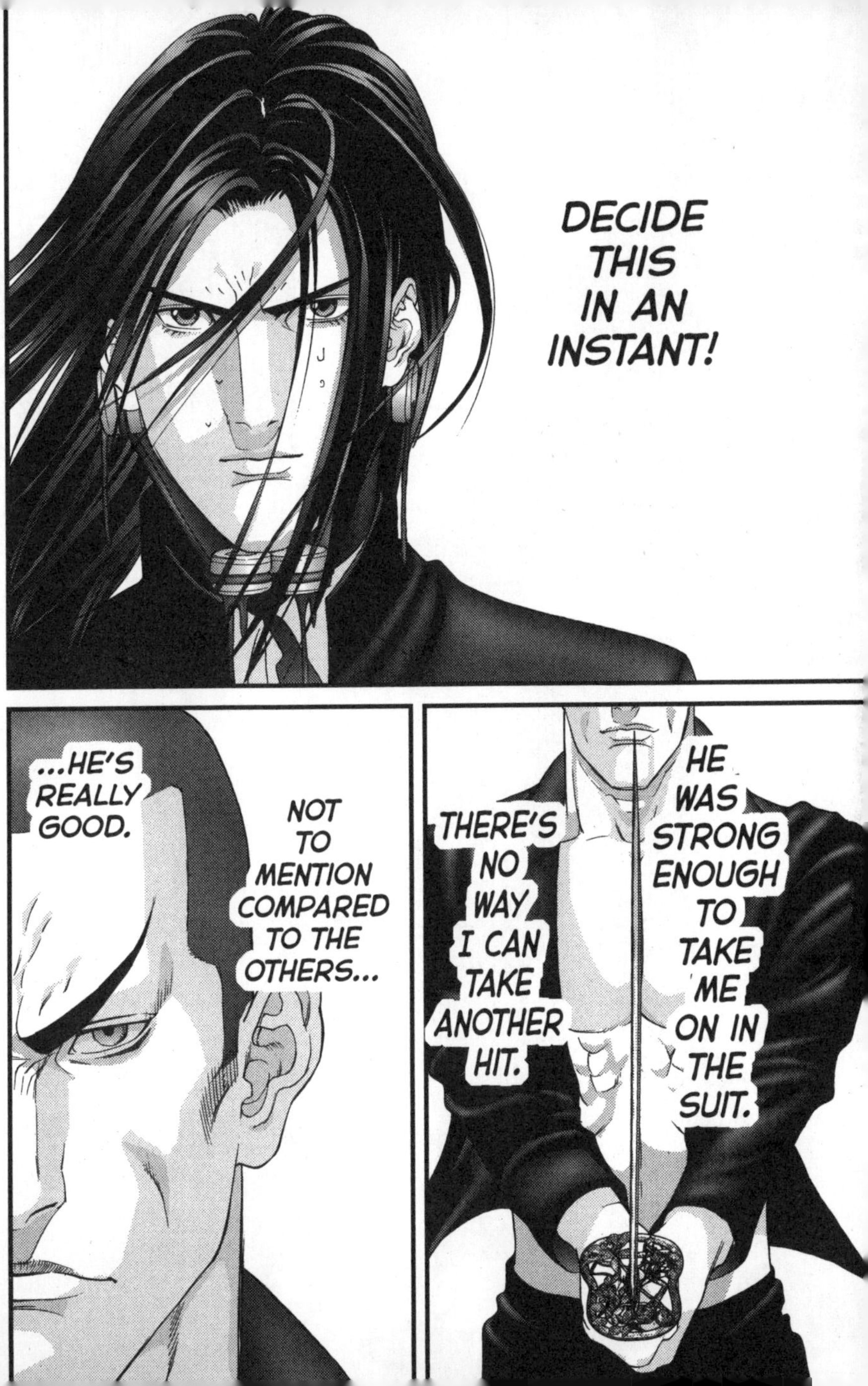
DECIDE THIS IN AN INSTANT!
HE WAS STRONG ENOUGH TO TAKE ME ON IN THE SUIT.
THERE'S NO WAY I CAN TAKE ANOTHER HIT.
...HE'S REALLY GOOD.
NOT TO MENTION COMPARED TO THE OTHERS...

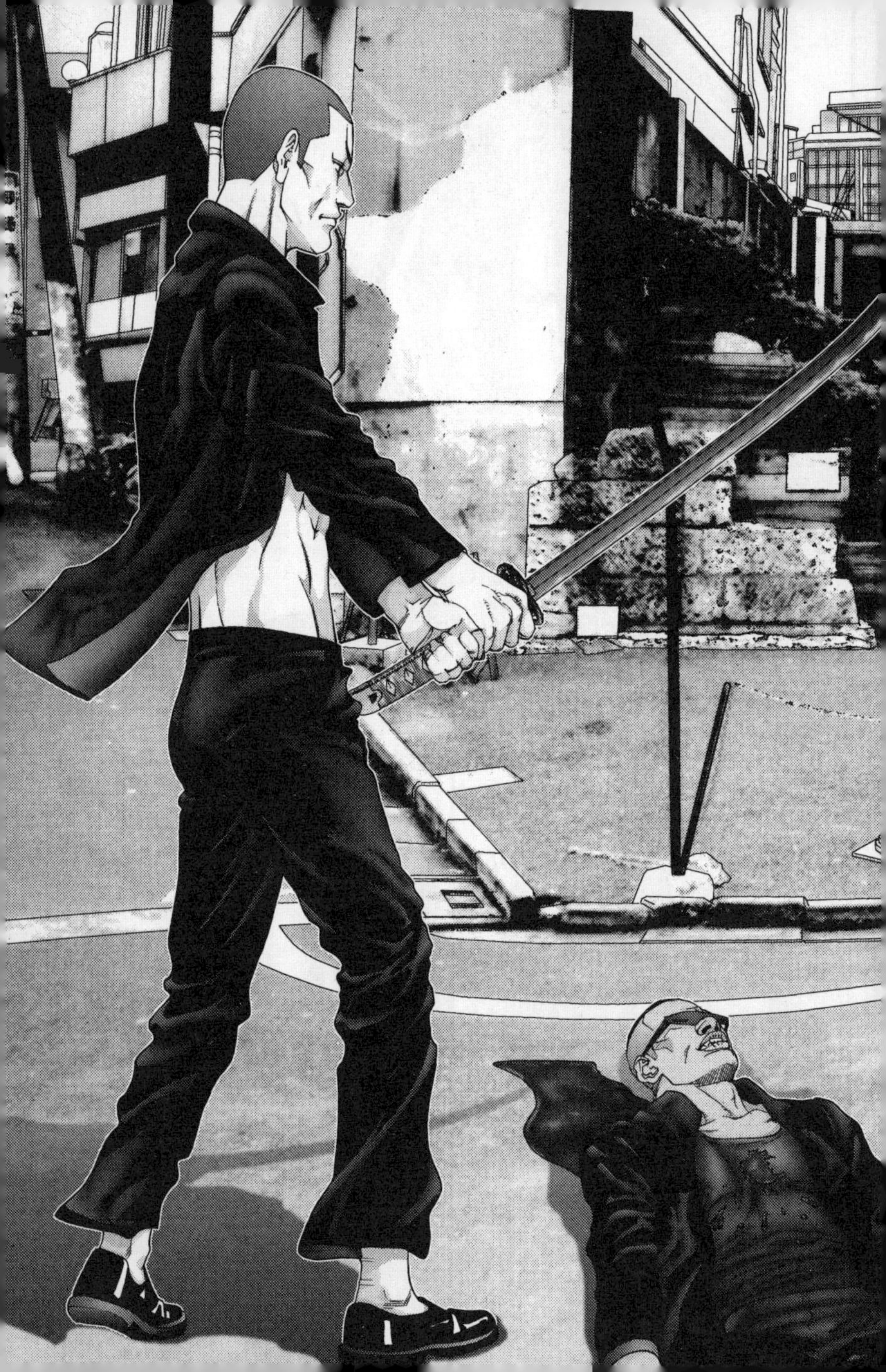

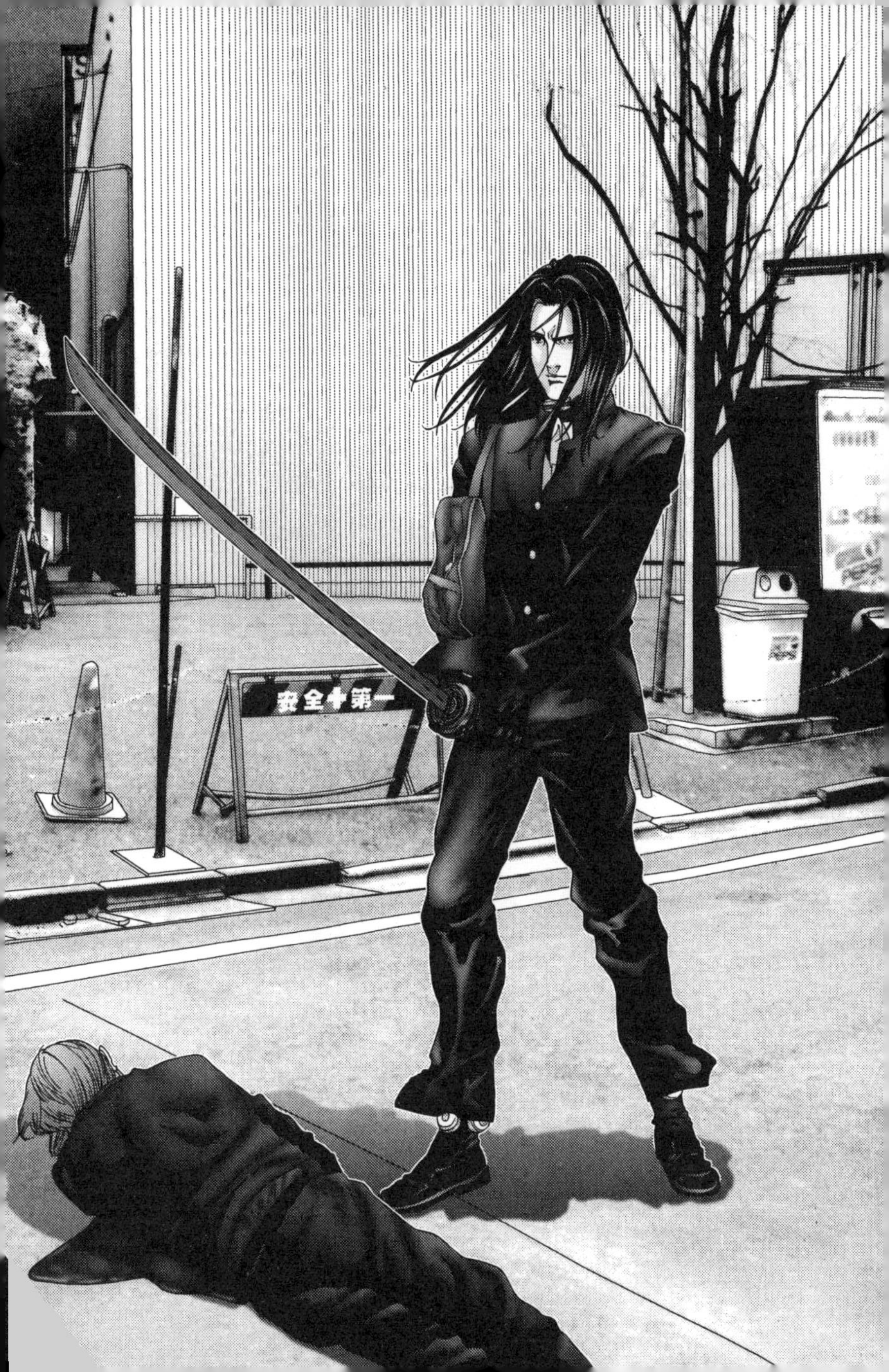
安全第一

0167
GAME OF DEATH

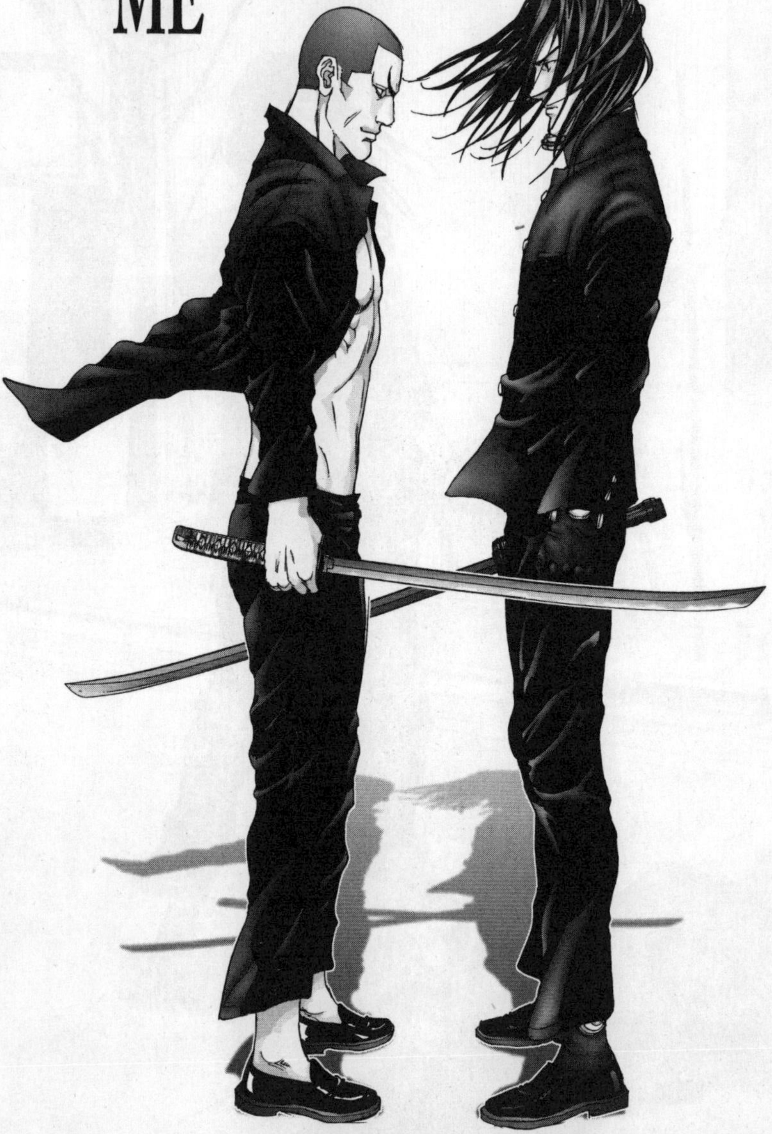

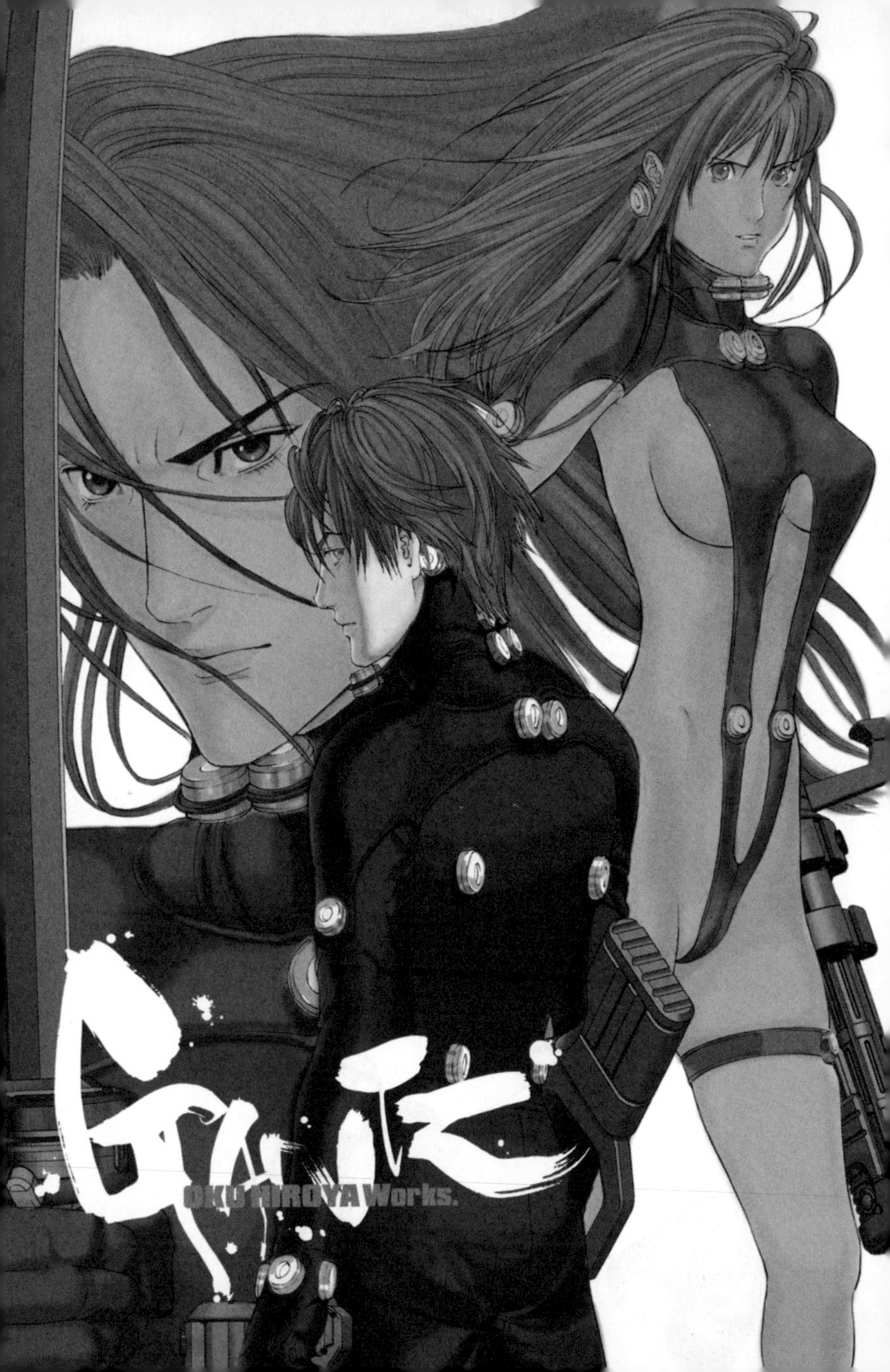
GANTZ
OKU HIROYA Works.

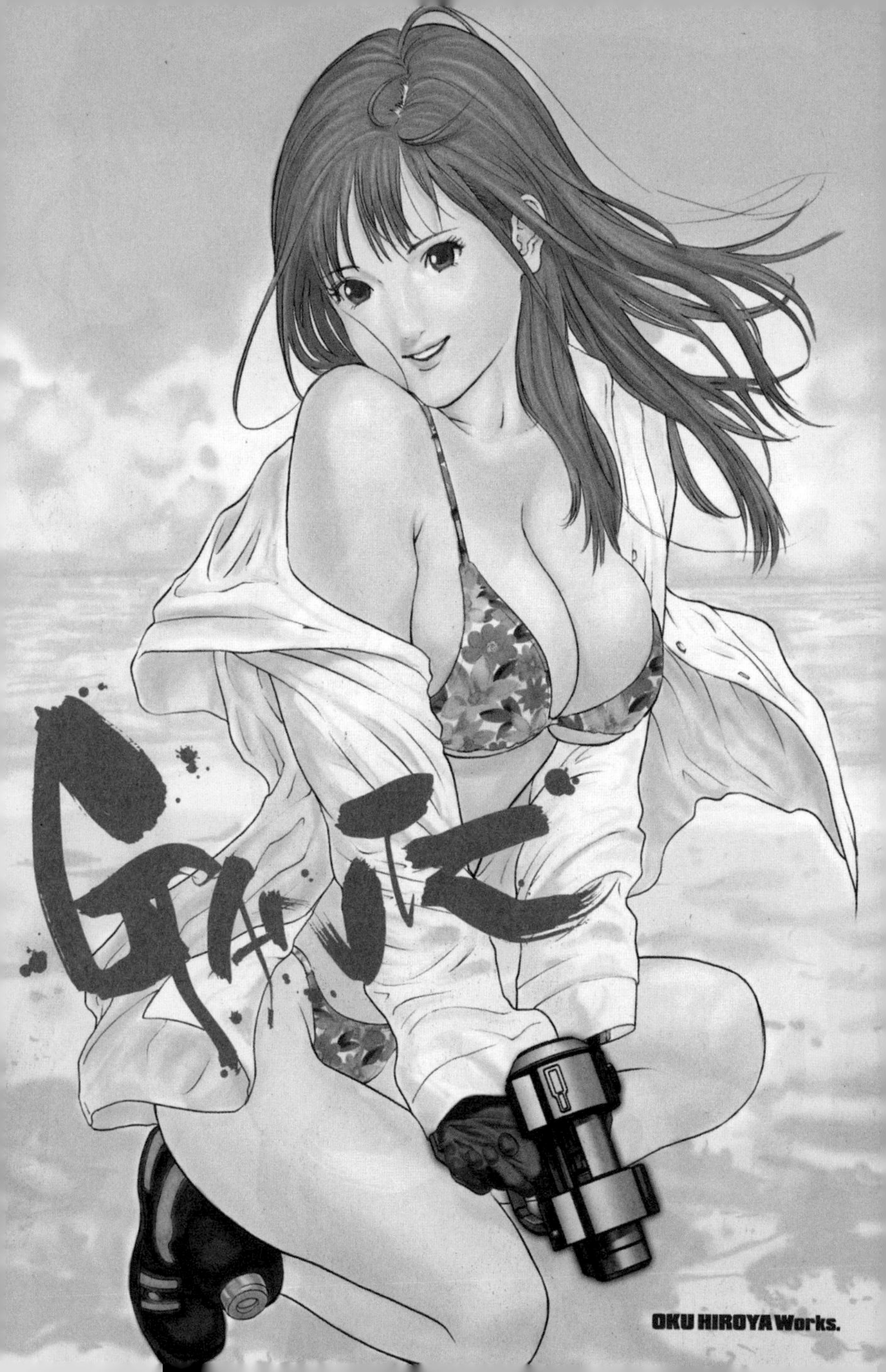
OKU HIROYA Works.

CONTENTS

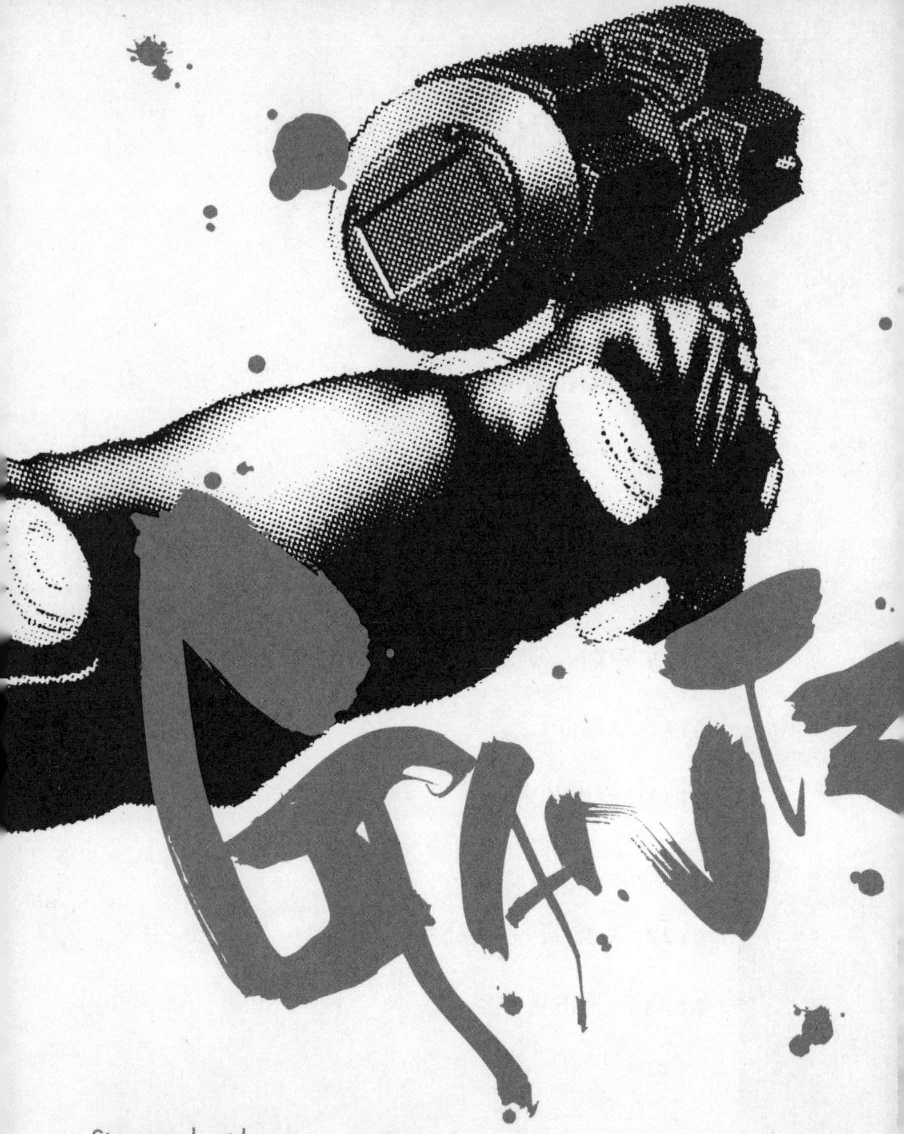

Story and art by

HIROYA OKU

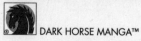

DARK HORSE MANGA™